CHAIN LETTER

ALSO BY
Christopher Pike

THE THIRST SERIES

REMEMBER ME

THE SECRET OF KA

UNTIL THE END

BOUND TO YOU

WITCH WORLD

CHAIN LETTER

INCLUDES *CHAIN LETTER* AND *THE ANCIENT EVIL*

CHRISTOPHER PIKE

Simon Pulse
New York London Toronto Sydney New Delhi

This book is a work of fiction. Any references to historical events, real people, or real places are used fictitiously. Other names, characters, places, and events are products of the author's imagination, and any resemblance to actual events or places or persons, living or dead, is entirely coincidental.

SIMON PULSE
An imprint of Simon & Schuster Children's Publishing Division
1230 Avenue of the Americas, New York, NY 10020
This Simon Pulse paperback edition July 2013

Chain Letter was originally published in 1986 by Avon Books, a division of the Hearst Corporation.

The text of this book was set in Adobe Garamond.
Manufactured in the United States of America
10 9 8 7 6 5 4 3 2 1
Library of Congress Control Number 2012943074
ISBN 978-1-4424-7215-0
ISBN 978-1-4424-7216-7 (eBook)
These books were previously published individually.

Contents

CHAIN LETTER

For Ann

Chapter One

Alison Parker saw the letter first. Normally, she wouldn't have checked on her friend's mail, but the mailbox was slightly ajar, and she couldn't help noticing the off-purple envelope addressed to Fran Darey. It was a peculiar letter, taller than it was long, with no return address. Alison wondered if it was a love letter. Whatever it was, whoever had sent it had lousy taste in color. The off-purple envelope reminded her of spoiled meat.

"Do you need help?" Alison called. She was standing on Fran's porch, holding an assortment of books and bags: enough for three girls' homework and personal items. Fran Darey and Brenda Paxson were unloading a half-painted set from the back of Alison's station wagon, trying to maneuver it into the garage with a minimum of damage. The prop was for a play the three of them were involved in at school: *You Can't Take It with You.*

Fran was in charge of special effects. Brenda had a small, wacky role. Alison was the star.

"Whatever gave you that idea?" Brenda gasped, swiping at her overly long bangs and losing her grip on a portion of their characters' living room. It hit the concrete driveway at an unfavorable angle, and a strip of wallpaper bent back.

"I took this home to finish it, not destroy it," Fran complained in her quick, nervous voice. Fran fretted over everything; it was a quality that made her excel at detail work. Brenda *professed* to be the opposite. She worried only about "things of importance." Still, on bad days, it was hard to tell the two of them apart. They were always arguing. They were Alison's best friends.

"I'm coming," Alison said, setting aside her gear and hurrying down the steps. It was hot and smoggy, not the best of days for heavy labor. Yet Alison didn't mind the weather. It reminded her of summer—only a few weeks away—and of their quickly approaching graduation. Lately, she had been anxious to finish with high school, to begin her *real* life. Her game plan called for four years in UCLA's drama department, followed by forty years starring in Hollywood feature films. Her chances were one in a million, so her parents often said, but she liked a challenge and she loved acting. Besides, when had she ever listened to her parents?

"Grab here," Brenda said, wanting help with her end.

"No, Ali, come over here," Fran said.

"Why should she help you?" Brenda asked. "This is your

project. I'm just a volunteer. I'm not even getting union scale."

"But you're stronger than me," Fran said, straining.

"I'll get in the middle," Alison said, her usual position when the three of them were together. With a fair quota of groans and curses, they got the makeshift wall into the garage. If the truth be known, and Brenda was quick to point it out, there was absolutely no reason for Fran to have brought the set home. *You Can't Take It with You*'s opening night was not for over a month.

Because they entered the empty house through the garage, Fran didn't immediately check on her mail. Only when they were seated at the kitchen table drinking milk and eating Hostess Twinkies and complaining about how many miserable calories were in each bite did Alison remember the books and bags she had left on the porch. While fetching them, standing just outside the kitchen window, she called to Fran, "Do you want me to bring in your mail?"

"She doesn't care," Brenda said. "No one sends real mail these days."

"Ain't that the truth," Fran said. "Sure, Ali."

Alison waited expectantly while Fran dawdled over the front cover of a *Glamour* magazine that promised an exciting exclusive on Princess Kate's tastes in sweaters and an in-depth article by a prominent psychiatrist on why women didn't trust their husbands. Finally Alison got fed up and, clearing her throat, pointed out the purple envelope to Fran.

"That letter has your name on it," she said.

"Are you serious?" Brenda asked between mouthfuls of cream and cake. "Who's it from?"

Fran did not immediately answer, examining the envelope slowly, apparently savoring hopes that would almost inevitably be disappointed when she opened the thing. Not having a boyfriend, not having ever been asked out on a date, Fran had to make the most out of the small pleasures in life. Not that she was ugly. Her clear-skinned oval face and wide generous mouth gave her the foundation for an above-average appearance. Plus her light brown hair had a natural sheen that none of them could duplicate with expensive shampoos and rinses. Yet she was shy and high strung. She was a gifted artist, a B-plus student, but when she got around the guys, she inevitably wound herself into a catatonic cocoon, and couldn't say a word.

"There's no return address," she said finally.

Alison smiled. "It must be a love letter. Why else would someone use snail mail?"

Fran blushed. "Oh, I don't think so."

"Open it," Brenda said.

"I will." Fran set the letter aside. "Later."

"Open it now," Brenda insisted. "I want to see what it says."

"No."

"Why not?"

"Brenda, if it's personal . . ." Alison began. But Brenda had long arms, excellent reflexes, and—suddenly—the letter in her hand.

"I'll spare you the trauma," Brenda told hysterical Fran, casually ripping open the top.

"Give that back to me!" Fran knocked over her chair and tore into Brenda with a ferocity that must have surprised them both. There ensued a brief brawl during which Alison finished her milk and Twinkie. Fran emerged the victor, her short hair a mess and her cheeks pounding with blood but otherwise none the worse for wear.

"I was just trying to be helpful," Brenda said, fixing her blouse and catching her breath.

Fran straightened her chair and sat down, staring at the envelope. "Well, it's none of your business."

"I'm also curious who it's from," Alison said casually.

"Are you?" Fran asked meekly. They had grown up together, but for reasons that always eluded Alison, Fran took her opinions seriously and was at pains to please her. Alison didn't mind the minor hero worship, but she was generally careful not to take advantage of it. So she felt a little guilty at her remark. She knew Fran would open the letter for her.

"Never mind," she said. "We don't have time to read letters now. We should start on our biology notes. I have that long drive home."

Her father had recently changed jobs and they'd had to move. Because graduation was so near, she hadn't wanted to transfer to another school. It was thirty-five miles of highway to her house, out in the boonies of the San Bernardino Valley.

Their house was brand-new, part of a recently developed tract, an oasis of civilization in a desert of dried shrubs. To make their isolation complete, they were the only family to have moved into the tract. Lately, at nighttime, being surrounded by the rows of deserted houses made her nervous. The empty windows seemed like so many eyes, watching her.

"If you really want to read it . . ." Fran said reluctantly.

"I don't," Alison said, opening her textbook. "Let's study photosynthesis first. I still don't understand how chlorophyll turns carbon dioxide into oxygen. On page . . ."

"I can open it," Fran said.

"Don't bother. On page . . ."

"Open the blasted thing and be done with it," Brenda grumbled, pushing another Twinkie into her mouth. "Why am I eating these things? They're just going to make me fat."

"You'll never be fat," Alison said.

"Want to bet?"

"So what if you gain weight?" Alison said. "Essie is played better chunky." Essie was Brenda's part in the play.

"That's not what the book says and don't give me the excuse," Brenda said, adding, "I wish that I'd gotten the Alice role, then I'd have a reason to stay on my diet."

Alice was Alison's part. Alison wondered if there hadn't been a trace of resentment in Brenda's last remark. After all, Brenda also wanted to study drama in college, and their school nominated only one person for the Thespian Scholarship program. They both needed the money. As *You Can't Take It with You* was the last play of the year, and since Alice was one of the leads, Alison had maneuvered herself into a favorable position to win the scholarship by landing the role. Brenda had tried out for it but had been passed over because she didn't—in the words of Mr. Hoglan, their drama instructor—have the "right look."

Alice was supposed to be pretty. Having known Brenda since childhood, Alison found it difficult to judge whether she was more attractive than herself. Certainly Brenda had enviable qualities: a tall lithe figure, bright blond hair and green eyes, sharp features that complemented her sharp wit. Yet Brenda's strengths were her weaknesses. Her cuteness was typical. She looked like too many other girls.

Fortunately, she had none of Fran's shyness and guys—particularly Kipp Coughlan—brought out the best in her. Brenda could sing. Brenda could dance. Brenda knew how to dress. Brenda knew how to have a good time. Brenda was doing all right.

If it was difficult to judge Brenda's appearance, it was impossible to be objective about her own. Her black hair was long, curly and unmanageable—contrasting nicely with her fair complexion. Throughout her freshman and sophomore years, she had worried about her small breasts but since that Victoria's Secret model had become a big star and the guys had flipped over the curve of her hips—Alison figured she could have doubled for her from the neck down—the concern had diminished. Her face was another story; *nobody* looked like her. She couldn't make up her mind whether that was good or bad. Her dark eyes were big and round and she had a wide mouth, but the rest of the ingredients were at odds with each other: a button nose, a firm jaw, a low forehead, thick eyebrows—it was amazing Nature had salvaged a human face out of the collection. Quite often, however, complete strangers would stop her in stores and tell her she was beautiful. Depending on her mood, she would either believe or disbelieve them. Not that she ever felt a compulsion to wear a bag over her head. Plenty of guys asked her out. She supposed she was doing all right, too.

"I may as well open it," Fran said, as if the idea were her own. Using a butter knife, she neatly sliced through the end opposite where Brenda had torn and pulled out a single crisp pale green page. Brenda waited with a mixture of exasperation and boredom while Fran silently read the letter. Fran was taking her time, apparently rereading. Alison watched her closely. She could not understand what the note could say that could so suddenly drain the last trace of color from Fran's face.

"Who is it from?" Brenda finally demanded.

Fran did not answer, but slowly set down the letter and stared off into empty space. Alison sat up sharply and grabbed the page. Like the address on the purple envelope, it was neatly typed. With Brenda peering over her shoulder, she read:

My Dear Friend,

You do not know me, but I know you. Since you first breathed in this world, I have watched you. The hopes you have wished, the worries you have feared, the sins you have committed—I know them all. I am The Observer, The Recorder. I am also The Punisher. The time has come for your punishment. Listen closely, the hourglass runs low.

At the bottom of this communication is a list of names. Your name is at the top. What is required of you—at present—is a small token of obedience. After you have performed this small service, you will remove your name from the top of Column I and place it at the bottom of Column II. Then you will make a copy of this communication and mail it to the individual now at the top of Column I. The specifics of the small service you are to perform will be listed in the classified ads of the Times *under personals. The individual following you on the list must receive their letter within five days of today.*

Feel free to discuss this communication with the others on the list. Like myself, they are your friends and are privy to your sins. Do not discuss this communication with anyone outside this group. If you do, that one very sinful night will be revealed to all.

If you do not perform the small service listed in the paper or if you break the chain of this communication, you will be hurt.

Sincerely,
Your Caretaker

Column I	*Column II*	*Column III*
Fran	____________	____________
Kipp	____________	____________
Brenda	____________	____________
Neil	____________	____________
Joan	____________	____________
Tony	____________	____________
Alison	____________	____________

For a full minute, none of them spoke or moved. Then Brenda reached to tear the letter in two. Alison stopped her.

"But that's insane!" Brenda protested. She was angry. Fran was shaking. Alison was confused. In a way, they all felt the same.

"Let's think a minute before we do anything rash," she said. "If we destroy this letter, what advantage does that give us over the person who sent it?" Alison drummed her knuckles on the table top. "Give me that envelope." Fran did so. Alison studied the postmark, frowned. "It was mailed locally."

"Maybe it's a joke," Brenda said hopefully. "One of the guys at school, maybe?"

"How could they know about *that* night?" Fran asked, her voice cracking.

With the mere reference to the incident, the room changed horribly. An invisible choking cloud of fear could have poured through the windows. Brenda bowed her head. Fran closed her eyes. Alison had to fight to fill her lungs. Whenever she remembered back to last summer, she couldn't breathe. Were this letter and her recent nightmares connected or coincidental? Seven of them had been there that night. The same seven were listed at the bottom of the letter. She had felt the empty windows of the neighboring houses staring at her. Did this *Caretaker* wait behind one of them?

Alison shook herself. This was not a nightmare. She was awake. She was in control. The hollow, bloodshot eyes and the lifeless, grinning mouth were only memories. They couldn't reach her here in the present.

"We should have gone to the police." Fran wept. "I wanted to, and so did Neil."

"No, you didn't," Brenda said. "You didn't say anything about going to the police."

"I wanted to, but you guys wouldn't let me. We killed him. We should have . . ."

"We didn't kill anybody!" Brenda exploded. "Don't you ever say that again. Are you listening to me, Fran? What happened was an accident. For all we know, he was already dead."

"He wasn't," Fran sobbed. "I saw him move. I saw . . ."

"Shut up!"

"He was making gurgling sounds. That meant . . ."

"Stop it!"

"Quiet down, both of you," Alison said, knowing she had to take charge. "Arguing won't help us. We had this same argument a hundred times last summer. The fact is, none of us knows whether he's dead or alive. . . ." She froze, aghast at her slip, at the idea that must have formed deep in her mind the moment she had read the letter. Fran and Brenda were staring at her, waiting for an explanation. She had meant to say: The fact is, none of us knows whether he *was* dead or alive. Of course, he must be dead now. They had buried him.

"What do you mean?" Fran asked, shredding her palms with her clenched fingernails.

"Nothing," Alison said.

"You mean that *he* wrote this letter," Fran said, nodding to herself. "That's what you mean, I know. He's coming back for revenge. He's going to . . ."

"Stop it!" Brenda shouted again. "Listen to yourself; you're babbling like a child. There are no ghosts. There are no vampires. This is nothing but a joke, a sick, sick joke."

"Then why are *you* so upset?" Fran snapped back.

"If I am, you made me this way. It's your fault. And that's all I'm going to say about this. Alison, give me that letter. I'm throwing it away, and then I'm going home."

Alison rested her head in her hands, massaging her temples. A few minutes ago, they had been happily gossiping and stuffing their faces. Now they were at each other's throats and had the dead haunting them. "Would you two do me a favor?" she asked. "Would you both please stop shouting and allow us to discuss this calmly?" She rubbed her eyes. "Boy, have I got a headache."

"What is there to discuss?" Brenda asked, picking at a Twinkie with nervous fingers. "One of the others, either Joan, Tony or Neil sent this letter as a joke."

"You didn't mention Kipp," Fran said. Kipp was Brenda's boyfriend. He was also, without question, the smartest person in the school.

Brenda was defensive. "Kipp would never have written something this perverse."

"Would Neil or Tony have?" Alison asked. Tony was the school quarterback, all-around Mr. Nice Guy, and a fox to boot. She was crazy about him. He hardly knew she was alive. Kipp and Neil were two of his best friends. "Brenda, you know them best."

"Neil wouldn't have, that's for sure," Fran cut in. She shared Alison's problem. Fran was crazy about Neil and he hardly knew she was alive. It was a mixed-up world.

Alison had to agree with Fran. Though she had spoken to him only a few times, Neil had impressed her as an extremely thoughtful person. Besides Fran, he had been the only one who had wanted to go to the police last summer.

"Yeah," Brenda agreed. "Neil doesn't have this kind of imagination."

"How about Tony?" Alison asked reluctantly. It would be a shame to learn her latest heartthrob was crazy.

Brenda shook her head. "That guy's straighter than Steve Garvey. Joan must have sent it. She's such a jerk."

As Kipp was the Brain and Tony was the Fox, Joan was the Jerk. Unfortunately, Joan was also the unrivaled school beauty, and she was *extremely* interested in Tony. And Joan knew that Alison also liked Tony. The two of them hadn't been getting along lately. Nevertheless, it was Alison's turn to shake her head.

"Joan's a cool one, but she's not stupid," she said. "She knows full well what would happen if that night became public knowledge. She wouldn't hint at it aloud, never mind have put it in print." She drummed her knuckles again. "The only possibility left is that one of the seven of us intentionally or unintentionally leaked some or all of what happened that night to someone else. And that someone else is out to use us."

"That makes sense," Brenda admitted. She glared at Fran. "A lot more sense than a vengeful corpse."

"I didn't say that!"

"Yes, you did!"

"Shh," Alison said, her nerves raw. "Do you have a copy of today's *Times,* Fran?"

Fran was anxious. "You don't think they would have what they want me to do in the paper already?"

"I would just as soon look and see than have to think about it," Alison said. "Do you have the paper?"

"We get it delivered each morning," Fran stuttered, getting up slowly. "I'll check in the living room."

Fran found the paper and Alison found the proper section

and a minute later the three of them were staring at a very strange personal ad.

Fran. Replace the mascot's head on the school gym with a goat's head. Use black and red paint.

"Who would want to ruin Teddy?" Brenda asked. They had a koala bear for a school mascot, first painted on the basketball gym by Fran, her single claim to fame. Yet, perhaps not surprisingly, she appeared more than willing to sacrifice Teddy to avoid the letter's promised hurt.

"I'll have to do it at night," Fran muttered. "I'll need a ladder and a strong light. Ali, do you know when the janitors go home?"

"You're not serious?" Brenda asked. She addressed the ceiling. "She's serious; the girl's nuts."

"But Kipp has to get his letter within five days," Fran moaned. "That means I have to paint the goat head and move my name and everything by Thursday." Fran grabbed her hand. "Will you help me, Ali?"

"What kind of nut could have written these things?" Alison wondered aloud. The tone was of a psychotic with delusions of godhood. A genuine madman could be dangerous. Now was the time to go to the police . . . If only that wasn't out of the question. "What did you say, Fran? Oh, yeah, sure I'll help you. But not to paint the goat's head. We need to tell the others. Then we'll decide what to do. Who knows, one of the others might burst out laughing and admit that it was just a joke after all."

"I can see it now." Brenda nodded confidently, pouring another glass of milk and ripping into a packet of Ding Dongs.

"I hope so," Fran said, dabbing at her eyes with a tissue and blowing her nose.

"So do I," Alison whispered, picking up the off-purple envelope and the pale green letter. The line: "What is required of you—at present—is a small token of obedience," bothered her. Painting a goat's head on their school mascot was no major demand. Some people might even consider it humorous. Perhaps all the demands would be similar. However, when they were all in Column II, the chain would be complete. Then maybe it would start over again, and the "small token of obedience" might no longer be so small.

Chapter Two

"Everything looks the same, Kipp," Tony Hunt said, standing at the window of his second story bedroom, looking west into the late sun. Some kids were playing a game of touch football in the street; their younger brothers and sisters sat on the sideline sidewalks on skateboards and tricycles, cheering for whoever had the ball—a typical tranquil scene in a typical Los Angeles suburb. Yet for Tony it was as though he were looking over a town waiting for the bomb to drop. The houses, trees and kids were the same as before, only seen through dirty glasses. He'd felt this way before, last summer in fact, felt this overwhelming desire to go back in time, to yesterday even, when life had been much simpler. Chances were the chain letter was a joke; nevertheless, it was a joke he'd never laugh over.

"We won't have such a nice view out the bars of our cell, that's for sure," Kipp Coughlan said, sitting on the bed.

"I'm telling my lawyer I won't settle for a penitentiary without balconies," Tony said.

"A while back, they used to hang convicts from courthouse balconies."

Tony turned around, taking in with a glance the plain but tidy room; he was not big on frills, except for his poster of a *Sports Illustrated* swimsuit model, which hung on the wall at the foot of his bed and which greeted him each morning with an erotic smile. "You know, we're not being very funny," he said.

"Really. Has Alison gotten hold of Joan?"

"Not yet. Joan's away with her parents at Tahoe. She wasn't at school today. But she should be home soon."

"She'll freak when she hears about the letter," Kipp said.

Tony thought of Joan, her angel face and her vampish temperament, and said, "That's an understatement."

"Will Neil be here soon?"

Tony nodded, stepping to a chair opposite his bed, sitting down and resting his bare feet on a walnut case where he stowed his athletic medals and trophies. It drove his mom nuts that he kept the awards locked up where no one could see them; he liked to think it was beneath his dignity to show off. Of course if that were true, why did he collect them at all? When he was honest with himself, he had to admit a good chunk of his self-image was built on his athletic successes. Grant High had won the league title in football last fall, and it had been his passing arm that had been hugely to thank, a fact that was often mentioned but never debated at school. At present, running in the quarter mile and half mile, he was leading the track team to a similar championship. What made him slightly ashamed of his accomplishments, he supposed, was his being a hero in a group he couldn't relate to. He was a jock but he really didn't give a damn what NFL team acquired who in the draft. He could never carry on a conversation with his teammates, and he despised their condescending attitude toward nonathletic students. That was one of the reasons he felt comfortable with Kipp and Neil. Neither of them could hike a football, much less score a touchdown.

"Neil called just before you arrived," Tony said. "He should be here any minute."

"Does he know that he now has a *Caretaker*?"

"Yeah. Alison gave him the gist of the letter over the phone."

Kipp grinned, which was always a curious affair on him. He had a buffoon's nose and a rabbit's ears, plus fair hair that had an unfortunate tendency to stick up, all of which at first glance made him look like a clown. But his intense black eyes belied the comparison. Even when he laughed, which was often, he looked like he was thinking. Kipp may not have been a genius, but he was close enough to make no difference. He had a 4.0 average and was going to M.I.T. come fall to study aeronautical engineering. He and Tony hadn't been friends for long; they had gotten beyond the superficial "Hey, what's happening?" level only after the incident last summer—nothing like a shared trauma to bring people together. He had the rare wit that could ridicule himself as comfortably as it did others. He loved to talk and, being a prodigious reader, usually knew what he was talking about. Tony was hoping he could shed some light on their dilemma.

"Why didn't you invite Alison to this discussion?" Kipp asked. "She wanted to come."

"Did she?"

"Brenda told me she did. And Brenda never lies, usually."

"Brenda's your girlfriend," Tony said. "Why isn't she here?"

"She says she's not scared, but I'm not sure I believe her. I didn't want us to have to have a hysterical female's opinion to deal with."

"Alison said Fran was the one who was most upset."

"You don't know Fran, she's always upset. She wouldn't even give Brenda the original letter for us to study." Kipp leaned forward and pulled a folded sheet of notebook paper from his back pocket. "Brenda copied it down word-for-word. Do you want to read it?"

"Alison repeated it to me twice on the phone. But let Neil read it. Then destroy it. I don't want copies of that blasted thing floating all over the place."

Kipp nodded. "So answer my question: Why not have Alison here?"

Tony shrugged. "At this point, what does she know that we don't?"

Kipp snorted. "Her liking you is no reason to be afraid of her. Look, you have no excuse to suffer the usual adolescent insecurities over creatures of the opposite sex. You're built like an ox, have apple pie in your blond hair, and the flag in your blue eyes. You're as All-American as they make them."

"How do you know she likes . . . oh, yeah, because Brenda told you and Brenda doesn't lie." Tony scratched his All-American head and tried to look bored. Actually, he always felt both elated and annoyed whenever he heard of Alison's interest in him: elated because he was attracted to her, annoyed because she was fascinated with someone who didn't exist. She saw only his image, the guy who could throw the perfect spiral to the perfect spot at the perfect time. If she were to get to know the real Tony Hunt—that shallow insecure jerk—she would be in for an awful disappointment. Besides, Neil had a crush on Alison and he never messed with his friends' girls. Indeed, Neil had asked Alison out a couple of weeks ago. She had turned him down but only because she was busy with drama rehearsals. He would have to get on Neil to try again.

"This is not the time to worry about starting a romance," Tony added, glancing out the window and seeing Neil Hurly limping—he had a bum knee—his way around the touch football game, his shaggy brown hair bouncing against his old black leather jacket, which he wore no matter what the temperature.

Neil was four years out of the back hills of Arkansas and still spoke in such a soft drawl that one could fall asleep listening to him. They had met the first week of their freshman year, sharing adjoining home room lockers. Tony had started the relationship; Neil had been even more shy then than he was now. What had attracted him to the guy had been clear to Tony from the start: Neil's rare country boy combination of total honesty and natural sensitivity. Usually kids who spoke their minds didn't give a damn, and those who did care deeply about things inevitably became neurotic and clammed up. Neil was a gem.

"Come right in, the folks are out!" Tony called. Neil waved and disappeared under the edge of the garage. A minute later he was opening the bedroom door.

"Hello Tony, hello Kipp," he said pleasantly, hesitating in the doorway. On the short side and definitely underweight, with features as soft as his personality, he was not a striking figure. Still, his eyes, a clear warm green, and his smile, innocent and kind, gave him a unique charm. If only he'd get a decent haircut and some new clothes, he would be more popular.

"Pull up a chair," Tony said, nodding to a stool in the corner. "Kipp, give him Brenda's copy of the letter."

"Thank you," Neil said, taking a seat and accepting the notebook page from Kipp. Tony studied Neil's face as he read the Caretaker's orders. Neil was not as bright as Kipp but he had an instinct for people Tony had learned to trust. He was disappointed when Neil did not dismiss the letter with a chuckle.

"Well?" Kipp said, growing impatient.

Neil carefully refolded the paper and handed it back to Kipp. His pale complexion seemed whiter than a couple of minutes ago. "The person who wrote this is seriously disturbed," he said.

Tony forced a smile. "Come on. It's a prank, don't you think?"

"No," Neil said carefully. "It sounds . . . dangerous."

Tony took a deep breath, holding it like it was his slipping hope, knowing he would have to let go of both soon. He turned to Kipp. "You're the scientist. Give us the logical perspective."

Kipp stood—perhaps for dramatic effect, he loved an audience—and began to pace between the door and the bed. Almost as tall as Tony but thirty pounds lighter and hopelessly uncoordinated, he moved like a giraffe. "I disagree with Neil," he said. "I think it's a joke. That's the simplest explanation and it does away with us having to search for a motive. What probably happened is that one day one of the girls was feeling particularly guilty and blabbed about the accident to a friend, who in turn told God knows who about it. Somewhere along the line, the information got to someone with a kinky sense of humor."

"Alison was very firm that none of them had spoken about the accident to anyone outside the group," Tony said. "Unless Joan did, which seems unlikely."

"Naturally they would deny it," Kipp said. "Girls can't be

trusted, and here I'm not excluding Brenda." He paused, leaning against the bookcase, thinking. "Or maybe they blabbed about it accidentally . . . Say Fran was talking to Alison in the library about last summer and they didn't know they were being overheard."

"Have either of you ever discussed the accident in public?" Tony asked.

"Are you kidding?" Kipp said.

"I would be afraid to," Neil said, glancing at the closed door. "I feel bad talking about it now."

"I know what you mean," Tony said. "I'm sure the girls feel the same way. I can't imagine them gossiping about it with even the slightest chance of being overheard."

"Then let's return to one of them doing it intentionally," Kipp said. "That medieval urge to go to Confession could be at work here. One of the girls must have felt they had to unburden themselves on someone unconnected with the deed."

"I can't help noticing how you keep blaming the girls," Tony said. "Do you have one in particular in mind?"

"Fran," Kipp answered without hesitation. "She's high-strung; she speaks without thinking. She could have told anybody. I think a couple of us should take her aside and squeeze the truth out of her."

"But even if she were to admit to telling someone," Tony said. "That doesn't mean that *someone* wrote this letter. Like you said, the information could have passed through several hands."

"We can only hope it hasn't gone outside a tiny circle of people," Kipp said.

"And what if this Caretaker is not joking?" Tony said. "What if he or she really would try to hurt us?"

He had not expected an answer to that question and he didn't get one. A minute passed in silence, during which Tony had a vivid mental image of the expression on his parents' faces if the truth were to come out, their shock and disappointment. More than the others, he had been to blame. Certainly a judge would see it that way. He might be sent to jail, and if the family of the man came forth, his parents would probably be saddled with a heavy lawsuit. College would have to be put on the shelf for years, and his record and image would be permanently ruined. Above all else, the incident could not be made public knowledge.

"We'll question Fran," Tony said finally. "But we'll let Brenda and Alison do it, and no one's going to *squeeze* her. And I don't think we should count on a confession. Let's look at other alternatives. What do you say, Neil?"

Neil appeared momentarily startled by the question, as if he had been lost in his own thoughts and had not been listening to the discussion. He fidgeted on his stool, said hesitantly, "I think the Caretaker might be one of us."

"You mean that one of us is playing a joke on the rest?" Kipp asked.

"Not necessarily."

"I don't understand," Tony said, not sure he wanted to.

"Someone in the group might be out to hurt someone else in the group," Neil said. "Or maybe everyone in the group. The Caretaker could be right in front of us."

"That's ridiculous," Kipp snapped. "What would be their motive? They would only be hurting themselves by revealing the incident."

Neil reached out his hand, indicating he wanted another look at the letter. Kipp was quick to oblige him. Neil read it at least twice more before speaking. "The way this is worded—the paragraph structure and all—the Caretaker seems to be separating the revelation of the accident from the manner in which he would hurt us. He could hurt us without telling a soul about the man."

"How?" Tony asked.

Neil shrugged. "There's hundreds of ways to hurt someone if you really want to."

"But who in our group would have the motive to do so?" Kipp asked, dismissing the possibility with his tone.

Neil gave a wry smile. "A crazy person wouldn't need a motive."

"It's illogical," Kipp said. "None of us fits the psychological profile. Now I say we—"

"Just a second," Tony interrupted. "The theory simplifies things in a way. We wouldn't have to explain how someone else came to learn about the man. Who do you think it could be, Neil?"

"I can't say."

Kipp went to speak but changed his mind. There followed another lengthy pause. In many ways, Neil's suggestion was the most disturbing; it was always worse to be stabbed in the back by a friend. Yet, try as he might, Tony could think of no one in the group who could write such a letter. On the other hand, he scarcely knew Alison and Fran, or for that matter, Joan and Brenda. He needed more information and wondered how he could go about getting it. He also wondered why Kipp was so anxious to dismiss Neil's suggestion.

The warm orange light slipped off Tony's face as the sun sunk below the city's false horizon of smog. In spite of the fact that he was sweating, he shivered. The day would be gone soon and they still had no clear idea what to do about tomorrow.

"Fran is frightened," he said. "If she doesn't confess, let's have her repaint the mascot tomorrow night and then pass the letter on. This will give us a breathing space to find more clues. You don't mind if the Caretaker comes after you, do you, Kipp?"

"As long as it's like Neil thinks, that he or she won't retaliate against me for not doing my duty by spreading the word about last summer." Kipp took the letter back and reread it closely. "Hmm, yes, it does seem that the phrase, 'You will be hurt,' is pointed toward the individual while the other threat is there to keep the group as a whole from seeking outside help."

"It's like we're in a haunted house we can't leave," Neil said.

A haunted house we're afraid to leave, Tony thought. They

could end their dilemma this minute by going to the police. But the threat of harm seemed preferable to certain disgrace.

The phone rang. All three of them jumped. Boy, they made lousy heroes. Tony leaned over and picked it up. "Hello?"

"What is this crap about the hourglass and our sins?" Joan demanded in her throaty voice. In spite of the situation, Tony had to smile. Every high school needed a Joan Zuchlensky. She separated the jerks from the phonies from the wimps. She was gorgeously gross; her angelic face let her get away with her crude personality—at least as far as the guys were concerned; she didn't have many girlfriends. And her coarseness just made her all the more attractive. Her eyes were a darting gray, her lips thick and sexy, her hair a taunting platinum punk-cropped masterpiece. More than anything, she looked nasty, and Tony could attest to the fact that the package could live up to its wrapping. He had gone out with her a few times with the excuse that she was "an interesting person," but in reality to see if he couldn't further his sex education. Their last date, they had gotten into some heavy fooling around. If he hadn't started rehashing in his mind all the sound advice he'd read online, frustrating Joan in the extreme, they would certainly have gone all the way. There was always next time. . . .

"I take it you heard the news," Tony said.

"Yeah, Brenda told me all about it." She paused and lowered her voice, and perhaps a trace of anxiety entered her tone. "What are we going to do?"

"Fran will repaint the mascot, then we're going to see if the ax falls on Kipp."

"Why don't we go after the guy?"

"As soon as we figure out who it is, we will." What they would do with the person if they did find him was a question Joan thankfully didn't ask.

"As long as that mess in the desert stays secret. You know my old man's a cop? I swear, he'd have me locked up if he found out."

"If the truth did come out, we could just deny it," Tony said. That was not really as simple as it sounded. If they were questioned by the police, their guilt, especially Fran's and Neil's, would be easy to read. And the Caretaker might very well know where they had buried the body.

Joan laughed. "And here I was getting so bored with these last few weeks of school! It looks like they're going to be wild." She added, "Hey, I've got to go. Let's talk tomorrow at lunch. And let's get together some other time, huh?"

"Sure." Lust was not at the forefront of his mind. Whoever had said danger was an aphrodisiac had said so in safe surroundings.

They exchanged good-byes, and Tony turned back to his companions. Kipp was meticulously shredding his copy of the chain letter. Neil was massaging his right leg just beneath the knee. He had injured the leg in P. E. a couple of months back and was supposed to have arthroscopic surgery on the cartilage sometime soon. Neil was having a lot of health problems. He had recently been diagnosed as diabetic. He had to inject himself with insulin daily and had to monitor his diet religiously. He said it was a hassle but no big deal.

"When are you going to get that joint worked on?" Tony asked.

Neil quickly withdrew his hand from the sore area. "My mom and I are still trying to put together the doctor's fee. We're almost there."

Neil's father had died when Neil was three, and his mother had never remarried. She worked two waitress jobs—lunches at a Denny's Coffee Shop, dinners at a Hilton restaurant—and Neil put in long hours at a twenty-four-hour gas station. They barely seemed to get by. Tony had a couple of grand in the bank, but knew it would be useless offering it to Neil, who could be unreasonably proud at rimes.

"The way your body's falling apart, pretty soon we're going to be measuring you for a box," Kipp said good-naturedly, though Tony would have preferred if he had kept his mouth shut. Kipp's sense of humor did not always run the right side of good taste. Sometimes he sounded like . . .

Like someone who could write a weird letter?

Tony knew he had better stop such thoughts before they could get started. If he didn't, he'd never get to sleep tonight.

"Ain't that the truth," Neil agreed, not offended. "I've had so much bad luck lately . . ." His eyes strayed to the remains of the letter. ". . . I sometimes wonder if someone ain't put a hex on me."

The opposite of hardheaded Kipp, Neil was superstitious. Kipp often teased him about it, and he had the bad sense to do it now.

"A ghost, maybe, in a tan sports coat?"

"Kipp, for God's sake!" Tony said, disgusted. The man had been wearing a tan coat.

"It's possible, I think," Neil said softly, his eyes dark. "Not the type of ghost you're talking about, but another kind, I mean."

Kipp giggled. "What *do* you mean?"

"Hey, let's drop this, OK? It's dumb and it doesn't help us." Tony stood and went to the window. The football game had ended and the kids had disappeared. The street was quiet. Soon his parents would come home. He wanted the guys gone before they arrived. It was getting dark.

"I mean, none of us is a doctor," Neil continued as though he had not heard him. "You read online how someone's heart stops, their breathing stops, and then, a few hours later, they're up and walking around. It happens quite a lot, I understand. And sometimes these people talk about the strange things they saw and the strange places they went to while they were dead. Usually, it sounds nice and beautiful. But this one man I read about who tried to commit suicide talked about a place that sounded like hell. It made me sick reading about it. But what I wanted to say was that these people who die and come back sometimes develop powers. Some can heal, while others can read minds and transmit thoughts. It's supposed to depend on how they died, whether they were scared or not."

Could there be a death worse than premature burial? Tony asked himself. Edgar Allan Poe had spent a lifetime obsessed with the idea, and he had been a devotee of horror. It was obvious that this is what Neil was driving at.

And the grave they had dug had been shallow.

Shallow enough to escape from? Maybe . . .

Dead dammit!

He simply could not allow these paranoid possibilities a chance to start to fester. They had checked and rechecked: No pulse, no breathing, no pupil response, no nothing. Dead, absolutely no question.

"And what else have you learned reading *The National Enquirer*?" Kipp asked sarcastically.

Neil did not answer, hanging his head toward the floor. Tony crossed the room, put his hand on his shoulder. Neil looked up, his green eyes bright.

"The person who sent this letter is alive," Tony said firmly. "It might even be, like you suggested, someone in the group. But it's certainly not a psychic zombie who can give us diabetes from a distance or force us to turn ourselves in against our will."

Neil smiled faintly, nodded. "Sure, Tony. I'm just sort of scared, you know?"

Tony squeezed his arm. "You're no different from the rest

of us. No different from even Kipp here, though he would be the last to admit it."

"Judges and juries frighten me more than witches and werewolves," Kipp muttered.

On that pragmatic note, the discussion came to an end. Tony walked them both to the front door and told them that as long as they stuck together they'd be all right. It sounded like a decent send-off remark.

He had been worried about getting to sleep that night but as he climbed the stairs back to his room, he felt suddenly weary and collapsed on his bed with his pants still on, his teeth unbrushed and his window wide open. Coach Sager had put them through a grueling workout in track practice that afternoon, but Tony knew it was wrestling with the unknown Caretaker that had worn him out. If only he could sleep now he could recover his wits for tomorrow.

And he got his wish, for within minutes he began to doze, or rather, he started to dream, which must have meant he was asleep. But the sleep was anything but restful. A shadow stood over him all night, forcing him to labor on a task that seemed impossible to complete. They were in a deserted field and he was working with his bare hands, digging a grave that would never be deep enough.

Chapter Three: Last Summer

The concert had been great. Tony's ears were ringing and he couldn't hear himself think, much less hear what the others were talking about. The crowd was thinning but it was still hard walking. There were no lights in the Swing Auditorium parking lot and out here in the valley there wasn't nearly the background glow of electric L.A. It was like being stuck in a black cave with a herd of cattle. He stumbled on broken asphalt and almost tripped Joan, who was holding on to his hand. He felt loaded and hadn't even had a drink. Then again, there had been enough dope smoke in the air to waste the security guards.

"What did you say?" Tony yelled at Joan.

"I didn't say anything!" Joan yelled back, sounding ten miles away but leaning close enough to make him wonder if the evening's fun wasn't only beginning. She was wearing tight white pants, a skimpy orange blouse, and her hair was all over the place, including in his face.

"It was I!" Kipp giggled, hanging on to Brenda, the two holding each other up. They had sure put away the beer on the long drive out to the auditorium. There were still several six-packs left. "Where the hell did I put my car?"

"There it is!" Brenda laughed, pointing so vaguely that she could have meant half the parking lot.

"I drive a Ford, not a Volkswagen!" Kipp shouted. "Hey, Neil, do you remember where my blue baby is?"

Neil did not have a date but they had brought him because he loved music and because he was such a great guy to have around when you were trying to find your car. He didn't drink and appeared impervious to marijuana smoke. He answered Kipp, but his voice was lost in the crowd and the ringing ears.

"You're going to have to speak up!" Kipp shouted.

Using hand signs, Neil managed to get across the message that they should follow him. Tony stumbled obediently on his heels, bumping into Joan whenever possible, with her hanging on to his pants pockets, giggling and cursing up a storm as they dodged people and slid between jammed cars. The maze seemed endless. Finally, however, Neil halted and by golly if they weren't standing next to Kipp's pride and joy—a super-charged '97 Ford. Kipp had parked at the far end of the lot where they could supposedly enjoy a quick getaway. Too bad the exits were all on the other end of the lot.

The wait in the traffic was tedious. The concert had strung them all up and now they had to move like snails. A half hour later and they were still captives of the carbon-monoxide-spouting train. To pass the time, Kipp—who was driving, naturally—and Brenda set to work on the remainder of the beer. Joan even had a couple of cans, though her dad always gave her a sobriety test when she got home from being out late, and Tony thought what the hell and put away a couple of beers himself. The alcohol seemed to dull the ringing in his head. Neil took a can, too, after prodding from Brenda, but nursed it carefully.

They were on the verge of a breakthrough to the street that led to the freeway when someone knocked on their window.

"Alison!" Brenda squealed when Kipp rolled down the window, letting in a fog of exhaust. "Wow! It's *sooo* amazing running into you here!"

"Brenda, I was with you when we bought tickets for this concert," Alison said, ducking her head partway into the car. Her curly black hair was held back with a pin and there were oil stains on her hands. She looked slightly exasperated, unusual for her—Alison always impressed Tony as being in control. He was sitting in the backseat and, for reasons known only to his sober mind, he immediately took his hand off Joan's knee. "Hi Neil! Hi Joan!" She smiled. "Like the concert, Tony?"

He grinned. "Wasn't loud enough."

"Having car trouble?" Neil asked from the dark corner of the backseat. The car in front was moving and if they didn't move too, the horns would start quick. Alison held up her oily hands.

"Yes. Fran and I are killing the battery. It just refuses to turn over. Could you please . . ."

"Call the auto club," Joan interrupted. "I've got to get back soon or my old man will be out on the porch with his shotgun." The car behind them honked. "Come on, Kipp. Move it."

"Pull over to the left," Tony said, though he knew Joan's dad disliked him and would only be too happy to have an excuse to castrate him with buckshot. Joan scowled but held her tongue.

"Sure," Kipp said. Alison stepped back and he swung out of line, their personal slot vanishing quickly. The glaring rows of headlights at their back made it a sure bet it would be a while before they got another shot at the freeway.

Fran's car was a Toyota Corolla, and Kipp promptly snorted his disgust for Japanese workmanship. While he tried jumping the battery, Tony checked for loose wires and Neil peered in the gas tank. All systems appeared go until Kipp put the jumper cables directly on the starter. It didn't so much as click, and they knew where they stood.

"Call the auto club," Joan repeated when they paused for a hasty conference on what to do next. "You're a member, aren't you, Fran?"

"I don't know. Am I?"

"I am," Alison said. "I guess I could call . . ."

"No," Tony said quickly. "It would take one of their men forever to get through this traffic. This is a run-down area. Neither of you would be safe waiting around. You're coming home with us."

"But my dad will have to drive all the way out here tomorrow to fix it," Fran complained.

"He won't mind the inconvenience once he understands it was to insure your safety," Tony said smoothly, having absolutely no idea about Fran's father's position on such matters.

"There's no room in Kipp's car for seven people," Joan growled.

"No problem," Kipp belched, swaying. "You can sit on my hands." Brenda punched him. "My lap, I mean." Brenda hit him again.

"Joan," Tony said with a trace of irritation, "auto club employees do not install starters, especially in the middle of the night. It's settled; now let's get back in line. And Kipp, give me your keys. You're drunk."

"If I was drunk," Kipp mumbled indignantly, "would I have trouble seeing like I am now?"

He handed over his keys a minute later.

Two hours had gone by and they were lost. At least the traffic had disappeared. They hadn't even seen another car in twenty minutes. Tony was sure he had gotten on the freeway going west toward L.A., but he wasn't sure when *or how* he had switched freeways—not all the signs were lit up in this crazy part of the country—and Alison's shortcut on the surface roads back to the correct freeway had definitely been a mistake. She was in the back this minute, poring over a tattered map with a flashlight, telling him to turn this way and that. The first gas station he saw, he was pulling over. In fact if he saw an ordinary house, he might stop. The surrounding fields seemed to stretch to infinity. They could have stumbled into the heart of the Australian desert.

Nevertheless, they were having fun. They had plenty of gas and fine conversation and the beer tasted good and he was no longer worried about the alcohol slowing his reflexes. He'd only had a few cans, anyway, and he was a big boy and had a hearty liver. He knew what he was doing and as soon as he knew where he was going he would be just fine. Joan's mood had lightened considerably—her old man was away fishing, she had remembered—and she was laughing and the way her legs were rubbing against his was distracting but he wasn't complaining. Even Fran was full of holiday cheer—she was unmistakably loaded—and Kipp had taken to reminiscing, which was always a riot. No one could lie with a straighter face than Kipp.

"Should I tell them, Tony, about the time we snuck into Coach Sager's house to steal his kitchen sink and caught him seducing one of Grant High's teenyboppers?"

"Tell them the whole story." Tony nodded. Coach Sager

was the football and track coach. They had never been within a mile of his house, wherever that was.

A road was approaching, narrower than the one they were on but running north and south. As the silhouette of the mountains was nowhere to be seen, Tony decided they must have come too far south. "Think I should make a right here, Ali?" he asked, slowing.

"Is there a sign?" she asked, apparently lost in a part of the map that was mostly gray. He could see her in the rearview mirror. She'd let her hair down and was looking all right.

"No sign."

"Might as well give it a try," she said. "We *must* be too far east."

"But this road runs north." Tony squinted. Either it was taking a long time for the brakes to take hold or else the road was approaching amazingly fast. He had to hit the pedal hard at the last instant to make the turn. There was a screech of rubber, and gravel sprayed the Ford's underbelly. He flipped on the high beams, rubbing his eyes. The night seemed to be getting darker.

"It was a Saturday night," Kipp began. "We thought the coach was gone for the evening, you see, and we wanted to unhook his kitchen sink and put it in the attic so when he called the cops he'd have to tell them that they took *nothing* but the kitchen sink!" Kipp laughed at the prospect and the rest of them laughed with him.

"Give me another beer, Fran," Brenda said.

"Have mine," Joan said. "I'm full."

They hit a bump and Tony's head hit the ceiling. The road was uneven but straight as an arrow and looked like it could stretch across the state. He decided to accelerate.

"At first he *was* out," Kipp continued, burping. "We practically had the last bolt unscrewed and hadn't even scratched the blasted sink. Then we heard the garage door opening and wc knew we were in trouble. But we didn't panic, we were cool. We raced upstairs and hid under the bed in the master bedroom. We could have snuck out the back door—that's how we came in—but we knew we were on to hot stuff when we heard female squeals coming from the garage."

"Get off it," Joan muttered.

"It's true! It's true! Now here comes the good part. When we were lying under the bed, what do we hear but Coachy bringing the young lady upstairs. I tell you, my gut almost split holding back the laughter. Especially when I remembered I had my phone. When I pushed the record button, I knew I was capturing something for posterity."

"What did they do?" Fran gasped.

The white strip disappeared from the center of the road. Tony was bothered at first but then figured he now had the whole road to himself. It was nice not having to stop for lights and pedestrians. All he had to watch out for were the tumbleweeds. A wind must have kicked up outside; the big thorny brown balls kept bouncing across his path, forcing him into an occasional swerve. The dust was also a pain, the headlights straining through it as they would have through filthy fog. But neither the weeds nor sand was a major problem. Joan put a beer in his hand and he sipped it gratefully. They may not have been heading in exactly the right direction but they were making excellent time.

"Everything," Kipp said. "They did things I haven't even done with Brenda."

"Kipp!" Brenda said.

"Brenda!" Fran said.

"What a crock of B.S." Joan said.

"Tony," Kipp said, "have I or haven't I spoken the sacred truth?"

"To the finest detail." He yawned, checking his watch. It was two-fifteen and it felt like it. He could have closed his eyes this second and gone to sleep. Maybe, he thought, he should let Alison drive.

"Where's your phone?" Joan asked.

"Huh?" Kipp said.

"If it's true, I want to hear it."

Kipp caught them all off guard. "All right," he said, pulling his phone from his pocket. "You'll have the rare and exciting privilege." After a quick search, he got the recording started. "This is confidential information, you understand."

There came a sound of sloppy footsteps, two pair, both anxious to get up the stairs, overlaid with fuzzy male and female voices. As the footsteps got louder, the voices grew clearer. To Tony's inestimable pleasure, the guy sounded like Coach Sager. The girl, also, seemed familiar.

"How old are you?" the coach was asking, his voice slurred as if he had been drinking, the lousy no good tyrant. They hit another bump and Tony vaguely wondered if it had been a rabbit.

"Eighteen," the girl crooned.

"I thought you said you were a junior?"

"So I flunked."

Wet kisses and lots of heavy breathing followed. Except for Fran's heavy breathing, the car was silent.

"Have you done this before?" Coach Sager muttered.

"Yeah, this afternoon."

"With who?"

"Some jerk on your team."

"All the boys on my team are jerks."

The realization hit Tony with a wallop and he almost went off the road. It was Kipp! He was a master at imitations. The others, except perhaps Brenda, didn't know that. Clothes rustled and stretched through the car's speakers. Zippers slowly pulled down. This was *soo bitchin'*!

"Let me do that." The girl sighed. "Oh, that's nice. Oh, I like that."

"Ain't I great?"

"I've heard you're the best." The girl groaned. "Ahhh."

"You heard right, baby," the coach whispered. "I love you, Joan."

The pandemonium was instantaneous, louder than any of the chords pounded out during the concert. The passionate couple continued their pleasure in relative private; who could hear them? Naturally, Kipp was laughing the hardest, but Joan's vehement denials—the girl who had played her part could have been a twin sister—pierced through the uproar.

"I never!" Joan swore. "I hate that bastard! Kipp!"

"I love you, Joan!" Kipp shouted with glee, knocking Brenda off his lap onto the floor where she sat giggling in a puddle of spilled beer. A tumbleweed somersaulted across the road, and Tony swerved neatly to avoid it. The traction on the tires, he observed, was superb.

"Wow, that's neat, do it again, Tony!" Fran cackled, her personality having done a one-eighty. "I knew it was you, Joan!"

"How was he?" Brenda yelled.

"Shut up!" Joan snapped. Kipp turned up the volume.

"We were meant to be lovers," Coach Sager said.

"Destiny." The girl moaned. "Ohhh."

"Turn that off, dammit!" Joan shouted. Four tumbleweeds squaredanced in front of the headlights, and Tony dodged them as he would obstacles on the arcade game, Pole Position. Joan fought for the switch on the tape player.

"You should never wear clothes, Joany," Coach Sager whispered loudly.

"Some jerk on your team!" Kipp jeered.

"Turn it off!" Joan swore, so furious she was unable to do it herself.

"Turn off the lights!" Fran cheered.

"Ahhh."

"Stop this, Tony!" Joan yelled. "Stop it this second!"

"I can't! I'm driving!" Tony yelled back, trying to stop laughing and failing miserably.

"You're like me, Joan," Coach Sager mumbled. "You're the best."

"Ahhh . . . ohhh . . ."

"I said stop!!!" Joan screamed. Then she did a very strange thing. She reached over across the steering wheel and punched out the lights.

Had the circumstances been normal, Tony would have flicked the lights back on, found his way to the freeway, taken everyone home and lived happily ever after. Unfortunately, he had three strikes against him. First, at the instant Joan did what she did, he was in the midst of avoiding still another scraggly tumbleweed and consequently was not driving perfectly straight. Second, no matter how many touchdowns he had thrown last fall, he was not such a tough dude that the forty plus ounces of beer in his bloodstream had not dulled important centers in his brain. Finally, had there been a speed limit in this godforsaken place, he would certainly have been in violation of it. Nevertheless, despite these handicaps, the night might have ended well if he'd had even a microsecond more time. His left hand had actually closed on the light switch and was pulling it out when the front right tire caught on the right edge of the road.

Tony did not know if he screamed, but if he didn't he was alone. The sounds of terror erupting from the throats of his friends signaled the beginning of the countdown of the twilight seconds. Time went into a slow-motion warp. When the tearing of the rubber against the asphalt started, he seemed to have all the time he needed to turn a bit to the right to take the car slightly further off the road, where it would be free of the sharp shoulder. But the edge must have had more drop than he realized, for it prevented the front wheel from turning as it should have. He succeeded only in trapping the back wheel. It was like riding a surfboard at midnight through a closing-out twenty-foot wave. He had both hands fastened to the steering wheel and there was no possibility of making another grab at the lights. At the first jolt, Alison's flashlight had smacked the dashboard and had gone out. Inside and outside, all was deathly black.

His friends began to scream his name. But so quickly, and so slowly, was everything happening that they were only pronouncing the *T* and had not yet moved on to the rest when he developed an alternative strategy. It was the exact opposite of the first one. He jerked the steering wheel to the left, intending to jump the irritating right edge of the road. And it worked—

too well in fact. They tore off the shoulder and plunged right off the other side of the road.

"Ahhh."

That was pseudo-Joan in the arms of Coach Kipp, her sighs of ecstasy miraculously making it through the howls of the others, at least for Tony's ears. His mind went right on assessing the situation and it was becoming more and more obvious it was time for plan X. When the roller coaster had started, he had immediately removed his foot from the gas, and the subsequent haggling with the shoulder of the road and the current cremation of the shrubs under the front fender had killed a fair percentage of their speed. A spinout now, so he figured, probably wouldn't tip them over. He slammed his foot on the brake.

The roar was deafening, made up of many ugly parts: burning rubber, shattering branches, blasting sand, screams and more screams. Tony closed his eyes—they were of no use anyway—and hung on for dear life.

Twice the car began to spin, but either because of his mastery of the steering wheel or because of blind luck they did not go completely out of control. They were grinding to a halt, heaving precariously in both directions, nevertheless looking as though they would live to tell the tale, when they hit *it.*

Soft, Tony thought, *too soft.*

The blow was nothing like impacting rock or tumbleweed or cactus. It felt bigger and heavier and, at the same time, more delicate. The shock wave it sent through the frame of the Maverick was one Tony would never forget.

The car stopped and stalled.

I hate driving.

Fran and Brenda were whimpering like small scared children, the rest of them gasping like big scared teenagers. The air stunk with sweat and the buzz had returned to Tony's head, only now it resembled more of a roar than a ring. He felt limp, the way he did after games against teams with three-hundred-pound defensive linemen, when every muscle in his body would cry not to be disturbed. The group's collective sigh of relief hung in suspension; it had been *too* close.

"Oh, Joan," Coach Sager whispered, "you were born to be naked."

Calmly and quietly, Joan turned off the recording.

Kipp began to laugh. It was such an outrageous thing to do that it was surprising no one told him to shut up. But then it began to sound, as gaiety often does in the worst of circumstances, strangely appropriate, and they joined in, laughing like maniacs for several minutes, hysterics close to weeping, the tension pouring out of them in loud gobs. When they were done and had caught their breaths and had thoroughly reassured themselves that they were alive, Tony flipped on the headlights. They were only a yard from the edge of the road, lined up parallel to the asphalt. Not too shabby for a drunk, he thought. He turned the key. The car started without a hitch.

"Anyone hurt?" he asked. No one spoke up. "Good." He slipped into gear, creeping onto the pavement. The frame was not bent, the wheels were turning free. All he wanted to do was get a couple of miles away before the next person spoke, to where it would make no sense to turn around and go back and look at . . .

What you might have hit.

"Don't you want to check for damage?" Brenda asked, nestling back into her boyfriend's lap.

"No," Kipp and Tony said simultaneously. They looked at each other, Joan sitting straight-faced between them, and Kipp nodded and a thousand unspoken imperative words were in the gesture, all of which could be summed up in a simple phrase: *Let's get the hell out of here!*

"I got to get home," Joan said quickly. "My dad will be furious. He'll take your head off, Tony. Let's go, let's go now."

"Right. Here we go." Tony nodded, pressing down on the accelerator. Fifty yards. Don't turn around. One hundred yards. It was just a cactus. One hundred and fifty yards . . .

"Tony," Neil said.

Tony hit the brake, threw the car in park and turned off the engine. His head fell to the steering wheel. Neil was like his conscience: quiet and soft-spoken and impossible to ignore. Tony took a deep breath, clenched his fists and sat upright. "Give me the flashlight." Brenda slipped it into his hand. "All of you, stay here," he ordered. "I'll be back in a few minutes."

"No," Kipp protested.

"Yes," Tony told him, reaching for the door.

Outside was a full-fledged dust storm. His eyes stung and he quickly had a dirty taste in his mouth. The flashlight flickered as he hurriedly retraced the deep grooves the tires had eaten into the dirt. A branch flung out of the shadows and slapped him in the face and he jumped twenty feet inside and the soles of his shoes didn't leave the ground. He was in a state a hairline beyond scared, where shock and dread stood as equals. A part of his mind he did not want to listen to was trying to tell him exactly what he would find.

Two hundred yards behind the car, he came to the man.

He lay on his back in a relatively casual position, no limbs bent at radical angles, his tan sports coat flung apart, untorn but filthy with dust. He was not old, thirty perhaps, nor was he tall, having Neil's slight build. The eyes were wide open, drawn up, focused on the mythical third eye, the gaze unnerving in the trembling light and the haunting wind. It was the mouth, however, that dropped Tony to his knees. A ragged trail of blood spilt out the corner of the slightly parted lips, and still, the guy looked like he was grinning.

Tony did not know how long he sat there, the flashlight

forgotten in the dirt. The next thing he was aware of was Kipp shaking him, seeming to call his name from the other end of a long tunnel. He raised his head with effort, found the others gathered in a half circle at his back.

"Is he dead?" Kipp asked. He was sober. His eyes had never looked so wide. He knelt by the man and felt for a pulse at the wrist.

"Looks it," Tony heard himself say.

Kipp touched the blood at the mouth. It was *not* dry. "Looks like he's been dead awhile."

The hope that swelled in Tony's chest was as bright as it was brief. "I don't think so," he said softly.

"You're saying *we* hit him?" Kipp asked, startled. Tony was thankful for the *we.* Before he could respond, Fran, Brenda, and Joan freaked out.

"I told you to slow down, Tony!" Fran squealed. "I told you when we were leaving the parking lot. I said, 'Tony, you're driving too fast.'"

"You imbecile." Joan swore. "*You* told him to turn off his lights."

"I never said that! I didn't mean it!"

"But it was *you,* Joan, who turned off the lights!" Brenda shouted. "You were so mad and drunk that you . . ."

"If I was drunk, who gave me the beer?" Joan shot back. "You! You brought the beer. You kept shoving it down our throats. No wonder Tony didn't know where he was going.

Which doesn't leave you out, Ali. You're the one who told him to come down this damn road."

"You're right," Alison said. The acceptance of responsibility had a quieting effect on the group. Alison came and knelt beside him, touching his arm. "What should we do, Tony?"

"I don't know. Find out who he is, I suppose." Tony was hoping Kipp would take the initiative. He didn't want to touch the guy. Kipp understood and began to go through the pockets. He should have closed the eyes first. With each touch of the body, they rolled slightly.

"He doesn't have a wallet," Kipp pronounced a minute later. "How could a guy this well dressed not be carrying a wallet? Someone must have raked him over, already. I tell you, we didn't kill him."

The sand was working its way under Tony's collar. The wind was warm and dry, a desert wind, uninterested in human affairs, hard to breathe. Like giant web-weaving spiders, dark tumbleweeds scraped the edge of their tiny circle of light. The man stared on, fascinated with what they couldn't see.

"It may have fallen out," Tony said. "Let's look for it."

Kipp was the only one who searched for the wallet. He found nothing. He hiked back to the car to check the fender. That piece of evidence was crucial. Had the man been standing or lying down when they had hit him?

There was a dent in the fender, Kipp reported when he

returned, but he said it was the same dent that had always been there. Tony could have sworn that there had not been a scratch on Kipp's car when the evening had begun.

Fran and Brenda began to cry. Joan started to pace. Neil maintained his motionless stance outside the glow of the flashlight and Alison continued to kneel by Tony's side, her head bowed. Kipp finally closed the guy's eyes. Not a car came by, not a person spoke. Tony checked his watch. They were running out of night, running out of time to . . .

Get rid of the body?

"We'll put him in the trunk," he said finally. "The authorities will be able to identify him." He waited for an objection and he probably would have been willing to wait till tomorrow night to get one. Kipp did not disappoint him.

"No way, you're not putting him in my car."

"Kipp, we can't just leave him here."

"Sure we can!" Joan cried, stopping her pacing and taking up a defiant stance on the other side of the body. She was no longer a sexy seventeen year old. She was a desperate woman. "My old man's a cop. I know those jerks. They'll question us separately. Fran and Alison will blab their mouths off. The cops will put the story together. Look, I admit it, I was the one who turned off the lights. I could be laid with a real heavy rap. Let's just get out of here. Let's just forget it."

"I agree completely," Kipp said. "Tony, someone else killed this guy. He was probably killed miles away and dumped here.

Listen, there's no parked car in the vicinity, there's no wallet, there's no dent . . ."

"There is a dent!" Tony exploded, and perhaps it was a last grasp at sanity. This craziness they were talking about, he knew, would follow them from this spot. But it was so tantalizing, so easy.

"There already was a dent!" Kipp yelled back. "I should know, it's my car. Don't you see, *it's my car.* Even if I was too drunk to be driving it, I'm as guilty as you are. We all are."

"I'm not," Fran whined.

"Shut up, or we'll run you over next!" Joan snapped.

"I'm for splitting," Brenda said. "He's already dead, what can we do for him?"

They thought about that for a minute and at the end of the minute, nothing had changed.

"I was driving," Tony said, forcing the ugly words out. "This was my fault. I should have . . . I shouldn't have drunk . . . I say we . . . We have to . . ." His throat was so dry, he couldn't finish. It was this damn wind, blowing straight up from hell. Kipp grabbed his arm and began to plead. He was given a sympathetic ear.

"You're eighteen, legally an adult. I know the law. You'll get manslaughter. And for what? Something you might not have done? Brenda's right, he's dead, we can't help him. We can only ruin our lives. Listen to me, Tony, I know what I'm talking about!"

Tony did not answer. He was waiting for Neil to speak. A word from Neil and he would turn himself in. But Neil trusted him to do what was right. Neil had always thought he was one super hero. Neil did not give him the word.

"If we won't go to the police," Alison said finally, "then we must at least bury him. We must show some decency."

"Would that be OK, Tony?" Kipp asked desperately. "We could say a prayer?"

So sorry, young sir.

Tony nodded, closing his eyes. That's how it was with prayers. They were always said when it was too late.

They carried the body fifty paces into the field, the skeletons of the sun-baked bushes grabbing for them like the claws of the cursed. They did not have a shovel. They used the bar that undid the wheel bolts, a large screwdriver and their bare hands to dig with. The ground was hard. The grave was shallow.

Fran gave them a brief scare when she suddenly jumped and screamed that the man was groaning. A quick check, however, showed that that was nonsense, and Joan belted Fran on the back of the head and dared her to open her mouth again.

They lowered him without ceremony, folding his hands across his heart, leaving what could have been a wedding ring on his finger. They begged Neil not to do it, but he insisted upon draping his crucifix around the man's neck just before they replaced the soil. They said one Our Father.

They found the freeway with remarkable ease. The return route was not complicated. Tony remembered it well. Had he a desire or a need to return to the gravesite, he would have had no trouble.

Chapter Four

The rehearsal was going lousy. This early in the morning—before first period—it was always hard to concentrate. Alison would have preferred working on *You Can't Take It with You* after school, but their drama teacher, Mr. Hoglan, had the erroneous belief that they were freshest closest to sunrise and could give him their best effort only when the birds were singing. Fran's swiping of the living room props was not helping matters. Alison had difficulty getting into her Alice role when she was supposed to look out the window and she had to stare into a featureless wall. But the biggest problem this morning was Brenda, who was playing Alice's sister, Essie. Essentially, the play was about Alice's introduction of her fiancé's super-straight parents to her own super-wacky family. Brenda, though she would never admit it, was effective only when playing weird characters. Essie's constant spastic dancing and frequent airhead one-liners created a role perfectly suited to her talents. Brenda, however, had already made it clear she disliked portraying "an unattractive geek." She was going out of her way this morning to reemphasize the point. She had added loudmouthed brain damage to Essie's character. In other words, Brenda was trying to drown out the rest of the cast. She was getting on Alison's nerves.

Normally, Alison loved being on stage. Turning into someone else seemed entirely natural to her. In her brief career she had played a conniving cat, a seductive vampire, a spoiled daughter, and even a psychotic murderer, and she had had to wonder if she hadn't at one time been all those things in past lives—she had felt so at home in their brains. But she realized a lot of her pleasure from acting came from simple ego gratification. She loved having people's attention totally focused on her.

"Let's go again," Mr. Hoglan called from the last row of the small auditorium. A short, pear-shaped middle-aged man with a thin gray beard and a thick jet black toupee, he was a superb instructor, knowing how to offer advice that did not cramp one's individual style. He was being very patient with Brenda this morning.

"From the top?" Alison asked. She was the only one on stage not holding a copy of the play. She always made it a practice to immediately memorize her lines. This also annoyed Brenda.

"No, start from: 'He's vice-president of Kirby & Company.'"

Alison nodded, taking her position. Mr. Hoglan gave a cue and she walked toward the coffee table—or where the coffee table was supposed to be—saying, "'No, he's vice-president of Kirby & Company, Mr. Anthony Kirby, Junior.'"

"'The boss's son?'" Brenda asked, with way too much enthusiasm.

"'Well,'" their mother said. Penny was played by Sandra Thompson and overweight Sandy already looked like someone's mother. She was a fine actress, though.

Alison took a step toward her mother and smiled. "'The boss's son. Just like the movies.'"

"'That explains the new dress!'" Brenda shouted. Alison grimaced, coming out of character; she couldn't help herself. Fortunately, at that moment, they were interrupted. It was not Mr. Hoglan, but a kid—a freshman, probably—in running shorts, standing at the open back door. He was talking excitedly about something on the gymnasium.

"What is it, young man?" Mr. Hoglan asked, unperturbed as ever.

"You've got to see it!" the kid exclaimed, and then he was gone.

Alison did not know why Brenda and she did not immediately put two and two together. As they hurried into the hallway after the rest of the class, the Caretaker was not even on their minds.

"You sure are in a bad mood this morning," Brenda said as they strode from beneath the wing of the auditorium into the bright morning sun. The day was going to be another cooker. Built in the fifties of red brick and austere practicality, Grant High did not have air-conditioning. During the months close to summer, sitting in class was more a dehydrating experience than an educational one.

"Thank goodness, we can't say the same about Essie."

"And what's that supposed to mean?"

"Get off it, Brenda, you'd think your character was doing a monologue."

"Not all of us have as many lines as some people. Some of us have to do the most with what we've got."

"Some of us shouldn't try to substitute volume for quality."

Brenda ran a hand through her blond hair, which looked oily and uncombed. "Don't hassle me right now, I'm exhausted. I hardly slept last night."

The Caretaker came back then, not that he'd been far away. Alison was also tired; she'd seen every hour on the clock between two and six in the morning. Twice she'd gone to the window to stare at the empty tract that surrounded her house. The moon had been full, bathing the neighboring fields—shrub-packed fields not unlike where they had gotten lost coming home from the concert. It was weird how fate had brought her to this spot that so resembled that one place in the whole world that filled her with dread.

They rounded a corner, almost colliding with the group that had gathered, and discovered that Fran had not gotten much sleep last night, either.

Their mascot, sweet smiling Teddy, now had a rather sinister black and red goat's head.

Lunch at Grant High was usually a humdrum affair. You either bought a greasy hamburger at the snack bar and went to a preordained clique or else you took a hop over to a nearby mall and had a greasy hamburger there and talked to much the same people you would have talked to had you stayed at school. The mall was nevertheless the preferable place to hang out. The courtyard in the center of school was cramped and the benches were the grossest obscenity-etched pieces of wood in all of California. When Alison grabbed Fran, prior to bawling her out, she planned on getting off campus the instant she was sure Tony was not staying. If nothing else, the chain letter had given her a great excuse to talk to him.

"Fran, you could have killed yourself doing the job alone," she scolded in hushed tones, glancing around to make sure they were not being overheard, searching for Tony.

"Do you like it?" Fran asked, dark circles under her eyes.

"What do you mean? Of course I don't like it. It's disgusting!"

Fran was very sensitive to criticism of her artwork. "I don't care! As long as *he* likes it!"

"And how do you know it is a *he*? Kipp is of the opinion

one of us girls blabbed about the accident. He thinks *you* were the one."

"I know what he thinks!"

"Shhh."

"I didn't tell anybody!" Fran said in a loud whisper.

Alison studied her pinched face, her trembling lips, and believed her. Fran would more likely have talked about the nude poster of Brad Pitt that she had painted. The only reason Alison knew about it was because Brenda had told her. She did not know how Brenda had found out about it.

"OK, don't get upset. I know you're good at keeping secrets. But why did you have to keep this a secret? I would have helped you."

"I didn't want you to get in trouble if a janitor came by."

The bravery was uncharacteristic of Fran. It made Alison wonder, just a tiny bit. "Did you send the letter to Kipp?"

"This morning. I whited out my name and typed it in the second column."

"You could have just given it to him."

"But the instructions said to mail it."

"How would whoever know? Oh, never mind . . . Oh, damn!"

"What is it?" Fran asked, springing to her toes. Joan Zuchlensky, strutting a black leather skirt and a silky white blouse, was plowing toward them.

"Here comes the Queen of the Roller Derby," Alison whispered. She smiled brightly. "Hello, Joany!"

Joan hated being called Joany. She wasn't fond of small talk, either. "Where's Tony and Neil?" she demanded.

Alison put her hand to her mouth. "Why, for the life of me, I can't remember where I tied their leashes." Nowadays, it was always this way between them. "Why ask me? I'm not their master."

Joan smiled slowly, chewing her lower lip, not out of nervousness, but because she was *bad*. "That's right, you don't got no guy at your beck and call." She shifted her gray eyes. "I loved your goat, Fran."

"Thank you," Fran mumbled, eyes downcast.

"It looks just like you." Joan went on, "So, Ali, what do you think of this Caretaker?"

"That he might be the perfect one to put you in your place."

Joan liked that and laughed. "Whatever he wants me to do, it won't be bad enough." She glanced at her hand, which she had propped against the tree, and her face changed. Joan had a phenomenal tan—rumor had it that she sunbathed nude in her backyard, and not always alone—but suddenly she turned bedsheet white. "Eeeh!" she shrieked, slapping her hand frantically.

"What's wrong?" Alison asked, at a complete loss.

"A spider!" Joan stamped the ground with her hard-tipped black leather boots.

Alison chuckled. Big Bad Joan. "So what? It won't bite."

"It did bite me!" Joan stopped her tribal dance and took

a couple of hot breaths, quickly regaining her composure. She knew she'd overreacted and was embarrassed. "So," she said evenly, "you don't know where Tony is?"

Alison turned to Fran. "Do you think we should insist she go to the hospital? Before the venom can reach her heart?" She couldn't resist the prodding, though she knew from experience it was not a good idea to humiliate Joan. The jerk had a long memory.

Joan raised one finger. "This letter reminds me of something I always wanted to tell you. I know you purposely faked car problems that night of the concert so you could ride home with Tony. What do you have to say about that?"

"That you're absolutely right," Alison lied.

"Ali!" Fran whined.

"Sounds like you're pretty hard up," Joan said.

"Sounds like you're afraid of losing what you don't have," Alison said.

Joan moved her finger to within an inch of Alison's nose. The purple nail was long, sharp. "Just keep your distance from Tony," she said coldly.

Alison threw her head back and laughed. "Why? Will I be . . ." The Caretaker's letter flashed before her eyes. "Will I be *hurt*?"

Joan smiled again, a sly sort of smile that seemed to cherish forbidden pleasure. "Remember," she said. "You've been told." She patted the top of Fran's head as if she were a pet, then walked away.

Just words, Alison thought, doubtful.

They saw Tony and Neil minutes later, approaching from opposite the direction Joan had disappeared. Alison had never before had the pleasure of having Tony walking straight toward her.

Neil struggled by his side, a head shorter, his long brown hair in need of a brush. Yet he was the first to smile, and Alison was quick to smile back. Neil's smile, next to Joan's, was like putting the Easter bunny beside a boa constrictor.

"Neil's with him," Fran whispered nervously.

"This is the chance you've been waiting for," Alison whispered back, speaking for both of them, her heart cruising along at a comfortable eight hundred beats a minute.

Fran gulped. "I could wait a little longer." She began to inch away. Alison grabbed her arm.

"If you split now, I'll tell Neil that you had an erotic dream about him last night."

"You wouldn't dare!"

"And I'll tell him you drew a picture about it when you woke up."

Fran decided to stay. The boys arrived moments later. Alison was pleasantly surprised when Neil offered his hand to both of them; politeness was never out of place in her book. Tony looked *sooo* cool.

But before they could so much as finish their hellos to one another, the principal of Grant High, Mr. Gregory Hall, joined their foursome. No doubt Alison would have panicked and Fran would have fainted had he looked the least angry. A tall thin man with a scarecrow face, Mr. Hall took care of his duties from behind the scenes. Less than half the student body even knew he existed. He must have had a photographic memory, however, for he greeted each of them by their first names.

"It was mainly you, Fran, that I wished to speak to," Mr. Hall said when they were through saying hello and commenting on the hot weather.

"Me?"

"Yes, about the terrible thing that happened to the gymnasium mascot." Fran went as still as the tree beside them. Mr. Hall nodded sympathetically, for all the wrong reasons. "I know how you must feel. I can promise when I find out who was responsible for this desecration, I will personally see to it that he is expelled."

"Personally," Fran said.

"What I was wondering is, would it be possible for you to redo the picture? Not necessarily right away, but whenever you feel sufficiently ahead in your schoolwork. I'm meeting with the board of supervisors this afternoon. I'm going to ask if we couldn't pay you for the job." Mr. Hall smiled. "How does that sound?"

Fran could have swallowed her tongue. Alison spoke up. "She would be happy to do it, wouldn't you, Fran?" Fran nodded. Alison added, "I think the job should be worth at least a hundred bucks."

"I was going to ask for two hundred." Mr. Hall looked hopeful. "So, do we have a deal?" Fran managed to move her head up and down a couple of times. "Wonderful! Now if I could steal you away from your friends for a few minutes to sign a paper to that effect, it would make my proposal to the board that much easier."

Mr. Hall practically had to carry Fran to the administration building. He must have thought the poor girl was heartbroken over the ruin of her creation. The three of them got a good laugh out of it. But once again, before they could even start a conversation they had another interruption—Neil this time, trying to excuse himself.

"Where do you have to go?" Tony asked, surprised.

"My locker." He flashed a quick smile. "Have a nice lunch." He turned to leave.

"Hey!" Tony said.

"Got to go," Neil called over his shoulder, limping away.

"Could he be chasing after Fran?" Alison asked hopefully.

Tony stared at her thoughtfully, a strand of blond hair touching near one of his blue eyes. She had to resist the temptation to brush it aside. "No, he's not," he said quietly.

His seriousness, his certainty, startled her. "She likes him at any rate. I wasn't sure if he knew."

Tony went to speak, caught himself. "Neil likes everybody," he said.

"He's a great guy." She hardly knew him.

Tony leaned against the tree and smiled. "Not wishing to change the subject, but isn't this a fine mess we're in? Any profound revelations strike you during the night?"

"Not really, unless you call nightmares revelations." During the brief spells when she had dozed off, she'd had this dream, over and over, where she had been trying to open the front door of her new house. What had been disturbing about the scenario had not been so much that the door had been stuck but that her hand had been stuck to the door.

Tony nodded. "I had a few of those myself."

"No," she said in disbelief. He seemed so much in command, it was hard to believe he was scared. On the other hand, he had been driving and stood the most to lose. It occurred to her then that, although she had watched Tony Hunt for four years, she knew absolutely nothing about the way his mind worked. He reinforced the idea when he remarked:

"You would be surprised."

"One thing did come to me. Maybe we weren't alone that night. It would explain a lot, someone watching us, I mean."

"No car drove by, I'm sure of that. But it's as reasonable an idea as any we kicked around yesterday."

"Brenda and I both gave Fran the third degree. I don't think there's much chance she talked." Tony nodded quickly, like he hadn't put much credence in the possibility. Alison continued, "What did you guys come up with? I would be very interested to know."

Tony shrugged. "The obvious, mostly. Except for Neil. He had two interesting theories. He thinks the Caretaker might be someone in the group, and that he or she is serious with their threats to harm us."

Alison thought of Joan but decided it would be a mistake to mention her name at this point. She didn't know how involved Tony was with her. Many times Joan had hinted that they were lovers—perish the thought. Tony seemed too discriminating to become that involved with someone whose only redeeming quality was that she did not carry a gun. Still, Tony was a guy, and Joan was so obviously available . . .

"What was Neil's other theory?"

"It's . . . hard to explain." He cleared his throat. "Hey, have you eaten?"

She shook her head. This was it! He was going to ask her out. He was going to fall in love with her.

"Would you like to go have a greasy hamburger at the mall?"

"No." *What?* She had meant to say yes! Of all the moronic times for the connection between her brain and her mouth to fizzle. "What I mean is," she stammered, "I'm on a diet."

He looked her over. "Are greasy french fries on your diet?"

"Oh, yes!"

He took her by the arm. "You're an unusual young lady, Alison."

Chapter Five

"It's been seven days," Kipp said with satisfaction, "and lightning hasn't struck yet. I tell you, the Caretaker was bluffing."

Four of them, Tony, Neil, Brenda and Kipp, were hanging out in the school parking lot next to Kipp's car. The early summer was showing no sign of an early departure. Heat radiated off the asphalt in rippling waves. A film of sweat had Tony's shirt glued to his chest and he was having a hard time imagining that in less than fifteen minutes he would have to start working out on the track.

The week-old event to which Kipp was referring was the appearance of the second command in the *Times.* It had employed initials rather than a name but otherwise it had been like the first, brief and to the point.

K.C. Flunk Next Calculus Exam

Kipp had gone right ahead and gotten an A on the test.

"No time limit was put on when you would be hurt," Neil said, brushing brown hairs off his shoulders. The diabetes or the stress or simply bad genes had him shedding like crazy. Tony was worried about him. Neil had been out of school all last week and he'd dropped five pounds from his already famished frame. He'd had the flu, he said, and was having trouble sleeping.

Kipp laughed. "It was a joke. Isn't that obvious?"

"I hope all this blows over before the play opens," Brenda said. "Neil, I saw you at our rehearsal this morning. What did you think?"

Neil beamed. "I thought you were wonderful. I left laughing."

Brenda fairly lit up. "Thank you. How sweet."

"I really like Alison as Alice," Kipp had to go and say. "That girl's got talent. You can see it just in the way she walks across the stage." He patted Brenda on the back. "I think you're great, too."

Brenda's lightbulb dimmed. "But not as great as Alison."

"Now I didn't say that."

"She has better lines than me! She's the star! What am I supposed to do? It isn't my fault that fat phony teacher thought I didn't look the part."

"Please," Kipp said, "let's not start this again. You're a fine actress. Alison is a fine actress. You're both fine actresses. In fact, you are probably the *finer* actress."

"You mean my style is not dramatic enough. That's what you mean, I know."

Kipp groaned, wiping the sweat from his forehead. "Look, let's fight about it on the way home. I'm tired of standing in this oven."

Brenda folded her arms across her chest. "I'm not going home with you. Who said I was?"

"I give you a ride home every day. I assumed . . ."

"Well, you assumed wrong, porpoise nose!" Brenda whirled and stalked away.

"I love you, too!" Kipp called. He shook his head. "I sort of hope the Caretaker is for real. Maybe he could scare her out of a few personality quirks." He climbed in his car, fastening his seat belt.

"Can I have a ride?" Neil asked. He usually walked home. His leg must be bothering him.

"Just don't ask me to comment on your talents," Kipp said, starting the car. Neil got in the front seat.

Tony leaned on the open window. "I notice you're buckled up. Since when did that start? Last week, maybe?"

Kipp was not amused. "I've always worn a seat belt." He put the car in reverse. "Have fun killing yourself in practice."

"Thanks," Tony muttered, not sure if he was being insulted. The car heaved back and charged forward, jumping the first speed bump, heading toward the steep exit at the rear of campus.

"Take care!" Neil called out his window.

Tony was crossing the parking lot, aiming for the boys' locker room, when Joan popped out of the metal shop, striding toward him. Joan was the only girl in the school taking metal shop. She was fond of making heavy brass necklaces and stainless steel arm bands. Wearing an assortment of the metal armor, tight red shorts and a loose purple blouse, she looked ready for fun and games. Tony was not happy to see her.

His lunch last week with Alison had been great. She'd been so interesting to talk with. He had been surprised. He had gone out with a number of girls and had always viewed them as people—not necessarily an inferior class, you understand—who were there to have fun with. The thing was, they always treated him as a celebrity. Joan, for all her bizarre quirks, was not an exception. Indeed, more than any girl he'd known, she saw him as some kind of sex god; that was beginning to annoy him.

On the drive to the mall, Alison had seemed to fit the standard mode. She told him how she had seen every touchdown he had ever thrown, how he would undoubtedly be drafted by the NFL in his freshman year in college and how Steven Spielberg would probably be looking to use his face in a movie sometime soon. Then she must have sensed his lack of interest for she settled down and started to talk like a *real person* who had not been preprogrammed by MTV and *People* magazine. She was so funny! Every bit as witty as Kipp and a hell of a lot better looking. They had talked about everything except football and the Caretaker, and after taking her back to school, he had found himself replaying in his head over and over again their time together. He'd read the literature—he had the classical symptoms of infatuation.

He hadn't spoken to Alison since. Neil might get upset. Joan might kill him.

"Tony!" Joan said, kissing him on the lips before he could defend himself. "Have you been avoiding me?"

"Of course not."

"Liar." She poked him in the gut. "Tell me why and tell me straight."

"I'm in love with Kipp."

"So you're gay?" She asked slyly, leaning close. "Can you prove that you're not? Say, in about two hours? My parents . . ."

Lightning hasn't struck yet.

Something large and loud crashed.

The explosion came from the direction of the steep exit his friends had just used.

Tony forgot about Joan. He was running the sprint of his life. No tumbleweeds obstructed his path. The sun was out and he knew where he was going. No sharp edge of the road tried to catch him looking. Still, he was on *that* road again, feeling the same time-warping panic.

At the crest of the hill that fell beneath his feet at a forty-five degree angle, he ground to a halt. The car had plowed into the fifteen-foot brick wall that theoretically shielded a neighboring residential area from the noisy antics of the student body.

The front end was an accordion, and cracked bricks littered the ruined roof. The windshield was gone. Tony covered the rest of the way at a slow walk, afraid of what he would find.

Neil was picking glass out of his hair. Kipp was changing the station on the silent radio. "Do you want a ride home, too?" he asked casually.

Tony discovered he had been holding his breath and released the stagnant air. No, this was not that night. This was only a warning. "What happened?" he asked.

"My brakes took a holiday on the hill," Kipp said, demonstrating the mechanical failure by pushing the unresisting brake pedal to the floor.

"Coincidence?"

"I don't think so," Neil said, putting his hand to a bloody spot on his forehead.

"Are you OK?" Tony asked.

Neil nodded. "Just banged my head. I should have had my seat belt on. I'll be all right."

Kipp and Neil carefully extricated themselves from the front seat and sat on the curb. Tony could see others approaching in the distance—Joan included—and wanted to make a quick inspection before he had an audience. Crouching to the ground, wary of the glass shards, he scooted under the back wheels. The front tires were totaled but he would be able to see if the rear brakes had been tampered with. At first he was confused—relieved, in a sense—to see that the screws that bled the brakes had not been loosened. Then he noticed the dark red fluid smeared over the lines themselves. A closer inspection revealed that they had been minutely punctured. The saboteur had been clever. Had the screws simply been loosened, the fluid would have run out the first time Kipp had pumped his brakes and he would have become suspicious. As it was, with the tiny diameter of the holes, he had had to hit the brakes four or five times—about the same number of speed bumps between where Kipp *always* parked and the hill—before losing them altogether.

"Were they fixed?" Kipp called.

"Yeah." Tony pulled himself back into daylight. From the expression on his face, Kipp could have just finished tea with his mother. Neil, on the other hand, looked like he was about to be sick. "The lines were punctured—a nail, maybe even a pin. Didn't you notice them slipping?"

"Nope. My favorite song was on the radio."

"For heaven's sake," Tony said, "you both could have been killed. And look at the mess your car is in."

"I can see," Kipp replied calmly. "But neither of us *was* killed, and I have insurance. Don't misunderstand me, I'm not taking this lightly. I have another calculus exam tomorrow, and I think I'll flunk it." He stood, brushed off his pants. "Now if you will excuse me, I have to go to the bathroom. Hitting walls at forty miles an hour always does that to me."

Tony watched him leave with a mixture of admiration and exasperation. He helped Neil to his feet. Neil's head had stopped bleeding but he must have banged his leg. His limp was much worse. "You should just rest here," Tony said. "Somebody has probably called the paramedics."

Neil shook his head, his arms trembling. "I hate doctors, I don't want to see them. I only want to get to a bathroom."

"Neil . . ."

"Tony, please?" he pleaded, adding quietly, "I think I peed in my pants."

Tony tore off his shirt and wrapped it around his friend's waist. "I'll help you, don't worry. I have extra sweats in my locker that are too small. You'll be OK."

"Thank you," Neil whispered, his eyes moist.

They huddled across the street. An ambulance could be heard wailing in the distance. Half the track team was pouring down from the stadium and Joan was leading a contingent of teachers and students out of the parking lot. "You both got off lucky," Tony said. "Your face could have gone through the windshield. Kipp could have cracked his skull on the steering wheel. It's a good thing he started wearing his seat belt."

Neil nodded weakly. "It's a good thing Brenda refused to get in the car."

At the foot of the hill, they stopped and stared at each other.

Chapter Six

Brenda handed Alison the early edition of the *Times* the following Monday morning and sat down without comment beside her in the fifth row of the theater. Alison opened to the classified section and searched for a minute before finding the ad.

B.P. Tell Mr. H. Worst Director World Front Everyone

"You cannot tell Mr. Hoglan that," Alison said, not really surprised. This was only number three, but in a queer sort of way, she was already getting used to the Caretaker's messages. "It would hurt his feelings."

"I'm not worried about his feelings. I'm worried about getting kicked off the play."

"But you hate playing Essie."

"How can you say that? Or are you just so anxious to run the whole thing?"

"Right. I'd look real cute on stage answering my own questions." Alison was getting a mite sick of Brenda's jealousy. "So, are you going to do it?"

"Do I have a choice? I don't want a brick wall to fall on me." Brenda glanced at the door, their sleepyhead cast stumbling in followed by their bright-eyed teacher. She added, "I just hope the jerk gives me half an excuse to chew him out."

With the opening night of *You Can't Take It with You* rapidly approaching, Mr. Hoglan wanted them to run through all of act one today, finishing the other two acts Tuesday and Wednesday morning. Everyone seemed comfortable with their lines. Unfortunately, Fran had yet to return the props—God knew what she was doing with them. So far, Fran had been able to stall Mr. Hall. She didn't want to repaint Teddy until she was sure the Caretaker was through enjoying the goat. Kipp thought she should go ahead with the job, collect the money, get another command to restyle it as a pig, receive another request to fix it, and keep collecting the money. Fran did not think that was funny.

Alice did not appear on stage until approximately ten minutes into the play so Alison sat in the seats not far from Mr. Hoglan and waited to see if Brenda had the guts to carry through. Since there were few nondrama students present, she briefly wondered how the Caretaker would know if Brenda had committed the foul deed or not. Then she had the disturbing idea that the Caretaker *must* be present. She scrutinized the six people unconnected with the play who were watching the rehearsal—three girls, three guys—and didn't recognize a single one. They must be either freshmen or sophomores, aspiring actors, too young, so it would seem, to be behind such a complex scheme. Then she realized that if Brenda did tell Mr. Hoglan off, the whole school would know about it by break, and the rest of the city by lunch. One way or another, if he or she had listening ears, the Caretaker would know what had gone down.

One thing you had to give Brenda, she didn't hesitate. She had hardly appeared on stage when she began to do Essie's idiotic stretching exercises in an unusually obscene manner—spread-eagled and the like. Mr. Hoglan called for a halt.

"Brenda," he said kindly, waddling his way to the front, tugging thoughtfully at his gray beard, not knowing he was about to have his professional qualifications severely questioned. "This is not an audition for *Hair.* Why are you being so . . . suggestive?"

"I don't know what you mean," Brenda said.

Mr. Hoglan did not like to argue. "Could you please perform Essie's limbering exercises as you have done for the last three weeks?" He turned back toward his spot in the last row. Brenda stopped him with a word.

"No."

Mr. Hoglan paused. "What did you say?"

"I'll do them the way I feel is best. You're the one who's always telling us to be natural on stage. Well, that's exactly what I'm doing, letting it all hang out. Although I don't know why I listen to you at all. To tell you the truth, I think you're the worst director in the entire world."

Fine, Alison thought, she had got the line out. Now if she could tactfully withdraw, Mr. Hoglan might let it pass.

But either Brenda thought the Caretaker would want more blood or else she really was speaking her mind; and when Brenda started on the latter, a brick wall couldn't have shut her up. Alison began to squirm in her seat.

"Brenda," Mr. Hoglan said, startled, "that's very unkind of you. I think you should apologize."

"This is a free country. I can speak my mind. You have your tastes and I have mine. And our tastes are far, far apart. Of course, I'm not a perfect Essie. I was never meant to play such a dumb cluck. But you said I didn't 'have the right look for Alice.' What's that supposed to mean? Alice is pretty. I'm pretty. So why did you pick Alison over me? I'll tell you why. Because you're a talentless, pompous, burned out—"

"Enough!" Mr. Hoglan said sharply, his red cheeks puffing up like a beaver's. Alison felt terrible for him. "Since that is how you feel, young lady, your part will go to someone more appreciative. Please excuse yourself from the room."

Brenda swallowed painfully, lowering her head, realizing

she had let herself get carried away. But as she trudged down the stage steps, passing the instructor, she did not stop to apologize. She walked straight for the door. Alison flew after her, catching her in the hallway. Tears were forming at the corners of Brenda's eyes but she would not let herself cry.

"Are you OK?" Alison asked.

"I'll live." Then she stopped and gave a lopsided smile. "How was I?"

Alison put an arm around her shoulder. "It was a great performance. I'm sure the Caretaker would be proud."

Tony asked Alison on a formal date the day after Brenda's parents grounded their daughter for two weeks for shooting her mouth off. The proposal happened under fairly trite circumstances. They were passing in the hallway and she just happened to drop all her books. He stopped to help, and when she was all in one piece and through thanking him, he asked if she was busy Friday night. She did it again. She said "yes" when she meant "no." But he got the picture.

Alison dressed for the date with care, several times in fact, hampered by a lack of information on what Tony had planned. She donned an expensive flowered dress, squeezed into a pair of tight jeans, finally settling on what seemed a compromise, a green plaid skirt and a light turtlenecked sweater. She worked on her makeup for an hour and discovered when she was cover girl perfect that she was allergic to an ingredient in a previously untried blush—she couldn't stop sneezing. She was washing it all off when she saw Tony's Ford Tempo cruising up her deserted block. She was lucky to get on her lipstick.

Tony charmed her mother and reassured her father, and still Alison was glad when they were out of the house and seated in his car. He was wearing dress slacks but an undistinguished short sleeved shirt, and she decided their attire was fairly matched. The upholstery had a fresh new smell.

"Is this car yours?" she asked.

He smiled. "That's right, I had this Tempo when we went to the mall. It actually belongs to my dad. My car looks like Kipp's did after it hit the wall."

She liked how he was not out to impress her with what neat wheels he drove, like so many other guys. When he had taken her out to lunch, she had been amazed to discover he was not even remotely like she had imagined. Where had her suave iron-nerved athlete gone? She didn't know and she didn't care. He was very much the dreamer. One revelation had summed up the afternoon. He had told her he hated football.

He started the car. "What would you like to do?"

Make out, Alison thought. "I'm hungry, that is, if you're hungry . . . would you like to eat?"

"Sure. I know a joint that serves Weight Watchers french fries."

She laughed. "My diet, oh yeah. I'm over that. Right now, I could eat a cow. That is, if we can find a restaurant around here. You know, Tony, I could have met you back in a normal section of town. You didn't have to drive all the way out here."

They rolled forward, Tony studying the empty houses, the wide blank windows, the unstained concrete driveways, the deserted sidewalks. "Are you still the only people in this tract?"

"Nobody here but us chickens. It looks like it's going to stay that way for a while. I went for a walk around sunset yesterday and ran into one of the brokers who has been showing the houses. Before, he'd told me that difficulties with a group-financing package were slowing buyers from moving in. But now it seems the developers are having major cash-flow problems. The contractors haven't all been paid and there're lawsuits and liens and bad blood and I can have my choice of over two hundred different bedrooms!" She made the joke to soften the edge that had automatically begun to creep into her voice. At first the empty area had spooked her, the way her steps echoed like pursuing footfalls, how her words called back to her as they rebounded off the silent walls. But now the lack of humanity was outright weighing on her soul. More and more, she felt she was being watched.

Still, she continued her twilight walks. The fright drew as well as repelled her. It was as if she were searching for *something* she intuitively felt she needed to find to be safe.

"Do they have a guard to protect against vandalism?"

Alison nodded. "Harry, yeah. He drives around in this tiny

security cart. He's always drunk. The Hell's Angels could show up in force and he probably wouldn't notice them."

"I'll be careful not to run him over," Tony said, picking up speed, wrapping through the maze to the street that led to the freeway a few miles south. "And don't worry about me having to come out this way. I enjoy driving." He grinned. "Especially when I can see where I'm going."

It was the only reference made to the incident all night. They both deserved a break.

They drove forever and ended up in a restaurant not far from Grant High. Tony explained that, since he was such a local hero, the meals would be on the house. It was a joke she believed while she was ordering her lobster. But he had New York steak so she didn't feel so bad, and she really was starving. She'd read that love—or maybe it had been lust—stimulated the appetite. They planned to go to a movie after dinner but they talked so long over dessert that they missed the last show. They ended up flying a kite in the park across from the school. Alison had never flown a kite at night. You couldn't see the silly thing and knew it was up there somewhere only by the tug on the string. When they were done, Tony simply let it go.

The evening went by in a flash. On the drive home, Alison began to worry what was going to happen. She had no intention of giving up her virginity on the first date—she would put up a fair fight, so she told herself—but she was kind of hoping to put some tarnish on her good girl image. With Tony, knowing he had gone out with Amazon Joan, she wasn't sure what to expect. He had in fact talked about Joan over dinner. He had said dating Joan was more like being in a war than being in a relationship, and he was, "filing for conscientious objector status," which sounded encouraging to her.

He parked directly in front of her house and she was disappointed. Necking would have been much simpler around the block. They certainly wouldn't have had to rent a motel room. He turned off the ignition and looked at her for a long time. The streetlights weren't working and she couldn't read his expression. "I had a great time," he said finally.

"I bet you say that to all your girls." She smiled, clasping her hands together to keep them from shaking. The move only caused her arms to start shaking.

"You're right," he said. He reached over and pulled her toward him. He had his arm around her and had kissed her once before she knew what had happened. Just her luck, her first important kiss and she had missed it. His lips, however, were still only inches away and she prepped her brain to make a permanent record of all the sensations to come. "What was your name, anyway?" he asked.

"Ralph," she whispered. She could see his eyes—that was all. His hand had slipped down her right side. It kind of tickled but she didn't want to laugh and spoil the mood.

"You know," he said, running his other hand through her

curls, "you have incredibly beautiful hair for a Ralph."

"My middle name is Susie." And that was the honest truth. She wanted him to kiss her again, preferably soon. Her parents would have heard the car pull up. Their bedroom was on the opposite side of the house but her dad might, if she didn't come inside shortly, come to the front door. But Tony seemed content to play with Ralph's hair. "I had a great time, too . . . ahh . . . what was your name?"

"Call me Tony."

"Tony. Tony?"

"Yeah?"

She kissed him. It was a hard deep one and it lasted a while and as the seconds turned into minutes, she felt a pleasant falling sensation, like she was a warm tropical cloud and another part of her was rain that she was releasing to earth. Perhaps she was being overly romantic. She decided it was a distinct possibility when she slipped off the seat and bumped her head on the dashboard, her legs bunching around the stick shift. So much for her falling rain. Her skirt ran up her legs practically to her hips and if her dad decided to check on them now, her relationship with Tony would be history.

"You have nice legs," he observed, offering his hand. She made it back into her seat without major difficulty.

"Thank you."

"Are we in danger here?"

She laughed softly. "It depends on what you're afraid of."

He had a hand resting on her bare knee and the other one was tracing erotic circles inside her ear and this was not her imagination; his touch was a pure delight. "If it's of my dad, yes."

"Dads don't frighten me. I'm bigger than most of them."

"What does frighten you?" she asked absently, leaning back, closing her eyes, his hand moving from her leg to her chin. She waited for a kiss that never came.

"You. It's easy to be with you, too easy, maybe." He traced her lower lip lightly, sending a nice shiver to the base of her spine, then withdrew both of his hands and sat back. She opened her eyes, feeling a pang. He was staring up the road.

"What is it?" she asked.

"Nothing."

This uncomfortable moment wasn't supposed to be in the evening's script. He was hers tonight, wasn't he? "Joan?" she mumbled, feeling sore.

"No."

"Tony, you can tell me."

"No," he said, raising his voice. He added quietly, "It isn't another girl."

Now wait a second, she thought. Tony wasn't . . . his calling her Ralph . . . he couldn't be . . . what the hell was going on here? "Is it *Ralph*?"

That caught him off guard and she was infinitely relieved to see him smile and shake his head. "No, I'm old-fashioned. I still think girls are prettier than boys."

"Then what is it? Can't you tell me?"

He did not answer right away. His attention seemed drawn far off, or perhaps he was so closely considering her question that he had forgotten her. The effect was the same and she no longer felt his closeness. "It's not my place to talk about it," he said finally. "I shouldn't have brought it up. I'm sorry." He touched the keys. "I should be getting home."

"Tony?" she pleaded softly, putting her hand on his shoulder. This was no way to say good-bye. Left this way, up in the air, she might not be able to get to sleep tonight. He wouldn't look at her.

"Sweet dreams, Alison. I really like you."

"But can't we go out together again?" she asked, dying a bit waiting for his answer. He glanced up the road, at the rows of empty houses, and frowned.

"That might not depend on you or me," he said.

Chapter Seven

Neil's "small token of obedience" was demanded and carried out without injury or insult to anyone. The Caretaker wanted him to get sick in class. The group debated whether it was actually necessary for him to vomit on somebody—"How gross!" Brenda had remarked—before deciding a fainting spell would probably be sufficient. Neil chose Algebra II to throw the fit. This was ironic—the math teacher was none other than Coach Sager, whose imaginary seduction they had been listening to when they had hit the man. Neil's selection, however, had been logically arrived at. His algebra class was immediately prior to lunch, just when a diabetic would be prone to trouble with his blood sugar level. Alison did not see the faked collapse but Tony was there and told her about it afterward.

"I knew it was coming and he still scared me. Neil should

be in one of your plays; he's an incredible actor. He started by swaying in his chair, trying to catch a few people's attention that something was not right. But you know the kids at our school—they went right on minding their own business. Then he turned white—how, I have no idea. Still, no one spoke up and Sager went right on lecturing about *X, Y,* and *Z*. Finally, Neil just went ahead and did it. He groaned loudly and pitched forward onto the desk, rolling to the floor. The back of his head hit the tiles with a loud thud. You should have seen Sager; he reacted as if Neil had caught fire. He ripped off his sweater and draped it over Neil's body and started fanning him with an algebra book. Coach was about to try mouth-to-mouth resuscitation when I stepped in, explaining about the diabetes. Someone ran for orange juice and as soon as we put it to Neil's lips, he opened his eyes and smiled. He hadn't even drunk any of it! The whole thing was pretty funny in a way. That is, until his mother showed up. I was sitting with him in the nurse's station when she came in. She was very upset. You would have thought her son had died. She started crying and shaking, and you could see how much this bothered Neil. He was furious with himself. I guess, one way or the other, the Caretaker is letting none of us off easy."

Joan's command sounded inoffensive enough: *Come School Dressed Bozo Clown.* Alison wouldn't have minded that order. She might even have enjoyed it. But to punk, tough Joan, used to wearing leather and metal, it cut to the core of her image.

"No way," she swore. "Let that bastard try what he wants."

That had been last week. But something had happened between then and now that worried Joan. She wanted a meeting of all seven of them. Fran's parents both worked, so they decided to gather at her house on a Wednesday afternoon after Tony's track practice. It was to be the first time since the accident that they were all in the same spot at the same time.

"Would anyone like some homemade chocolate chip cookies?" Fran asked, bustling about the kitchen table—the same table where they had opened the Caretaker's original letter—like the typically overly anxious hostess. "How about you, Neil?" she asked, reaching for a winning smile. "You don't have to worry about your weight."

Neil looked up, rubbing his eyes. He had been resting his head in his arms. He smiled. "Homemade? Sounds wonderful."

"But all that sugar . . ." Tony began.

"One or two won't hurt," Neil said.

Fran brought out a warm plate of three dozen cookies and a half-gallon carton of milk. Alison helped herself—she always craved sweets when she was worried. Why had Tony chosen to sit next to Joan?

"We should get together like this more often," Kipp remarked, his mouth full.

"We always *do* have such an exciting time," Joan said sarcastically.

"I see you got a new car, Kipp," Alison said. He had driven up in a red Ford, a later model. "The Caretaker didn't do bad by you, after all."

Tony and Neil exchanged glances. Alison wondered what she was missing. Unconcerned, Kipp continued to dunk his cookies, muttering, "The old one had sentimental value."

Alison noticed Neil playing with a ring, twisting the band on his middle finger as if he were winding it up. The fit was poor, loose. She had never seen him wearing it before. She was fond of jewelry. "Neil, can I try on your ring?"

He looked pleased. "I doubt it will fit you," he said, handing it over.

"But it does." Her hands were not nearly as bony as his, and the fit was snug. The stone was an emerald—an expensive one, she knew her gems—cut in a sharp triangle, mounted in gold. "Has this been in your family?" she asked.

Neil nodded. "How did you know?"

"The green matches your eyes." She gave it back. "It's beautiful."

"Let's cut out the small talk," Brenda said. "Remember, I'm grounded. I've got to get back before my mom discovers I'm gone. Why did you want this meeting, Joan? You don't look like anything has fallen on you."

"The suggestion was mine as much as Joan's," Tony interjected. "We should have been gathering and working together since this started, instead of purposely avoiding each other."

"Does Joan need help with her clown outfit?" Kipp asked.

"Tell them what happened," Tony said.

Joan put down her cookie and beer—yes, she had wanted beer with her cookies—and coolly eyed everyone at the table. "Let me say up front that I don't think what happened to me was funny. If any of you laugh when I tell you, especially you, Kipp, I'll put this plate of cookies in your face." That said, Joan lowered her voice and said, "Last night I went to bed about twelve, my usual time. My folks were home but they were bombed from a police ball they'd gone to earlier. A gunshot couldn't have woken them. They didn't hear what happened and they still don't know about it.

"I must have been in bed about half an hour—I wasn't asleep yet—when my window just exploded. The glass sprayed all over my whole bed. I had it on my pillow and in my hair and, when I sat up, I could feel it cutting my arms." Joan rolled up her right sleeve and it was indeed badly scratched. "But I didn't care. I thought, if that's the worst that damn Caretaker can do to me, I have nothing to worry about. I would have jumped to the window right away to see if there was anyone there, but I was in my bare feet and I knew there must be glass all over the floor. So I decided to first get to the light switch, which is by the door opposite the window. I carefully slipped out of the sheets and was tiptoeing across the floor, when I feel this"—she made a face—"this *thing* crawl up my leg. I tell you, I forgot all about the glass. I pounced on that light switch quick. Then . . . I saw what was there." Joan stopped, taking a swig of beer.

"Please continue," Kipp said. "The suspense is killing me."

Joan glared at him. "There were cockroaches all over the room! They were in my bed, crawling through my clothes, running over my desk, and trying to get up my legs." She chewed on her lower lip, and this time, it wasn't because she was *bad.* "If I live till I'm thirty, I'll never get over feeling as nauseated as I did then."

"And as scared?" Alison asked.

Joan nodded faintly. "Yeah, and as scared. I was scared." She took a deep breath. "It took me half the night to kill those buggers, if I even got them all. I used my old man's CO-2 fire extinguisher. Hell help us if the house catches fire next."

The group silently considered the Caretaker's latest ploy. Finally, Tony asked, "Are you particularly afraid of cockroaches?"

"I hate all bugs," Joan said. "Doesn't everybody?"

"I'm sure none of us here like insects," Tony said. "But disliking and being afraid of are two different things. My point is, the Caretaker appears to have hit you where you're weak." He had to quickly raise his hand to prevent Joan from defending her weakness. "We all have our secret phobias—don't be embarrassed. Now I know you're afraid of bugs because of what you said just now. But how did the Caretaker know this?"

The question brought no ready answer. While they racked their brains, Fran's cookies enjoyed another wave of interest.

Only Neil abstained, toying with his milk, looking exhausted. But it was he who spoke next.

"The Caretaker must know Joan," he said. "The Caretaker *must* be one of us."

More silence, everyone looking at everyone else, everyone looking equally guilty.

"There is a pattern, of sorts here," Kipp said with some reluctance. "Fran was proud of Teddy, I was proud of my Ford. More than anything, Brenda wanted to do well in her play. And Neil hates how Tony and I are always hassling him about how sickly he looks. This last ad maintains this pattern. Joan—and please don't hit me—loves her mean street girl image. Dressing like Bozo the Clown wouldn't exactly reinforce that image."

"Let's look at a specific case," Tony said. "Which of you knew that Joan was afraid of bugs?"

"I hardly think the Caretaker will admit to knowing about it," Kipp said.

"But you were the one who said the Caretaker can't be one of us," Tony said.

"I haven't changed my mind," Kipp said. "When I mentioned the pattern, I was merely stating the obvious. Lots of people at school are aware of our likes and dislikes, probably some people we don't even know. Still, I'll go along with your questions. For myself, Joan has always struck me as someone who would love insects." Suddenly, Kipp grimaced, bending over and grabbing his leg. "I asked you not to hit me," he breathed.

"You said nothing about kicking you," Joan said.

"I didn't know our darling Joan was afraid of bugs," Brenda said.

"We knew!" Fran said. "Alison and I both knew. Just the other day, we saw Joan scream at a spider."

Just the other day, Alison thought. That had been a very timely demonstration of Joan's phobia. Had she purposely jumped at the spider to show she was afraid of bugs so she would fit right in with the pattern? Had she really had a bottle of cockroaches thrown through her window?

"Joan," Alison said, "did you cut your feet getting to the light switch?"

"You better believe it. I cut the right one real bad."

"May I see it?" Alison asked.

"What?"

"I'd like to see the cut."

"You calling me a liar?" Joan said savagely.

"Not yet," Alison said.

Joan steamed for a moment then reached down and slid off her right boot. The rear section of the foot was heavily bandaged, the gauze wrapped many times around the ankle. "Are you satisfied?"

"No," Alison said. "Anybody can put a bandage on. You weren't limping when you came in. Take it off."

"No! You're sick. You like looking at bloody scars?"

"Alison is just trying to collect more information," Tony interrupted smoothly. "I can understand why you don't want to expose the cut to possible infection, but eliminating suspects is as valuable as finding them."

Joan stared at him in disbelief. "She's really got you wrapped around her little finger. You're already parroting whatever she says. I know you two went out. She couldn't help but tell the whole school."

"What was that?" Neil asked, coming back from a daydream.

"I'm no one's parrot," Tony said firmly, staring Joan in the eye. She hardly met the gaze before looking down, scowling at her beer bottle. Tony added, "Put your boot on. We can check your window after the meeting."

Joan chuckled, once. "Don't. I already fixed it. By myself."

"How convenient," Alison muttered.

"Is this Down on Joan Day, or what?" Joan complained, her voice shaky. Tony's harsh tone must have gotten to her. Alison felt a pang—a rather small one—of guilt. "I came here for help."

Tony softened, squeezing her arm. "We shouldn't be singling you out. That's largely my fault and I'm sorry. We're just trying to learn what we can. Let's get back to this bug thing."

"I knew Joan was afraid of insects," Neil said. "I'm not sure how I knew."

"Who knew I liked my car?" Kipp asked, rhetorically. "The whole school. Who knew Brenda wanted to be in the play? The whole school. I tell you, Tony, this is not the way to go about it. Granted, the Caretaker probably knows us. But let's look to our enemies."

"Who hates Joan?" Joan mumbled. "The whole school."

"Joan." Tony frowned. "I said I'm sorry."

"I love you, Joan," Neil said sweetly.

Joan's pleasure at the remark was obvious. "That's because you're such a far-out guy, Neil," she said.

"Can any of you think of someone who hates us all?" Tony asked, trying to keep the discussion on track.

"Joan," Kipp blurted out, quickly moving his chair lest he absorb another kick. The joke went over well, even with Joan, and they all enjoyed a good laugh. Neil cut it short, however, with his next remark.

"Maybe the man hates us," he said.

"What do you mean?" Fran asked, her eyes wide.

Kipp snorted. "Don't bring up that nonsense again."

Neil shrugged. "You asked."

"Let Neil talk," Fran said. "All of you think you know everything. I've seen lots of shows on TV, real documentaries, where weird things start happening to a group of people. And what they find out is that a dark power is at work on them. Maybe that man has—"

"There are no dark powers," Tony interrupted. "People who talk about them are usually trying to scare you into sending them money." He added, "The man is dead."

"Not in our memories," Neil said. His words, gentle as usual, carried unusual force. "See how he haunts us still. And is that right? Does it have to be this way?" He turned to his best friend, and Alison could see the pain in his eyes. "Tony, all this talk ain't helping us. It doesn't clear our conscience. But if we face what we have done, we can take away the Caretaker's hold on us. We can be free. Go to the police. Tell them we made a mistake. This whole thing is killing me. *Please,* Tony, tell them we're sorry."

Tony stood and went to the window. A car door had slammed and he was probably checking to see if Fran's mother had returned home. Alison stared at him, hoping she knew not what, only that he would make the right choice.

"I can't," he said at last. "It's too late for that."

"And what if the Caretaker really does hurt one of us?" Neil asked.

"Then it will be all my fault," Tony answered.

"All we can do is hope to find the Caretaker," Kipp said.

"Will we kill him, too?" Neil asked sadly.

Chapter Eight

Tony always spent a long time warming up before a race. His distances were the quarter mile and the half mile, but before he even stepped to the starting line, he would have jogged two miles and run a dozen sets of wind sprints. His teammates thought he carried the warm-up too far, especially when he sweated so much that he always needed to drink before he ran, which to them was a sure prescription for a cramp. His stomach didn't seem to mind. He favored a particular brand of lemonade that came in eight-ounce clear plastic cartons that could be purchased only at gas stations. Jogging toward the ice chest in midfield, he felt exceptionally thirsty. The sun had the sky on fire.

"How do you feel?" Neil asked, sitting beside the ice chest. He came to all the track meets. He helped keep stats, measured the shot put tosses, and reset the high jump and pole vault bars. He was a big fan, though on this particular afternoon, he was only one of many. Today's track meet was the biggest of the year. Over half the stadium was filled.

"Are you referring to my mental or physical state?" Tony asked. Three days after Joan had put on her homemade Bozo outfit—much to the delight of the entire senior class, which was catcalling Joan to this day—and the day after he had received the chain letter from her, a not unexpected ad had appeared in the paper.

T.H. Come Last Next Races

The meet was against Crete High, which was tied with Grant High for first place in the league. If he did not win both the quarter mile and the half mile, Grant would probably lose the title. Coach Sager had already penciled in the sure ten points to the final score. Tony could not lose, it was as simple as that.

He was getting a crick in his neck guarding his back.

"Both," Neil said, hugging his knees to his chest. He did not seem so down today, and Tony was glad.

"Great." Tony smiled, flipping open the chest, reaching for his lemonade. There were four cartons on ice, all for him—no one else could stand the stuff. He tore off the tinfoil cap and leaned his head back to finish it in one gulp. Neil stopped him.

"Let me taste it. You never know."

"Are you serious?"

Neil plucked it from his hand. "Just a sip, to be sure it's kosher." He took a drink, rolled it around inside his mouth and made a face. "It tastes sour."

"It's lemonade, for godsake." Tony took the carton back and downed it quickly. Reaching for another container, he hesitated. Was that an aftertaste in his mouth or what? He decided he was the victim of suggestion. He didn't, however, take any more. "Where are the others?"

"Keeping their distance. They're afraid the earth's going to open up and swallow you." Neil laughed. "Not really. Kipp and Brenda were here a few minutes ago. I told them you like to be by yourself before a race. They're in the stands somewhere. I hope you didn't mind my speaking for you." He added, "I told Alison the same thing."

Although his friend was acting nonchalant, Tony could hear the tension in his last line. He had told himself he wouldn't do this to Neil, and he had gone right ahead and done it just the same. He was an SOB, why didn't he just accept the fact and have the initials tattooed on his forehead so he wouldn't be able to fool anyone else? The problem was, Alison was the first girl he had found who made him feel important without having to swell his already bloated ego. Quite simply, he was happy around her. But these feelings, they seemed to totter on a balance: Add a gram of joy to this side and you had to put a pound of misery on the other side. That is what he had been trying to tell Alison that night in the car. *I feel guilty, baby.* He would have, except it would have been like stealing a piece of Neil's pride, and he would never do that.

"I should have told you I went out with her," Tony said. "I meant to."

"That's OK. You better keep stretching. The starter is . . ."

"It's not OK. I stabbed you in the back. But . . . I didn't even intend to ask her out. I just did it, you know?"

"Did you have fun?" Neil sounded genuinely curious.

He hesitated. "I did."

"Are you going to go out with her again?"

Tony sat down on the ice chest and yawned. The sun must be getting to him; he felt like he'd already run his races and was recovering. "Not if you tell me you don't want me to."

"If you had fun, why not?"

"Neil . . ."

"I would never tell you what to do."

I wish you had, Tony thought, *a year ago.* Almost involuntarily, he found himself searching the stands for Alison. Dozens of people waved to him but none of them looked like her. One of the reasons he was defying the Caretaker, petty as it sounded, was so that he could show off in front of her. "When are you going to get that leg fixed?" he asked, as if that were relevant to the topic.

"Soon. Why?"

"So we can run together."

"I could never keep up with you."

"You wouldn't have any trouble today, I don't feel so hot."

"But you said you felt great." Neil reached for the empty carton. "The lemonade! Maybe there was something in it."

Tony laughed. "Would you stop that! I mean, I don't feel so hot because of what I did to you. I think it would help if you'd at least get mad at me."

Neil was hardly listening. "Another time, maybe." He pointed to the starting line, where a half dozen young men in bright colored track suits were peeling off their sweats. Crete High had a quarter miler who had not lost this year. Tony could see him pacing in lane two, a squat, powerfully built guy. Tony knew he would snuff him. "You better get moving," Neil said.

Tony stood. "Will you cheer for me?"

Neil grinned. "Only if you win."

While the other contestants fought with their starting blocks, Tony stood patiently inside lane one behind the white powdered line, taking slow deep breaths, wanting to be mildly hyperventilated before they took off. Blocks had never helped him in a sprint as long as the quarter mile and he doubted they would be helping anyone else in the race. Being in lane one, he had the disadvantage of the tight turns but he always opted for the position for it gave him a clear view of the other runners. This fellow from Crete High—Gabriel was his name, Tony remembered—would feel him on his heels until the last turn. That is when he would blow past the guy. He would rely on his kick. He had to save himself for the half mile. He wasn't feeling any surplus of energy at the moment. Yawning, he pulled off his sweat pants and put his right foot a quarter of an inch behind the starting line.

"We'll go at the gun, gentlemen," the starter said, a short fat man with a cigar hanging out the corner of his mouth. He pulled out his black pistol and aimed at the sky. "Set!" Tony took a breath and held it, staring at a point ten yards in front. He thought he heard Alison shout his name and smiled just as the gun went off. The distraction cost him a tenth of a second before he could even begin.

Gabriel was either a rabbit or else he was extremely confident of his endurance. Tony was two strides in back of the guy's stagger going into the first turn. And he was working. No matter how he trained, some days he was simply flat, and he knew this was one of those days as he reached the first quarter-lap white post. He was not unduly concerned. He had such faith in his superior physique that he was still positive he would win.

Yet when they straightened into the backstretch and he saw that he had failed to gain ground on Gabriel's stagger, which he should have done automatically, he began to worry. His breathing was ragged and he couldn't seem to get his rhythm. He would have to gut this one out. Driving his arms, he *willed* the gap between them to close.

The final curve was agony. The quarter mile, which

required as much strength as speed, was never easy, but this was ridiculous. Each gasp squeezed tighter a red hot iron clamp around his lungs. He must be coming down with something, he thought, a heart attack, maybe. Hitting the straightaway, he finally managed to draw even with Gabriel, which is exactly where he wanted to be at this point. The problem was, he couldn't get in front of the dude. His legs were—in the words of the sport—going into rigor mortis. All the way to the tape, which had never approached so slowly, he thrashed with his arms, the only thing pulling up his knees. Five yards from the finish, he had somehow managed to slip a body width behind. He had no choice. He threw himself at the line. The tape did nothing to break his fall. Nevertheless, it was a relief to feel it snap across his chest. He had won.

The cigar-puffing starter helped him up and slapped him on the rump, congratulating him on a thrilling victory. His teammates jubilantly pumped his hands and Coach Sager went so far as to hug him. Tony received the gratitude in a hazy blur of oxygen debt. But he distinctly heard his time—49.5. He had run 48 flat last week and had finished waving to the crowd. He had to be sick. He couldn't be getting old.

The half mile was in half an hour. Normally, he jogged steadily between the two events. Today he staggered about unable to find his sweats. He had another lemonade from the ice chest and had to struggle to keep it down. His digestive tract felt like it was digesting itself. Had this not been such a crucial meet, he would have called it a day.

"You looked like you were running in mud," Neil said unhappily, popping out of nowhere, holding his sweats. Tony took them but felt too weak to put them on. "Are you OK?"

"I've felt better."

"You've *looked* better. I'm glad you won but don't you think you should forget the half?"

He leaned over, bracing himself on his knees, shaking his head, which seemed to be coming loose. "We need the points."

"Then at least get out of the sun for a few minutes. Go sit under the stands."

That sounded like good advice. "I will."

Neil turned away. "I'm going to help at the pole vault. I tell you again, don't run if you're sick. It's not worth it."

Tony dropped his sweats and stumbled toward the seats. Several people, mainly girls, shouted his name and he answered with a vague wave. By sitting down he was running the risk of tying up, but he felt he had no choice. He found an unoccupied spot in the shadow of the snack bar and plopped to the ground, leaning his back on the cool concrete wall, closing his eyes. He wouldn't have minded just sitting there for the next eight hours.

He might have dozed. The next thing he knew, Alison was kneeling by his side. She had on a green T-shirt and sexy white shorts that showed her legs to the point where his imagination could comfortably take care of the rest. Green was one of Grant High's colors and the green ribbon in her curly black hair was the best piece of school spirit he'd seen all day. She leaned over and kissed him on the forehead.

"You were wonderful." She smiled.

"I stunk." Sweat dripped off his arms. "I still do."

"But you won."

"But I should have won easily." He rested his head on his knees. "I feel like a space cadet."

Alison put her arm around him. Her flesh was cool like the wall, soft like he remembered from their kisses in the car. "I'll walk you down to your car. You should get home, take a shower, and lie down."

"I have to win the half," he mumbled.

"You have to run again? That's crazy, you're exhausted. You've done enough." She paused. "Are you doing this to show the Caretaker?"

"To show you." This was a fine time he had picked to pour out his feelings. He felt like he might throw up.

"I don't care how many races you win."

He had expected her to say that, and still she had surprised him. She had said it like she had meant it. He sat up, saw her concern. He was still playing the game of trying to impress the girls. "I know you don't," he said, taking her hand, seeing past her to center field where Joan and Kipp were rampaging the ice chest. Unlike Neil, they were not helping put on the meet and did not belong out of the stands. "But I have to run. For the team's sake and for the sake of my Algebra II grade. Remember, Sager is also my math teacher." He went to stand and without her help he would have had trouble making it.

"But how can you possibly win like this?"

He smiled. "I was born under a winning star, don't worry."

He spent the next ten minutes plodding up and down the football field, searching for his legs. A tall lanky fellow in Crete High colors, loosening up near the starting line, caught his attention. Tony groaned; he recognized him—Kelly Shield. The guy was traditionally a miler, very strong. Crete High must be dropping him down, hoping for an upset. Tony leaned down and massaged his knotting calves. This was going to be harder than the last one.

The fat starter called his number and Tony found himself being placed in lane two. Kelly Shield was at his back and that bothered him more than it should have. He did not feel the perspiration roll in his eyes but his vision blurred and he assumed it must be from stinging sweat. His usual routine of mild hyperventilation started to make him dizzy and he had to stop it.

"Set!"

Tony crouched down, swaying slightly. The bang of the gun made him jump up rather than forward. Like before, he was off to a bad start.

Naturally, the pace was not as frantic as the quarter mile

and he did not feel as quickly winded. On the other hand, he didn't feel very swift, either. Striding down the first backstretch of the two-lap race, he was amazed to find that Kelly Shield had already made up his stagger. Going into the second turn, the guy had the nerve to pull slightly ahead. This time, Tony did not press the pace. Mr. Shield was making a mistake. He would go through the first lap like a hot dog and die on the second lap. Then Tony glanced to the fourth lane, where his teammate Calvin Smith was running, and began to have doubts. Taking into account the varying staggers, Calvin was also ahead of him, and Calvin normally couldn't have beaten him on a motorcycle. Could they *all* be off pace?

You just keep telling yourself that, buddy.

Passing the timer, Tony heard numbers being called out that he hadn't heard since his freshman year when he'd run a race with a sprained ankle. By then, however, the clock was not necessary to tell him that he was out of it. The entire pack was in front and pulling away with what seemed like magical ease. Kelly Shield would romp. It struck Tony then with complete clarity, just when his mind started a headlong dive into a fuzzy gray well, that the Caretaker had gotten to him. If he'd had double pneumonia, he wouldn't have felt as he did now: trapped in slow motion, his chest filling with suffocating lactic acid, hopelessly out of control. He had probably been poisoned, maybe even hexed.

I won't quit, he swore. His last place was assured but what was left of his fading mind and will wanted a morsel of satisfaction. He would lose but he wouldn't be beaten.

But it was not to be. He was a hundred yards from the finish line, weaving over the brittle reddish clay, wandering in and out of lanes, when his right knee buckled and he hit the ground. The last thing he saw was a crowd of anxious people running toward him. One of them was probably the Caretaker.

Chapter Nine

Opening nights always made Alison nervous. There were so many things that could go wrong. She could miss an entrance, forget a line, trip on the carpet, or burp when speaking. And tonight, on top of everything else, she had to worry about getting shot. The Caretaker's ad had been clear.

A.P. Flub Lines Opening Night

No way. Famous last words.

"I'm so scared," Fran whispered. They were standing in the backstage shadows. On the other side of the living room wall, they could hear the audience settling. Curtain was soon. "What if they don't like my walls?"

"In the entire history of the theater," Alison said, "I've

never heard of a set being booed. By the way, it was nice of you to finally decide to bring them in. Rehearsing without them was uninspiring."

"Two minutes," Mr. Hoglan whispered, moving like a ghost in the dark. He had replaced Brenda the day he had dumped her. The new Essie was standing in the corner with a penlight, frantically studying the script. Alison felt sorry for her.

"Mr. Hoglan, did you find your keys?" Alison asked. He had complained about having misplaced them earlier in the week. In her opinion; that was a bad omen.

"This afternoon," he said, his eyes twinkling. "They must have been on my desk all along. I don't know how I could have missed them." He patted her arm affectionately. "I know you'll be wonderful tonight."

"Thank you." What if the Caretaker had simply duplicated the keys or had already planted his bomb? She wished her parents had not insisted on coming tonight. But her dad would soon be going to New York on a business trip, and her mom would be accompanying him. They felt they had to see the play now or else possibly miss it altogether.

Mr. Hoglan went off to encourage the new Essie and she and Fran were left alone again. "Is the gang all here?" Alison asked. "Come to watch the latest sacrifice?"

"I haven't seen Brenda, Kipp, or Joan. But Tony and Neil are here." Fran's eyes lit up. "Neil's sitting in the front row!"

"Did you talk to him?"

"No! I can't do that."

"How do you expect to seduce him if you won't talk to him?"

Fran surprised her. "Can't talk and kiss at the same time."

"Touché. Now get out of here. I have to psych myself up."

Fran was used to working with temperamental actresses—this one in particular—and was not offended at the brush-off. But when Fran was gone and Alison was left alone in the dark corner—the bulk of the cast was already in place next to the entrances and she did not wish to disturb them—she almost went searching for her. Around other people, her chances of getting hurt were small.

Of course, Tony had been in front of two thousand people.

Alison was still furious with herself for having allowed him to run the second race. She had known he was ill, he had told her as much. She would have gone to Coach Sager and insisted he be withdrawn. She had hesitated because, if she knew nothing else about him, he was a determined fellow and would not have wanted anyone to stand in his way. No one else she had ever met could have pushed himself as he had over that last lap. His willpower almost frightened her.

Alison heard the curtain rise and the opening antics of her stage mother but her mind was back in the stadium with the shocked crowd. When Tony had lapsed into his drugged stride, clawing at the air as if for invisible strings that could hold him up, she had cried. And she had not cried since last summer.

Maybe the Caretaker had done what he had for that very reason, to keep afresh their memories.

The meet officials and coaches had prevented anyone from getting near while he lay unconscious on the track. When the paramedics had arrived and loaded him in the ambulance without even a brief examination, she had thought he was dead. If Neil had not taken her by the arm, she might have wandered around the stadium until the sun had gone down.

The hospital had been jammed. Anyone else, and a dozen kids might have come by. But for Tony, half the student body showed up, and there was no horsing around. "He is alive and recovering nicely," the doctors had announced to a loud ovation not long after their arrival. Most had left then, but she had hung around with the rest of their unlucky group, and eventually they had learned of the diagnosis from Tony's parents.

Someone had spiked something Tony had either eaten or drunk with codeine, a powerful painkiller. Neil mentioned a suspicious-tasting lemonade, but when he went to search the ice chest back at school, he found it empty. The police made inquiries, but no one (i.e., none of them) who could have presented a motive spoke up.

Crete High had won the track meet by two points.

With his stomach still recovering from a thorough pumping, Tony had left the hospital the next morning.

"'God is the State; the State is God,'" Alison heard in disbelief. Had she been woolgathering a whole ten minutes? Someone must have slipped her codeine, her entrance was in a few seconds! Quick . . . Where was the script? What was her first line? What was her character's name? What was she doing here?

Love it, Alison thought, laughing to herself. The last-second anxiety attack was an old friend; she didn't feel comfortable without it. Stepping confidently to the side of the front door, she heard the sound effects of a real door opening and closing. She paused momentarily on the threshold, took a deep breath, and then swept into the lights.

"'And so the beautiful princess came into the palace,'" she said, allowing her tension to flow into her character, who was supposed to be a shade nervous. She kissed Alice's mother, father, and grandfather, saying, "'And kissed her mother, and her father, and her grandfather.'"

The magic started. She was not a deliberate actress. She was at her best when she let herself go. This style always contained its element of doubt: What if she cut free and whoever took over had decided to take the night off? Fortunately, tonight, that was not the case, for Alice—a lovely fresh young girl—had dropped by for a visit.

This did not mean that she went into a careless void. Her spontaneity needed to consciously avoid certain dark paths and steep ditches while frolicking on stage. One wrong turn for her was to look at the audience. It was fine to *see* them, but thinking who they were and what they thought of her was never wise. This was particularly difficult not to do tonight, knowing

Tony was watching. When she was not speaking, she found her mind turning his way. This drifting was partly brought on by the fact that Alice's love in the play was named Tony. He was a poor imitation of the real thing.

Her first stint on stage, when she told her wacky family about her new love and her plans to go out with him that evening, went over without a hitch—at least as far as her part was concerned. Brenda's stand-in for Essie forgot two lines, one being a question she was supposed to ask Alice. Immediately recognizing the vacant panic in the girl's eyes, she had covered for her by asking herself the question and then answering it. "'And I bet you wanted to know if he is good looking? Well . . . yes, in a word . . .'" Waiting for her next line, Alison distinctly heard a chuckle coming from the rear rows. It was Brenda, wallowing in her poor replacement's misery.

Alice went to get dressed and Alison went up a flight of stairs that started down after the fifth step. She stood in the dark to the side of the front door, off stage. She had to call, "Is that Mr. Kirby, Mother?" a couple of times, but otherwise she had a few minutes break. She felt high as the kite Tony and she had flown on their date. He had confessed wanting to impress her with his athletic ability, and she was no different when it came to her acting. He would *have* to love her. She was hot.

"How did you like the way I arranged the tiny paintings above the fireplace?" Fran whispered, popping out of the shadows.

"The whole time I was out there, I couldn't keep my eyes

off of them. What kind of question is that? Had you hung a *Playgirl* centerfold over the fireplace, I wouldn't have noticed."

Fran's patience with temperamental actresses apparently had its limits. She was insulted. "Brenda's right; all you care about is being the star." She whirled and stalked off.

Sorry! Alison thought, afraid to say it aloud lest the audience hear. Is that how her friends saw her, as an egomaniac? It was a depressing possibility. But she couldn't worry about it now.

Collecting her boyfriend from the clutches of her eccentric relatives also went smoothly. But coming up was her big love scene. The young man who played Tony was named Carl Beet. He was a nice enough looking guy—dark, strong, about her height—but his every move on stage was exaggerated, and he had a tendency to mumble. Also, there was absolutely no chemistry between them. Mr. Hoglan knew all this; he had simply cast Carl out of desperation for anybody else. Carl was essentially a humble young man but, it was funny, when it came to his acting, he thought he was blessed; the disease must be contagious. Alison wondered what the real Tony would think when she kissed Carl. The intimacy always grossed her out. Carl had bad breath.

Yet once again in the spotlight, she slipped comfortably into Alice's mind, and for a few minutes, actually found Carl desirable. "'I let myself be swept away because I loved you so.'" The lines were a bit mushy in places, but what the hell, it had only cost a couple of bucks at the door.

They decided to get married. It was inevitable—it was in the script. She walked Carl to the door, kissed him good night, and floated back into the living room. Still under love's spell, she softly leaned against the wall in the same spot she had leaned against during yesterday's rehearsal. Granted, the set was canvas and, under the best of conditions, could not withstand much pressure. Still, she only put a portion of her body weight against it. There should have been no problem.

The wall fell down. Alison fell with it.

The disorientation was similar to being sound asleep and then suddenly being awakened by a bucket of ice water. Alice was a dream character falling into a nightmare. She did not know what was happening, only that she was hitting the floor hard. Pain flared through her ribcage as she rolled on her back, hearing a loud ripping of canvas and a muffled gasp from the audience. The part of the living room wall that was still upright sagged away from the top of her head. Her vision seemed to telescope on a glint of metal where the ceiling would have joined the wall, had the room been real. It was a chain, hooking the lights to Fran's set, a stainless steel loop that refused to give under the pressure. Since it wouldn't give, the thin cable that suspended the row of stage lights did, snapping cleanly. The heavily wired metal bar and its accompanying electric bulb fell directly toward her face.

There was no time to get out of the way. Instinctively, she threw up her arms, her hands catching a wide, yellow light, the glass cracking around her knuckles, the splinters raining about her closed eyes. Her back arched with a sudden spasm. Her fingers were entangled with exposed wires, the hot current vibrating up her nerves to her spinal cord. Letting out a cry of disgust as well as pain, she pushed the bar aside, cutting herself twice over. Blood dripped from her mangled hands onto her costume.

Tony was the first to reach her side. Grabbing the light support, he angrily pulled it away from her. "I did this," he said, helping her up, his face ashen, the crowd gathering at his back.

She would probably cry in a minute, but right now she couldn't help laughing. In a perverse way, the same way all the Caretaker's tricks had seemed to her, it was funny. "Looks like I flubbed my lines, after all," she said.

Chapter Ten

The cycle was complete. As the Caretaker had said nothing about restarting it, Alison did not try to second guess him by mailing the original letter to Fran. Instead she did what Brenda had wanted to do at the beginning. She tore it into tiny pieces. The gesture was a weak one and she knew it. Standing at a comfortable distance, humiliating them all, their foe had easily moved each of their names to Column II.

The Monday after the fiasco at the play, Fran received a pale green letter in a purple envelope. It had been mailed locally and had been postmarked the previous Friday afternoon—the bastard sure had been confident the lights would fall on cue.

My Dearest Friends,

No longer can I say you do not know me. In these last few weeks, I feel we have come to know each other intimately. The closeness both stimulates and disgusts me. While I can now more readily share your zest for the performances of the tasks that will be set before you, I must also wallow lower and lower in your evil. But this is to be a temporary situation. The hourglass runs low.

At the bottom of this letter is a list of your names. The directions and conditions will be as before, only now your names are to find their way from Column II to Column III. Due to the delicate nature of your tasks, they will appear in the paper in a secret code befitting a secret society such as ours. Starting with the first letter, every third letter will help make clear your duty.

Some of you have sought to defy me. From experience, you have learned how uncomfortable that can be. As your tasks will now be more exciting, your punishment, should you choose to be stubborn, will be equally exhilarating. Remember, you have been told.

It has come to my attention that you suspect I am one of you. Let this be made painfully clear: I am not.

Love,

Your Caretaker

Column I	*Column II*	*Column III*
__________	Fran	__________
__________	Kipp	__________
__________	Brenda	__________
__________	Neil	__________
__________	Joan	__________
__________	Tony	__________
__________	Alison	__________

The ad, as it appeared in the *Times* the same day the letter arrived, read:

Fran: syrtlorryeunahokltnieaesknaesedrl
supcoehycomoaidollpulonitcwohig

Deciphered with the code, it said: Streak naked school lunch.

Alison sat alone with Fran in Fran's kitchen. The purple envelope and pale green letter lay on the table beside the paper. Alison had just finished telling Tony over the phone the details of the Caretaker's latest exercise. Within the hour, probably within ten minutes, the rest of the gang would know what was happening. Fran was crying.

"Tony is going to the *Times* offices this afternoon to see if he can't trace who's placing the ads," Alison said, taking a drink of her sugar-saturated Pepsi. She'd given up on diet colas. Why worry about a few miserable calories when a madman would probably be executing her before school got out? "He'll call if he learns anything."

Hot air breezed through the open front door. The rest of the house was empty. Somewhere upstairs, a clock chimed two o'clock, causing Fran to lift her tear-streaked face off her damp arms. "I can't do it," she whispered.

"What if you were to wear a mask," Alison said, not trying to be funny. Since reading the task, she had been turning over in her mind whether she would have what it takes to run naked through school at lunch. Given a choice between doing it and dying, she still couldn't decide. All she knew for sure was that she was glad she wasn't Fran.

"Everyone would know it was me. No one has hair like mine."

You mean, no one has a body like yours.

"You could pin it up, or cut it even. I think a mask would be permissible. The Caretaker has not struck me as inflexible."

Fran groaned, her hands gesturing helplessly. "But I would still have to do it! And I would get stopped before I could get away. I can't run very fast. One of those gorillas on the football team would grab me and rip my mask off."

"You're probably right, there," Alison agreed. Out of habit, she went to drum her knuckles on the table, as she often did when she was thinking hard. The bandages across her fingers stopped her. *Alice* had performed Saturday night wearing gloves. Friday's performance, of course, had never reached Act II. The same doctor who had treated Tony had taken care of her. They would probably be seeing more of the guy. "You know, Fran, you don't have a bad figure. Would it be so terrible if everyone saw . . ."

"No!" she cried desperately. "I can't do it! Don't you see? Why aren't you helping me? You're supposed to be my friend." Her head fell back onto her arms and she wept uncontrollably. A couple of minutes went by as a wave of compassion stole over Alison. She reached out and stroked Fran's hair as she would have a child's.

"I do have an idea," she whispered.

Fran, sniffling, raised her head. "What?"

"That you go away."

"Where?"

"Anywhere, it doesn't matter. Remember last Friday how you told me your parents keep hassling you about visiting your senile grandmother in Bakersfield? Why not call the poor lady tonight and then tell your parents that you feel so sorry for her that you really must go and stay with her for a week or so? You're finished with the courses required for graduation. And your electives are pretty much winding down, especially now that you have completed the sets for drama. They'll let you go."

Unlooked for hope dawned on Fran's face. It didn't last. "The Caretaker will find me. He knows everything we do."

"Don't tell anybody where you're going."

"But you know!"

"I won't even tell Tony where you're hiding, trust me."

Fran thought about that for a minute, when suddenly, a peculiar expression darkened her features. To Alison, it looked positively fiendish. "You really like Tony, don't you?" Fran asked. "You're in love with him, aren't you?"

"He is important to me," she answered carefully. "Why do you ask?"

"No reason." Fran shrugged, averting her eyes. Alison was suspicious of the sudden shift in tone and believed she had a glimmer of what Fran might be considering.

"You're my friend, Fran, and you're in trouble," she said quietly, firmly. "And I intend to do everything possible to help you. But if you want my help, or the help of anyone else in the group, then you better remember where your loyalty lies."

Fran folded the newspaper and went to stand. Alison stopped her. "What are you doing?" Fran cried, trying to squirm away. "Let go of my arm! I don't know what you're talking about."

Her obvious guilt confirmed Alison's suspicion. Staring her in the eyes, she let go of Fran and Fran stayed where she was. "You're thinking of going to the police."

"No, I'm not!"

"Yes, you are. You would turn Tony in and hope . . ."

"Neil says we should! And he's a good person."

Alison nodded. "But Neil has *not* gone to the police, even though he thinks Tony should. He's too honorable to do anything behind his friend's back. He's not like you. You think if you report the crime, you'll be absolved of all responsibility. I know how your mind works."

"You know nothing of my mind!" Fran swore, proud and bitter.

Is that true? This was a side of her friend she had never seen before. Fran whined, worried, and wept. Fran did not shout out pronouncements, that is, not to anyone's knowledge. Alison picked up the Caretaker's letter. A tiny seed of doubt, like so many others she had collected of late, sprouted in her mind.

"Maybe I don't," she said quietly.

Fran went to the sink and started, of all things, to wash the dishes. Alison studied the list of names and wondered if there was a significance in the Caretaker's choice of who went first, and who went last.

"So what are you going to do?" she asked when Fran was done with the dirty plates and glasses. Drying her hands on a towel, Fran came back to the table. Her burst of authority appeared gone and she was the same old twitching adolescent.

"Your idea sounds good. I guess it's my only choice."

"Do you swear that you won't go to the police?"

Fran hesitated. "I won't."

"I hope for your sake you don't."

Chapter Eleven

We have to talk," Tony said, coming out of a lengthy kiss in the cramped confines of the front seat of his car, taking back his left leg which had somehow intertwined with Alison's right leg. They were not lying down but they were far from sitting. Neither of them was missing any articles of clothing, though Alison's blouse was halfway unbuttoned. They were both soaked with sweat—the afternoon sun pouring through the windows had the greenhouse effect in full gear—but that did nothing to diminish his enjoyment of her skin, which was unimaginably soft and sensitive. Making out with Alison was a new experience for him. She seemed to melt right into him, unlike other girls—Joan for instance—who had always been anxious to have as many buttons pushed as quickly as possible. But the lot at the back of the city park was no place to get too carried away. They could get a ticket.

"No," Alison protested, tightening her embrace, her eyes closed. He didn't resist and in fact began to fiddle with the belt on her pants. What prevented him from investigating further was the sudden appearance of a jogger, who seemed to come out of nowhere.

"Got the time, buddy?" The guy—couldn't he see what was going on here?—was leaning against the car, his middle-aged beer gut hanging over the door handle. Tony sat up quickly and checked his watch.

"Three-fifteen."

"Thanks, bud." The jerk poked his fat scruffy face closer. "Hey, aren't you Tony Hunt?"

"No," he said flatly, staring straight ahead. Out of the corner of his eye, he could see red-faced Alison trying to fix her bra.

"Sure you are! I was there when you threw that seventy-yard bomb against Willmore High. I never thought that ball was going to come down. You were great!"

"Thank you."

"I bet you'll be a pro one day. Hey, can I have your autograph?"

Tony looked directly at him. "No. Get the hell out of here."

The man's proud grin disappeared. He spat on the ground. "Sorry to take up your precious time."

When he was gone, Alison asked, "Do people often recognize you?"

He shrugged. "Only when I'm trying to hide." He laid his head back on the hot seat. "Where were we?"

Alison chuckled. "You were trying to make a fallen woman out of me."

He smiled. "You'll have your chance later."

"My chance!" She socked him. "The gall of this jock."

He laughed. "Just kidding." He rechecked his watch. He had lied to the guy, it was three-forty-five. With the exception of Fran—tucked away only Alison knew where—the group was scheduled to meet in fifteen minutes in the rocket ship in the children's playground, a hilly quarter-mile walk from where they were now parked. He scanned the area to make sure none of the others were visible. If Joan caught him necking with Alison, that would be bad. If Neil saw him . . . it was best not to think about it. He added, "We have to talk."

She was wearing tight blue jeans and a stretched yellow blouse, looking irresistibly cute with her sudden seriousness.

"You said that already. About what? Us?"

"All of us," he said. "You and I have to compare notes. We can't do that when we're all together. There're always too many petty interruptions." He paused. "Do you have any idea, Alison, who the Caretaker is?"

She scratched at the healing cuts on her hands. "He says he's not one of us. If that's true, where can we begin?"

"Why do you suppose he used the word, 'painfully,' when making that clear?"

"I don't know," she said. "But, it's weird, when he said he wasn't one of us, I believed him! Everything he's done to us so far has been to expose us for what we are. I can't help feeling he would tell the truth when talking about himself."

"If the Caretaker is as complicated as he appears, his *truth* might also be complicated, and mean more than one thing. Also, he may have made a slip. He broke his pattern. He drugged me *before* I tried to win the races. He tampered with the set *before* you had a chance to flub your lines. It was like he knew what we were going to do, like he was one of us." He pulled a tattered piece of the *Times* from his pocket, smoothing it on his leg. Fran hadn't sent him a letter; nevertheless, Kipp had received one this morning. It had been identical to Fran's except Fran's name had been missing. The accompanying ad in the paper had been given in the familiar code. Translated, it read:

K. C. Tell Everyone Cheated SAT Tell M.I.T.

Such an announcement, Kipp said, would ruin his academic career. He refused to do it. He did not appear worried about the consequences of his refusal.

"Let's go through the group one by one and bring up anything even remotely suspicious," he said. "Let's start with Kipp."

"You start; you know him better than me."

Tony hesitated, reconsidering what he was doing. A few

kissing sessions and here he was ready to pour out his deepest suspicions to this girl he had scarcely spoken to up until a few weeks ago. Then he looked at her again and decided if she was the Caretaker, he was already done for. "Kipp is smart," he began. "More than any of us, he could have planned this. His kinky sense of humor reminds me of the Caretaker. I like him a lot, I assume he likes me, but he can be indifferent at times. I'd never seen him wearing a seat belt before, but he had his on when he hit the wall. When you and I were sitting by the snack bar during the track meet, I saw Kipp and Joan going through the ice chest. Also, right from the beginning, he was opposed to the possibility of the Caretaker being one of us."

"He sounds guilty as sin. What's his motive?"

"I can't see us coming up with a motive for any of us. Tell me about Fran."

"A couple of weeks ago, I would have put her at the bottom of the list. But now, I'm not so sure." She began to count on her fingers. "Fran did not seem to mind painting over Teddy. She constructed the set that gave out on me. I told her to leave and told her where to go, but she could have put the idea in my mind a few days before when she mentioned someone she felt obligated to visit. She's smart, too, even if she doesn't act it. Most of all, she's always been the odd one out: never gone out with a boy, never been given much respect. Isn't that the standard B-movie background for a vengeful teenager?"

"Does she like you, really like you?"

"I'd always thought she looked up to me. But lately, I've been sort of putting her down. It's a bad habit I've gotten into." She shook her head. "You know, this is freaky having to look at your friends this way."

"That's why we've postponed doing it."

"Tell me about Neil?"

"Before I do, tell me if you suspect him."

She seemed reluctant to answer. "I do. It's nothing he's done, it's the way he is: quiet, thoughtful, polite."

"And those qualities make him suspicious?" he asked coldly. Why was he so keen to protect Neil? Because he was his friend? That was the obvious reason and it was probably true, and yet, as he thought about it, a deeper more disturbing motive came to mind.

Neil speaks for me; he says what I'm ashamed to say.

"I'm sorry." Alison touched his hand. "You really care about him, don't you?"

He nodded. "Do you?"

"I . . . I hardly know him."

"Of course, silly of me to ask." He wiped his brow, rubbed the sweat into his palms. "The only thing I can think of that makes Neil a possible candidate is that he was alone beside the ice chest just before I drank the lemonade. In fact, he was the one who stocked the chest."

"That's pretty incriminating"

"But he's always taken care of our drinks."

"Still . . ."

"The police didn't blame him," he interrupted.

"Tony, I . . ."

"I'm sorry, I know I'm not being objective about this. It's instinct with me, I suppose, to watch out for him. He's always watching out for me. Did I tell you he insisted on sampling the lemonade before I drank it? He warned me to leave it alone. He's warned all of us that the Caretaker must be one of us." Tony shifted uncomfortably. "Let's go on to Brenda."

"She's as old a rival as she is a friend. She really enjoyed what the Caretaker told her to do. She went above and beyond the call of duty. Lately, she hasn't been getting along with Kipp, and I'm not sure why. She's a complicated person. I thought I heard her laugh when I crash-landed during the play."

"Interesting," Tony muttered. "Just before he hit the wall, Brenda refused to get in Kipp's car. Tell me, did you trust Brenda before all this craziness started?"

"Ninety percent."

"What does that mean?"

"I wouldn't have trusted her with my life."

"Was Brenda at the track meet?"

"Yes. She was wandering around a lot."

"On the field?"

"I think so."

"What does Brenda think of me?"

Alison smiled. "You wouldn't know, would you? Brenda

has a crush on you, or at least she used to. Most of the girls at school have a crush on you. She always used to talk about what it would be like to get you alone."

He was mildly flattered. "*Used* to? Does she still talk about me?"

"No. When I told her you had asked me out, that first time, she just said, 'That's nice,' and went on to something else. It's possible she resents the two of us. Very possible."

"Hmm. Which of us should do Joan?"

"Have you already *done* Joan?" she asked, tickling his leg.

"That's a secret. Hey!" She started poking at him something fierce and he had to use both hands to contain her. She sure was quick; she should have been one of his receivers. "I don't kiss and tell."

"But I need to know for the sake of the investigation!" she protested, fighting against his hold. A slight downward turn at the corner of her mouth made him realize it was troubling her.

"There's nothing to tell."

"Are you sure?"

He grinned. "Nothing to brag about." He cautiously released her and she immediately slapped him on the top of the head.

"There had better not be." She appeared satisfied. "Joan could fill a book. Even if you were driving, I don't think there's any question that it was mainly her fault. Maybe she figured that the truth would eventually come out, and she set up this whole thing to make us do something that would somehow implicate us further." Alison stopped suddenly.

"What is it?"

"Something that Joan said to me once." She put her hand to her head. "Something that reminded me of the Caretaker." She pounded her knee lightly with her fist. "I can't remember. It's there, but it won't come out."

"It will, eventually."

"Yeah, probably when the guillotine blade is falling toward my neck. Did you check on Joan's window?"

"Closely, last night when I was in her bedroom . . ." Alison reacted quickly but he was waiting for her. "Jealous, aren't you? Kipp went over, not into her house, but by her street. He brought binoculars. He couldn't tell whether the window had just been replaced. It didn't look like it. There wasn't a single putty stain on the glass. But he did learn that Joan wears purple lace underwear, not that that was news to me . . ."

"Would you stop that!"

He laughed. "Don't be so much fun to tease and I will." He checked his watch. "We had better be going. We don't seem cut out to be detectives."

"They all sound guilty. Tony, did you read *Murder on the Orient Express*? What if it is *all* of them?"

"Then we had better leave the country." He didn't seriously consider the possibility. But the question did raise another idea that he took very seriously, one he kept to himself.

I am not one of you.

That would not be a lie if the Caretaker were, say, two of them.

The meeting at the rocket ship was going as Tony had feared it would. Joan kept throwing Alison nasty looks, Kipp kept ridiculing Joan, Brenda kept complaining about the time they were wasting, and Neil kept looking sad and miserable. No one even thought to ask Tony how he had fared at the paper and he had to bring it up himself.

"They wanted to know if the ads were personally harassing me or if they were connected with an illegal activity. I had expected as much going down there, but I had also hoped to talk to the person who had taken the ads, to see if they remembered if it had been a male or female on the phone. But the supervisor wouldn't let me in the back without 'good reason.' If I had told her the truth, it would have been the same as going to the police."

"It was a nice try," Neil said, sitting on the sand, leaning against the low wall that enclosed the rocket ship. He was holding a half-peeled orange, nibbling on it like a bird. Last week, Tony had brought Neil's mother over a fortified protein powder, but it did not look as if Neil had been taking it.

This whole thing is killing me. Please, Tony?

"Chances are a different person took each ad," Kipp said, relaxing at the end of the slide, looking perfectly jovial for someone whose life was in danger. "Those people take thousands of ads a day."

"But how many in code?" Tony asked.

"Half the ads in the paper are incomprehensible to me," Kipp said.

"Aren't you even a little scared?" Alison asked.

Kipp smiled. "I'm sleeping with my night-light on."

"I don't know why you just don't admit to cheating on the SAT," Joan said, her bare legs hanging through the bent bars on the third stage of the rocket. Taking a drag on her cigarette, she sprinkled the ashes toward Kipp's head. "A perfect score, hah! The whole school knows you had a black market answer sheet."

"I could have gotten 2400 on that test after finishing a six-pack," Kipp said, leaning his head back, shielding his eyes from the sun. "I like that skirt, Joan, it goes with your purple underwear."

"I'm not wearing any underwear."

"Where's Fran?" Brenda asked, shouldering a clay fort, standing away from the rest of them when one would have expected her to be holding on to her boyfriend. Tony cautioned himself, however, that he might be overstressing the unimportant. Brenda and Kipp were not a touch-crazy couple. They often sat apart. "Why isn't she here?"

"She's in hiding," Alison said. She was sitting beside him on the monkey bars. "Don't you remember?"

"Oh, yeah. Up . . . wherever she went."

Alison jumped on that. "Why did you say *up*?"

"Huh?"

"How did you know she had headed north?" Alison insisted.

"I didn't," Brenda snapped, annoyed. "I just said up. I could have said down."

Neil lost his orange and it rolled in the sand. He picked it up and began to brush it off. The fruit was obviously ruined. "Bakersfield isn't exactly north," he said casually.

Alison was shocked. "How did you know she went to Bakersfield?"

Neil looked up, startled, and lost his orange again. Her tone—*his angel's harshness,* Tony thought—seemed to bruise him. "Wasn't I supposed to know? I was talking to Brenda yesterday and—"

"Brenda?" Alison interrupted. All eyes went to the clay fort. Brenda no longer looked bored.

"F-Fran's parents told me," she stuttered. "Big deal."

"But you just denied knowing where Fran was!" Alison said.

"Because I thought that's what you wanted me to do!"

"Who else knew where Fran is?" Tony asked. Kipp and Joan remained silent. He glanced at the rest room down the hill by the lake. There was a phone attached to the ladies' side. "Do you have Fran's grandmother's number?" he asked Alison.

"In my purse. But I just called her yesterday. She was fine."

"Call her again, please, right now." He nodded toward the phone, fishing change from his pocket. "Use this. We'll wait here for you."

While Alison was gone, Tony studied the faces of each member of their gang and tried to imagine which two could make up a conspiracy. None matched, possibly because it was impossible to forget that he trusted these people.

Alison was back soon, too soon. Looking lost, not saying a word, she sat down beside him. He did not have to ask.

"Well?" Kipp said.

"Her grandmother doesn't know where she is," Alison said. "When the woman got up this morning, Fran was gone."

"She probably went home," Brenda said.

Alison shook her head. "I called there."

"Maybe she went out for a long walk," Joan said.

"No," Alison sighed. "She's gone."

Chapter Twelve

A loud noise woke Alison. She sat up in bed. It was dark in her room but she could see. This did not seem strange to her, not as strange as the knocking on the door downstairs. It was loud, and the house cringed at each blow. She waited for it to stop, to go on to another house, but it stayed. It wanted her to answer the door.

She got out of bed. Her feet hardly seemed to touch the floor. She was surprised to discover that she was dressed. She could not remember when she had gone to bed but she was puzzled that she had not changed out of her clothes. She always did. Why then, she asked herself, was she wearing the same clothes she had worn to the concert last summer? They were covered with dirt. And her nails were black, like she had been digging with her hands.

She walked to her bedroom door and stepped into the hall. All the lights in the house were out but the walls, the ceiling, and the floor were emitting a dull gray glow, a questionable improvement over utter blackness. Her feet were bare, except for a film of dust, but she was not cold. The house temperature was difficult to gauge. She was certain, however, that it was freezing outside. That was one of the reasons the person knocking wanted to get inside. The other reason was he wanted to get to her. She knew who this person was, though she could not remember his name. He was not someone she wanted to meet in a dark and lonely place. The person was dangerous.

The knocking got louder, more insistent, and she began to feel afraid. The person was not knocking with his hands. He was using something heavy, something he might want to use to crush her head to a pulp. She hurried down the hall to her parents' bedroom. The door was open and she peeked inside. The room was empty, the bed bare of blankets and sheets. Her parents were long gone. There was no one to protect her, no one else who could answer the door.

She started down the stairs. She wanted to return to her bedroom and lock the door and hide in the closet but she knew that would make her a sitting duck. She had to get out of the house. Once outside, she would have the whole tract to hide in.

Halfway down the stairs, she realized the banging was at the back door, not the front. The blows were changing, as the wood began to soften and splinter, giving in under the beating.

She quickened her steps, passing through the empty living room. A faintly luminous, red-tinged gas had filled the lower portion of the house. She could not imagine what it was or where it had come from. Yet it was familiar, smelling of dry weeds and parched earth, making it difficult to breathe. But she could not hear her panting lungs, only feel the suffocation. All she could hear was her pounding heart and the pounding on the disintegrating door.

The front door would not open. It was not locked and the knob was not stuck; it simply would not open. She began to panic, especially when the banging suddenly halted. Terrifying as the pounding had been, its abrupt stopping could only mean the final obstacle to getting to her had been removed. She closed her eyes, cringing into the corner, waiting for the blade that would split her skull in two.

But it never came. No one crossed the astral lagoon that was the living room. Praying for a second chance, she again tried the front door. Then something terrible happened, something worse than waking up in the middle of the night to the sound of an ax murderer chopping his way inside.

Her hand stuck to the doorknob.

It would not come off.

On the other side of the door, someone began to knock, a polite civilized knock.

"Who is it?" she cried.

"You know," the person said. "You have always known."

It was true, she did know, and the knowledge filled her with horror. She began to scream. And the door began to open.

"Don't come in!" Alison gasped, bolting upright in bed, her nightmare momentarily superimposed over her waking state, the cold, etheric light giving way in halting steps to the warm blanket of the normal dark room. Her right hand was interlocked with her left hand, losing an impossible tug-of-war. She relaxed her fingers and placed her palm on her moist forehead, the pounding blood reminding her all too clearly of the pounding on the dream door.

The phone was ringing. Which had awakened her, the call or the terror? She glanced at her digital clock, saw it was 3 A.M., and reached for the phone.

"Hello?"

"Alison?"

"I think so . . . Tony?"

There was an eternal pause. "There's been an accident. It's Kipp."

She was slipping back into her nightmare. "Is he dead?" she whispered.

"We don't know." He sounded crushed, defeated. "I'm calling from his house. The police are here."

"I'm coming."

"Don't." But the word had no force behind it. "Oh, if you want, I guess. But don't speak to anyone till you talk to either Neil or me."

Putting down the phone, crying a little, she remembered the question.

"Who is it?"

But she could not remember the answer.

The ax-wielding psychopath and the ringing phone had not awakened her parents, and she was able to get away without having to make impossible explanations. Although it took her better than an hour to reach Kipp's house, two police cars were still there, their red lights spinning like maddened phantasms. She coasted by the house and parked up the street, using her rearview mirror to search for a glimpse of Tony. Somehow, she missed Neil's approach, and when he knocked on her window, her taut nerves rammed her head into the car ceiling.

"Sorry," Neil said.

Rubbing her bruised scalp, she rolled down the window. "It wasn't your fault." He leaned against the car as if he would otherwise fall down. Kipp's street was old and the lights were dim. She could scarcely see Neil's expression, but she saw enough to know it was bad. Kipp's big-nosed face sprang into her mind, laughing in the sun, chewing on a blade of grass in the park, totally unconcerned that he was next on the list.

You brilliant fool, what have they done to you? "Tony didn't tell me . . ." she began.

"He should be here soon," Neil answered, obviously wanting to spare her details she was in no hurry to hear. Neil moved aside, and she climbed out of the car and it cut her to the heart to see how he hobbled on one leg. She hugged him with her right arm.

"We're losing, aren't we?" she said.

He looked at her with what seemed surprise, and for a moment, depended solely upon her for support. She could feel him trembling. "It seems that way," he said.

That she could have mistrusted him, as she had told Tony, filled her with shame. A breeze, warm but still causing her to shiver, blew from the direction of Kipp's brightly lit house, and she hugged him closer. "I'm sorry, Neil," she said.

"I am, too."

"I mean, I'm sorry for not understanding you."

There was no moon, but a snow white light gleamed deep in his eyes as he peered at her, inches away. "Alison?"

"I wish we had talked more before all this started. You're a great guy. I wish . . . I wish my dreams were different." She winced, close to crying. She was making no sense but, for Christsakes, they were only kids! "I had a nightmare tonight. I've had it before. I'm alone in my house at night and someone is trying to get me—hacking at the door with an ax." She closed her aching eyes for a moment. "And the worst part is, I know who it is."

"Who?"

"I can't remember."

"The man?"

"Neil?" she said suddenly, and she was almost begging. "Are you having nightmares?"

"Not all the time." He tilted his head back, staring at the hazy black sky. "I have some wonderful dreams. They're full of colors and music and singing. When I'm in them, I wish they would never end. They remind me of the days before all this started." His voice faltered and he lowered his head. "But I'm like you, I've been forgetting." He frowned. "Yeah, I've been having nightmares."

"We shouldn't talk about them. It doesn't help. Tell me something happy. Was I . . . ?"

Was I in your wonderful dreams?

She didn't get a chance to ask. Maybe she wouldn't have, anyway; it was sort of a sentimental question to put to someone she knew only because she'd helped kill a stranger with him. Tony interrupted at that point, walking quickly up the street. She released Neil and he returned to leaning against her car. Wearing cutoffs, his sweatshirt inside out and backward, the tag hanging at his Adam's apple, Tony embraced them both. His eyes were dry and when he spoke, his voice was calm. He had been hit hard but had mastered himself.

"Do you know what has happened, Ali?" he asked.

She shook her head. One of the patrol car's red lights had

come to a halt pointed directly at them, making the street look like Lucifer's Lane. A policeman came out of the house and stared their way. Tony shifted his body in front of hers. "Kipp has disappeared," he said. "He left behind . . . a lot of blood."

Sleeping with my night-light on.

The shadowed street, the shining house, even Neil and Tony, receded and took on an unreal quality. She was watching a badly filmed colorless movie that ran on an unending reel. She was slipping away, feeling she had to get away. She had to force herself to ask, "How much is *a lot*?"

"The police believe he could still be alive," Tony said quickly. "We just don't know. Somehow, without a lot of noise, he was overcome and dragged out his bedroom window. The trail of blood leads from the backyard to the street. His mother woke up when she heard what sounded like a truck starting up out front. She was the one who found the soaked mattress." He added quietly, "She had to be sedated and taken to the hospital."

"How did you two come to be here?" she asked. The answer to the question did not really interest her. The puddle of blood said it all. She sought for the picture of Kipp in her head, but he was no longer laughing, fading as if even the life were running out of his memory.

"After our meeting this afternoon," Tony said, "Neil and I decided we wouldn't let Kipp out of our sight. We came back to his house with him and sat around listening to music, talking, whatever. Then about nine Brenda came over with some beer. We were all so uptight with Fran disappearing, I guess we drank too much and forgot that we were supposed to be protecting Kipp. When he told us to leave so he could get some sleep, we figured no one would come after him in his own bedroom." Tony ran his hand through his hair. "Then a couple of hours ago, when I was in bed, I got this call. It was a detective. Since Neil and I were the last ones to see him—Brenda didn't stay long after bringing over the beer—he wanted to question us. He wanted to know if Kipp had any enemies." Tony stopped and pulled a purple envelope out of his pocket. "I swear I would have told him the whole story, but I found this on my car seat when I went to drive over here."

The page inside the envelope was the familiar pale green. This time, the Caretaker came right to the point:

If you are not certain they are dead, do what you know you shouldn't, and be certain.

Your Caretaker

"What are we going to do?" Alison asked miserably.

"I don't know," Tony said. "Not yet."

Chapter Thirteen

They sat in the deserted courtyard of Grant High on the raunchy wooden benches Alison had always despised. The bell signaling the end of break had rung ten minutes ago, and Brenda and she had watched without moving while the other students had migrated to their next classes. The day was like every other day had been for what seemed like the last ten years: a little smoggy, a lot hot.

"You don't have to come with me," Brenda said, refolding the morning paper. As with Kipp, none of them had passed on the letter to her, and still, she had not been spared. Fran's and Kipp's names had been blanked out but otherwise the Caretaker was sticking to his formula. Decoded, the ad in the paper read:

B.P. Tell Every Teacher School Go To Hell

Brenda had spent last week in a trance after learning the circumstances surrounding Kipp's kidnapping. She was a fair actress but Alison had mentally crossed her off her list of suspects. No one could fake the anguish she was going through. The only thing that had got her back on her feet was her strong desire to do her "duty."

"I'll wait outside each classroom and give you pep talks in between teachers," Alison said.

"Who should I start with?" Brenda's hair was unwashed and she wore no make-up. Incredibly, in the space of the last few days, gray hairs had begun to show near her ears.

"Start with someone you hate. You may as well get some satisfaction out of this." She added, "You won't get far."

Brenda nodded wearily. "As long as I get an *A* for effort." She climbed unsteadily to her feet. "Let's go to Mrs. Franklin's art class. That bitch gave me a *D* on a pretty giraffe I made my freshman year."

Waiting outside the door, Alison anticipated a loud commotion a few seconds after Brenda's entrance. But she heard nothing and when Brenda reappeared a minute later, her expression was little changed. "The moron just stared at me like she didn't understand," she explained. "The class was too busy painting to notice."

They went to Mr. Cleaner's history class next. Young and precise and as bald as an egg, he had made fun of Brenda's choice of lipstick her junior year. He was not one of her favorite people. This time, Alison kept the door open a crack. It was terrible of her, but she really wanted to see the look on the teacher's face.

Brenda had not made it all the way to the front when Mr. Cleaner broke from his lecture and said, sounding slightly annoyed, "Yes, Miss Paxson. What can I do for you?"

Brenda cleared her throat. "I wanted to tell you that you can go to hell."

The class went very still. Mr. Cleaner frowned and scratched the top of his shiny head. "Are you preaching, or what? This is hardly the time for it."

"No, no. I'm not trying to save your soul. I'm telling you that you can go to hell, and that I hope you do."

He responded briskly. "In that case, you can go to hell yourself. And while you're at it, get the hell out of my class."

The kids started laughing. Red faced—she had not got the best of it—Brenda turned and ran for the door. Alison took her by the arm and pulled her outside and around the side of the building, where they hid between the bushes.

"At least he won't report you to the principal," she said.

Brenda gave a wan smile. "I think he was glad I stopped by."

Miss Fogleson was the next victim. A grossly overweight lady in her mid thirties, she taught English literature and made it seem like a foreign language class. No one liked her because unless you read and reported on *Moby Dick* and *Tale of Two Cities* and similar classics, she thought you were a tasteless waste who certainly deserved a poor grade. Once again, Alison held the door slightly ajar.

Miss Fogleson was grading papers while her senior class was pretending to read Hemingway and Dickens. All was quiet. Brenda had reached the front desk when Miss Fogleson, without glancing up, said in her crass voice, "Yes, what do you want?"

"I want you to go to hell," Brenda said, loud and clear.

Miss Fogleson's right hand twitched and her red pen dropped and rolled off the desk and fell on the floor. Alison felt a nasty tickle of pleasure. Miss Fogleson looked at Brenda in amazement. "What did you say, young lady?"

"You heard me. I told you to go to hell."

She heard her all right; her fat neck began to swell up like a red balloon. The class put down their books and watched. "How dare you!" Miss Fogleson said furiously.

"I'm just speaking for all of us kids," Brenda went on, getting revved up. Alison did not cringe as she had with Mr. Hoglan. Then the poor man had been innocent, and back then there had been a chance Brenda would get off clean. Today, she was doomed before she started; best to get it over and have it done with. She gestured dramatically, "We all hate you. You have lousy taste, no patience, and you're ugly! You should be a character in one of those boring books you make us read. Then we could rip out the pages you're on and wad you up and throw you in the garbage where you belong!"

Miss Fogleson climbed to her elephant legs, and her mouth dropped open wide enough to swallow in one bite the doughnut she had on a napkin on her desk. "You cannot say these things! You will be severely punished!"

"Hah!" Brenda snorted. "Take me to court! Any jury will be able to see you're the fat slob I say you are. This is a free country. I can call a pig a pig when I see it. Pig!"

Gyrating like a rippling bowl of Jell-O, Miss Fogleson appealed to her class. "Steve, Roger, get the principal. Get the security guard. Get her out of here!"

It was then things got real interesting. A short, black-haired boy, whom Alison recognized but whose name she could not place, stood in the back and said with a straight face, "Miss Fogleson, I don't believe that Brenda has done anything that could be called illegal. She is, after all, only expressing an opinion. And who knows, there may be some merit in it. I suggest we listen with an open mind to whatever she has to say and don't get upset." He sat down without cracking a smile.

The class went berserk. They did not merely start laughing as they had in Mr. Cleaner's room, they positively freaked with pleasure: falling out of their chairs, jumping up and down, even throwing things. Miss Fogleson was like a thermometer thrust into fire, the red blood swelling in her head, ready to burst. It was Brenda who waved for order.

"Let's take a vote!" she shouted. "All those who think

Miss Fogleson's worth a damn, raise your hand." Whatever hands happened to be up, came down. "See!" Brenda pointed at the teacher. "I told you I speak for the masses. You're out of it, lady. You should roll your fat ass down to the administration building this minute and hand in your resignation." She bowed to the applauding class. "Thank you for your time."

Alison caught her—or tried to catch her, Brenda came storming out the door—as she spun into the locker room, leaving a riot at her back. "I think you deserve a break after that one," she said.

"No breaks," Brenda said, her eyes narrowed. "These teachers are going to pay for what's happened to Kipp."

"But *they* didn't do anything to Kipp."

"Well, they didn't help him any." She barreled around the corner and flung open the first door she came to. Too late, Alison reached to stop her. The class was Algebra II and the teacher was Coach Sager whose no-nonsense "slap them till they get in line" attitude was notorious. Alison put her back to the wall and closed her eyes. This one, she couldn't bear to watch.

She did not have long to wait. A thick palm on her shoulder, the other hand pinning her arms behind her back, a stern mask of discipline riding shotgun above her white face, Brenda reappeared thirty seconds later, Coach Sager manually steering her in the direction of the administration building. Alison was thankful the coach's feet pounded past her without notice. She slumped to the ground, losing the laughter she had found only a moment ago. A student poked his head out the door.

"Wow!" he exclaimed. "Did you hear what that girl told Coach Sager?"

"I can imagine," she muttered.

Chapter Fourteen

The days had been hot since the Caretaker's appearance, and today had added a stilling humidity, a leaden front up from a tropical storm in Baja, to make sure they did not forget that they were not far from burning in Hell. At least that's how Neil saw it, though he had always been religiously inclined. It was his turn. The Caretaker hadn't done him any favors.

N.H. Burn Down School

Fran and Kipp were nowhere to be found. The police had returned twice to question the others, but the interviews were obviously uncoordinated. They had asked Brenda and Alison about Fran and had spoken to Tony, Neil, and Brenda about Kipp. No one had thought to quiz Joan. Why should they, the police didn't know of the existence of their cursed group. The kidnappings were big news locally.

Neil and Tony were sitting in Tony's room, Neil on the corner stool, Tony on the floor. The window was open and the sun had a bird's-eye view of their heads. Both of them were sweating but neither of them was bothering with his drink. There was a lot they had to talk about but they were letting it wait. Tony wished he could shut off his mind as easily as he could his mouth. He kept rehashing the events that had brought them to their current dilemma, trying to find the turn he had missed that would have taken them all to safety. But the only exit he could see was the obvious one, Neil's trap door: Confess and face the consequences. Now, with the Caretaker's last threat, even that way was blocked.

"How is Brenda?" Tony asked.

"Expelled, grounded, depressed, and alive," Neil answered.

Tony half smiled. "In order of importance?"

"No."

"It was a joke. I'm sorry; it wasn't funny." He wiped at his face with his damp T-shirt. For a moment, he considered calling Alison. Their romance had been put on hold since the pints of blood—the police had confirmed that it had been human blood—had soaked through Kipp's bed sheets. He wanted to be big and strong in front of her, and he had nothing to offer that would make him appear that way. And he wanted to be with Neil. "How's your leg?"

"Sore."

"You still don't have enough money to get it fixed?"

Neil took a sip of his orange juice and coughed. "My mother's gone to Arkansas to visit her brother. The strain was wearing her out. I gave her what money I had."

"How does she feel the strain we're under?"

"She feels it," was all Neil would say. Putting his lips to the glass for another drink, Tony could see every bone in his jaw through his pallid skin. Neil would soon be a skeleton.

If he lives that long, Tony thought, shamefully.

"You wanted to get her out of the way in case something happens to you, didn't you?"

"Yes."

"Nothing's going to happen. I'm not leaving your side."

Neil pressed the cool glass against his cheek and closed his eyes. "I'd rather be alone. It's strange, but I don't feel as afraid when I'm alone, not anymore." He opened his eyes. "But you can give me one of your father's guns."

Tony nodded. He had already lifted one from his dad's collection and hidden it under his bed. But rather than reaching for it, he picked up a Bic lighter instead, striking the flame up to maximum, as if they really needed more hot air. He was staring at the flame when he said, "It could be done."

"No."

"We have a small pump in the garage. I could take my car from gas station to gas station and use the pump in between stops to siphon the fuel into a bunch of old five gallon bottles we have out back. If we hit the school at, say, three in the morning, drove through first and dropped the bottles off, then came back on foot and broke a window in a classroom in each wing, and then poured the gasoline inside, it could work. When everything's set, I could take a flare and a box of Fourth of July sparklers and make one mad dash around the campus. The place would be an inferno before the first fire truck could get there."

"No."

"I'll do it myself then, dammit."

Neil sighed, wiping his thinning hair out of his sunken eyes. "And what will you do for me when I'm in Column III?"

The question was as honest as it was fatalistic. Tony leaned his head back and stared at the ceiling. The worst thing was this waiting and doing nothing . . . no, that was the second worst. Neil's refusal to blame him ate at him more than anything the Caretaker had dreamed up. "I got you into this predicament, I'm going to get you out of it, at least for this round. I'm burning the blasted place down. It deserves it, anyway." Neil said nothing. Frustrated, Tony threw the Bic lighter at the door, half hoping it would explode. "One word from you that night and I would have turned myself in. I swear, one word and I wouldn't have given in to Kipp and the others."

"I'm sorry."

"I'm not blaming you, don't get that idea." He chuckled without mirth. "How could I blame you?"

"Tony?" Neil asked suddenly. "Do you ever think about the man?"

"I think about nothing else. If we hadn't hit him, life would be about ten thousand times rosier."

"No, I mean think about who he was: whether he was married and had kids, what kind of music he liked, what he hoped for in the future?"

"I would like to say I do but . . . I don't."

Neil hugged his glass tightly. "Since the accident, even to this day, I read the paper in the morning and look for an article or picture about the man. In the days following that night, I was sure there would be something about him, at least one person looking for him. But there was nothing."

"We were lucky."

"No," Neil said sadly. "It made me feel worse that no one cared for him, that only I cared." He put his drink on the floor and tugged at his emerald ring, which could now have fit on his bony thumb. "It must be lonely to be buried in a place where no one ever goes."

"Personally, I would prefer it." Tony wanted to get off this morbid bent so he changed the subject to a much cheerier topic—guns. He leaned over and pulled the walnut case from beneath his bed, throwing back the lid. "This is one of my father's favorites." He held up the heavy black six-shooter. "It's a Smith & Wesson .44 special revolver. The safety is here." He pointed to the catch above the handle. "This is a mean weapon.

Just be sure before you pull the trigger." He handed the gun to Neil, along with a box of shells. Neil looked at it once with loathing before tucking it in his belt, hiding the butt beneath his shirt. "Remember to load it," Tony added.

"You don't think it would scare the Caretaker, empty?"

"Not if he knew it was empty."

Neil swallowed painfully. Reality was hitting home. A tear started out of his right eye. He wiped it away and another one took its place. At that moment, Tony would have given his life to know for certain that Neil would be safe. Cowards like himself, he thought, were always heroic when it was too late to make any difference.

"I guess I should be going," Neil said.

"Won't you stay, please?"

"I can't." He took hold of the shelf and pulled himself up. It struck Tony then, only after all this time, that Neil's leg could not possibly have simple cartilage damage.

"Thank you for everything. I won't forget you, Tony."

Tony stood and helped him to the door, where he hugged Neil. "Of course you won't forget me. You'll see me tomorrow, and the day after."

"But if something should happen . . ."

"Nothing will happen!"

"If it should," Neil persisted in his own gentle way, "I want you to do something for me."

Chapter Fifteen

The clouds rode high and swift in the sky, covering and uncovering the sun, casting the sloping green cemetery in shadow and light. Life was like that, Alison thought, the world one day a dark and dreary place, the next day bright and full of promise. But death she couldn't think about right now. It all seemed so black and hopeless.

Neil was dead.

They stood by the grave, dressed in mourning, atop a low hill that looked through tall trees to an orchard and a wide watermelon field beyond. It was a pretty place, she supposed, if you had to be buried. Neil's mother was present, as were Tony and a minister, but pitifully few others had come to pay their last respects. Brenda and Joan had both bowed out, pleading too much emotional distress. Alison did not doubt the validity of their excuses. She was beyond wondering and worrying.

The minister read a psalm about the shadow of the valley of death and having no fear, and Alison felt that for Neil it was a proper reading, for his life, more than anyone's she had ever met, had been truly righteous. At the close of the prayers, they each stepped forward and laid a rose atop the casket. The casket was not an expensive one—Neil's mother hadn't much money—nor was it very big. But it was enough. The Caretaker had not left much, anyway.

"Thank you for coming," Mrs. Hurly told her as they hugged at the end of the service. "My son often talked about you."

The lady's quiet strength, her calm acceptance of the tragedy, both strengthened and confused Alison. She stopped crying. "I thought about him a lot," she said truthfully. "I'm going to miss him."

Tony came next, at the end of the line. The last two days, Alison had not seen him shed a tear, nor had he at any time failed to say the right words. He did not ask for sympathy and he continued to stand tall. Yet he had become a robot. His spark was gone. Perhaps it would be gone for a long time. "If there is anything you need help with at the house," he said, embracing the tiny, gray-haired lady whose eyes were as green and warm as Neil's had been, "let me know."

That had been a minor slip, though an understandable one. There wasn't a Hurly house anymore.

Mrs. Hurly nodded kindly. "Please walk me to the car. I would like to speak with you and your girlfriend."

Alison would have preferred not to have been invited. Though on the inside she had felt drawn to Neil, she had not really been a close friend. If his mother was going to bring up sensitive, sentimental memories, Tony alone would be the right one to share them with. But she could not very well say no to the lady, and she trailed a pace behind as Tony escorted Mrs. Hurly, arm in arm, to an aging white Nova.

"I don't know how best to put this," Neil's mother said as they reached the narrow road that wound through the cemetery, the sun temporarily out, warm on their faces, the overlong grass rippling in green waves in the shifting breeze. "When I received the call at my brother's place in Arkansas that our home had burned to the ground and that Neil had been caught asleep in bed and had perished in the flames, I refused to accept it. I thought the officer had the wrong address and that it was the family next door or the one across the street. God forgive me for praying that this was so."

As Mrs. Hurly paused to find the right words, Alison was forcibly drawn back to two days ago. The phone call had come in the early morning instead of the middle of the night, and it had been Brenda, not Tony, who had brought the news of the fire. Brenda had rattled off the facts with what had seemed mechanical precision but which in reality had been emotionless shock. Neil's home was a smoldering ruin. So far, the firemen going through the debris had found only one body, the charred and scattered pieces of a skeleton of an individual approximately five-and-a-half feet tall who had worn an emerald ring on his left hand. All the evidence was not in, but the fire marshal was inclined to rule out arson. There were no signs that combustibles such as gasoline or kerosene had been involved. The blaze appeared to have started in the kitchen, probably triggered by faulty wiring. And it must have spread quickly to have caught the resting occupant—as the expert had called Neil—totally unaware. It was the gentleman's opinion, Brenda said, that Neil had probably not even awakened.

Listening to the account, Alison had felt a corner of her being cracking, the tight place where she had hemmed in the panic that had been growing since the Caretaker's first letter. Released, the fear had rushed through her like an icy wave, leaving her shivering but strangely unafraid. She had probably felt that now, with this murder, things could get no worse.

Remember, you have been told.

Each passing day inevitably decreased Fran's and Kipp's chances of being alive. Three scorched skeletons in the rubble would not have surprised her.

Yet the game rolled forward. Joan had received a letter and her task had been in the paper this morning.

J.Z. Spread Rumor You Are Gay.

Joan had been prepared to model naked in the mall, slap the principal in the face, and burn down the whole city. This demand, however, she simply could not meet. She was sleeping with a police-trained German shepherd, her bedroom windows covered with shutters that had been nailed shut. Her law-enforcement father didn't even know his daughter was in danger.

Alison was not looking forward to her own turn.

"All parents react that way to accidents involving their children," Tony said. "Don't blame yourself."

Mrs. Hurly patted his supporting arm. "It was still wrong of me, especially given the circumstances. After I had a chance to be by myself, to put the accident in perspective, I saw that it was a blessing in disguise."

God's will, fate, destiny . . . Alison could see it coming. Nevertheless, she nodded in understanding. Metaphysical rationalizations were a comfort this poor woman deserved, and she was not going to argue with her personal philosophy at a time like this. A minute later, however, she realized she had totally misjudged the lady.

"I'm afraid I can't see it that way," Tony said.

"Because Neil never told you the truth," Mrs. Hurly said, glancing in the direction of the lonely coffin lying beside the pile of brown earth that had seconds ago lost its green plastic cover to the wind. A brief shudder shook her. Around the curve of the bluff, a worker waited impatiently in his tractor. He was probably supposed to be out of sight, but the message was still clear: They were in a hurry to get the body in the ground. Mrs. Hurly continued, "He didn't want your sympathy, he didn't want you treating him any differently in the time he had left. Remember once when you were at the house, Tony, and the two of you were going to see a movie? Neil was broke and I was behind on the bills that month. You offered to take him, but he wouldn't even accept a couple of dollars from you. You remember how proud he was in that way. I think that's one of the reasons he kept his illness a secret and made up those stories about having diabetes and cartilage damage. He couldn't totally hide what was happening inside his body, but he thought he could camouflage it with lesser complaints. I went along with his wishes, but it was hard, harder than I can say with words, especially toward the end when he was in so much pain he could hardly walk."

"What are you saying?" Tony whispered.

"Neil had cancer. It started in his leg. Those weeks when he was out of school, that's when he was receiving chemotherapy. That's why he lost so much weight. The doctors tried, but it just spread everywhere. The last X rays they took showed tumors in his brain." She bowed her head. "You see how I could be grateful for this accident. At least he doesn't hurt anymore."

She broke down then and Alison wept with her, filled with shame for all the times she had been with Neil, watching him deteriorate before her very eyes and not once stopping to ask him or herself if he was OK.

"But I could have helped him," Tony said, choking on the revelation. "He should have told me." He clenched his fists and yelled, "Neil!!"

The cry echoed over the cemetery and through the orchard. Of course, there came no answer. The fury left Tony's face as quickly as it had come. "I'm sorry, Mrs. Hurly," he said softly.

"Most of all," she said, dabbing at her eyes, regaining her composure, "Neil didn't want to have you sitting around worrying about him. He was a brave kid." She handed Alison a handkerchief and Alison took it gratefully, blowing her nose. His suffering in silence filled her with as much awe as sorrow. When she had a cold, she called all of her friends and cried on their shoulders. Neil had taught her a lesson about nobility that she would never forget.

Tony offered to drive Mrs. Hurly to the home of the friends she was staying with, but she refused, reassuring them that she would be all right. They watched her drive away in silence. With a wedding you could always throw rice, but there seemed to be no good way to end a funeral.

Tony walked her toward his car, which was a respectable distance—he had parked on the far side of the cemetery by the chapel and had ridden to the gravesite in the hearse. By unspoken consent, they did not hold hands or talk until they were out of sight of the casket.

"It's funny the way your mind plays tricks on you," he said finally. "Just for a moment there I was thinking how sad this day is and how I would have to call Neil when I got home to tell him about it. That's what I've always done these last four years." He shrugged. "Now I don't know what I'll do."

She wanted to tell him that she would listen. But she was afraid how poor a substitute she might be. "I wish I had called him a few times," she said instead. "Just to chat, you know. I always meant to."

A scrawny rabbit, looking anxious to get to the neighboring farm fields, cut across their path. "He would have liked that a lot. He liked you a lot, more than you know, I think." He stopped her and reached into his coat pocket. "That's what I was trying to tell you that night in the car in front of your house. You were his . . . love."

"Me?" Neil had found a shallow phony like her attractive? "I never even suspected." The information hit her as hard as the fact of his cancer.

"But he asked you out."

"Yeah, just to the movies. I didn't think anything of it. I . . . I . . ." Her tears—she should have run out of them yesterday—bubbled up again. She sought the handkerchief Mrs. Hurly had given her. "I turned him down. *Damn*."

Tony hugged her gently. "He didn't hold it against you.

The last time we were alone together, he asked me to do two things for him should the Caretaker get to him. One of them was to give you this."

He placed a warped lump of blackened metal in her hand. It took her a moment to realize it was Neil's emerald ring. The heat had distorted the gold band but the stone had not shattered. "Did he have this on when . . ."

"He was wearing it, yes. He was going to give it to me to keep for you but he said he wanted to get it cleaned first." Tony added softly, "It made the identification easier."

"But I can't take this."

"If I'd had more time, I would have had it cleaned up. I think a jeweler could reset the stone."

"No. I don't care that it's no longer beautiful. I just don't deserve it."

Tony smiled, and she knew before he spoke that it was from a sweet memory. "He used to see you as a goddess. To him, you had everything: beauty, poise, good humor, love. He loved you, and although he was never really able to express it to you, I like to think it made him happy just being in the same world as you. For that, you deserve the ring."

"Was he . . . jealous of us?"

"Not Neil."

The question had been unworthy. She held the ring tightly. "I'm honored to know he saw me that way. I'll keep it safe."

They resumed their walk toward the chapel. For the last

several minutes, the sun had been hidden behind the clouds and it appeared that a storm truly was on its way. Here they'd been cooking for the last few weeks and now when summer was about to officially begin, they were going to get rained on. Graduation was just around the corner. There would be a few empty seats at the ceremony.

"What else did he want you to do for him?" she asked.

He shook his head. "It's a long story."

"Were you able to do it?"

"No, I'm afraid not."

"Did you check with Mrs. Hurly to be sure it was OK that I keep the ring?"

"Yes, and it was fine. Please don't feel guilty about it."

"I was just afraid that she would feel uncomfortable losing a family heirloom."

"I don't think Neil's mother even knew he'd had it."

"Oh, for some reason I assumed it had been in the family."

Tony stopped.

"What is it?" she asked.

He shrugged. "Nothing important."

Chapter Sixteen

The thunder rolled toward the house without haste, starting far off in the mountains, flattening and building over the empty fields that surrounded the deserted housing tract, reaching her ears and filling her head with a lonely, inhuman roar. The storm was thickening, the rain pelting the roof harder with each passing minute. The sun had hardly set, and it was black as midnight outside the drawn curtains. Alison was alone. But it was not yet her turn. She was safe. . . . *Sure.*

Earlier in the day, her parents had left for New York, her mother accompanying her father on an important business trip. Her mom had been reluctant to leave her alone, and Alison herself had not been wild about the idea. But she had refused to let her secret situation interfere with her parents' plans; they intended to turn the trip into a twentieth-anniversary second-honeymoon combination. They had been looking forward to it for some time. Nevertheless, her mother had almost stayed. Fran's and Kipp's kidnappings had been on the other side of the county and Neil's supposedly accidental death had not even been indirectly connected with the abductions, but mothers have strong intuitive radar when it comes to danger. Only when Joan—of all people, they were getting desperate—had called and promised to bring over Brenda to spend the night had her mother left feeling comfortable. Joan and Brenda would be arriving soon, Alison thought, rechecking the clock, moving magazines from one corner of the coffee table to the other, polishing tables she had polished already, unable to sit still. She was not scared, just uneasy, terribly uneasy.

Part of the problem was that there were no ceiling lights in these new houses. All they had were lamps, dim, yellow, old-fashioned ones that cast as many shadows as they alleviated. She contemplated unscrewing a couple of shades but she didn't want the others to see how much the gloom bothered her. They might laugh.

Searching for something to occupy her mind, she spotted the DVDs she had bought yesterday on her way home from school. The choices were two extremes: *The Wizard of Oz* and *Emanuelle.* She had wanted something light and something dirty—both helped one forget. Since Joan probably wouldn't let them watch the adventures of Dorothy and Toto, she slipped the fantasy tale into the DVD player and turned on the TV, making herself comfortable on the sofa.

"Are you a good witch or a bad witch?"

When she had been small and had first seen the movie, the witch, the wizard and even the tornado had given her nightmares. Since then, she had caught the flick or pieces of it several times, and the magic and terror of believing had never come close to the initial experience. But tonight, with the hypnotic strumming of rain on the windows, the bare drafty spots of the half-furnished house all around her, her isolation and the recent tragic events of her life, the impossible appeared not so intangible, and all adventures, good and bad, seemed just around the corner. Indeed, the accidental landing of the house on the wicked witch's sister that started Dorothy's perilous journey closely paralleled their own accidental killing of the man. Now if the man had had a brother . . .

Or a sister!

The lights and the TV went out.

"Eeh!" Alison cried, swallowing her heart.

The lights came back on, followed by a wall-shaking boom. She eased back into the cushions, trying to catch her breath. Lightning was responsible, nothing more. Brenda and Joan would be here soon. No one was going to kill her.

I wallow in your evil. You are a bad witch.

The TV was full of static. At the power surge, the DVD had automatically turned off. Reaching for the PLAY switch, she decided to take a break before traveling any farther along the yellow brick road. She turned off the equipment and picked up the phone.

Tony had been avoiding her since the funeral. Appreciating his need to be alone, she had tried not to be a burden. Still, she had called occasionally; she was getting low on friends, too, and needed support from someone. It would have been unnatural for him to act normal after the loss of his best friend; nevertheless, his self-absorption, his long blank pauses while speaking, frightened her. Something bizarre was percolating deep inside him.

There was no answer at his house. His parents had gone to San Diego to visit his brother, but he had specifically told her he would not be accompanying them. She had been calling since eight this morning and had still to receive an answer. Where could he be? It wasn't his turn, either.

Joan was a week past the deadline. None of them had gone that long without paying for it. Maybe it had been a mistake to invite her over. After all, when you got right down to it, Joan hated her guts. Then again, she had not invited Joan or Brenda. They had invited themselves.

Alison called Brenda's house and got her mother. Yes, Brenda had left a while ago. No, Brenda had said nothing about picking up Joan. Yes, it was terrible weather they were having . . . Thank you, Mrs. Paxson.

Whenever she was uptight, a hot bath always helped. Figuring she'd hear the girls' knock even if she were upstairs, she decided to squeeze in a quick one. Before she climbed the stairs, however, she rechecked the locks on the front and back doors.

The wet warmth was a delight. Slipping all but her kneecaps and face beneath the bubbly surface, she closed her eyes and thought of how when she was a rich and famous actress, she would have a Jacuzzi installed in her Beverly Hills mansion where she could entertain Tony in the way she had seen on *Real Housewives*. The erotic daydream was only half over—they still had their bathing suits on—when the phone rang. Reaching for a towel and groaning, she pulled herself up. This had better be Tony. She could tell him she was talking to him in the nude.

She did not waste time drying and got it on the fifth ring. But the instant she picked it up, the party on the other end put the phone down. Whoever it was must not have been that anxious to talk.

Standing naked and dripping next to her bed, she had the sudden uncanny sensation that she was being watched. Her rational mind knew that eyes perceived only light and could project nothing that could be felt; yet it was as if twin fingers were lightly tracing down her spine.

Cold air shook her from her frightened pose. The window was open, that was it. Her subconscious had registered the fact before her conscious mind and had been reminding her via her paranoia that she was standing naked in a lit room where anyone out on the street could see her. That sounded reasonable. Hugging the towel to her breasts, she hastily closed the window, pulling over the curtains.

She dressed warmly, in a heavy pair of corduroy pants and a thick woolen sweater. She was pulling on a second pair of socks when the lights went out for the second time. The darkness lasted and lasted. She'd noticed no flash of lightning, and she counted to thirty and heard no thunder. Having no natural explanation for the loss of power, she began to imagine a dozen unnatural ones, with a sharp blade and a puddle of blood in every one. But once again, before she could go off the deep end, the lights snapped back on. Her tension burst out of her in a cackle of a laugh that sounded alien to her ears. Where were those stupid girls?

The downstairs TV was also back on, full of static. From experience, she knew the power switch was tricky, and could pop on if not pressed hard enough. But she could have sworn she'd hit the thing squarely. Fretting over the tiny irregularity, she made another check on the doors. What she found did not soothe her nerves. The dead bolt knob on the back door was turned up, which is where it normally should have been to be locked. When it had been installed, however, the carpenter had been either drunk or unfamiliar with the brand and had arranged matters so that the door was locked when the switch was horizontal. Her father had reminded her of this flaw, this morning in fact, and she was almost positive she had turned it sideways before going for her bath. But could she have, out of habit, done the opposite? She must have. What alternative was there?

Oh, say, the Caretaker just happened to be in the neighborhood.

"Shut up!" she told herself, twisting the lock, yanking on the knob to prove to herself the door couldn't budge an inch.

She went into the kitchen and poured herself a glass of milk. There was a phone next to the microwave and she tried Tony again. Three tries got her nothing. The wind raking the outside walls howled softly, sad and forlorn. Closing her eyes, she strained her ears to detect a trace of civilization beyond: the hum of the distant freeway, the drone of an overhead plane, the passing of a nearby motorist. But there was only the cold storm, and the beating of her heart. She tossed the milk down the sink.

The static on the TV was disquieting, so she restarted the DVD and huddled in the corner of the couch. Just her luck, the heroes were creeping through the witch's wicked woods, about to be attacked by monsters. Although she knew everyone would live happily ever after, she couldn't entirely dispel the irrational possibility that this was a black market version of the story, with a different ending, a violent and bitter ending.

"Nuts, you're nuts," she muttered, picking up the phone and setting it on her lap like it was a pet that could comfort her. This time she gave Tony thirty rings. No dice.

She found herself in the garage before she would admit to herself what she was doing there. The excuse of wanting to make sure it was locked didn't fool her. Without checking the garage door, she had gone straight to the cabinet where her father kept his sporting equipment. He played tennis, golf, and skied. But his hunting enthusiasm was all that was relevant to her at the moment.

Where is that bazooka?

She found the shotgun in a maple box at the back on the floor. The black over-and-under twin barrels were cold to touch. Lifting the smooth oak stock, she marveled at its weight. From having watched her dad, she knew it split in the middle and took two shells, both of which were controlled by a single trigger. Once, when she had been a child, he had caught her playing with it, and although it had been unloaded, he had yelled at her something fierce, yet not nearly as fierce as her mother had yelled at him later on. Hopefully dear daddy would forgive her tonight if she brought the gun in the house to keep her company. When the girls arrived, she could keep it in the hall closet for handy reference.

She was searching for the box of shells when she heard the knock at the door. Whether the sound filled her with relief or the opposite was hard to say. Joan was an old nemesis and was not to be trusted, but Brenda was a good friend. There was no reason not to welcome her arrival. They'd known each other since childhood. Sure, they'd had their arguments, quite a few of them lately, but so did all old pals. Then again, Brenda sure had enjoyed her tasks. Who else of them could say that? She had suffered the consequence of expulsion from school, but there had been a streak of strange satisfaction in that also, judging from how she had joked about it afterward.

Alison took a long time to make it from the garage, through the kitchen and living room, to the front door. And once there, she paused, wondering why they hadn't rung the bell.

"Brenda?" she called. "Joan?"

No answer.

Stay cool, don't freak, you're not going to die.

She pressed her ear to the door. She couldn't even hear the rain over the roar of the blood in her head. "Hello?" she croaked.

Whoever was there, if there was anybody there, was playing it mean. All right, she was a big girl, all she had to do was . . . what was she supposed to do? She didn't know. Turn on the porch light, *yes,* and peek through the glass at the side of the door, *yes,* and be careful she saw them before they saw her, *yes,* and then scream bloody murder.

She had a hard time with the switch, her hands were shaking so. But finally the porch light went on, spilling a bloody glow on either side of the door. Wishing she had a miniature periscope, she inched her eyes toward the smoky panels of glass. If this was a joke they were pulling, Brenda and Joan were sleeping in the garage.

But there was no one there, no one she could see. To be absolutely sure, she needed to open the door; the house was more likely to be struck by a meteor than were the chances of her doing that. Yet she had not imagined the knock. It had been as clear and distinct as . . .

Oh, God.

. . . the knock at the back door.

She began to pant on air that seemed to turn into a vacuum in her lungs. No one with any scruples or benign intentions would have gone to the back door. Only psychotics with masks over their grinning skulls and sharp cutting implements in their greasy hands used back doors after dark. She'd seen the movies; she knew the score. The hatchet man would get his due, but only after he'd garroted and dissected a half dozen coeds. And a character as crafty as the Caretaker, why his quota would be bigger than average, at least everyone on the list, not to mention a few possible bystanders.

This is only a play, and I am the star, and I had better move my ass!

Two loaded barrels could make her odds a lot better. Picking up her feet, placing one in front of the other, she plodded back into the living room. The Great and Terrible Oz was threatening them not to look behind the curtain. I guarantee you, you won't like what you see.

She had rounded the kitchen counter and was passing the oven when the knock came again, loud and insistent. For a moment, what was left of her courage ran out the bottom of her feet, collecting in a sticky puddle on the floor, preventing her from budging an inch. Then a slight peculiarity in the origin and quality of the knocking squeezed its way into her thoughts. As it sounded again, she listened closely, and it seemed to be coming, not from the back door, but from the far den. Also, the texture was not of knuckles on wood, but of wood striking itself.

The shutters?

The innocent solution to the deadly dilemma brought a flood of relief. She cracked a smile big enough to permanently stretch her face and forgot all about the shotgun. Turning, she hurried back the way she had come, striding into the rear hall and opening the den door. A glance out the room's windows confirmed that the shutters were loose and banging in the wind. Parting the glass, she reached out into the wet night air and fastened them tightly in place with a metal clasp. She felt about ten million times better.

The phone rang.

"Tony!" She called, bouncing into the living room toward the couch. She would have to tell him about the mysterious knocks, leaving out the shutters. Maybe it would inspire him to come over and spend the night. If that didn't work, a few nasty suggestions might bring him running. Too bad Joan was already on her way.

Where were those girls, anyway?

"Hello, Tony?" she said, picking up the phone. "Hello?"

There was breathing, not heavy and pornographic, but

ragged and faint. Her own breathing stopped. The fear she had seconds ago sidestepped struck her full on. There was nothing to be gained by not hanging up the phone, but she simply could not bring herself to do it. A childish prayer kept her frozen. As long as the person was on the phone, he was somewhere else, and he couldn't break through the door and split her open like a side of beef. The problem was, he was probably thinking along similar lines. As long as *Alison* continued to listen, *Alison* was a sitting duck for any attack.

"Brenda? Joan?"

They hung up, but not before she heard what sounded like a sigh. She put down the phone and instantly picked it up again. When they had moved in, she had memorized the housing tract's security number. Their guard, Harvey Heck, was an alcoholic, and if he was stone drunk right now, he would never forgive himself when he read in the morning paper about the cute teenager who had bought it while he was on duty.

"Harvey!" she shouted when she heard the tenth unanswered ring. She was on the verge of cursing his name, when it occurred to her that the Caretaker might have already paid him a visit. Harvey might be unable to answer. Feeling a despair that threatened to transform her into a whimpering vegetable, she slowly replaced the receiver.

But it's not my turn! I would have done whatever you asked!

She had two alternatives: call the police or load the shotgun. Both of them sounded like fantastic ideas. She got out the local phone book and it took her four tries to punch out the correct number. Finally, she reached another human being, an elderly lady with a faint English accent.

"San Bernardino Police Department. May I help you?"

"Yes! My name is Alison Parker and I live at 1342 Keystone Lane in a housing tract five miles north of the 10 freeway. There is someone trying to kill me! I'm all alone. PLEASE send somebody . . . Hello? *Hello!*"

The phone was dead. The connection had not been simply interrupted. There was no dial tone, no static, nothing. And hadn't it gone dead the second she had started talking? The police hadn't even gotten her name.

And she had no idea where she'd left her cell phone.

Clutching her abdomen, she bent over and put her head between her knees. Purple dots the same shade as the Caretaker's envelopes danced behind her closed eyes. She was going to vomit. She was going to faint. She was going to die.

I'll get you my pretty, and your little dog too.

The TV hummed happily along. The witch's hourglass, like the Caretaker's, was running low. But unlike Dorothy, no one was coming to her rescue. Sitting up and staring at the screen, she tasted blood in her mouth. She had bitten her tongue.

But I'm the star, I'm not supposed to die.

She forced herself to think. The only way her antagonist could have called one minute and cut the line the next was by being at one of the places where the phone company had been working installing new cables. Several times, while on her daily walks, she had passed the gray electrical boxes and noticed the numerous available plug-ins. That meant the Caretaker was definitely in the tract. There was a phone company box up the street. The Caretaker could be a couple of hundred yards away, and closing in on her.

At the realization that the final confrontation was about to begin, Alison experienced an unlooked for charge of defiance swell inside. It was not as though her fear left her—if anything it intensified—it was simply that anger and vengeance demanded equal time. The cowardly bastard had taken the others unaware. But she was awake, she would not bleed or burn to death so easily. She had not played the role of the pursued heroine before but she would play it well. As long as the curtain stayed up.

She ran to the garage. The shotgun was where she had dropped it, cracked open and ready for loading. Unfortunately, her father's sporting equipment cabinet was in disarray, crowded and dark. Digging through wet suits and basketballs and rackets, she couldn't find the box of shells. Was it possible that there were none?

She had exhausted the cabinet to the last inch and was considering searching the drawers beneath the workbench when the lights went out for the third time. Her heroic resolve of a minute ago swayed precariously. Angry thunder—and now it sounded like the sky was tearing in two directly overhead—slapped the garage door, followed by a torrent of falling water. But in her shrinking heart, she knew the storm was not responsible for the sudden darkness. The power had been cut. The blackness was as featureless as in a cave ten miles beneath the earth, smothering her like a demon's cloak.

The Caretaker could not have interrupted the electricity as easily as the phone lines unless he had reached the circuits under the metal panel outside the back door. And a dead bolt would not stop someone who had stolen kids right from beneath the eyes of their loving families. She had to find those shells!

The magic slippers were always right under her nose.

Her one hand was balancing the gun, the other was squeezing the arm of an old polyurethane jacket, when something about the jacket began to demand attention she was hardly able to spare, and the missing clue was stuck on the tip of her mind when a *sudden pounding on the back door* jarred it free. Her dad always wore this coat when hunting! And sportsmen always liked to keep their ammunition in a handy place.

There were two shells in the coat's front right pocket. Relying solely upon feel, she guided the cartridges into the rear of the barrels and, disengaging the safety, she snapped the shotgun straight. One glance at that maniac's face to know forever who he was and then she would splatter his features so his own mother wouldn't be able to recognize him.

The garage was strategically a terrible place to be and she

did not entirely want to wait for him to come to her. Positioning the stock into the soft flesh beneath her shoulder, holding the twin barrels aloft with her left hand and putting her right finger on the trigger, she silently slipped out of the dark garage into the dark kitchen, crouching down, using the stove as cover. She couldn't even see the end of her weapon and was sorely tempted to turn on the light for a second to get her bearings. But that would only serve to make her an easy target. The blind waited a lifetime in the dark. She would be patient. Soon, very soon, they would have to show themselves.

Her plan lasted exactly two seconds.

The back door convulsed from a splintering blow.

Oh, please, good God, don't be a bad God.

It sounded like an ax. It wasn't the Tinman's ax.

Frantically she began to reconsider waiting. There were a lot of cons. She was depending on a weapon she had never fired. What if it jammed? What if she missed? There was an alternative she had never considered before because it meant going outside. But at this instant, when she knew exactly where the Caretaker was, it didn't seem like such a bad move to grab her keys, quietly open the front door, run out to the street to her car and put her foot on the accelerator and keep it there.

The boom from the second blow of the ax reverberated through the house and promptly settled the issue. She scurried around the oven and made a beeline for the couch, catching her purse on the run. The showdown could wait for another day when she had reinforcements. She hurried to the front door. To undo the stubborn dead bolt, she had to set down the gun, which she did reluctantly. Careful, lest she interrupt the Caretaker's efforts to turn the back door into firewood, she twisted the lock.

Did you hear about that girl who was stuffed up her own chimney?

It was stuck. Something, a bobby pin probably, had been jammed into the lock from the outside. A hard slap could knock it out but she would do almost as well calling out, *Going out the front door, sorry I can't stay.*

A portion of the back door cracked inward.

She started pounding on the lock. And still, it would not turn. First she had been afraid of someone getting in and now she couldn't get out. Well, if that maniac could force his way inside, she could force her way outside. Dropping her purse, grabbing the shotgun, she swung the stock into the glass panels that lined the entrance. The resulting jagged hole was tight but she was in a hurry and a scratch was infinitely preferable to a hack. Once again setting down the weapon, she dropped to her knees and thrust her arm outside into the cold air, feeling for the lock. Her fingers had lightly brushed the keyhole—and there was indeed a pin stuck there—when she realized the chopping on the back door had stopped. That meant . . .

Someone grabbed her arm.

She was yanked, hard. Her head smacked the door and she saw black holes instead of stars, pain exploding behind her eyes. Had she not been so damn disgusted at being caught so easily, she might have passed out right there and then.

"Screw you!" she screamed, desperately trying to position her feet against the glass and door where she could use the strength in her hamstrings to push and hopefully get her arm back while it was still attached. But the bastard's hold was firm and she was too cramped to maneuver her legs into place. After several agonizing seconds of the insane tug-of-war, what finally came to her aid was her own blood. With every yank and pull, the teeth of the cracked glass dug deeper into the flesh of her left arm, bringing a flow of the oily red liquid from her elbow to her wrist, finally causing the Caretaker's viselike grip to slip slightly. This slip didn't set her free, but it did give her the space she needed to plant her feet. Throwing back her head, she shoved with every muscle in her body, instantly snapping loose and landing on her butt over ten feet from the door. Dazed, her arm on fire, she climbed up on her elbows, seeing the blurred silhouette of a moving ax through what was left of the glass panels.

Yeah, I read about that poor girl. What a mess.

She rolled onto her belly, turning her back to the door, feeling for the gun with her right hand. She would fill the SOB full of lead, she swore to herself, but not just this second. If she turned around now, she knew she would pass out.

Her bedroom had always been her place of escape when things were not going well and tonight definitely qualified as a bad night. Dragging the shotgun like it was a broken leg, crawling on all fours, she began to pull herself up the steps. She was going fairly fast for a quadruped, but if she could only stand, she would have done much better. But she couldn't get up and she did not know why, other than that her entire body was a quivering mass of protoplasm. As she conquered the last step, she heard the front door swing open.

But did you hear exactly what was done to her?

One more brief postponement of the final shoot-out, and she thought she would be able to pull the trigger. Digging into the carpet with her elbows, slithering like a snake with a broken spine, she squirmed into her bedroom. Throwing the door shut, she fell away from it onto the floor. She was crying, she was bleeding, and she had nowhere else to go.

No, and I don't think I want to hear about it.

He was coming up the stairs, slowly, pausing between each step. She could hear his breathing, just as it had been on the phone, thin and scraping. Whether he was male or female was impossible to tell. The house was new and still the boards creaked with each plodding footfall. That meant either the building contractors had ignored the county codes or else the Caretaker was huge—and maybe not even human. If Fran and Neil had guessed right, she would need silver shot in the shells to stop it, if it could be stopped.

I'll tell you, anyway. Hope you've got a strong stomach.

He knew which room was hers. He knew everything about her. The steps came to a halt on the other side of the door. Breathing pushed through the cracks and she thought she could hear a heartbeat, a ribcage pressed against the wood, the beats echoing like radar sent out by a bat, rebounding back to the source, telling him exactly where she lay. If he had a gun, he wouldn't even have to open the door. He could simply point and fire, and afterward do what he would with her body at his leisure.

Her blood was everywhere, on the carpet, the curtains, the ceiling.

One good shot, she told herself, climbing to her knees. If she could get that, she could make her graduation and pick up her diploma in person. The door could stay shut for her, too, and not be a problem. Clapping down on her wheezing breath, she inched forward, hugging the left, where a centered bullet wouldn't catch her begging.

At first, the police weren't sure if it hadn't been an animal.

She propped herself up on the wall behind the door and held the shotgun straight out like it was a weight bar she was doing exercises with, pointing the muzzle toward the exact middle of the door, squeezing the trigger to within a millimeter of contact. The malevolent breathing puffed on, inches away, and all she had to do was close that millimeter. But she couldn't do it. A sudden memory flattened her will.

The day after the first letter had arrived, Joan had approached her and Fran in the school courtyard. They had fought, as they usually did, and Joan had warned her to keep her distance from Tony. In response, she had laughed. *"Why, will I be hurt?"* And Joan had smiled and said, *"Remember, you have been told."*

The same line in the letter.

Joan was the Caretaker. She was a kidnapper, a pyromaniac, and a murderess. But she was also a sick girl, and Alison simply could not pull the trigger.

"Joan," she whispered, "I know it's you."

The breathing quickened. Alison pulled the gun back and let it hang at her side. "I know you hate me," she said. "I know I've given you a lot of reasons to hate me. But I *do* want to help you."

The door bumped slightly, as if Joan had let her head fall against the wood. Alison felt perhaps it was a sign of surrender. Then the doorknob began to turn.

"Don't!" she shouted. The knob stopped. "Don't come in. I've got a gun. I don't want to hurt you, but if you come in right now, I'll shoot."

The breathing stopped. Joan must be thinking, so Alison started to think some more herself. Pity, like all virtuous feelings, was delicate and quickly scattered by a strong gust of reality. Fran had disappeared without a trace. Kipp's blood had soaked all the way through his mattress to the floor. And what had been left of Neil had been hard to sort out from what had been left of the house. Joan was ill, true, but Joan was still awfully dangerous.

And they say she almost got away.

"Damn you for everything!" Alison cried, and whether she did so the instant before the knob turned again and the door began to open or the instant afterward was not clear. The compassion that had touched her heart evaporated, in a boiling wave of bitterness. Her leg lashed out, slamming the door shut in the Caretaker's face even as she pivoted on the ball of her foot and brought the gun to bear. Ramming the wide barrels into the wood at chest level, she pulled the trigger.

The recoil was cruel, slapping her aside like she was a paper doll. She landed on her shoulder blades, the butt of the shotgun striking her jaw with a loud crack. She did not lose consciousness, but her hold on it slipped several notches. Her eyes remained open, rolling in a mist. A numbing sheet wrapped her brain. And yet, the unhappy triumph pushed its way through. The breathing on the other side of the door had stopped for good.

Your hourglass just ran out, baby.

How long she lay there, she was not sure. There seemed no hurry to get up, not even to bandage her mangled arm, which continued to bleed. A cool current of blessed relief flowed through her nerves. If not for the dread of what she would find on the other side of the ruined door, she could have laughed. Instead, and not for the first time that night, she cried.

Should have told someone else, Joan.

When her heart had finally slowed from its shrieking pace and her eyes had run dry, she sat up. A glance at her arm brought a rush of nausea; there would be scars, and a lifetime of having to explain where they had come from. Stretching forward, a half dozen vertebrae popped in her back. She looked up. Even with the absence of streetlights and the closed curtains, the hole in the door was impossible to miss. She reached for a sheet on her bed. She would not look at the body. If she did, she would never be free of this night. She would cover it, immediately.

She kept her gaze up when she opened the door. The damage the buckshot had done to the hall closet door stared her in the face, shredded and blackened towels hanging through the ruptured boards.

But where was the blood? Feeling tentatively with the tip of her toe, her almost forgotten panic escalating in quantum leaps, she swept the floor and hit nothing. There was no choice. She had to look down.

There was no body.

The Caretaker was still alive.

The phone beside her bed began to ring.

Alison did not want to answer it. The only one who could be calling was the one who had originally interrupted the line. And suddenly she began to doubt very seriously that it had been Joan she had been talking to on the other side of the door.

Joan was tough but even she couldn't swallow a twelve-gauge shell at point-blank range with no ill effects.

But her will was crushed. She felt herself drawn toward the ringing, unable to resist. She was a pawn. Her master wanted to have a word with her. She picked up the phone. "Hello?"

The voice was weak, on the threshold of hearing, possibly because of a bad connection, probably because he wished it so. The tone was neither masculine nor feminine, cleverly disguised, a barren neuter. And yet it was a voice that was not necessarily unkind. Once, so it seemed, she had heard it before.

"Do you know who I am?" the voice asked.

"The Caretaker."

"Yes." The voice sighed. "I am here to take care of you."

"Don't kill me," she breathed, tremors starting in her feet, rising swiftly.

"You kill yourself." In the background Alison heard a cough, and then thunder, at the exact moment she heard it outside her own window. "Come to me. I have your task. Hurry . . . not much time."

"But I don't want to die!" she cried, her knees beginning to buckle.

When the voice spoke next, it was clearer. And it was true, she knew this person. She just couldn't remember who it was. "You are dead."

The Caretaker hung up, and no dial tone came on. She did not replace the phone. She backed away from it as if the cord might come alive and strangle her. There was nothing to be done. He *knew* her. If they said she was dead . . .

But I live! I'm the star! And I'm only eighteen years old!

Her courage wavered like an uncertain candle, but it wasn't ready to go out just yet. The Caretaker was not omniscient. He had tried once to catch her and had failed. He had in fact retreated, at least far enough away to make the call. It was possible he was wounded. And she had the gun, and one shot left, and could wound again.

Taking hold of herself and the shotgun, she ran down the stairs. The front door lay wide open and she found her purse where she had dropped it. The Caretaker had made a mistake. Her car keys were still inside.

She was only ten strides outside before she was soaked, the cold rain stinging her gashed arm. Lightning flashed before her eyes and thunder punched her eardrums. Her soggy socks supped on the concrete walkway and she almost saved the Caretaker a return visit by breaking her neck. Nevertheless, getting out of the house was like climbing out of a coffin.

The car door was locked. Her chain had three keys on it and two of them were almost identical. She tried one. It didn't fit. She glanced around. No one in sight. She tried the other key. It didn't fit! She had it upside down . . . no, she'd had the first one upside down. The door opened and there was no one in the backseat and she climbed inside, immediately pressing down the lock. She was going to make it. Pumping the gas, she turned the ignition. Nothing happened.

She was *not* going to make it.

Her head hit the steering wheel with a thud. Upside down, inside out—there were no more ways for her to be torn. She could look under the hood but she knew that would be futile. The battery cables, the spark plug wires, and probably the fan belt would be cut. The Caretaker had made a mistake, sure Ali.

She slowly got out of the car, leaning on the door window, the rain melting her wax limbs—she could scarcely move. She tried to consider her options but she had to wonder who she was fooling. Whatever course she picked, it appeared she would end up in exactly the same place. Where was that Caretaker, maybe he wouldn't be so harsh on her if she turned herself in.

Huh?

She heard music.

Someone farther down the street was playing the Beatles.

Her spark had died a thousand deaths tonight and she was afraid to let it rekindle once more, but hadn't her mother mentioned something last week about another family that was ready to move in? And wasn't that an inhabited house, complete with lit windows, in the same direction as the music? And did this mean that safety had been only a hop, skip, and a jump away all night?

Alison took a quick three-hundred-and-sixty degree scan of the area and bolted. Tony had run some excellent times in his track career, but even he could not have caught her now. Her socks began to loosen, the stretched toes slapping the pavement, and her drenched hair obscured her vision. Twice she slipped, once taking the skin off her right knee. But none of this slowed her down.

As she reached the driveway, she felt a tiny, wary thread tug at her expanding balloon of joy. She was not a man dying of thirst in a desert seeing a lake. This music was real. She could see the light pouring out the windows. This was, however, very convenient, and coincidence often bespoke of cunning plans. Above all else, the Caretaker was crafty.

Was this a trap?

Without forethought, she had brought the shotgun, and it comforted her as she crept up the walkway toward the front door. But before the pulse of her terror could beat aloud once more, it began to fade. Above the music, sweeter than any melody ever composed, were dozens of human voices: laughing, dancing, happy. She passed under the porch out of the rain, knocking at the door and smiling. A voice shouted, as always happened at parties, for her to come in. Turning the doorknob, she almost burst out laughing. How welcome would she be toting a shotgun! Leaning the weapon against the wall beneath the mailbox, she opened the door and went inside.

The house was empty: No people and no furniture, except for three unshaded lamps sitting on the floor, connected by one long extension cord that looped beneath her feet and under the back of the door. The music seemed to come out of the walls. The celebrating crowd was all around but conversing on the astral plane. She stood there for perhaps five seconds, not knowing which corner of the twilight zone she had stumbled in, before turning to look behind the door. It was then the extension cord jerked under her heels, causing her to lose her balance. The music stopped. The lights went out.

Come to me.

Darkness had fallen on her on several occasions tonight, but none compared to this, for previously each time she had been alone.

An arm encircled her neck, locking tight.

In a flash her pendulum of despair and resolution swung to both extremes. She went limp, giving up, letting her windpipe be closed off. A prayer started in her head and she had all the words in the past tense. Then she thought of Tony, how kind and beautiful he was, how much she would miss him, and how he would be the next victim. And that, more than anything, brought her back to life.

She cut hard and sharp with both elbows, catching ribs, the Caretaker's breath whistling in her ear. The hold on her neck loosened slightly and she was able to refill her lungs. "Nooo!!!" she screamed, planting her feet firmly on the floor, shoving up and back. One bang followed the other, a head smacking the wall, her head smacking a jaw. The arm around her neck slipped once more and she jumped forward, grasping for the half-open door. But she was not totally free and the hands that clung to the back of her sweater regrouped quickly, clawing into the material, catching hold of her flesh. *So play dirty,* she thought, *and while you're at it, take this!* Swinging through a wide arc, she caught the Caretaker squarely on the nose with her right fist. Warm blood spurted over her stinging fingers and the shadow, *her* shadow for the last two months, let go and staggered back. Almost, she could see who was there.

Had Alison immediately struck again and pressed her advantage, she might have gotten away. But she lacked faith in her strength and she was anxious to end things once and for all. Jumping out of the doorway, she grabbed the shotgun. And she had enough time. She had the barrels up, the stock stabilized on her shoulder, her finger on the trigger and the Caretaker in her line of sight. Then the figure stepped forward, closer to the door, and what light the stormy night could spare caught the face.

No, she whispered in a cold place deep in her soul.

The Caretaker was someone impossible.

Eyes stared into hers and nodded.

Goddess.

Her paralysis ended. "It makes no difference!" she screamed. Taking a step forward, she pulled the trigger.

The Caretaker repaid her earlier favor. The door slammed in her face. Before the shot could spray its flashing orange tunnel of death, the doorknob caught the tip of the gun, tilting the barrels upward, discharging the shell into the ceiling. Since the weapon was not jammed against a relatively immovable object as it had been the first time, the recoil was minimal. That made her downfall, after all her struggles, all the more ironic. Turning to flee, she simply slipped and fell, and hit her head on a brick planter wall and was knocked out.

Chapter Seventeen

Tony found the spot without having to search. Even with the storm and the dark, there were visible signs: the tracks on the soft shoulder of the road that the winter's worst had failed to obliterate, scraped rubber on the asphalt that would probably be there at the turn of the century. But had there been no evidence, he still would have recognized the place where he had lost control of the car. For him, it was a haunted place, and his ghost, as well as the man's, often walked there at night. He stopped his car, grabbed his shovel and flashlight, and climbed outside.

The rain was lighter here in the desert and his waterproof coat was warm. The daylight hours probably would have been a less morbid time to have come but he had wanted the cover of night. Besides, grave robbers should work the graveyard shift. Plus it had only been a little while ago that he had deciphered the Caretaker's hidden messages. He hadn't known for sure until then, or so he told himself, as he turned the flashlight on the trembling tumbleweeds; it was a poor excuse. He should have come to this grave immediately after he had left Neil's grave. But he had been afraid. He was still afraid.

Slamming the car door shut, taking a firm hold of the shovel, he pressed forward, his tennis shoes sinking in the listless mud, the damp but still sharp shrubs clawing at his pants. A year ago, he had counted fifty paces that they had carried the man into the field, and tonight he counted them again. When he reached the magic number, he found himself standing in a small rectangular clearing of uneven footing. The soil here did not look like it had been left a year to settle, and that reassured him as much as it oppressed him. Finding out what a corpse looked like after a lengthy decay would be about as pleasant as confirming his hunch. Either way, he was going to be sick.

Confirm what? He gave you his name!

He set the flashlight down and thrust the shovel into the ground, throwing the earth aside. With the rain and the sandy mixture, it should have been easy going, but each descending inch wore on him. Soon he was sweating and had to remove his jacket, the wind and rain pressing through his shirt. When they'd buried the man, they'd had little to work with and hadn't dug deep; each stab of his shovel carried with it the fear he'd cleave into something dead. His thoughts were a whirlwind of wordless dark images: vultures circling above parched bones, men in tuxedos holding stakes and bibles in black and white cemeteries, and, worst of all, scenes from his life before the man and the Caretaker—disturbing because the scenes seemed the most unreal.

He had dug himself waist deep when he stopped to stretch his tiring muscles. Was it possible he had the wrong spot? He had been drunk that night and the terrain here was fairly undistinguished and what did tumbleweeds do if not tumble all over the place? There was no way the man could be under his feet, not this far down.

Had he not a minute later found the crucifix that Neil had draped around the man's neck in the mud under his shoes, he might have talked himself into digging a few more holes. But with the tiny gold cross in his hand, still bright in the flashlight beam, he knew his trip had been in vain. The man was not here. What was left of his burned skeleton was in a casket six feet under in Rose Memorial Lawn.

Tony rested his head in his arms at the edge of the empty grave. He was tempted to replace that which had been taken and lie down in the hole and cover himself. He might have wept had he not known the worst was yet to come.

He did not remember walking back to the car but a while

later found himself exhausted, soaked and muddy, sitting behind the steering wheel. The faded yellow piece of newspaper that had brought him to this forsaken place and that should have spared him the journey lay on the passenger seat. He had only studied the first of the Caretaker's column two ads, but that had been sufficient.

Fran: syrilorryeunahokijnieaesknaesedrl
supwehycoeiojlldoilpulonitcwohig

Using the given key, starting with the first letter and including every third letter, the message told Fran to streak naked through school at lunch. As the Caretaker's notes had always been terse, it should have been obvious he was not one to waste words or letters. But surprisingly, none of the group had thought to study the extra letters. What had brought Tony to re-examine the ad had been a desperation to do anything *but* return here to where they had buried the man. That desperation had been growing all along but it had peaked sharply during his walk back to the cemetery chapel with Alison.

"I was just afraid that she would feel uncomfortable losing a family heirloom."

"I don't think Neil's mother even knew he'd had it."

"Oh, for some reason, I assumed it had been in the family."

He had known for a fact Neil's mother had not known about the emerald ring because before going to the funeral, he had asked Mrs. Hurly if it would be OK if he gave it to Alison. Also, at Alison's remark, he had specifically remembered that Neil had nodded during their meeting at Fran's house when Alison had asked if the ring had been in his family.

"How did you know?"

"The green matches your eyes. It's beautiful."

Had Neil lied, or had he, in a deranged way, in a manner they were all familiar with from the chain letter, told the truth? Standing on the cemetery road with Alison, surrounded by rows of tombstones, he had realized that only someone who cared deeply for the man, whose soul wept for the man, *who actually in some incomprehensible way identified with the man,* could refer to the man as family. And on the coattails of the realization he had remembered that the man had been wearing an expensive ring, and that Neil had been the last to touch him when he had folded the guy's hands over his heart.

The hourglass runs low.

Neil had been dying. Neil *was* dying.

In more ways than one, Neil had warned them that the Caretaker was right in front of them. Starting backward, using every third letter, Fran's ad had read:

> *Go To Police Please Tony Or I Will Die Yours*
> *Neil Hurly*

. . .

There was pain. At first it was everywhere, heavy and unbearable, and she struggled to return to unconsciousness. But her aching body dragged her awake, taking back its many parts, each with its own special hurt: her head throbbing, her arm burning, her back cramping. She opened her eyes reluctantly, feeling the sting of a grating, white glare.

She was in a small square unfurnished room with people that looked familiar, sitting on the floor beside an unshaded lamp that seemed to be emitting an irritating radiation. Her hands and feet felt stuck together and, looking down, she noticed without much comprehension that metal bands joined her ankles and wrists together. Turning her head, a sharp pain in her neck made her cry softly. The people, also arranged on the floor, looked her way, their forms blurring and overlapping before settling down. The face closest to her belonged to someone she remembered as Joan.

"What are you doing here?" Alison whispered, her throat bone dry. Trying to swallow, she began to cough, which made her head want to explode. It felt as if someone had beaten her repeatedly with a club. Then she remembered that it had been a brick. The rest came back in a frightful rush. She closed her eyes.

Neil, it was Neil. Of all people. He was dead.

"Keeping you company," Joan said. "Wake up, Ali, naptime's over."

"Shh." That was Brenda. "She doesn't look so good."

"That's because she didn't have a chance to put on her makeup," Kipp remarked. Alison ventured another peek. Except for Neil and Tony, the whole gang was present, each bound as she was, each with two sets of interlocking handcuffs. Both Brenda and Joan looked miserable, and Fran, looking thinner than she had ever seen her, appeared to have been crying. Kipp, on the other hand, wearing bright green pajamas with an embroidered four leaf clover on the shirt pocket, seemed perfectly at ease.

"My God," Alison breathed.

Kipp smiled. "I told you she'd think that she'd died and gone to heaven." He spoke to her. "Do you feel well enough to start worrying again?"

"How's your head, Ali?" Brenda asked, concerned. Alison tried to touch it to be sure it was all in one piece, but her hands stayed stuck down by her calves. Flexing her jaw, she felt dried blood along her right ear.

"Wonderful. How long have I been here and where is here?"

"Almost two hours," Kipp said. "You're in a house down the street from your own. Would you like to hear our stories? We're tired of telling them to each other."

She reclosed her eyes. If she remained perfectly still, it wasn't so bad. "The highlights," she said.

"You go first, Fran," Kipp said, playing the MC.

"He's going to kill us!" Fran cried. "He's going to take us

out to where we hit the man and dump us on the road and run us over."

"Now, now," Kipp scolded patiently. "Don't ruin the story for her. Start with how you were kidnapped." Fran tried to speak but only ended up blubbering. Her outburst didn't initially faze Alison. That the Caretaker wanted to kill them sounded like old news. But as the information sunk past the layers of bodily misery, she decided that whatever they had to tell her had already been ruined.

"Fran's story isn't really very interesting," Kipp picked up. "She was in Bakersfield at her grandmother's house when her sweetheart Caretaker dropped by for a friendly visit. She was so flattered that when he asked her for a walk and offered her a spiked carbonated beverage that tasted like a codeine float, she didn't think twice. At least I had an excuse, I was drunk when I downed the drugs Neil must have slipped into my beer. Naturally, this is only Fran's version of the story. Personally, I feel Neil simply kissed her and she swooned at his feet."

"I did not kiss him!" Fran said, indignantly.

"But did he kiss you?" Kipp asked. "All those hours you were unconscious in that van he stole, he might have done all kinds of nasty things to you."

"Neil would never have . . ." Fran began, before realizing that defending Neil's personal integrity at this point would be a losing proposition.

"Kipp," Alison groaned, "just the facts, please."

"But aren't you happy to see that I'm still alive?" Kipp asked. "Joan wasn't, but Brenda gave me a big kiss."

"I'll give you a kiss later, if we don't all end up getting killed."

"Actually," Kipp said, thinking, "none of our stories is very interesting. I went to sleep one night in my bedroom and woke up the next morning in this bedroom. Fran and I have been keeping each other company ever since. She's not the girl I thought she was. Did you know she once painted a nude poster of Brad Pitt?"

"Kipp!" Fran whined.

"Neil's been feeding us," Kipp went on without missing a beat. "For lunch this afternoon, we had apples, and for dinner last night, we had apples. He's not big on condemned prisoners enjoying delicious final meals. Last week, though, he brought us a bunch of bananas. He even lets us go to the bathroom whenever we want."

"Neil flagged us down a few hours ago about a block from your house," Brenda said. "Joan was driving. She almost ran him over. Man, we were spooked. I practically peed my pants."

"You did pee your pants," Joan growled. "All over my upholstery. But I wasn't that scared, not till he pulled out that damn gun."

"He has a gun?" Alison asked, her alertness growing with each revelation. She did not have to ask why Joan had used the same line as the Caretaker. When she thought about it, Joan was always talking that way. Neil could have swiped any of their remarks for his chain letter.

"Yes," Kipp said. "Didn't he show you the nice black hole at the end of it? Tell us how he captured you. We heard him play the music and people tape. I bet you thought you were coming to a party."

"I thought I was coming to a party," she muttered.

"We heard a shot," Brenda said. "What happened?"

"I missed, twice. It's a long story." It struck her then that her room, minus the furniture, was identical to this one. A pair of binoculars lay discarded beneath the cardboard-covered windows, and even before the arrival of the first letter, she had felt as if someone had been watching her. "How did you survive losing all that blood?" she asked Kipp.

"Brenda told me about that," Kipp said. "What a dramatic exit! A trail of blood reaching to the street! You got to grant Neil one thing, he's got style. But to tell you the truth, I didn't lose any blood, not as far as I know."

"Interesting," Alison said. The police had verified that the blood had definitely been human. With his illness, it was relatively easy to understand how Neil had obtained the drugs. And he had probably picked these cuffs up at a swapmeet or an army surplus store. But where did he get the blood? From his own veins? Siphoning it off over a period of time? If that were so, it provided a unique insight into his madness. He would torture himself as readily as he would torture them. “Has Neil talked to you much?” she asked.

“Brenda has explained his cancer,” Kipp said, catching her drift. “Watching him these last couple of weeks, Fran and I had pretty much figured on something like that. He doesn’t complain but that guy is really hurting. I think it’s obvious that the disease is to blame, the malignancy has gone to his brain. I don’t hold any of this against him. He doesn’t know what he’s doing, the poor guy.”

She nodded, though that sounded a bit pat to her: tumor in the head and the sick boy goes on a rampage. It also sounded self-serving, The Caretaker—she couldn’t quite interchange Neil’s name with the villain’s—had repeatedly spoken of their evil. Was it possible he had a—granted perverse, but nevertheless—consistent motivation for what he was doing? If that were so, and she could understand what it was, perhaps she could get through to him. “Where is he?” she asked.

“Downstairs,” Fran said. “He’s got a terrible cough. I think he’s dying.”

“Pray that he hurries,” Brenda said.

“What a terrible thing to say!” Fran said.

“You’re the one who’s worried about getting squashed out on that desert road,” Brenda said.

“Well, so are you!” Fran shot back.

“My point exactly,” Brenda said. “He’s nuts. He’s . . .”

“Would you two please shut up,” Alison said, and it seemed

when they had first received the chain letter, Brenda and Fran had been arguing and she had had a headache. "Kipp, has Neil spoken to you using the Caretaker's style of language?"

"Not exactly, but he has said things like having to 'balance the scales,' 'purge our filth,' and 'pay for our crime.'"

"Have you tried to talk sense into him?"

"Endlessly. And he sits and listens to every word we have to say. Neil always was a good listener. But he doesn't let us go, doesn't even argue with us, just brings us fresh bags of apples." Kipp stopped suddenly. "But maybe he will listen to you. He's brought you up a few times, not in any specific context, just muttered your name now and then."

"Favorably or negatively?"

"Both ways, I would say."

"Do you really think that he intends to kill us?" she asked.

Kipp hesitated. "I'm afraid so. I think he's just been waiting to get us all together. The guy's gone."

"But *could* he kill us?"

"Alison, anybody who could pull off what he has could probably do anything he damn well pleases."

"But we're not all together," she said. "Where's Tony?"

"Dead," a sad and worn voice coughed at the door. To say that Neil did not look well would have been the same as addressing such a remark to a week-old corpse. His yellowish flesh hung from his face like a faded and wrinkled oversized wrapper. His back was hunched, and it was obvious that his right leg was painful. The once irresistible green of his eyes was a pitiful blur, and the left shoulder of his dirty leather jacket was torn and bloodied. Back at her house, when Alison had thought she was giving Joan her due, he must have shoved open her bedroom door and then jumped back, but not quite quick enough. That she had wrestled him and come out the loser was a testament to how driven he must be. An ugly black gun protruded from his belt.

Tony, she wailed inside. No matter how badly she had been flattened tonight, each time, her strength had returned. But if Tony was gone, she was gone. Mist covered her eyes, and she heard crying, not Fran's, but Joan's.

Neil limped into the room. In one hand he carried a hypodermic needle, in the other, a medicine bottle filled with a colorless solution. Obviously, he intended to sedate them before dragging them down to the van and driving them out to the desert road. He knelt unsteadily by her side and, it would have been funny in another time and place, pulled a small bottle of rubbing alcohol and several balls of cotton from his coat pocket. His breathing was agonizing. He refused to look her in the face.

"Neil," she whispered. "Did you really kill Tony?"

"He killed himself," he said quietly, arranging the cotton balls in a neat row, as a nurse might have done.

"Is he really dead?" she pleaded. Neil nodded, his eyes down. A pain, bright like a sun rising on a world burned to ruin, overshadowed the injuries in her body. All that kept her from giving up completely was that Neil might be lying. "You would not," she stammered, "have killed your friend."

He didn't respond, just kept rearranging his cotton balls. She leaned toward him. "Dammit, you answer me! Tony was your best friend!"

Endless misery sagged his miserable face. He sat back and stared at her. "He killed himself," he repeated.

He was speaking figuratively, she realized, and it gave her cause to hope. "Neil," she said patiently, "when Tony and I were at your funeral—when we thought you were dead—he told me how you felt about me. He said that I was important to you. Well, you are important to me, too."

He glanced at the covered window. In the lower right hand corner was a bare spot, probably through which he had watched her. "I wasn't," he said. "Only the man cared for me."

"The man? Neil, the man was a stranger."

"He was somebody. And he was wronged, and he never complained. How could he? He was never given the chance." Neil lowered his head. "He would have been my friend."

The emotion in his voice made her next step uncertain. Even as she sought to reach his old self, her eyes strayed to the revolver in his belt. Her hands and feet were bound, but her fingers were free and the weapon was not far. "I am your friend," she said carefully. "We are all your friends. Hurting us will not bring back the man."

"That's what I told him," Kipp remarked cheerfully.

"We don't want to bring him back, I just want all of us to be with him." Neil nodded, a faraway look in his eyes. "You're very pretty, Alison, and you see, he's very lonely."

She thought she saw perfectly. She shifted position slightly, angling on a clean approach to the gun. The maneuver made her next words sound hypocritical to her own ears. "He's not lonely. It's you, Neil, who's lonely. Let us go. We'll stay with you."

"You would?" he asked innocently, mildly surprised.

"Yes. Don't be afraid. We'll help you with the pain."

A shudder ran through his body. "The pain," he whispered dreamily. "You don't know this pain." His eyes narrowed. "You never wanted to know me."

"But I did," she said, striving for conviction. This was not going to work. She was having to use half truths and he was, even in his deranged state, extraordinarily sensitive to deceit. "I thought about you a lot. Just the other day I was telling Tony that . . ."

"Tony!" he yelled scornfully. "Tony knew how I felt about you! But he didn't care. He took what he wanted. He took the man's life. He took you. He took and took and gave nothing back. He wouldn't even go to the police." A spasm seemed to grip his stomach and he bent over in pain. She squirmed closer. The gun, the gun . . . if she could just get her hand on it, this would all be over.

"He was afraid, Neil. He was like you. He was like me. You can understand that."

He shook his head, momentarily closing his eyes. "But I don't understand," he mumbled. The gun handle was maybe twenty inches from her fingers and the interlocked handcuffs had about ten inches of play in them. If she could keep him talking . . .

Good God, be good to me this one time.

Unfortunately, just then, Neil sat back and picked up the hypodermic. "We need to return to where all this started to understand, to the road," he said, regaining his confidence, sticking the bottle with the needle, the clear liquid filling the syringe. He pulled up her pants leg and picked up a cotton ball.

"But you promised to tell me your dream," she said quickly, playing a desperate card. A drop oozed at the tip of the needle, catching the light of the naked bulb, glistening like a deadly diamond. It was very possible be would simply finish them here and now with an overdose. Yet Neil hesitated, and the play went on.

"When?"

"When we were standing on Kipp's street in the middle of the night. Before Tony came over, we were alone, and I told you about my nightmares and how they were frightening me. You tried to cheer me up. You started to tell me about a wonderful dream full of colors and music and singing."

"What a night that must have been." Kipp sighed.

"So?" Neil said. He lowered the needle.

"I asked you if I was in it," she said.

Neil winced. "No."

"Yes! I started to ask. Remember, just when Tony interrupted us? I wanted to know if I was that important to you that you would have dreamed about me." She swiveled her legs around, disguising the overt movement with an expression of pure sincerity. Neil was listening and she prayed that Kipp kept his mouth shut. At Neil's next solid blank spell, she was going for the gun.

"I dreamed about a lot of things," he admitted. "You were one of them. But I can't see that mattering to you."

She held her tongue. In spite of his words, she could see that he wanted to believe her. His madness and sickness aside, he was just like everyone else: He wanted to know his love had not been wasted on someone who couldn't have cared less. He ran an unsteady hand through his tangled hair, fidgeting. "You were always too busy," he said, raising his voice. "I tried to talk to you. I called you up. But you always had things you had to do. That was OK, I could understand that. I could wait. I could have waited a long time. But then . . . I saw I couldn't wait forever; not even until the summer when you would have had more time . . . I saw I was going to end up like the man."

"How was it different in your dreams?" And surely her soul would be forever cursed, for as she asked, she leaned forward, gesturing that he should whisper his answer in her ear, stopping at nothing to get next to the hard black handle. Neil was too much of a child to succeed as a murderer. He did exactly what she wanted.

"I was never sick in my dreams," he began. "We were . . ."

I'm listening.

She grabbed the pistol. Next to the shotgun, it was a cinch to handle, and she had her finger on the trigger and the barrel point between his eyes before he could even blink. "Sorry," she whispered.

He absorbed the deception silently, sitting back, his sore leg jerking once then going as still as the rest of him. Before, he had been ashamed and had had trouble looking her in the eye. Now the roles were reversed. He said nothing, waiting.

"I want the key to these handcuffs," she said. "That's all I want."

"That's all you want," he echoed.

"Don't shoot him!" Fran cried.

"Neil," she said firmly, "I've shot at you twice tonight. I won't miss a third time." She shook the gun. "Give me the key!"

"No."

"Don't be a fool!"

He raised the needle. He was not afraid of her. In her rush to get the gun, she had never stopped to consider that she might have to use it. He squeezed out what bubbles may have been in the syringe, a couple of drops of the drug dribbling onto the floor. "I don't have it," he said.

"Get it!"

"The man has the key."

"Listen to me, you're going to be as bad off as the man if you don't get it!"

Neil nodded. "That's what all this has been about." He unscrewed the cap of the alcohol jar and dabbed one of the cotton balls.

"Kipp?" she moaned.

"Don't give him the gun, whatever you do," Kipp said in his most helpful manner. Unreality rolled forth unchecked. Using the moistened white ball, Neil sterilized a spot on her calf. He was asking to be killed, she told herself. She could close her eyes, pull the trigger and never see the mess.

He's going to die, anyway. It would be quick.

"Neil?" she pleaded, trembling.

He shook his head. "I'm not listening. Everything you say is a lie. You don't care about me." Like a nurse administering an injection, he pinched her flesh.

"I swear!" she cried. "I'll kill you!"

"I know you will," he said sadly, pausing one last time to look her in the face. "You're like Tony, just like him. Since last summer, he's been killing me."

She cocked the hammer. He had terminal cancer. His mother had already buried him. Tears had been cried and respects had been paid. She would just be doing what was already practically done.

You were his love.

But staring into his eyes, it seemed impossible that she could snuff out what dim light remained there. She had brought herself to this terrible decision as surely as he had.

"Hello, Alison, this is Neil. Would you like to go to a movie with me this Friday?" "How sweet! I would but I'm busy Friday." "Would Saturday be better?" "It would be better but not good enough. Sorry, Neil." "That's OK."

"I'll give you the gun," she whispered, the narcotic inches from her bloodstream: "If that will prove to you that I do care."

"Nooo!!!" Kipp, Brenda, and Joan howled.

Neil considered for a moment. He nodded.

She gave him the gun. He took it and set it down behind him. "Thank you, Alison," he said, and taking the needle, he stabbed it in her leg.

The rain had begun to ease and the freeway was empty and fast. Tony remembered the night of the accident when he'd been driving and had thought that, although he didn't know where he was going, he was making good time. He was beginning to feel that way now. The proper one to see at this point was Neil's mother, it was the obvious thing to do, and yet, with each passing mile, his doubts grew. Telling Mrs. Hurly her son was still alive would also mean she would have to be told about the Caretaker's mad plot. How could he possibly make up a story to cover the facts? On the other hand, how could she possibly accept the truth? The only part she probably would believe, or that would at least give her cause to wonder, was that her son was somewhere in hiding, still hurting. Neil would die on her twice and whatever followed could only tarnish her memories of her son.

Should I do the right thing for the wrong reasons or should I do the wrong thing for no clear reason at all?

About the same time his indecision was reaching a climax, he was closing on a fork in the freeway. Alison's house was over twenty miles out of his way, but just the thought of her got him thinking of all the times Neil had talked about how beautiful she was. Neil had once said he could stare at her all day and not get tired.

"That would be my idea of heaven, Tony."

Where does a guy go after his own funeral if not to heaven?

Tony swerved onto the north running interstate, picking up speed. He hadn't spoken to Alison all day.

A half-hour later he was cruising up Alison's submerged street; this new tract still had a lesson or two to learn about flood control. He noticed lights on in a house a couple of hundred yards before Alison's, but only in passing. He assumed another family had finally moved in.

Her place was dark as he parked across the street. Her parents were out of town, he knew, but it was close to midnight, and if he went knocking on her door, he would scare her to death. Then again, it might not be a bad idea to wake her and take her to Brenda's or even to his own house. His folks were gone, too, but that didn't mean his motivation was in any way remotely connected with sex. They could sleep together in the same room for protection, maybe even in the same bed, and not actually . . .

Oh, Neil, no.

The front door was lying wide open. He was out of his car in a moment, running to the porch. The glass panel next to the door was cracked. Dark stains tipped the jagged glass—blood. Steeling himself as best he could, he went inside. For now, he would do what was necessary. Later, he told himself, he would feel what he had to feel.

None of the lights would go on. He did not need them to know the house was empty. It was not the absence of noise that told him, it was the feel of the place—like its life had been yanked out of it. He went to the back door, in spite of his resolve, his heart was breaking at the splintered shambles that he found. Forcing himself forward, he stepped outside to the circuit breakers, finding each one snapped down. He restored the power and returned inside, heading upstairs to Alison's bedroom. There wasn't a step that wasn't smeared with blood.

His nerve almost deserted him when he saw the hole blasted in her door. The fact that the shot had been fired from the inside out, and that the hall was not soaked with blood, was all that kept him together. He turned on her nightstand lamp and sat on her bed, seeing a picture of himself on her desk. He felt as if he was back in the man's grave, only now all his friends were with him, and they were unable to get out of the hole, and they were asking him again and again why he had brought them to such a terrible place.

Minutes, like those ticked off by watches with dead batteries, dragged by. Somewhere amid his grief he took out his phone. He was going to call the police. He would tell them everything. Then he would lie down on her bed and try to pretend she was there beside him.

But his phone was dead, and suddenly, it didn't matter. He was remembering the night in his car with Alison not fifty yards from where he now sat. He had kissed her and he had wanted to continue kissing her. But then he had thought of Neil and had felt guilty. Only he just hadn't started to think of him, he had actually felt as if Neil was in his head, like that crazy way he had occasionally felt on the field during a game when he had just *known* that there was this one fat slob in the audience who was praying to God and Moses that that hotshot Tony Hunt would suddenly get an acute attack of arthritis and maybe have his right arm fall off. It had been like Neil had been near at hand, watching him defile his goddess.

Tony slipped the phone back into his pocket and went to the window. *That* house with the light on, *that* was the house that had drawn his attention the night of their date. He had driven by the place and not even slowed down. *Fool!*

He ran down the stairs and out the door, but not so fast did he go that he missed the soggy sock lying in the road halfway between the two houses. It was blue, Alison's favorite color, and the evidence was piling up quickly. There was a shotgun resting in the grass near the house porch. He cracked it open, sniffed the chamber. Both barrels had recently been fired.

He did not knock. The front door was unlocked. Except for a few lamps, he found the living room and den empty, but rounding into the kitchen, he stumbled across a makeshift bed: a thin piece of foam rubber, a tattered blanket, and a slipless pillow covered with long brown hairs. Beside the bed were Neil's phone and a ring of miniature keys, which he pocketed. There were also a bottle of cough medicine and two prescription pill containers. The latter reminded him of many things, not the least of which was that, of all the people he had ever known, he had loved Neil the most.

His next move was to go upstairs, and he did so cautiously, hearing voices before he reached the top step. They were faint, muffled by a closed door, but he recognized one as belonging to Alison, and his relief broke over him like a warm sweet wave. Almost, he rushed to be with her; the sound of Neil's voice stopped him cold. He tiptoed to the door and peered through the crack. The whole group was assembled. Fran appeared well if a bit skinny and Kipp's big nose had never looked so good. Only Alison had been banged up—her left arm looked like it had been put through a meat grinder—but she was alive and that was what mattered. Neil was not a murderer after all and Tony was thankful. Yet Neil had a gun in his belt—a revolver

Tony had more than a nodding acquaintance with—and it might be a mistake to trust Neil while overlooking the Caretaker. Who were these two people? How were they connected?

"I wasn't," Neil told Alison. "Only the man cared for me."

"The man? Neil, the man was a stranger."

"He was somebody. And he was wronged, and he never complained. How could he? He was never given the chance. He would have been my friend."

"I am your friend. We are all your friends. Hurting us will not bring back the man."

Listening, watching, two things struck Tony. First, Alison was as much intent on reaching the gun as she was on reaching Neil. The movement of her eyes betrayed her. Second, in spite of her itchy fingers, she was doing a master psychologist's job of forcing Neil to confront the truth, and she was doing it quickly. As the conversation progressed, Neil answered less and less with incoherent remarks. In fact, he started to get painfully clear.

"Tony! Tony knew how I felt about you!"

He took and took and he gave nothing back.

Tony could not have defended himself. It was all true. He had always been nice to Neil. Yet, at the same time, in a very quiet way, he had taken advantage of him. Neil had not always acted like a saint. He could get angry like anybody. But no matter what the situation, whether he was laughing or yelling, he had always been more concerned about how he was affecting Tony Hunt than he had been worried about how he might be hurting Neil Hurly. While Tony Hunt had usually been pleased as pie to congratulate himself on how neat a guy he must be to bring out this devotion in Neil Hurly. His friend's affection had just been another *thing* to boost his self-image. Nevertheless, he felt there was something else that was necessary to explain the craziness, something that Neil was not saying. Neil obviously blamed him for the death of the man and for stealing Alison, but these were effects, not causes. He was sure of this for the simple reason that Neil had never blamed him for anything before.

". . . I wanted to know if I was that important to you that you would have dreamed about me."

"I dreamed about a lot of things. You were one of them. But I can't see that mattering to you."

Alison was so blatantly baiting him that Tony had trouble believing Neil wasn't aware of the deception. Could it be that he wanted her to kill him? Or was it that thc gun was not what it appeared?

"You don't think it would scare the Caretaker empty?"

"Not if he knew it was empty."

". . . But then . . . I saw I couldn't wait forever, not even until the summer when you would have had more time . . . I saw I was going to end up like the man."

"How was it different in your dreams?"

"I was never sick in my dreams. We were . . ."

Oh, God, she had the gun. That Alison sure had nerve. Now

all he had to do was fling open the door and play the big hero. He stayed where he was. If he interrupted this fine edge Alison had led Neil to, this place where Neil wandered lost between pain and sanity, truth and insanity, he might never be able to take Neil back there, and Neil might never open up again, and he might die misunderstood. Tony knew it was ludicrous to risk what was at stake—he was banking on an unloaded gun—for an insight that might never be found. Nevertheless, he did not interfere.

A moment later, he was given Neil's *why.* It cost him.

"Give me the key!"

"No."

"Don't be a fool!"

You can't threaten him, Ali; he has nothing to lose.

Tony dropped to his knees, digging holes in his palms with his clenched fingers. The cold draft from the open front door felt like Death's breath on the back of his neck.

"I'm not listening. Everything you say is a lie. You don't care about me."

"I swear! I'll kill you!"

"I know you will. You're like Tony, just like him. Since last summer, he's been killing me."

Divine vengeance . . . all along, he's been telling me.

At last, he thought he understood. He did not fool himself that he was a psychiatrist, but he could see a pattern. Neil had sympathized with and related to the man to an unheard of extent. Much of the Caretaker's strange language in the chain letter probably came from that unnatural identification. Plus Alison's rejection of him in favor of the person who had killed the man couldn't have helped matters. Yet it appeared that the main cause of the whole mess was very simple. Neil thought that he had become sick because he had done a serious wrong, that the cancer was his just punishment. As the disease had progressed and the pain had intensified, he had probably begun to believe that if they confessed, particularly his best friend who had after all been the main instigator of the crime, he would be healed. Of course the confession would have to be to the police instead of to a priest, and it would have to be sincere. That is why the Caretaker hadn't just told them to turn themselves in. Repeatedly, Neil had warned them that the chain letter's only hold on them was their guilty conscience. Maybe the accident *had* caused the disease. Who knew how much deep guilt could contribute to an illness?

So caught up was Tony in his analysis that he did not immediately respond to Alison's surrender. But when Neil set aside the gun and reached for the hypodermic, he decided enough was enough. He was a bit late with the decision. He kicked open the door just as the needle plunged into Alison's calf.

Neil did not react like a sick man. One glance at his unexpected company and he was on his feet, backing into the corner, dragging Alison by the throat. With her two sets of handcuffs still in place, her arms stretched halfway to her feet, she was a clumsy burden. The syringe swung haphazardly out of her leg, the majority of its dosage unadministered. The gun lay forgotten on the floor. Neil had no need for it. Tony was surprised at the switchblade that suddenly materialized in Neil's hand. There was no question that the razor tip was sharp.

"Hello, Neil," he said, keeping his distance. Neil had the knife pressed against Alison's neck. Her eyes were wide, but she was keeping very still.

"Hello," Neil answered, uncertain.

"How ya doin', Tony?" Kipp said. "I bet you're glad to see me."

Tony ventured a step forward, two steps. Neil poked Alison slightly and she stifled a cry. He halted. "I read your secret message in the paper," he said. "Can we talk about it?"

"We have talked," Neil said. "You love to talk."

The room was claustrophobic, the walls seeming to press in from all sides. The tension was so thick it was like a mountainous weight, smothering all external sounds. He could hear his heartbeat, the anxious breathing of his friends, nothing else. The rest of the world could have ceased to exist. "I'm willing to go to the police," he said honestly. "Let Alison go."

"It's too late for that."

"It's not too late. We're still friends. No matter how you feel, you're still one of us."

"I am not one of you!" Neil shouted, his knife hand trembling. A pinprick of red appeared under Alison's chin, a thin streak of blood staining the collar of her sweater. She remained

silent. "I would never have done what you did. The man . . ."

"Forget the man," Tony interrupted, afraid Neil would slip into the Caretaker's prattle. He noticed Kipp's fingers creeping toward the plug that juiced the room's only lamp and stopped him with a slashing hand signal. He took another step forward. "Let's talk about you, Neil, and about me. This is between us. You don't want to hurt Alison."

"I want to hurt you all!" Neil cried. "You hurt me! All of you with your M.I.T. scholarships, your great paintings, your star performances, your big trophies! I wanted all of those things! And I would have gotten them for myself! But none of you would give me the chance!" His eyes flashed on Alison, who had her own eyes half closed. "You had to kill me!"

The condemnation hit Tony like scalding steam. The switchblade was sharp, and an ounce of pressure could spill Alison's life over the floor. Nothing was more important than to insure her safety. All the things Neil was talking about were already lost. Still, Tony strove inside for the perfect response that would address both the past and the present. It never came; instead, out of the corner of his eye, he noticed Fran. Pale and frantic, she looked an unlikely hero, but the last couple of months had taught him well how deceptive appearances could be. He turned away from Neil and Alison and came and knelt by her side, pulling out the key chain he had taken from beside Neil's mattress downstairs. The first key he tried worked and Fran's cuffs snapped open.

"Go get Ali," he said gently, giving her the keys. "Don't be afraid."

"He's . . . he's sick?" she asked, unsure.

He nodded. "He's been hurt. He's been used. But never by you. He won't hurt you."

He helped her up—she was stiff from her captivity—and she composed herself admirably and crept toward Neil and Alison. Neil's anger changed to confusion.

"Stay back!" he said.

"She just wants Alison," Tony called.

Neil shook his head desperately. "I won't let go! I can't let go!"

"Then hold me instead," Fran said in her usual meek voice. Kipp went to laugh but wisely cut it off. The offer was not funny; it was genuine, and it touched Neil like nothing else they had said. Neil could hear things most people couldn't; he was practically a mind reader. Fran had always cared for him. She was not trying to manipulate him. He could see that. And he seemed to see something else. A glazed film lifted from his eyes. Fran held out her hand. As if in a trance, he took it and squeezed her fingers around Alison's hand, nodding in resignation. He lowered the knife and, using the keys, Fran released Alison's cuffs. But then neither of the girls moved, waiting for Neil to decide. He did so a moment later, when he pushed them aside and leaned alone against the wall, barely able to remain upright, the knife still in his hand.

His madness departed like a foul spirit, leaving an aching void. Another evil took its place.

Suicide.

"Leave," he whispered.

Tony moved closer. "I'm staying with you."

"For how long?" he asked, unbearable torment twisting his mouth. "Till the end?" Tears gushed over his wasted cheeks, his bloodshot eyes falling on the knife as it slowly bent toward his heart. "This is the end."

"But you did nothing wrong last summer," Tony pleaded, approaching to within an arm's reach, feeling his own heart being cut in two. "And you haven't actually hurt any of the girls, or Kipp, or me. How can you punish yourself for a crime you didn't commit?"

Neil's ravished body quivered. He looked to each of them, into them, and love, the old Neil, glimmered. But shame claimed it too soon, and the tip of the blade came to rest on the soft flesh beneath his sunken ribs. Tony went to grab the knife, but Neil raised his other hand, stopping him before he could try. "I've done enough," he said.

Tony shook his head, beginning to choke up. "You've done nothing wrong. Always, Neil, *always,* I thought you were the best of us. Don't end it this way, please?"

Neil leaned his head back, his eyes falling shut, lifetimes of care etched in his face. "The doctor didn't say the word," he whispered, "but I knew what it was, I had read about it. When

I went to bed at night, when it was dark, I tried not to think about it. Then I began to get sore, everything hurt, and I got scared. They gave me so many drugs, I was sick all the time. I kept wondering and worrying and I tried, but this thing got in my head and I couldn't get rid of it. I don't know where it came from. It was like a voice, saying this is true and this is a lie. It wouldn't shut up! I had to listen, and I did listen, and then . . . I did all this." He winced as though he had been struck and his grip on the knife tightened. "I'm sorry, Tony, I just can't take it."

Then I will take it from you, Tony thought. He could do that for his friend. He could kill him, and stop the pain. Fortunately, it was an offer he wasn't given a chance to make.

"Neil," Alison said softly from the corner. Neil's exhausted eyes opened slowly and followed her as she ignored the knife and came close enough to touch him. "I gave you back the gun because I really did want to be in your dreams." She brushed a strand of hair from his face. "Live a while longer, for me?"

Her concern, which hurt him, and saved him, was the final stroke. The switchblade dropped from his hand onto the floor as he sagged against the wall, the last of his strength departing. "Take me away, Tony," he moaned, sobs convulsing his body. Tony caught him as he fell, and cradled him in his arms.

"I'll take care of him," he told the others, and carried him out of the room.

Epilogue

It was a fine day to move into a new house. Although the sun was warm, the afternoon continued to savor the morning's freshness, the last traces of dew sparkling on the recently planted lawns, cool air pockets clinging to the shade and fanning Alison on each of her brief and repetitious treks from the moving van to the front door. As Mr. Hague, her new neighbor, had said, "It's the kind of day Adam and Eve probably used to enjoy."

Tony had reappeared this morning, looking fit and at ease, and she had been relieved. He was presently helping Mr. Hague, a jolly middle-aged man with a huge pumpkin head and an ingratiating laugh, maneuver an overstuffed refrigerator through a dieting front door. Tony had already helped Mr. Hague with three quarters of the house. In fact, had he not lent a hand, Alison figured her new neighbor probably would have had trouble unloading the drawers and cushions—which was OK, Mr. Hague was a most appreciative gentleman. She was looking forward to meeting his family.

"Can I help?" she asked, holding a box of books, standing on the walkway in shorts, the sun a sensual delight on the back of her bare legs, enjoying how Tony's muscles strained and bulged through his sweat-soaked green T-shirt—he was such a hunk.

"No," Tony breathed, positioning his body against the overloaded dolly for a burst of effort. "Ready, Mr. Hague?"

"What should I be doing?" Mr. Hague called back, hidden inside the house behind the bulk of the icebox. Tony looked at her and winked.

"Just step back," he said, and flexing his biceps and using a bit of he-man magic, the refrigerator did a tiny hop and rolled into the entrance hall from where he was able to easily wheel it into the kitchen. She followed on his heels, depositing her burden on the couch they had earlier squeezed through the window. Tony unstrapped the dolly belt and walked the appliance into the proper corner while Mr. Hague stood idly nearby, shaking his head in awe.

"I'd like to say when I was your age," Mr. Hague remarked, "I could have done that. But I was more of a wimp then than I am now." He laughed and picked up the loose electrical cord. "But I suppose I can manage to plug this in." He accomplished the simple task and reached for his wallet. "Let me give you a little something for saving me a couple of hernia operations."

"You spared me my afternoon workout," Tony said. "Let's call it even."

"Come, I insist, a few dollars." Mr. Hague pulled out two twenties. "You can take Alison to dinner."

She smiled. "But I'm on a diet."

"How about when I have to move," Tony said. "I get to call you?"

Mr. Hague scratched his big head, thought about that for a moment, and decided that that sounded fair. The heavy articles were all unloaded, and the three of them shared a pitcher of lemonade before Mr. Hague walked them to the door. Standing half inside, half outside, Alison glanced at the stucco ceiling. Not far from the entrance, there was a sloppy patch job—her second missed shot. Mr. Hague noticed her attention.

"The realtor told me the contractor's spray gun went on the blink," he said. "They'll be out soon to smooth out the spot."

She could understand why a salesman wouldn't have been wild about telling a client that their brand-new home had been shot at. "Nothing like a gun on the blink," she said, and Tony looked at the floor.

Mr. Hague thanked them profusely for a couple of minutes before letting them go. She had not had a chance to talk to Tony before he had started in on the furniture and she was anxious to get him alone. But as they walked down the driveway, they were stopped by a swiftly decelerating Camaro. A straw blonde with an excited face and a skimpy top bounded out the door. All of about sixteen chewing gum years old, she wasted no time raking Tony over with her dizzy blue eyes.

"Hiya!" She stuck out her hand. "I'm Kathy, your new neighbor!"

Tony shook her hand—Kathy had obviously been hoping he was a local boy—and introduced the two of them, adding quietly, "Alison is actually your neighbor. I'm from the other side of town."

Kathy let her disappointment show briefly, then turned and took in the empty street. She threw her hands in the air. "Lord, this place looks dull!" She popped her gum. "When are all the other people moving in?"

Alison hugged Tony's arm, noticing all of a sudden the far-away look in his eyes. "Soon," she said.

"Then again," Kathy mused, taking a different slant on things, "it's kind of neat, kind of spooky having all these empty houses to ourselves, huh?"

Alison pointed at the bedroom that overlooked the garage. "Is that going to be your room?"

"Hey, yeah, it is. Why ya ask?"

"Just wondering." She tugged on Tony, who was hardly listening. "Catch you later, Kathy."

"Nice meeting you! You, too, Tony. Great to see you."

Tony nodded silently.

They strolled up the middle of the street, hand in hand, not speaking, the brown fertilized plots on either side of them spread with bright green blades, sparrows skipping between the young grass, searching for unsprouted seeds. The sun was hotter out here on the asphalt, and she would have preferred short sleeves to complement her short pants. But her parents didn't know about the stitches and bandages on her left arm and she was still working on a good excuse. Fortunately, Kipp had helped her replace the back door, her bedroom door, the hall closet door and the glass panels next to the front door. The new back door was a distinctly lighter shade of brown than the old one, but neither her mom or dad had so far noticed.

She had spoken to Harvey Heck the day after all the excitement. He had been on duty solid for the last week, he had told her, but he had looked hungover and she hadn't bothered asking why he had failed to answer his phone at a certain crucial moment.

"I'll have to tell you about Fran's and Kipp's explanations to the police," she said finally. "They were pretty funny. Fran told them that she got kidnapped by a deaf and dumb old man who took her to his house in the desert and forced her to draw obscene pictures of him all day long. Of course they wanted to know where he lived and what he looked like but she just told them she couldn't remember. She told them she escaped when he wasn't listening. Want to hear Kipp's?"

Tony brightened. "This should be good."

She laughed. "Not one, but *three* beautiful girls were responsible for his kidnapping. He told the police he put up a good fight, that's how he lost all that blood in his bedroom, but they wrestled him down and tied him up and dumped him in their plushly carpeted and heavily perfumed van. They didn't take him to any one spot, just drove him all over the place."

"For two weeks?"

"Yeah! And whichever two weren't driving would amuse themselves by doing all sorts of atrocious things to his naked body. There was an amazon blonde, a large-chested redhead, and a tireless brunette. And here's the weird part—the police swallowed the whole story! It seems they have several adolescent male kidnappings on record that fit the same pattern."

"I don't believe any of this."

"I'm not so sure I do, but this is what Kipp has been telling everyone, that is, in between asking them if they aren't real glad that he's still alive."

Tony let out a hearty laugh, and she was happy to hear it. They reached her house a moment later and then decided that, since it was such a nice day, they would circle the tract on foot. Before continuing, however, she reached into the back seat of her car and pulled out two green vinyl folders. "I'm sure you hadn't forgotten, but graduation was a couple of days ago. I accepted your diploma for you." She handed him the two certificates, adding, "Fran accepted Neil's."

He glanced at both briefly, his expression unreadable,

before setting them on the car roof. "I'll get them on the way back." He took her hand and they resumed their walk. "How was the ceremony?" he asked casually.

She shrugged. "Boring, for the most part. They held it in the stadium, and had us sitting on fold-outs in the center of the football field. But there were a couple of neat things. One was that they had Brenda sing a song. To do that, they had to lift her suspension, but you know, she's the only one in the whole stupid school that can sing. I guess they figured they didn't have much choice. You'll never believe what material she chose! Alice Cooper's 'School's Out for Summer'! And it was Mr. Hoglan who accompanied her on piano!"

He smiled. "Did Kipp give the valedictorian's speech?"

A huge silver-collared German shepherd with a dinosaur's bone in his mouth leisurely crossed their path, regarding them suspiciously out of the corner of his eye. Another family besides the Hagues must have arrived. "He did," she said carefully.

"What did he talk about?"

"Neil. A recording was made of it, if you want to hear it later."

"You tell me."

"Just like Kipp, he tried to keep it light, but he said some real neat stuff. In fact, right in the middle, he lost his voice for a couple of minutes. He said afterward it was because his throat got dry, but everyone could tell there had been another reason."

She bent low as they passed a beginning planter, plucking a white daisy. Simply remembering had brought a lump to her throat. She continued, "He started off with the obvious stuff, how Neil had helped out at the football games and the track meets, what his favorite subjects had been, how he would have graduated on the honor roll. But then he just . . . started to talk about Neil." She sniffed. "He quoted you, sort of, saying that of all those at school, he had always seen Neil as the best example of what a person should be. He finished by telling this story of how you three guys were out hiking in the desert one day when suddenly he slipped and fell and twisted his ankle and wasn't able to walk anymore. He said that while you went searching for help, Neil stayed and took care of him. But then you were gone so long, and it was so hot, that Neil decided he had to try to carry him back to the car. He went on about how Neil wasn't very strong, but how he tried anyway, giving it everything he had, and how it almost . . . killed him." Her eyes burned with unshed tears and she had to take a couple of deep breaths to keep from crying. "I know it sounds mushy and I know Kipp probably made up the story, but when he told it at the graduation, it was just . . . perfect."

"I like the story," Tony said, hugging her as they walked.

She hesitated. "Can you tell me how it was?"

He did not answer right away and for a moment she was afraid she had trod where she shouldn't have. He was listening, however, to a train far off, miles it must have been, its fast and heavy passage rolling toward them like the thunder of a distant but approaching storm. Perhaps it reminded him, as it did her, of that terrible night. But of course no rain followed in its wake and soon it had vanished all together.

"We went to the mountains," he said finally. "It was a pretty place, next to a lake. Neil liked it. I used my parents' credit card and rented a cabin. I called my mom and dad and told them that I needed to be alone for a while and, what with all that had been going on, they thought that was fine. We stayed there the whole week, had great weather. In the morning, these deer would come right up to the door and we would feed them. At least Neil would—they always ran when they saw me." He shook his head, squeezing her arm. "Hey, this shouldn't sound so soapy. Neil was happy this last week. He was in a lot of pain, he refused to take any drugs, and he got so he couldn't walk, but he was his old peaceful self. The Caretaker, the man, all that garbage was gone. We didn't even talk about it. We just talked about old times: movies we'd seen, music we liked, places we'd gone. And we talked about you."

"What did he say?" she asked, smiling, wiping her eyes.

"Nice things. You would have been pleased." He let go of her and stretched his arms and spine backward, drinking up the sun like a man who had spent too long in a dark place. "Mainly, though, we just sat by the lake and skimmed rocks and that was good. I fixed him up this old cushiony chair next to the water and he was comfortable enough." A shadow, neither long nor deep, brushed over his face. "He was sitting in it yesterday morning when he died."

Their walk was taking them into a dead end and she pointed to a break in the wall that enclosed the tract, and they passed through it out into the tall dry grass and the low gnarled bushes, the field stretching practically unchecked to the mountains. Insects buzzed at their feet—none appeared bloodthirsty—and a large orange butterfly circled above their heads. Far to the right atop a low bluff, a clan of rabbits gave them a cursory glance before continuing with more important business. She felt her eyes drying and noticed that Tony's smile had returned.

"There was one thing he did that sort of reminded me of the Caretaker," he said. "It was quite clever. Before his *first* funeral, he asked me to do him two favors. One was to give you the ring, the other—I hope this doesn't *disturb* you—was to bury him next to the man in the event the Caretaker killed him."

"I'm fine now, really, go on."

He burst out laughing; it certainly seemed an unusual time to do so. "Well, before he died yesterday, he made me swear that I would bury him *in* the man's grave!" He paused, waiting for her reaction, which surely must have been inadequate—she didn't know what to say. "Don't you see, Ali, he knew I'd be feeling so guilty that I'd turn myself in when he was gone. And he was right, I was going to do that. But now how was I supposed to turn myself in without evidence? He'd disposed of the man's body in the fire—which, by the way, actually helped his mother out financially, what with the insurance money and all—and now he'd rigged it so I couldn't even take the police to the man's grave." He added wistfully, "When it suited him, Neil could be funnier than Kipp."

Their big orange butterfly escort landed on top of a huge yellow boulder. Alison stopped and rested her open palm near it and was delighted when it skipped into her hand. "That hasn't happened since I was a kid," she whispered.

"You must have gotten your innocence back."

"Do you think so?" she asked seriously.

He shrugged. "I was just mumbling."

She raised her hand and blew gently and the butterfly flew away. The last couple of months had been the most intense time of her life, and it seemed wrong that she could have learned nothing from the experience. She leaned against the boulder and looked up at the blue sky and thought for a moment, before saying, "I don't know about my innocence, but I know I'm not such a stuck-up bitch anymore."

He squeezed her shoulder. "I never saw you that way."

"A lot of people did."

"Neil wasn't one of them."

"But he was the one who made me aware of it. I'll never again brush someone off the way I did him. The next time someone cares about me, I'm going to know about it." She took his hand from her shoulder and kissed it lightly. She was feeling sad again, but it was a sweet sadness, and she was glad for it. "You've lost your best friend, and I've lost my greatest admirer. I can't take Neil's place, but can you take his?"

He stared at her for a moment, his eyes the same rich blue as the sky, then shook his head. "No," he said, and pulled her into his arms. "But I'll still do the best I can."

THE ANCIENT EVIL

For Neil

Prologue

The chain letter came as it had before. First to Fran Darey—in a purple envelope with no return address. It came totally out of the blue, and like the original letter, it carried with it a threat of danger. And like before, at first no one listened.

Until it was too late.

Fran Darey was just returning home from a morning of hard work when she collected the mail. Summer was almost over and so was her job at the local mall. She worked at the McDonald's, and although it would be fair to say she did not hate her job, it would also have been fair to say she was never going to work in a fast-food joint again. The job didn't allow her to use her full physical and mental potential. Heck, she was going to college in a few weeks. She was going to get straight A's and graduate in four years and make the world a better place.

She was never going to have to worry how many more fries there were in a big scoop versus a medium scoop—a question she had been asked three times that day by smart-mouthed junior high kids.

But too soon Fran would have wished to have such mundane problems.

A strange thing happened as Fran reached to remove the mail from her parents' mailbox. Even before she touched or saw the purple envelope, she thought of Neil Hurly. She had of course thought of Neil many times over the course of the summer, since he had died of a horrible cancer. But no thought had ever come to her so strong. A cold sweat rose on the back of her neck, and a tear formed in the corner of one eye. She had loved Neil, she thought, and she had never told him. She couldn't imagine what could be worse in life. Never once, in the weeks following the incident with the chain letter, had she blamed him for what had happened. He had been sick, after all. He had not been evil.

"Miss you," Fran whispered under her breath. She almost turned and glanced over her shoulder right then, his presence was so strong. He could have been standing right behind her.

It was a pity he wasn't. He might have stopped her hand.

Fran reached inside the box and took out the mail.

She noticed the purple envelope immediately.

No, Jesus, no, she thought.

Her heart almost stopped. But her hands did not. Dropping all the other letters and bills and assorted junk mail, her fingers tore into the purple envelope and pulled out the letter inside. She began to read.

My Dearest,

You thought you knew me, but you did not. You thought I was your friend, but I am not. I am the real Caretaker, and I am going to take care of you. Listen closely. . . .

Standing alone outside her house, Fran screamed. Her throat was tight; the sound came out pitifully thin and high. It was doubtful her nearest neighbor could have heard. But the sound of her scream was to echo over the next few days, until it became a full-fledged wail. Her scream was the beginning, if the chain of the letters could be said to have a beginning—or an end.

Chapter One

At the time the second wave of chain letters began, Tony Hunt and Alison Parker were trying to decide whether to make love or never speak to each other again. The situation was filled with contradictions. They were alone in Alison's house. Her parents were not going to be home for several hours. Neither of them was a virgin. In fact, they were each responsible for their mutual lack of virginity. They had been true to each other the few months they had been dating. They were both healthy, and in a sense they were both willing. But neither of them was happy. That was the main contradiction.

Alison thought the problem was Tony's fault, and although Tony was normally not one to place blame, he thought it was Alison's fault. It was she, after all, who had decided to go to college three thousand miles away instead of thirty. The situation had arisen only the previous week when Alison had received a rather surprisingly late invitation to attend NYU to study drama. That was New York University in New York City, on the other side of the country from UCLA, where Alison had been planning to go. Alison had already called the airlines. It took a modern jet five hours to get to New York. For Tony that was an awful long way to have his girl fly. He was going to miss her—boy, was he going to.

But Tony was not unreasonable. He could understand that it was a wonderful opportunity for Alison. She had initially applied to NYU and been turned down because the competition to get in their highly rated drama department was unbelievable. He knew there would be great teachers in New York, and she would learn great things. Yet he also knew that UCLA had an excellent drama department, and that when all things were factored in and set down in two lists—one of pros and one of cons—the fact that he was in Los Angeles, and not in New York, should have been a major factor. And that was why he was upset. Because Alison was acting as if she couldn't understand why he was upset. She was acting as if she didn't care.

He hoped she was acting. He really did love her, more than he liked to admit to himself.

At present Alison was pacing back and forth between the kitchen and the living room, wearing a towel on her head and a towel around her midsection and nothing else. She often paced when she was angry. Lately she had been wearing out the carpet. He was still fully dressed, but if they hadn't started fighting, he would have been in bed with her by now. That was another thing that bugged him. She was mad that he hadn't *at least* waited until they had had sex to bring up her relocation venture. Damn, he thought, wasn't that uncool of him. He didn't have one of those push-button physiologies they wrote about in *Cosmopolitan.* He couldn't be intimate when his mind was going ten thousand miles an hour. He wasn't a space shuttle, for godsake. But turmoil was no obstacle to her.

"We can talk all we want while I'm away," Alison said. "There are things called phones. People all over the world use them to stay close to the ones they love."

Tony grunted. "I've heard about them. You have to pay for minutes."

"We don't have to talk that much," Alison said.

"You mean, we don't have to stay that close?"

Alison finally sat on the couch beside him and angrily crossed her legs. The towel on her head was white. The other was pink. It went well with her very tan legs. She glared at him.

"I don't understand why you're trying to make me feel guilty," she said.

"I'm not trying to make you feel guilty."

"Yes, you are."

"No, I'm not."

"You are."

He shrugged. "All right."

"Don't just say all right. Answer me. Why are you doing this to me?"

Tony threw up his hands in frustration. "What am I doing to you? You're doing it to me. You're leaving me. I'm not leaving you. You have it backward."

Alison put on her patient face, which at the moment was a mask of poorly concealed exasperation. But he couldn't help enjoying her expression, maybe because it belonged to her. Her beauty was unusual, her features at odds with one another, but in a way that somehow brought them together into a whole that was greater than its parts. Her big eyes and her wide mouth were classics. The rest of her, though—her button nose and thick eyebrows—was supposed to be out of style. That was what *Cosmopolitan* would say. But Alison always had style. She had enough for the next sixty years, in his opinion.

And now her style will have a New York flavor.

Her only physical flaw was her left arm. It was badly scarred from her battle with Neil.

"We wouldn't be three thousand miles apart if you had accepted that football scholarship to Boston," Alison said with exaggerated patience. "That was your choice, not mine. Boston would have been just up the road. I refuse to accept full responsibility for this separation."

"They offered me that scholarship seven months ago," Tony said dryly. "Nobody was going to New York seven months ago. Nobody was even going together then."

Alison tapped his leg as if she had just received a brilliant idea. "I bet they still want you! Why don't you give them a call? We can call them right now." She stood. "I'll get their number."

He grabbed her arm, stopping her. "The football team is probably practicing as we speak. I can't just call them and tell them I want to be their next starting quarterback." He let go of her arm. "Besides, I told you, I don't want to play anymore."

She was impatient. "Why not? You're a gifted athlete. How many people are born with an arm like yours? Your talent can open up whole worlds for you. God gave you your abilities to use, not to run away from."

Now she was cutting low. She knew why he didn't want to play football anymore. In the middle of his fabulous senior season, he'd hurt his back. At first it had seemed like no big deal. In fact, he'd even gone out for track and done well. But backs were funny, his doctor told him. You could injure them and not feel the full impact of the injury for several months. Shortly after graduation and Neil's death, he started to wake up in the middle of the night in pain. It was mainly in his lower back, but if he turned the wrong way in bed or bent over too far during the day, the pain would shoot into his legs like burning needles slipped into his nerves. He was presently seeing a chiropractor three times a week, and that was helping. The chiropractor thought he'd heal up just fine, as long as he avoided being crunched by two-hundred-and-fifty-pound linemen. But Alison thought chiropractors were quacks, and she often hinted that his injury might be psychosomatic. Yeah, right, he thought sarcastically, it was all in his head. Somebody should tell his back that.

But sometimes Tony wondered if his pain was indirectly related to Neil's death. He often thought about Neil when he lay awake at night. Supposedly time healed grief, but if that was true, time was taking its sweet time. He missed Neil as much as he had the day Neil died.

But sometimes he felt as if Neil were still right there, beside him. Like a hovering angel. He would turn suddenly and expect to catch Neil's sweet sad smile. Of course he never did. It was all just wishful thinking.

"It seems to me," Tony said softly, "that we've talked for hours about why I don't want to play anymore. I'm sure you remember. It has something to do with my back."

"How do you know your back just doesn't need a little exercise?" Alison asked.

"Having your vertebrae pulverized by oncoming helmets does not constitute exercise."

Alison shook herself and almost lost one of her towels. "Why is it we can't talk without you getting sarcastic? You never used to be this way."

"I guess this is just the way I am." Tony was suddenly tired of the argument "What do you want to do? If you want to go to New York—go. I won't stop you."

"But you will make me feel guilty about it. You don't mind doing that."

Tony shrugged. "I guess I'm just feeling sorry for myself."

"Why?"

Tony looked right at her. A wet curl of her long dark hair hung over her right cheek, near her eye. He reached out and brushed it away, and for a moment he touched her soft skin and a thousand gentle memories flooded his mind. But he didn't let his touch linger because the memories only made him sad.

"Because I'm going to miss you," he told her. "I'm going to miss you more than I can stand."

She softened slightly. "I'm going to miss you, too, Tony. You know that."

He continued to stare at her. She was so beautiful. She would be just as beautiful in New York. The guys there would surely agree.

"You'll meet someone else," he said.

She was offended. "That's ridiculous."

"It's reality. You're young. You're pretty. I'll be on the other side of the country." He nodded. "It'll happen—sooner than you think."

She stood, mad. "You don't put much stock in my loyalty, do you? What do you think I am, a slut? I can't believe you just said what you did. You have some nerve."

Tony wondered if he had said too much. The problem was—he had just spoken his mind honestly. All during high school girls had pursued him. He had no false modesty about his good looks. He was a blond, blue-eyed, all-American boy, built like a stud. Alison had chased after him at first, too, but now that she was suddenly leaving, it was he who was attached. The experience was new to him, and he hated it. The thought of her dating other guys plagued him like a virus, and he couldn't be free of it. If he imagined her kissing another guy, he would actually become sick to his stomach.

And what made it all worse was that he *was* being realistic. Long-distance romances just didn't work, not when you were eighteen years old. She would meet new guys in New York, and that would be the end of Tony and Alison. In a way he was getting what he deserved. He had, after all, stolen Alison from Neil.

But that's not true. Neil and Alison were never a couple, except in Neil's head.

Then again, maybe he and Alison were only a couple in his head.

"You're not a slut," he said and sighed. "I'm sorry I said what I did."

She continued to stand. "You're trying to hurt me."

"I'm not. I said I was sorry."

"It's a great opportunity for me."

"I understand that."

"Then why can't you be happy for me?" she asked.

"I am happy for you. I'm just more unhappy for me. And I can't understand—Oh, never mind." He stood. "I should go."

It was her turn to stop him. "No. Say what you were going to say."

"It was nothing."

"I want to hear it. What can't you understand?"

Tony looked at her once more. The towel on her head had shifted to the right side and now there was a whole handful of wet hair he could brush away. But he couldn't bear to touch her again. If he did, he knew he wouldn't be able to leave, and he had to get away. It was better to end things between them now—so she wouldn't have to dump him later with a Dear John letter.

"I can't understand how you can just leave me," he said. When she began to protest, he raised his hand. "No. Let's not argue anymore. It's the difference between us. I would never leave you."

Alison's eyes moistened, and she clenched her hands in frustration. "I love you just as much as you love me. How can you say that?"

He shook his head. "I've got to go." He turned away. "Have fun in New York."

She called to him as he walked toward the door, and by now she was crying openly. "What's that supposed to mean? You're going for good? I don't leave for another two weeks. You're not even going to come back to say goodbye? Tony!"

He paused at the door, keeping his back to her. "You can do what you want," he said. "You have my permission."

"I'm not going to do anything!" she cried, moving closer. "I love you. I just want to be with you."

He glanced over his shoulder. "Then stay, Ali. Stay."

Her face was a mess of tears. Yet she was also wearing her old friend—her pride. Alison was a proud girl. He had recognized that about her not long after they had met. She wanted to be an actress. No, she wanted to be a famous actress. She wanted admirers. He'd had those once. He'd been the toast of the town when he'd led their high school team to the city championship. But being popular had meant nothing to him. Certainly it had not been worth the price of a bad back. That was another difference between them. Another reason why he should break it off now. Her tearful face was suddenly not so soft.

"I have to go," she said.

"Then go," he said. He opened the door. "Goodbye."

"Tony!"

He let the door close behind him without answering her. Had he paused on the porch, he might not have been able to leave. But he didn't pause, and the chain of letters had fertile ground to begin again.

Chapter Two

That same afternoon Alison Parker had a date with Brenda Paxson to go shopping for clothes for Alison—warm things to wear in the cold East Coast fall and winter. That morning Alison had had fun planning the stores they would visit and the money they would spend. Alison's mother had given her a gold credit card with the dangerous instruction to buy what she needed. To Alison that was the next thing to heaven. Yet as Alison drove toward Brenda's house, she was far from a happy camper. She was dismayed by Tony's reaction to her leaving. She thought he was being immature about the whole matter. He wasn't acting at all like the guy she had fallen in love with. That Tony had been as cool as an unlit candle and as secure as a rock. This new guy was clinging to her like an emotional cripple. Sure, he was going to miss her.

She was going to miss him. But life was like that. People had to go their separate ways sometimes. It didn't mean they had to break up. God, she hoped not. She wasn't interested in anybody except Tony. Even when he was in one of his moods, he was still pretty right on, and he was the only guy she had ever really cared about. She had been dying to hold him earlier, but he had walked out on her. He could be really weird at times.

Brenda was standing outside her house, watering the lawn, when Alison drove up. She had a red bow in her shiny blond hair and ass-kissing black shorts that showed off her lithe figure. She seemed to be happy, and Alison hoped she was. Brenda wouldn't be starting college with the rest of them. Her parents were having financial difficulties, and she had to work to help out. She was currently employed by a shipping company and making good money. She didn't seem to mind the work, and Alison wondered if Brenda wasn't relieved to be taking a break from studying. Brenda had never been one to hit the books.

"You're early," Brenda called, throwing down the running hose on the lawn. "I haven't had a chance to change."

Alison climbed out of her car and brushed her hair back. It was a warm day, but windy. It had taken her an hour to drive to her friend's house from her own. They had grown up around the block from each other, but Alison's family moved to a new housing tract just weeks before the two girls graduated from high school. The tract had been practically deserted back in June, and it had been there that Neil, in the guise of the Caretaker, had attacked her.

Poor Neil, she thought. He'd been so sick at the time.

Better not think about him. She knew Tony still did, which was probably a big part of his problem with her leaving. Neil had been Tony's best friend, and best friends were not easy to replace.

"You're dressed as well as you want to be," Alison said, walking toward her own best friend. "You love nothing better than sliding around the mall scantily clad."

Brenda turned off the hose. "Really, Ali, I think I have more dignity than that."

"If you do, you keep it well hidden."

Brenda wiped her hands on her shorts and reached for her sneakers, which were sitting on the front porch. "And what was Miss Conservative doing just before she drove over to pick up her loose friend? Enjoying carnal pleasures with her boyfriend perhaps?"

Alison felt her face fall, although she tried her best to hold it up. "No," she said softly. "Not really."

Brenda was instantly alert to the change in her tone. "Did you and Tony have a fight?" she asked, concerned.

Alison put a hand to her head. It was handy place for it—a moment later she was wiping away a tear. "He's mad at me," Alison said sadly. "I don't know—maybe I shouldn't leave. In a way I don't want to."

"That's nonsense," Brenda said, slinging an arm around her

friend's shoulder. "Going to NYU is a dream come true for you. Tony's just got to grow up and understand that he doesn't own you."

"But he's right, I could go to UCLA. They have a fine drama department, and then we could still see each other." She sniffed. "Maybe I am only thinking of myself."

"You have to think about yourself," Brenda said, turning once more for her shoes. "Now, I'm going to say something and don't take it wrong. What if you do decide to stay here, and Tony and you break up in six months?"

"We're not going to break up," Alison said quickly.

"But what if you do? People do, you know. Then what? You'll be mad as hell at Tony and yourself for ruining your big chance. You'll have thrown it away and gotten nothing in return. Take my advice, sister, and go to New York and find a new boyfriend there."

Alison shook her head. "You don't understand. I love Tony."

Brenda sat to tie her shoelaces. "So what? I love Kipp. That doesn't mean I let him run my life. Don't get me wrong. I like Tony. He's a babe, and he's got manners. But we're young. We're going to be in love dozens of times before it's all over."

Alison raised her eyes to peer at the sky, through the thin haze of smog that hung over the city. Everything Brenda said made sense. Yet it felt wrong. Alison lifted an arm to shield her eyes from the glare.

"There's only one sun," Alison said with feeling. "It's always the same, but it's always the best. Do you know what I mean?"

Brenda snickered at the sentiment as she finished her shoes. "Guys are a dime a dozen. They come and go like streetcars."

Alison lowered her hand, her eyes. "Tony's not a streetcar."

Brenda changed the subject. "Fran called. She left a message on our machine. She said it was vital I call her immediately. Sounds like Fran, huh? Should I call her before we leave?"

"No." Alison sighed. "Let's stop by her house. She might want to come with us."

"All right," Brenda said.

Fran didn't answer the door when Alison and Brenda knocked. When they peeked inside, they were surprised that Fran was sitting at the kitchen table. She should have heard them knocking. The *L.A. Times* lay spread out on the table in front of her.

"Hello?" Brenda said to Fran as Brenda and Alison stepped all the way inside. "Are we in? Are we happy? Is life good?"

Fran didn't answer. She continued to sit with her face buried in her hands. Fran was often overly emotional, so neither Alison nor Brenda was unduly concerned. Alison crossed to the table and touched Fran on the back.

"It can't be that bad," Alison told her.

In response Fran removed her hands from her face and stared at them both with red eyes. Without saying a word, she fished under the paper and withdrew a purple envelope. She held it out with a trembling hand for one of them to take. Alison felt afraid as her eyes fell upon it, even before she realized the envelope was the same color and shape as the ones Neil's chain letters had been sent in. She forced a laugh.

"Don't tell me it's another chain letter?" Alison said.

Fran nodded. Her voice came out like a croak. "Yeah."

"Let me see that thing," Brenda snapped, pulling the letter out of Fran's fingers. She ripped the letter out. Alison peered over Brenda's shoulder, and they read it together.

My Dearest,

You thought you knew me, but you did not. You thought I was your friend, but I am not. I am the real Caretaker, and I am going to take care of you. Listen closely.

At the bottom of this communication is a list of names. Your name is at the top. What is required of you—at present—is a small token of obedience. After you have performed this small service, you will remove your name from Column III and place it in the box. Once you are in the box, you will stay in the box. Then you will make a copy of this communication and mail it to the individual now at the top of Column III. The specifics of the small service you are to perform will be listed in the classified ads of the Times *under Personals—in backward code. The individual following you on the list must receive this letter within three days of today.*

Feel free to discuss this communication with the others on the list. Like myself, they are not your friends, but they do know all your sins. Do not discuss this communication with anyone outside the group. If you do, you will anger me.

If you do not perform the small service listed in the paper or if you break the chain of this communication, you will be horribly killed.

Sincerely,
Your Caretaker

Column III
Fran
Kipp
Brenda
Joan
Tony

For a full minute none of them spoke or moved. It was as it had been a few months earlier. They were in the same place. They had the same kind of letter in their hands—the same kind of fear in their hearts. Yet their fear was different, too. Months ago they'd had no idea of the horror that would follow the letter. At first they had thought it might be a joke. Now their fear was based on bitter experience. Yet it would lead them to the same conclusion as before. Brenda was the first to say it out loud.

"This is a bad joke," she said and crumpled up the letter. Alison stopped her.

"Wait a second," Alison said, taking it out of Brenda's hands. "I want to study this thing."

"What's there to study?" Brenda asked angrily. "One of the others sent it to scare us. It was probably Joan."

"What about Kipp?" Alison asked.

"It could have been Kipp," Brenda was quick to agree. "What did I tell you about guys? They're a pain in the ass all around. Let's toss this thing and get to the mall. I'm hungry."

"It's not a joke," Fran whispered.

"Of course it is," Brenda said, sounding as if she were addressing a small child. "Neil's dead. He's not sending any more letters."

Fran nodded to the paper. "There's an ad under Personals in there." Fran trembled. "It's for me."

Alison grabbed the paper. It took her only a second to spot the ad. Fran had worked out the code on the empty column beside it. The original ad read: NARFTHGINOTYPPUPRUOYNWORD. Decoded it said:

Drown your puppy tonight, Fran.

Alison's face twisted in disgust. "This is sick. Kipp wouldn't place an ad like this."

Brenda glanced at it and shook her head. "It must have been Joan, then. Anybody who dresses like her has got to be sick."

"But Joan likes animals," Alison said. "She has a dog. She wouldn't want Fran to drown her puppy."

Brenda was getting exasperated. "Of course Joan doesn't expect Fran to drown her puppy. She knows Fran isn't that stupid. She's just trying to scare us. She has to say something weird."

Alison stared once more at the letter. It was neatly typed, as Neil's had been. It was not a photocopy. "I don't know," she muttered.

Brenda lost her temper. "What don't you know? The wording and ideas of this letter are almost identical to the ones Neil sent us. The person who sent this couldn't even be bothered thinking up something original. It has to be someone in the group. We're the only ones who knew about the chain letters."

"Will you quit yelling at me," Alison said.

"I am not yelling at you!" Brenda yelled.

"Yes, you are," Fran said.

"Well, if I am it's your fault," Brenda yelled at Fran. "Why didn't you throw this thing away when you got it and not bother us with it? We've got stuff to do. We've got to go shopping."

Alison sat down at the table, studying the column of names at the bottom. "How come I'm not on this list?" she asked.

"It doesn't matter who's there," Brenda said impatiently.

"I think it does," Alison said. "If someone in the group was trying to play a joke on us, then he or she would have known to include my name. They would have known that I had been involved before."

"Are you saying that the person who sent this letter doesn't know exactly what happened before?" Fran asked.

"I think it's possible," Alison said, and the possibility filled her with dread. If someone outside their group knew even a little about what had happened the summer before, then they were in hot water. After all, they had accidentally run over a man in the desert.

At least, they thought they had run over him. They had been driving blind at night, with their lights out. For all they knew, the man could have been lying dead when they hit him. The man had had no wallet. They had never even been able to identify him. But one thing was for sure, they had buried him, and they hadn't told the police about it, and that was a punishable crime.

"Doesn't this discussion strike any of you as familiar?" Brenda asked. "We had it a couple of months ago. We thought the letter must be from someone in the group, but then we figured it couldn't be one of us 'cause it was too weird. Well, it turned out to be Neil, and he was with us that night. It'll be the same this time."

"Are you saying someone else in the group has gone insane?" Fran asked.

"Yes," Brenda said. "You and Alison for believing this garbage."

Alison stood. "We have to call the others. Let's call Kipp and Tony."

"I'd call Joan first myself," Brenda said. "She'll probably bust up laughing."

"I don't want to call Joan," Alison said. Tony had gone out

a few times with Joan before he had started to date her. Joan had never forgiven her for stealing the guy she considered to be her boyfriend. It was all absurd—Tony said he hadn't even made out with Joan.

Alison set the letter beside the phone and dialed Tony's number. She got his voice mail. She didn't leave a message. She tried Kipp's number. Tony had said something earlier about going over to see Kipp. But she got Kipp's voice mail as well. She left a message for him to call her. She didn't say anything about the chain letter. She called Tony back and left a similar message on his voice mail. Then, reluctantly, she tried Joan. She got another voice mail. The world was full of them. She left a message for Joan to call ASAP.

"I think we should wait here until we get one of them on the phone," Alison said, setting the receiver down.

"What?" Brenda complained. "We're going to blow out the rest of the day because of a stupid letter? Give me a break. If you're not going to the mall, I am. Give me your car keys."

"No," Alison said. "You're going to shut up and sit here and wait with Fran and me. This letter may be a joke. It probably is. But it might be serious, and if it is, we have to stick together. That's what we learned last time. All right?"

Brenda sat down with a big huff. "I didn't learn anything last time—except to stay away from the mailbox."

It may have been a coincidence, or the dog may have been psychic and known he was being discussed. In either case, Fran's puppy suddenly ran into the kitchen and began to lick his master's hands. Fran reached down and patted the cute little brown cocker spaniel on the head. An anxious smile touched her lips.

"It must be a joke," Fran said. "No one could want Barney dead. No one could think I'd actually drown him."

"I'm sure you're right," Alison replied. But a chill went through her as she thought about what Fran had just said. Alison stared at the letter again. The *small service* was absolutely unthinkable. Perhaps this Caretaker wasn't the least bit interested in seeing Barney dead. Maybe he was only interested in having an excuse to harm Fran.

Chapter Three

Tony Hunt didn't leave Alison Parker's house and drive straight to Kipp's. He stopped at the mall near his house first. He was hungry, and there were a dozen different places to eat there. Also, at the back of his mind, he hoped to *accidentally* run into Alison, who was supposed to go shopping with Brenda. He thought this was pretty ironic since he had just walked out on Alison. But he was beginning to accept as normal the contradictions between his thoughts and his actions. Nowadays his whole existence seemed one vast vat of confusion.

Tony didn't know what was wrong with himself. Alison was leaving town, of course, but if he was completely honest with himself, he had to admit that he had been feeling anxious even before her invitation from NYU arrived. He tried to rationalize that the pain in his back must be throwing him off more than he realized. Yet he had been hurt before and hadn't lost his sense of inner stability. As he examined his feelings, the clearer it became that his sense of confusion and foreboding had started with the arrival of Neil's chain letter. Yet his anxiety hadn't culminated with Neil's death and then begun to heal. It continued even now to hang over his head. He missed Neil terribly, sure, but why the continuing feelings of anxiety and foreboding? Why not simply sorrow and loneliness? Those emotions would have been natural and easily explainable. It was almost as if nothing had ended with Neil's death, except Neil.

Tony parked in the warm sun and walked into the mall. The cool air and shopper sounds enfolded him like a hug. He liked malls, which was odd because he seldom bought anything. But he could walk around in a mall for an hour and just observe people—so preoccupied with their latest purchases, so delighted with the silliest little things. He watched them but always felt separate from them. In fact, he felt closer to the mannequins in the windows. The silent observers. Hadn't that been a line from Neil's chain letter? *I am the Observer, the Recorder. I am also the Punisher.* Tony felt as if he were still being punished for a crime he wasn't even sure he had committed. This was another feeling that had only begun in the last few months, long after they had buried the man in the desert.

Tony went to the food circle. His tastes were uncreative. He ordered a hamburger, fries, and a Coke from the McDonald's—he figured he couldn't go wrong with that. He had hoped Fran

Darey might be working. The cashier told him that Fran had already left for the day. Fran was a high-strung worrywart, but she always had a smile and a kind word for him. Tony could hardly remember the last time Alison had looked happy to see him. God, girls changed when you got to know them. They turned into people with problems. People who wanted you to solve their problems.

Tony took his food into the center of the tables and sat beside the good-luck fountain, where for a tossed penny and a silent prayer all your wishes might come true. Tony pulled a nickel from his pocket and threw it into the splashing water. It was a good throw; it landed on the top circular tier. Alison was right—he had a hell of an arm. But no wish came to his mind, only the desire that his unhappiness be gone. He picked up his hamburger and took a bite. They had cooked it well done, just the way he liked it. A soft laugh sounded to his right.

"I make a wish every day at this time," a girl said. "I don't know if they don't come true because I don't know what I want or because I only use a penny."

Tony looked over and was surprised to see a beautiful young woman at the next table. Her hair was long and shiny, an odd maroon so deep red it was almost black. Her green eyes shone bright above her full lips, which were painted a warm red. Her face was pale, but cute freckles played around her shapely nose and her innocent dimples. She was drinking a cup of coffee and reading a magazine. Her dress was entirely white, like that of a nurse. She smiled as his eyes met hers, and he found himself smiling in return.

"Maybe we should use quarters," he said.

She nodded. "Then we could do a month's worth of wishing in one throw."

He gestured around them. "You come here a lot?"

"For lunch, yeah. I work near here. At the hospital."

"What do you do?"

She made a face. "Today I'm drawing blood. Exciting, huh?"

"You don't like your job?"

She shrugged. "It's a job. It pays the bills. What do you do?"

He didn't want to sound as if he'd just graduated from high school. He put her age at about twenty-one, two years older than he was. "I'm in college," he muttered.

"I was in college once. Where do you go?"

It was his plan to attend a local junior college for the first two years. Without an athletic scholarship, he couldn't afford anything else. But he gave Alison's first choice of schools because it sounded more impressive. He didn't know why he wanted to impress this girl. It wasn't normally his style.

"UCLA," he said.

"That's where I went to school! It's a neat campus, isn't it?"

"I like it."

"What's your major?" she asked. She had a wonderful voice. It conveyed warmth and excitement at the same time.

"I'd like to be a teacher," he said. "But I haven't settled on a definite major."

"It's a bitch having to choose, isn't it? I'm not even in school, and I'm still changing my major." She nodded to his food. "Your hamburger's getting cold. I should leave you alone and let you eat."

Tony paused. She was right. He should finish his food and get on with his day. Kipp would be waiting for him. But he suddenly realized he was enjoying himself, chatting with this stranger about odds and ends. He used to have fun with Alison like this, back when they could communicate.

"I can eat and talk at the same time," he said. "What's your name?"

"Sasha." She offered her hand across the five feet that separated them. "What's yours?"

"Tony Hunt." He shook her hand. Her skin was soft, like Alison's, but her grip was firm. "I'm pleased to meet you, Sasha."

She smiled again. Her teeth were a little crooked, but still nice. "You know, you look kind of familiar," she said. "Have I seen you before?"

He suspected she had seen his picture in the papers, extolling his accomplishments on the football field. He didn't want to tell her that though. Then she would know he had just graduated. Besides, she might want to talk about football, and nothing bored him more.

"You might have seen me here," he said. "I come here often enough."

"I suppose." She frowned slightly. "Is there something wrong with your neck or your back?"

She had caught him off guard. "Why do you ask?"

"The way you hold yourself. You look stiff."

His chiropractor had been able to spot the problem just by looking at him, but no one else had ever commented on it before. Sasha must be a very perceptive young woman, he thought.

"It's an old sports injury," he said. "It flares up every now and then."

"I'm considering being a physical therapist," Sasha said. "I'll have to go back to school to get certified, but I've been studying a lot on my own about deep-tissue massage. You should get a massage. It can give tremendous relief."

Tony smiled shyly but spoke boldly. "If you ever want someone to practice on, give me a call."

Sasha surprised him. "I could give you a massage." She reached for her purse. "You can give me a call if you want one."

Tony shifted uncomfortably in his seat. Although he was pleased that he might be seeing Sasha again, guilt weighed heavy on him. If Alison had solicited the number of another guy, and he caught her, he would have been furious. On the other hand, he thought, Alison would probably be giving out her number soon enough—in New York. Besides, it wasn't like he was making a date with Sasha. She was just going to give him a massage. . . .

"That's very nice of you," he said. "I wouldn't mind trying it— What did you call it?"

"A deep-tissue massage." She scribbled down her number on a scrap of paper and handed it to him. "It was nice to meet you, Tony." She grabbed her purse and stood up. "Call me any evening. I'm usually home."

He studied her number. It was local. He stood to say goodbye to her. "It was nice meeting you, Sasha."

She smiled one last time and tapped him lightly on the shoulder as she turned away. She had a sweet smile, innocent and carefree.

"Later," she said.

"Yeah, sure," he replied. He watched as she disappeared in the crowd. He had been so enchanted with her voice and face, he had hardly noticed her excellent figure, much fuller than Alison's.

Enchanted.

There had been something enchanting about Sasha. Tony looked once more at the number in his hand and stuffed it in his pocket. He left the mall without finishing his lunch.

Kipp Coughlan was pulling into his driveway when Tony Hunt arrived at his house. Tony parked behind him and got out of his car.

"I'm glad you weren't waiting for me," Tony said.

"Were you here earlier?" Kipp asked, his expression good-natured as usual. He had fair hair, a big nose, and even bigger ears, which made him appear silly. But his dark eyes were sharp, and so was his mind. Kipp was heading for MIT in a couple of weeks to study aeronautical engineering. He had been the class valedictorian.

"No. I stopped at the mall for a bite," Tony said.

"Too bad, I was hoping we could eat together." Kipp walked toward his front door, a brown paper bag in his hand. "I'm watching Leslie."

Leslie was Kipp's little sister. They were devoted to each other. She was seven years old and every bit as smart as her brother.

"Did you go out and leave her alone?" Tony asked, following Kipp into the house. Kipp gestured to the bag he was carrying.

"I had to," Kipp said. "She found an injured bird in the backyard. Its wing is broken. A cat might have got hold of it. Anyway, she ordered me to go get it birdseed while she tended to it. She said if she left the bird, it would die."

Just then Leslie appeared in the living room. She didn't have her brother's ears, but she had his nose. She could best be described as charming rather than pretty. Her fair hair was the same shade as Kipp's, and they had similar mannerisms, the most noticeable being the tendency to talk with their hands when they were excited. Leslie was excited now. She hurried to collect the birdseed.

"Hi, Tony," she said. "Did Kipp tell you about the bird with the broken wing that flew in my window?"

"Yes," Tony said, glancing at Kipp and smiling. "He told me you were nursing it back to health. That's kind of you—helping the poor thing."

"Did you get the baby bird kind?" Leslie asked Kipp as she peered into the bag.

"I didn't know baby birds ate different food from big birds," Kipp said. He gave the bag to his sister. "I bet the bird doesn't know the difference, either."

"I bet he does," Leslie said seriously, running off with the bag.

"Cute," Tony said, watching her go.

"Yeah. Too bad we can't bottle it and sell it." Kipp headed for the stairs. "Did you see Alison today?"

"Yeah."

"How was it?"

"How was what?" Tony asked, following him up to the second floor.

"The sex."

"We didn't have sex."

"Why not?" Kipp asked.

"We don't have sex every time we get together. I'm sure you and Brenda don't, either."

"Yeah, but we have an excuse."

"What's that?" Tony asked.

"Brenda isn't attracted to me."

They entered Kipp's bedroom. Tony noticed the faded bloodstain on the carpet. When Neil, in his Caretaker craziness, had abducted Kipp, he had soaked the bed and surrounding area with blood. Only later had they learned that the blood had been Neil's, slowly siphoned from his veins over a period of time. It still boggled Tony that Neil, in his weakened condition, had had the strength to kidnap Kipp. Neil had done a lot of amazing things back during the days of the chain letters—some were almost supernatural.

"I'm always happy when I come in my room and see that someone's called me," Kipp said, reaching for his phone. "Usually it's just Brenda or you or somebody trying to sell me life insurance. But just before I check the messages, I always have a hope that a gorgeous babe has seen me on the street, somehow found out my number, and has called to ask me out. I don't know why I never stop hoping."

"Aren't you and Brenda getting along?" Tony asked, sitting on the edge of the bed.

"We're going through a rough period right now."

"Any particular reason?"

"I think it's because she doesn't like me anymore."

"I know the feeling," Tony mumbled.

Kipp was surprised. "Is Ali still going to New York?"

"Looks like it."

"What a bitch. You're better off without her."

"I guess," Tony said miserably. He shook his head. "Doesn't

it depress you when Brenda acts like she doesn't care?"

"No. I'm used to it. It depresses me when she doesn't want to have sex. But I'm getting used to that, too. Just a second, let's see who called."

Kipp played his messages. There was only one. It was from Alison, and she sounded worried. She wanted Kipp to call her at Fran's house as soon as he got in. Kipp looked at Tony for an explanation. Tony didn't have one.

"I don't think it has anything to do with me," Tony said.

"Don't you want to call her instead of me?" Kipp asked.

"No."

"Come on."

"No, I don't," Tony said. "Honestly."

"What did you two fight about today?"

"Her leaving. My not wanting to play football anymore. Our sex life. Her wanting to date other guys."

"She wants to date other guys? Alison? Did she say that?"

"Not exactly," Tony admitted.

"I don't believe it. Forget what I said a moment ago about her being a bitch. Alison's a great girl. There's something special when you two are together. There's a kind of magic in the air."

"There won't be any magic in a couple of weeks. She'll be gone."

Kipp came over and sat beside Tony on the bed. He put his hand on his shoulder. "Hey, buddy, you sound really bummed about this."

Tony nodded weakly. "I am. I'm embarrassed by the way I feel because I've never felt this way before. I just feel like if she goes I'll lose her forever."

"It won't happen. I'm your friend and I'm leaving, but I'm still going to be your friend. Alison will be, too. She loves you. Anyone can see it."

Tony barely smiled. Before the chain letter began, he and Kipp hadn't been real close. Now Kipp was his best friend. There was nothing like a shared trauma to bring people together. He appreciated what Kipp was saying. The trouble was, he didn't believe it. Alison was attracted to him. She had fun with him. She might even have been attached to him, but she didn't love him. You didn't leave the one you love, not for any reason.

"We'll see" was all Tony could say.

"You sure you don't want to call her?" Kipp asked. "She does sound upset."

Tony shrugged. "I guess it wouldn't hurt." Tony reached for the phone. "Do you know Fran's number?"

"It's button number six."

Tony pushed the appropriate button. The phone rang only once before it was picked up by Fran. "Hello?" she said.

"Fran, this is Tony. Is Alison there?"

"Yeah."

"Could I speak to her?" Fran was slow in answering. "Is there something wrong?" Tony asked.

"Here's Ali," Fran said finally. Tony listened while the phone shifted hands. Alison came on the line. Her tone of voice was low.

"Where are you, Tony?" she asked.

"I'm at Kipp's house."

"Is Kipp there?"

"Yeah. He's sitting beside me. What's wrong?"

Alison paused. "I don't know how to say this."

Tony's heart pounded loudly in his own ears. Here it came—the big goodbye. We had some good times, Tony, but you're right. I should date other guys. I should have a variety of lovers. You just don't satisfy me anymore. Not like this guy I met this afternoon. Boy, does he have all the right stuff. I'll always love you, Tony, but you know a girl always says that when she's dumping a guy for another guy.

"Just say it," he whispered.

"Tony?"

"I'm here. Say it."

There was another long pause. "Somebody's sent us another chain letter."

Tony couldn't comprehend what she was saying for a moment. "What?" he asked.

"Fran got another chain letter in the mail this morning. It's a lot like the ones Neil sent. If Kipp's there, ask him if he sent it." Her voice was almost trembling. "Tell him it's not funny."

Tony put his hand over the phone. "Did you send Fran a chain letter as a joke?" he asked Kipp.

Kipp raised an eyebrow. "No."

"You're sure?"

"Yes. What's this about?"

"I'm trying to find out." Tony took his hand off the phone and spoke to Alison again. "Kipp did not send a letter to Fran."

"Could he be pulling your leg?" Alison asked.

Tony glanced at Kipp, who seemed to be worried. Kipp didn't worry easily. "No," Tony said. "Read me the letter."

Alison read it to him all the way through, and with each sentence Tony found himself sinking deeper into the bed. With Neil's first letters it had been the tone that was more disturbing than any specific threats. For they sounded as if they had been written by a brilliant madman, capable of great evil. Even after it had been revealed that Neil was the Caretaker, Tony had never been able to reconcile his friend with writing the letters. They had been so crafty, and Neil had always been so simple. It was almost as if the letters had been dictated to Neil by someone else.

"I kept wondering and worrying and I tried, but this thing got in my head and I couldn't get rid of it. I don't know where it came from. It was like a voice, saying this is true and this is a lie. It wouldn't shut up! I had to listen, and I did listen, and then . . . I did all this."

"Are you still there?" Alison asked.

"Yes." Tony swallowed. His heart continued to pound—

for a different reason now. Yet it was funny—the reasons may have been different, but the anxiety remained the same. It was almost as if his concern over Alison leaving and dating other guys had just culminated in the arrival of the chain letter. In a way he wasn't surprised another one had come.

"There's an ad in the paper," Alison continued. "It's in code like the letter said it would be. It says Fran has to drown her puppy tonight."

Tony had to take a breath. "That's pretty gross."

"Tony, it's got to be a prank. Do you think Joan sent this?"

"I don't know. I'd have to ask her. Have you called her?"

"No. I thought you should. You know her better than I do."

"I don't know her that well."

"I didn't mean anything by it," Alison said.

"I'm sorry."

"Yeah, well, so am I." Alison sighed. "This is the last thing I need in my life right now."

"At least this new Caretaker won't have your address in New York."

"Tony, I'm not even listed at the bottom of the letter. Did I tell you that?"

"No."

"It's interesting, don't you think?"

Tony stopped. When he spoke next, his voice was cold. "Are you suggesting that I sent that letter?"

Alison sounded dismayed. "I don't see how you can think

I'd even suggest that. Tony, what's wrong with you? Why are you treating me this way?"

Tony closed his eyes. They were in trouble again, and he had to be cool. Ultimately he was responsible for them being in this situation. After all, he had been the one who had been driving when they hit the man.

"I'm in a bad mood, that's all," he said. "Where was the letter mailed from?"

"Locally."

"Just like before. How's Fran holding up?"

"She's freaking. Who wouldn't? This letter's a lot nastier than the ones Neil sent. It says she's to be horribly killed if she doesn't drown her puppy. What should I tell her?"

"I don't know," he said. "I'll talk to Joan and get back to you. I'll try to get her right now. OK?"

"OK. Call me back even if you don't get her. And Tony?"

"What?"

Alison hesitated. "Nothing."

Tony hung up the phone and related the wording of the letter as best as he could to Kipp. His friend was not amused. He stood and paced the room.

"If Joan didn't send it, then someone outside the group must have got hold of one of Neil's letters," Kipp said.

"Is that possible?" Tony said. "His house burned down. He burned it down with the man's body in it. You remember how he tried to make it look like he had died in the fire? Then,

Neil didn't have any letters on him when he died later. I was with him."

"Did we destroy all the letters Neil sent us?" Kipp asked.

"Yeah, I'm sure we did."

"It doesn't really matter. Any one of us could have reconstructed those letters from memory." Kipp thought some more. "Call Joan right now."

Tony dialed her number. He knew it from memory. He had actually been closer to Joan than Alison realized. He had once come within a finger's inch of having sex with her. Sometimes, when things were rough with Alison, he fantasized about calling Joan again and continuing their affair. But he never did. Joan was so gorgeously gross, she intimidated him. Plus he would never cheat on Alison.

He got her mother. Joan was completely unavailable, Mrs. Zuchlensky reported. She was backpacking in Yosemite with friends and wouldn't be home for three days. Tony left the message that she should return his call as soon as possible. He set down the phone and turned back to Kipp.

"Joan's up in the mountains," Tony said. "She's unreachable until Thursday."

"That's convenient," Kipp said.

"Yes and no. If Joan was pulling a prank like this, she would have to stay around. Her absence would cast suspicion on her."

"That's true," Kipp said. "Is it possible Fran and Brenda and Alison are playing a prank on us?"

Tony remembered the fear in Alison's voice. "I somehow doubt it."

"But Alison is mad at you."

Tony shook his head. "This isn't her style."

Kipp walked over to his window and stared out. "Then we might have ourselves a big problem. Another Caretaker—Jesus, who would have thought. Alison's right, this guy sounds a lot nastier than Neil did."

"Do you honestly think Fran's in danger? I've got to call Alison back and tell them something."

Kipp smiled, but it wasn't because he was happy. "I don't think she'll be in danger if she drowns her puppy."

"Kipp! She's not going to do that."

Kipp was sympathetic. "I know. Call them and tell them Joan's in the mountains. Tell them it's probably just her idea of a sick joke."

"Alison won't buy it. This letter was mailed locally."

"How long has Joan been camping?"

"Her mom said a week already," Tony said.

"That's not good." Kipp sat down beside Tony. "Can I ask you a stupid question?"

"Sure."

"Do you want to go to the police with the letter?"

Tony was horrified by the idea. "If we do that we'll have to explain everything—the whole story will come out. They'll put us in jail."

"It was just a suggestion. It would be a crazy thing to do without talking to Joan first. When did you say she'd be back?"

"Thursday."

"When does the next person on the list have to receive the chain letter?"

"Thursday," Tony said.

Kipp laughed. It was his way of coping with the stress, Tony understood. Their situation was totally preposterous. "Then if Fran is still alive on Thursday, we'll have nothing to worry about."

Tony nodded. "She'll be fine."

But his words sounded hollow even to himself. Like when he was trying to tell himself Alison loved him, when he knew in the end she was going to leave him.

Chapter Four

When Eric Valence was ten years old, he read all of the Sherlock Holmes books. He walked around in an imaginary world fancying himself Dr. Watson and carrying on intricate conversations with the great detective. In high school he fell in love with Agatha Christie. He read all of her more than eighty murder mysteries word for word, and in over half of them he figured out who the villain was before the master herself revealed the truth.

After graduating from high school, he had his heart set on becoming a hotshot homicide detective. The problem was he'd had serious ear infections as a child, and as a result he was totally deaf in his right ear and had only fifty percent normal hearing in his left. Half a working ear was plenty to keep him from being seriously handicapped. He could enjoy movies and talk comfortably on the phone, as long as the other person spoke directly into the mouthpiece. Unfortunately he couldn't pass the physical to enter the police academy. He had tried three times and had even attempted unsuccessfully to bribe the administering physician. But the men in blue didn't want him, and it was difficult to study by himself to be a competent private eye. He'd planned to become a PI after he had honed his skills on the force. Not that he had given up on his dream. He would be a PI someday. It was just going to take longer than he hoped.

Eric had an uncle who was a cop with the LAPD—Sergeant John Valence. The man was neither a detective nor much of a police officer. He was basically a nice fat guy who had passed a civil service exam when he was twenty-four years old and out of work. Uncle John had driven around in a black-and-white for a few years and eventually found himself where he really belonged, behind a desk pushing papers and talking about all the great crimes other men had solved. Surprisingly, though, the man had done a brief stint with the homicide department, and the stories he could tell were wonderful. All the bodies and the coroners' reports and the smoking pistols—they made Eric's trigger finger twitch just to listen to the man.

But even better than all the talk was the fact that in his position as desk sergeant at the West Covina branch of the LAPD Eric's uncle had access to the computers where the files of literally hundreds of unsolved murders were stored. In a weak moment Eric's uncle had given him the secret codes that tapped into the files, a serious sharing of confidences because there existed tons of information in the files that had never been made known to the public. From that moment on, Eric was in heaven. He would drive to the station from night classes at Claremont College—Eric was majoring in computer science, which he felt was the future for detective work—chat with his uncle for a few minutes, then plug himself into a terminal at the back of the station. Some nights Eric stayed at the terminal until the sun came up and the morning crew came on. People had done so many horrible things to each other in L.A. over the past twenty years—it was wonderful.

Eric Valence was on such a late-night vigil with the police computer when he came across the file on the late Neil Hurly. Eric almost skipped over it. The file didn't appear to be that of an unsolved murder case. But a sentence did catch his eye. One from the county coroner. Apparently this Neil—he was only eighteen at the time of his death—had perished in a fire in his home. His body had been so badly burned that identification of his remains had been difficult. The situation had been further complicated by the fact that there were no current dental records available on Neil. In summary, the coroner wrote that an emerald ring on the victim's left hand had been used to substantiate that it was Neil Hurly who had gone up in smoke. The matter was further verified by the mother's testimony that her son had been sleeping alone at home when the fire broke out. In other words, case closed.

The thing that got Eric about the report was that it had been an emerald ring that had gone through the fire. Eric was no expert when it came to jewelry, but it just so happened that the year before he had been seriously involved with a girl named Meryl Runion, who had an expensive appetite for emeralds. Naturally, because he thought he was in love at the time, and because Meryl twisted his arm about the matter, he tried to buy her an emerald ring for her birthday. Being a practical man on a limited budget, however, he did a little research before making his purchase. One of the things he discovered about emeralds was that they did not make good stones to set in rings. They were soft, and they chipped easily. An expensive emerald could be ruined just by forgetting to remove it before washing the dishes. Eric decided that he should buy Meryl an emerald set in a necklace or a bracelet. But then Meryl met this young lawyer who drove a red Porsche and forgot to return his calls. Eric didn't buy her anything.

Eric was instantly suspicious of the identification of Neil Hurly's remains. If Neil Hurly had been wearing an emerald while lying in a burning house, the emerald should have been destroyed. Yet the coroner's note indicated the emerald had survived the fire intact. How many coroners knew of the softness of an emerald? Eric was only familiar with the gem's fragile nature by chance. It made him wonder if the ring had been placed on the body's hand after the fire. If that was so, it raised an even more startling question.

Was it Neil Hurly who had died in the fire?

The file contained X-rays of what was left of Neil's skull and teeth. As stated, the X-rays had done the coroner no good because he had no dental records for comparison. Eric doubted that the man had tried hard to find records. Why should he? The mom was probably right down the hall saying, "That's my son who died, I know it." Eric studied Neil's history. He had moved to Los Angeles from Canyon, Arkansas, at the age of fourteen. Canyon was listed as Neil's place of birth. In all those fourteen years Neil must have gone to the dentist at least once.

Eric sat back from the terminal. He had no idea where Canyon was in Arkansas. It was probably a small town, and that fact should help him. He didn't waste time speculating on the matter. He looked up the area code for Arkansas—it had only one. Then he called Information there. Canyon was tiny. All told, the information assistant gave him a list of three dentists, and two of those were a husband and wife team who shared an office. Eric jotted the numbers down on a notepad. He was already opening his own file on Neil Hurly. There was something not quite right—he could sense it. "Something's afoot," as Holmes might have said to Watson.

Eric was not able to call the dentists until morning. He did so from his apartment identifying himself as an assistant coroner with the LAPD. The lie went over well because he was able to use his uncle as a reference, calling him the officer in charge of the case. Eric had yet to tell his uncle what he was doing, but he doubted that the dentists would check. As it turned out the couple had no Neil Hurly in their files. But the secretary of the third guy, Dr. Krane, remembered the Hurlys well. She sounded about eighty years old but very bright.

"Of course I knew Neil," she said. "He was such a sweet young man. They moved to Los Angeles when Neil was about to enter high school. Would it be all right to ask why you need his X-rays?"

It was clear the woman knew nothing about Neil's supposed death. Eric made his voice sound older. "I'm afraid, madam, we have reason to believe that Neil Hurly has been the victim of a fire at his house. There are few remains, and we need the X-rays to make a positive identification."

The woman sounded distressed. "That's horrible. Was the mother killed as well?"

Eric didn't want to complicate the matter by having the mother alive. It was always possible Dr. Krane's secretary would want a permission note from the mother before releasing the X-rays.

"I'm afraid she perished in the fire," Eric said, feeling like a jerk.

"That's so sad," the woman replied. "Do you think it was an accident?"

"The case is still open." Eric cleared his throat. "Could you please mail the X-rays overnight express to the following address? It would be much appreciated."

"Of course." He could hear her reaching for a pen. "I'm ready."

Eric gave her the address of the West Covina police station in care of Sergeant John Valence. Then he got off the phone quickly. His heart was pounding, but he was feeling good.

He walked into the station the next evening beside his uncle. John was surprised when Eric snapped the overnight mail envelope out of his box before he could go through it.

"What are you up to?" his uncle asked with a twinkle in his eye. At the station Christmas party Sergeant Valence was always the first choice to play Santa Claus. There was a jolliness about him that Eric found endearing.

"I'll tell you when I know something exciting," Eric promised.

His uncle shook his head. "Just don't get me in trouble. I have only a year before my pension."

Eric hurried back to the computer and compared the dentist's X-rays to those of the coroner. The coroner's photographs of his X-rays did not have the high-quality resolution of the dentist's X-rays, but it didn't matter. Eric was no specialist, but even he could see at a glance that the X-rays were from two different people. Neil had had a series of fillings on the lower right side of his mouth when he was thirteen. The guy who had burned to death in Neil's house had no fillings on that side.

Neil Hurly had not burned to death in the Hurly home. But someone had wanted it to look as if he had.

Who?

Why?

The questions of an unfolding mystery. Eric was bursting with excitement. This was better than sex with Meryl Runion. Well, he wouldn't know that for sure. They had actually never done it. But it was better than making out with her. Meryl had always had bad breath.

Eric went in search of Mrs. Hurly's new address. He couldn't find it. She wasn't in the phone book. But he did have her old address, the place where the house had burned to the ground. If he went to the neighborhood and asked around, he should be able to find out where she was living. He had already decided that when he got her new address, he'd drop by the house rather than call her. He'd show the woman the evidence and see how she reacted. For all he knew, she might have been the one who set the whole thing up.

Eric briefly wondered if Neil would answer the door.

Chapter Five

For the gang Thursday came and left with no drama. Alison spent the day with Fran, going to the mall and the movies. Fran held up surprisingly well, only crying once over dinner. Alison stayed by her side until twelve midnight. It was Alison's plan to stay overnight, but Fran said it wasn't necessary. Her parents were home sleeping, and besides, Fran snored like a bear and was always embarrassed to have anyone else sleep in the same room with her. Alison left her with a hug and a promise to call in the morning.

Alison did call Fran on Friday morning, and her old friend was just fine. The news spread through the group, and Tony and Kipp began to relax. Brenda didn't, however. It was unnecessary, she said. She hadn't been worried initially. Joan had called her mom to tell her she had decided to spend an extra day in the mountains, so she was still unavailable.

Then Friday night arrived.

Alison went to bed early. Tony was still not talking to her, and the stress was wearing her out. She drank a glass of warm milk and crawled under her covers. The last thing she remembered before falling asleep was that Fran had told her she was going downtown that night to some party.

Then Alison was asleep, and she had no more conscious thoughts.

But curious images did float in her unconscious mind, bringing with them strange sensations. She was in a wide open space but felt claustrophobic. The air pulsed in nauseating patterns of red and purple light. A painful throbbing sound seemed to come from every quarter, totally out of sync with the oscillating colors. There was also a haze of smoke that stank of rotten eggs. But most of all was her intense feeling of despair. It wrapped like a steel coil around her heart and brought pain.

As Alison listened in her dream, she thought she could hear the distant wails of people in torment. Their faint cries came to her through the din of the throbbing and were so twisted they could have been the sounds of animals being tortured to death. But she could see no one, even though she herself felt watched. It was as if the horrible space had eyes of its own, made out of the sickening light and deafening noise. Eyes that were constantly aware and always displeased. Above all else, she wished to God she could be anywhere but where she was.

Then suddenly she was sitting bolt upright in bed—in the dark, where all bad things happened. The phone beside her bed was ringing, and her heart shrieked in her chest. She reached over and grabbed it.

"Hello?"

"Alison?"

"Yeah." She had to take a breath. "Who is this?"

"Mrs. Darey."

The fear came in a wash, instantaneously. "Is something wrong with Fran? What's happened to her?"

Mrs. Darey wept. "I don't know. The hospital called. They say she's been in a car accident. They wouldn't say how she was. They want me to come to the hospital, but my husband's not here, and I'm so upset I can't find my glasses. Ali, can you take me to the hospital? I don't think I can drive like this."

Alison realized the woman had momentarily forgotten that she lived almost an hour away in the valley. She spoke gently. "Sure, I can take you to the hospital. But it might take me a while to get to your house. I'm going to have my boyfriend, Tony, come over and get you instead. You've met him. Then I'm going to drive directly to the hospital and meet you there. Would that be OK?"

"I suppose." Sobs poured from the poor woman. "When they won't tell you how your daughter is, does that mean she's dead?"

"No, Mrs. Darey. It only means they're not sure yet what's wrong with her. There might be nothing wrong with Fran. I'm sure there isn't. Now give me the name of the hospital that called you."

Mrs. Darey was able to convey the vital information. Alison reassured her once more and then hung up and called Tony. He answered immediately. He hadn't been asleep—she could tell by his voice. She glanced at the clock. It was one in the morning.

"Tony, it's Alison. Bad news."

"Fran?"

"Yes. Her mom just called. Fran's been in an accident."

"What happened?"

Alison gave him what information she had. Tony said he could be at Fran's house in ten minutes. He sounded alert but calm, far from the way she felt. If anything had happened to Fran, she was never going to forgive herself for having let her go out alone.

"You were waiting for this, weren't you?" Alison asked. "You've been staying up."

"I was waiting for something," Tony said. "I didn't know what it would be."

Alison almost choked on the question. "Do you think she's dead?"

Tony sighed. "I try not to think these days. It makes my head hurt."

Fran Darey was dead.

The three of them got the news at the same time. Although Alison had considerably farther to drive to the hospital, it had taken Tony a while to get Mrs. Darey out of her house and into his car. She had been so overcome with grief. Fran's mother fainted when she heard the news. A team of white coats suddenly appeared and wheeled her away on a gurney. Alison's head was spinning. The doctor who had delivered the news to them could have been telling them Fran had a bad cold—from the tone of his voice. He was middle-aged, and his green surgical gown was splashed with dried blood. He worked the emergency room in the center of the city, where shootings and stabbings were a way of life. He probably told people their loved ones were dead all the time. No sweat off his back.

"How did this happen?" Alison moaned to the doctor as she sagged into Tony's strong arms.

The doctor shook his head. "Ask the police. They're out back with the ambulance drivers. I understand she drove straight into a tree."

Alison asked a stupid question. "Are you sure she's dead? I mean, couldn't she somehow be revived if you tried real hard?"

The doctor regarded her with a blank expression. "She's as dead as they come. We won't be able to revive her. I'm sorry."

Tony wanted to check on Mrs. Hurly. He looked shaken but still in control. Alison let him go. She wanted to talk to the police before they disappeared. She caught one of them in the parking lot as he was climbing into his squad car.

"Excuse me," she said. "I'm a friend of that girl who was just brought in. The one in the car crash. Were you at the scene of the accident?"

The officer was young and handsome. He had a neat brown mustache and a dark blue uniform that fit him perfectly. He stood outside his car with her. His face supplied the sympathy the doctor's had been missing.

"Yes, I was, miss," he said and touched her arm. "I'm very sorry your friend was killed. I understand she was only eighteen."

Alison nodded and sniffed. "I'm sorry, too. But I'm also confused. The doctor inside said Fran ran straight into a tree?"

"That's correct. The tree was a tall olive at the side of the road. She must have been doing sixty when she hit it. Both the tree and the car were destroyed."

"Do you think she was run off the road?"

"There was no sign of skid marks. Usually when someone runs you off the road, you have a chance to hit the brakes. But maybe not. The accident's going to be thoroughly investigated. I wish I could tell you more. I really am sorry."

Alison started to turn away and go back inside to find Tony. She needed his strong arms now more than ever. She just hoped that when she found him, he would open his arms to her. Yet she hesitated before leaving and asked the officer what was probably another stupid question. It was just something she felt she had to ask.

"How exactly did Fran die?" she asked.

The police officer looked uncomfortable. "From the force of the impact."

"Her body got smashed between the car and the tree?"

The cop fidgeted. "Not exactly, but close enough. I can tell you for certain that she died instantly."

The odd purple color of the chain letter envelope flashed in her mind, along with the sick purple and red lights of the nightmare she'd been having when the phone rang. She remembered the dream then—the invisible people crying in the smoky distance. It was a memory that made her shudder.

"Tell me exactly how it was," she said.

The officer looked down. "You don't want to know."

"I need to know."

"Her head went through the windshield and struck a thick branch of the tree at an unfavorable angle. That broke her neck and—"

"And what?"

The officer looked puzzled. "I've been to a hundred serious car accidents, and I don't know how it happened. It must have been the shattered glass of the windshield in combination with the impact of her skull on the tree."

"What are you saying?"

The officer lowered his gaze once more. "Your friend was decapitated in the accident. We found her head in a nearby bush."

Chapter Six

Saturday morning the surviving members of the original ill-fated "gang" met at the city park beside a kiddie rocket ship in the play area. Joan Zuchlensky was present, finally back from hiking in the mountains. The gang had met in the same spot a few months earlier, after Kipp received notice of his "small service" to perform. That time Kipp only had to tell everybody he cheated on his SATs to please the Caretaker. But life had become tougher. Kipp received a letter in the mail that morning, even though Fran hadn't passed hers on to him. Fran's name was no longer on the list, but otherwise the letter was identical to the one Fran had received. A coded ad had appeared in that morning's edition of the *Times.* Decoded it said:

Burn sister's entire right arm.

"Who wants to open this meeting?" Alison asked. She was sitting on the park bench outside the concrete circle that surrounded the rocket ship and the playing sand, Brenda beside her. Of them all, Tony decided, Alison looked the palest. Of course, she had been the closest to Fran. Yet none of them looked too hot. Even Kipp had lost his smile. He was very protective of his little sister.

"We don't need to formally open it," Joan said "We just need to start talking."

"Fine," Alison said. "We'll all start talking at once."

"Are you going to hassle me?" Joan asked Alison. "Because if you are, I'd just as soon leave now."

Alison seemed to be too hurt to argue. "I'm not going to hassle you."

"Good," Joan replied. She wasn't dressed in her usual leather and metal style. Her platinum hair was short and unadorned, almost as white as her T-shirt. She had on blue jeans, a shade too much lipstick, but a pound less makeup than when she was in school. Her voice sounded tough as ever, though.

"Why don't I start things off," Kipp said, sitting at the end of the rocket slide with the chain letter in his lap. "I'll list what we know about this letter and the situation as a whole. Then I'll list what we don't know."

"Sounds good," Tony mumbled. He was sitting in the sand, off to the side from everyone else. It was eleven in the morning, and he hadn't gone to bed yet. Maybe when the others left, he would lie down in the sand and take a nap.

"This new chain letter was written by someone who knew about Neil's chain letters," Kipp began. "The wording is almost identical. The envelope it came in *is* identical. But this chain letter can't have come from Neil because he's dead. That's a fact. Tony buried him. But the person who wrote this new letter also knows how far Neil took us through his 'Columns.' You'll remember we were all in Column Two when the truth finally came out. This person has started us off in Column Three. You all follow where this is leading?"

"Neil had an accomplice," Alison said.

"It seems like it," Kipp said. "And a mean one at that."

"Neil didn't have an accomplice," Tony said. "He was my friend. I was with him when he died. He would have told me."

"He didn't tell you he was the Caretaker to begin with," Brenda said.

Tony shook his head. "It's not possible."

"I have to agree with Brenda," Kipp said carefully. "Neil was physically and mentally ill. He was very weak toward the end. Having an accomplice would explain how he was able to do all the stuff he did before he died."

"If Neil had an accomplice," Tony asked, "how come this person didn't know about Alison? She's not on the list."

"I can't explain that," Kipp admitted.

"Wait a second," Joan interrupted. "We're acting like babies.

How do we know this new Caretaker was responsible for Fran's death? She ran into a tree. The police think it was an accident."

"It could have been an accident," Tony said. "We all know how upset she was. She couldn't have been driving very well."

"I suppose it's possible," Kipp said. "But it's a hell of a coincidence."

"Are you guys nuts?" Alison broke in. "The Caretaker promised Fran would die if she didn't drown her puppy. Well, she didn't and she's dead. That's not coincidence. That's cause and effect. And are you forgetting how she died? She was decapitated! Talk about a horrible death." Tears sprang into Alison's eyes. "Let's not fool ourselves that she wasn't murdered."

"I think you're being overly dramatic," Joan told Alison. "People lose their heads in accidents all the time. My dad's a cop, you know. He's told me plenty of stories like this."

"The cop who was at the scene of the accident didn't know how it could have happened," Alison said bitterly.

"He was probably a rookie," Joan said.

"Goddamn you, I talked to him!" Alison swore.

"Hold on, you two," Kipp interrupted. "Both of you are making good points. As I said, that Fran should suddenly die is an amazing coincidence. But if she was murdered by the new Caretaker, how did he do it? Fran was in a devastating car crash. The Caretaker couldn't have been in the car with her when she crashed. He wouldn't have survived. That leaves the possibility that she was run off the road. But even the cop Alison talked to didn't think that was likely."

"He didn't say it was impossible, though," Alison muttered.

"All right," Kipp said. "Let's say she was run off the road. What about her losing her head?"

"Would you guys please quit hammering that point?" Brenda asked, and now she began to get teary as well. "You're making me sick."

"We have to talk about it," Kipp said. "We have to talk about everything that's happened if we're to get out of this situation alive. Now, how was she decapitated if not by the accident alone? Did the person who ran her off the road stop and hack off her head?"

"It's possible," Alison said.

"Not really," Kipp said. "The guy would have had a few minutes at best. It's hard to cut someone's head off. You'd need a saw, and a coroner would spot saw marks immediately. It must have been the impact with the tree in combination with the shattered windshield—like the cop told you, Alison."

Alison stared at him. "I cannot believe that you of all people, Kipp, could turn this into a simple accident."

"I'm not," Kipp replied. "I believe she could have been run off the road. I'm simply not buying the scenario that she was purposely decapitated."

"Could we move on, please?" Brenda complained.

"We have to come to conclusions before we move on," Kipp

said. "Was Fran's death an accident or not? Let's take a vote."

"I say it was an accident," Joan said.

Brenda glanced at Alison. "Accident," Brenda said.

"Brenda!" Alison said in disbelief.

"It doesn't make sense she could have been murdered while driving down the street in her own car," Brenda said. She gave Alison a quick hug. "I'm sorry."

"It was no accident," Alison insisted, pushing Brenda away.

"What do you think, Tony?" Kipp asked.

The question startled Tony. He had been watching and listening but from a distance. He had almost forgotten that he was part of the group. It might have been the stress of Fran's death and the missed night of sleep, but his old friends all looked like strangers to him. These people he had gone to school with for years. Even Alison. They had hardly spoken to each other before they parted at the hospital the night before.

"I think we're not seeing the big picture," Tony said. "I think we're asking ourselves the wrong questions."

"Whether Fran's death was accidental or not is a vital question," Kipp said.

"Do you think it was an accident?" Tony asked him.

"I just don't know," Kipp said. "Do you?"

Tony shrugged. "Who knows? Who can know? Something weird is going on, that's for sure."

Kipp showed impatience. "What's your point?"

"Who's sending these chain letters and why?" Tony asked. "That's the only thing that matters. All this other stuff is just that—stuff."

"I agree," Joan said.

"All right," Kipp said. "We can talk about that. Do you have any suggestions, Tony?"

Tony nodded. "The loose end we had last time, after we found out the Caretaker was Neil, was that we never discovered who the dead man in the desert was."

"Do you think someone connected to him might be sending the letters?" Alison asked.

"Yes," Tony said.

"Why?" Alison asked.

"Revenge," Tony said. "We ran the guy over, after all."

"We don't know that for sure," Kipp said quickly. "Talking about him won't do us any good. We talked about him three months ago and went around in circles. We don't know who the man was, and we're probably never going to know who he was. We've got to take steps that can help us right now—"

"Last time it was one of us," Joan interrupted, eyeing Alison. "It could be one of us again."

"None of us would kill Fran," Alison said.

"She was scared," Joan said. "She ran off the road."

"Yeah, while you were conveniently unavailable," Alison snapped at her. Joan jumped up, fire in her eyes.

"Are you saying I wrote these sick letters?" Joan demanded.

"You're the only one in the group who's sick enough to have done it," Alison shouted back, and the fact that she was contradicting herself of a moment ago didn't seem to bother her.

"You bitch," Joan swore, taking a dangerous step toward Alison.

Alison stood slowly. "What are you going to do, Joany? Try to make my day?"

"Stop it," Tony said quietly. "Joan is not the Caretaker."

Alison gazed at him incredulously. "I can't believe you're taking her side."

Joan laughed. "Looks like you don't have him wrapped around your little finger like you thought."

Tony waved away both of them. "You two fight whenever you get together. Sit down and let's figure out what we have to do next."

Alison continued to stare at him before she nodded. "All right," she said and sat back down. Joan strolled over and leaned against the rocket ship, studying her nails and looking bored. Kipp resumed command of the group.

"The demands made in these new letters are much stronger than Neil's ever were," Kipp said. "In fact if they continue the way they're going, none of us is going to do any of them. I'm sure as hell not going to hurt Leslie."

"But what if it's a choice between hurting her and being killed?" Brenda asked Kipp, real anxiety in her voice. Kipp's reaction was a combination of fondness and surprise.

"But you said you thought what happened to Fran was an accident," he said.

"Kipp, I'm serious," Brenda said. "What if?"

Kipp was disgusted. "There is no *what if.* I'm not going to burn my sister's arm. It's as simple as that."

"Why don't we go to the police?" Alison suddenly blurted out.

Tony sat up with a start. "Are you kidding?"

"No, I'm not kidding," Alison said firmly. "With everything that happened with Neil, no one died. No one was even hurt, except Neil. But this round of letters has only begun, and already one of us is dead. We can't fool around this time. We have to go to the police."

"If we go to the police, I go to jail," Tony said flatly. "If that's what the rest of you want, tell me now. I'll have to find myself a lawyer."

"You don't have to go to jail," Alison said.

Tony felt a stab of anger. "You know what I love? I love it that out of everyone in this group, you're the one who's making this suggestion. I just love it, Ali."

His words pierced her like a sword. She shook her head slightly and stared at him some more, but now there were more tears to cloud her vision. He didn't care, he told himself. He couldn't believe that his welfare wasn't a prime consideration of hers.

"Tony probably would go to jail if we went to the police,"

Kipp said. "He was the one who was driving when we hit the man."

"But it was Joan who punched out the car lights on him," Brenda broke in. "If it weren't for her, Tony wouldn't have hit anybody."

"If it weren't for your beer, I wouldn't have been so drunk that I wanted to punch out the lights!" Joan yelled.

"Stop it!" Kipp raised his hand. "We're all involved in this. All of us helped bury the man. None of us reported what happened to the police. We could all go to jail. I was just pointing out that Tony is in the most vulnerable position."

"Yeah," Joan said to Alison. "You don't care what happens to your boyfriend. You're just interested in saving your own skin."

Alison closed her eyes and took a deep breath. Tears trickled over her cheeks. As angry as he was, Tony had to restrain himself from getting up and wiping her tears away. He hated to see Alison cry. Of course he cared. And maybe she was right. Maybe it was time to go to the police. But it was a suggestion he was not going to second. There had to be a better way out of this madness. They just had to find it. Alison reopened her eyes and scanned everyone.

"I'll go along with what the group decides," she said. "I'm not trying to hurt anybody, least of all Tony. But I want Kipp to go away for the next few days. I want him to disappear to a place none of us have heard of."

"I think that's a good idea," Brenda said, nodding in the

direction of her boyfriend. "You're getting out of here, Kipp."

"I can't go now," Kipp said. "I'm leaving for MIT soon. I have things to do."

Brenda got up. She walked over and slapped Kipp on the head. "You're not going to argue with me!" she shouted. "You're going to leave today because you're not going to die."

"All right, I'll go," Kipp said, trying to protect himself from another blow with a raised arm.

"When my turn comes, I'll split," Joan said. "It'll be better than running off and crying to the police."

Tony got up and wiped the sand off his butt. "Are we done? Have we decided to do nothing? If that's it, I've got to go."

Alison also stood. "Do you have any other suggestions about what we should do, Tony?" she asked.

He eyed her across the distance between them. It wasn't far—maybe fifteen feet. But she could have been on the far side of the moon as far as he was concerned. He felt no contact, no connection, between them. It made him more sad than angry. They were under attack, and from the outside. A common enemy usually brought people together, but that wasn't the case here. Maybe they'd been too quick to dismiss the possibility that the Caretaker was one of them. Tony's heart was aching so badly, it was as if the attack were coming from within.

"I have nothing else to say," Tony replied. He turned and walked away.

Chapter Seven

It was good to come home to the old school. It was only across the street from the park, and Tony walked there without going back for his car. He climbed the fence that enclosed the football stadium and track. Ah, the stadium—the site of his adolescent glory. It was good to see it, but at the same time it filled him with revulsion. All the things he had done in high school to construct an invincible self-image. Of what use was that image to him now? He was tired and his back ached and he had an unseen monster on his tail. He wished his name were at the top of the list instead of Kipp's. It would be good to see what his task was and get it over. It might be even better to refuse the task and meet the monster head-on. Sometimes he imagined he saw the new Caretaker when he looked in the mirror.

Tony walked out onto the field, marveling at the silence.

He couldn't remember a time when he had played football or run track with the stands completely empty. What a shallow jerk he'd been. He'd always needed an audience in order to perform.

A sudden desire to run came to him right then. He had shorts and running shoes on. Even though his spine hurt, his doctor had said light jogging shouldn't aggravate his condition. He'd been a good runner once—a great one, in fact. He'd won league championships in the quarter mile and the half mile. Some of that old endurance must still be with him.

Tony walked back out to the track and began to run around the cinder oval. His pace was slow at first, but it wasn't long before he found his rhythm and began to pick up speed. Soon he had his stride stretched almost to full. He was breathing hard, but it didn't feel hard. It was a release for him—driving his body forward, around and around the track. The exercise was like a penance—for all the real and imagined crimes he had committed. He ran a mile, then two, three. He ran over four miles, and by the time he stopped, every muscle in his body was limp. He staggered into the center of the field and plopped down flat on his back in the grass beneath the warm, clear sky. He didn't remember closing his eyes. His last conscious thought was of wanting to float up into the heavens, to leave the world behind.

Then he was asleep.

In his dream he was floating in an alien sky.

The space was not blue, but red and purple, filled with heavy pounding sounds and thick smoke that stank of sulfur. In this abyss of unpleasantness he floated like a drifting balloon, fearful of passing too close to a hidden flame. It wasn't as though the place was hot. It was simply that the threat of painful fire existed, just as the place existed. But perhaps it was the faint cries he heard in the distance that invoked his fear. They didn't sound like human cries, or rather, they sounded like cries of creatures that might have once been human but had now become twisted and evil. He didn't know how this sense came to him. It was just there, as he was there, without explanation. The consciousness brought no relief. It only deepened his horror.

His drifting continued. Yet he began to feel that there was a destination to his course. He sensed rather than saw the great wall that lay before him. He knew it was a wall to separate him from where he was and where he could end up—if he made the wrong choice. But as horrible as the space was in which he was floating, he knew that beyond the wall there existed true despair. For it was from there that the cries emanated. The cries that prayed only for a death that would lead to nonexistence.

Yes, there was definitely a wall ahead. He could see it now. It was dark, but not so thick that he couldn't catch a sense of what was on the far side. . . .

Tony awoke to find a sky the color of twilight above him. At first he couldn't believe he'd slept away the entire day. But then he sat up and looked around and the evidence of his eyes couldn't be denied. It was no wonder, actually. It had been so long since he'd rested.

Tony got up and walked to the fence that enclosed the stadium. He had trouble scaling the wire mesh—his limbs felt oddly disconnected from his torso. It took him half an hour to walk back to his car on the far side of the park, although the car was less than a mile from where he had slept. By the time he got behind his steering wheel, his legs were cold and he had a headache. He had been getting so many headaches lately that he kept a bottle of Tylenol on his dashboard. He took out a couple of tablets and chewed them slowly without water. They left a bitter taste in his mouth. He remembered then that he'd had a nightmare while lying in the center of the football field. But no details of it came to him.

Tony was putting the bottle of Tylenol back onto the dashboard when he noticed the scrap of paper sitting there. He picked it up and studied it in the stark halogen light from a nearby street lamp. It was Sasha's phone number. He smiled at the memory of her, and the smile felt like a welcome stranger on his face. She had told him to call him some night when he needed a massage. What was wrong with right then? He checked his watch. It was only seven o'clock. He needed someone to talk to, other than the people in the group. Certainly he didn't feel like talking to Alison. He couldn't get over how she had wanted to hand him over to the police, even before they were certain Fran's death was anything more than an accident. Alison had a thing or two to learn about devotion.

Tony took out his phone and dialed Sasha's number. He

didn't really expect to catch her in. It was, after all, Saturday night. She was an attractive young lady, and she probably had a line of men waiting outside her door.

She answered on the third ring.

"Hello?"

"Hi, Sasha? This is Tony. I met you at the mall the other day. Do you remember me?"

She took a moment, then said, "Tony, yeah, sure I remember you. How are you doing?"

"I'm all right. How are you?"

Her voice was warm and easy. "Fine. A little bored. What are you up to?"

"Nothing. Actually, I was wondering if you were doing anything?"

"No. Why? Did you want to stop by?"

"Not if it would be inconvenient."

"It's no problem. Come over. Maybe we can go out and have a drink together."

"That sounds like fun." Tony worried if he'd be able to get into a bar. He'd never been in one before. "Where do you live?"

Sasha gave him her address. It wasn't far from where he was. He said goodbye and hung up. He found himself smiling again. The thought of Alison tried to enter his mind, but he pushed it away.

Sasha lived in a new apartment complex not far from the mall where they had met. She greeted him at her door wearing black pants and a white blouse. Her maroon hair hung long down her back. Her green eyes shone as she looked at him, and her lips were a wonderful red around a friendly smile. Sasha invited him in.

"Forgive the mess," she said as she strode from the living room into the kitchen. The apartment was small but neat. The only mess was a couple of paperbacks and a half-filled mug sitting on a coffee table. The furniture seemed to be of high quality. Tony briefly wondered if her family lived in the area, and if they helped her out. He wasn't entirely sure what her job at the hospital was. She seemed a tad young to be a nurse.

The apartment had a faint medicinal smell to it—not alcohol, something else. He asked her about it as he sat at her kitchen table. She had made coffee and wanted him to have a cup before they went out. The question seemed to embarrass her.

"Is it noticeable?" she asked.

He wished he hadn't asked. "It's not bad."

She forced a laugh. "To tell you the truth, I think it's me. The smell of the clinic gets on my clothes and in my hair. I can't get it out. The only time I don't smell is right after I've taken a shower." She glanced over at him. "When I'm naked."

Tony grinned. "I guess I caught you at a bad time, then."

Sasha brought him a mug of steaming coffee. "It's a good time. Do you take it black or with cream?"

"I like a little milk and sugar in it, thank you."

Sasha turned back to the refrigerator. "I like it scalding hot and black. I like to feel it burn my insides as it goes down.

Pretty weird, huh? All the girls at work drink it the same way."

"What exactly do you do at the hospital?" Tony asked.

"As little as possible." She brought him milk and sugar. "I'm thinking of quitting my job and leaving the area."

"Oh, that's too bad."

She sat across from him and regarded him with her big green eyes. "Why?" she asked seriously.

He shrugged. "I just met you is all. You seem like an interesting person."

She liked that answer. "How did you like the way I asked you out at the mall?"

"Did you ask me out?"

"I did and you know it." She regarded him closely, in an oddly penetrating way that made him nervous. "But I could tell you liked me. I knew you'd call."

Tony blushed. "Does this mean I don't get a massage?"

Sasha blushed as well and was even more beautiful. For the blood gave color to her face, which was quite pale.

"You can have a massage and then some, Tony," she said.

They didn't go to a bar but to a nightclub that played music at several decibels above the comfort level. The lighting was a trip—brilliant strobes that were sequenced with the guitars and vocals. Tony had never been to such a place before and found it exciting. Sasha could really dance—he could hardly keep up with her. Her endurance was extraordinary. They danced fifteen songs in a row before taking a break. She ordered drinks for them while he ran off to the bathroom, and she paid for them. Maybe she did know he was under twenty-one and didn't want to embarrass him by asking. They each had a margarita and a screwdriver—heavy on the lethal fluids. Sasha downed her drinks and ordered another couple while he nursed his first one. He paid for this round, and no one asked any questions. Sasha lit up a cigarette and blew a cloud of smoke in his face. He was surprised a nurse would smoke.

"Are you having fun?" she asked. It was hard to hear her over the music.

"I'm having a great time," he called back.

She continued to peer at him, holding the fire of the cigarette close to her hair. "Something's on your mind," she said.

"No," he said. "I'm fine. I'm glad I'm here with you."

She nodded. "I want you to tell me about it later."

Tony didn't reply, not directly to her remark, and soon they were back out on the dance floor, and it was all he could do to hold himself upright. He had run too far that morning. He had run too fast. He felt as if he'd been on a treadmill for the last three months, and he wondered if this was his first chance to get off. He really liked Sasha. The whole time he was with her, he hardly thought of Alison, and that was a big relief. He could handle the new Caretaker, he thought, if he could just get his heart free of the pain he'd been feeling.

On the way home he was tired and drunk. For safety's sake

it would have been better if Sasha had driven. She had drunk twice what he had, but her system seemed to be able to handle it. But it was a masculine thing with him that he had to be the one to drive his car. It was close to midnight. On a long stretch of freeway Sasha again asked him what was on his mind.

"How can you tell something's bothering me?" he asked. He had to concentrate on the road. The red taillights of the cars in front of him kept blurring into bloated sunspots.

"I can see it in your face," she said simply.

He glanced over at her. Her mood was more serious than earlier, but still easy. She had a definite presence. When she asked something, it was hard to resist answering her truthfully.

"What do you see?" he asked.

"You're grieving over another girl."

Tony was shocked. "Huh?"

"What's her name?"

Tony stared straight ahead. "Alison Parker."

Sasha reached over and touched his leg. "You can talk about it. I don't mind."

"There's nothing to say." The car suddenly felt cramped. Yet the touch of her hand on his leg was nice. So nice he was able to lie—a little. "She was a girl I used to date. We broke up."

"You haven't broken up completely." Sasha took her hand back. "Was she unfaithful to you?"

"No. I don't know. I don't think so." He added, "She's leaving the area soon."

Sasha's next question hit him like a slap. "Do you think she's with someone else right now?"

Tony forced a smile. "I hope not."

Sasha leaned closer. He could smell the alcohol on her breath, but it smelled sweet not sour. "You're with someone. Why can't she be with someone?"

"She can. I just don't think she is."

Sasha sat back in her seat. "Let's swing by her house on the way to my place. We'll see if she's alone."

He glanced at her, uncertain. "Sasha?"

"It's just a hunch I have, Tony. We'll pay her a visit. Don't worry. She'll never know we were there."

"But I don't want to stop by her house."

"Yes, you do."

Chapter Eight

Alison left the park with a heavy heart. She got in her car and drove aimlessly around town. She felt torn apart. She had pain hitting her from all directions. Her friend Fran was dead. They had to bury her on Monday. The murderer was still on the loose, composing fresh letters and tasks for them to complete. Then there was Tony, her beloved Tony, who treated everything she said with distrust and contempt. She couldn't understand where his hatred for her was coming from. She had done nothing to him. She only wanted to live her life to the fullest with him still a big part of it. Of course, she had suggested they go to the police. It was the only rational thing to do. This Caretaker was not picking at their weak spots. He was going for the jugular, and he liked the taste of blood. Eventually Alison found herself heading for her house, more than thirty miles from the neighborhood where her friends lived. But when she reached her usual off-ramp, she kept driving. She couldn't face her parents the way she felt. She needed to get away, to get out of the city. She stayed on the freeway, and when the turnoffs came for the mountain resorts, she took one. The ground rose in front of her, and the air cooled. She saw a pine, then half a dozen. The forest thickened steadily the higher she went. Soon she was driving through mountains of green.

She finally realized she was heading toward Big Bear Lake. She didn't want to go there. It was a weekend, and the lake would be crowded. She spotted a sign pointing toward a Green Valley Lake. That sounded nice. She turned left off the main road. Five miles later she caught sight of a crystal-clear body of water. The valley was heavenly and appeared almost deserted. She parked and walked along the water. For the first time all day the lump in her throat began to shrink. There wasn't a cloud in the sky. She took a deep breath and picked up a stone and skimmed it over the glassy water. Five hops—she hadn't lost her touch.

She wasn't the only one skimming rocks on the lake. At the far end of the lake she could just make out a young man in blue jeans and a yellow shirt dancing his pebbles over the surface, too. He didn't throw his rocks hard, but they went forever over the water. *He* had the touch. He noticed her watching him and waved to her. He seemed to be harmless, about her age, with a slight build and light brown hair that was in desperate need of a trim. He smiled as she approached, and a powerful sensation of déjà vu swept over her. Yet she had never been to this lake before. Certainly she couldn't have met this guy before. She was sure of that—well, pretty sure.

"Hi," he said.

"Hello," she replied. She nodded to the rocks in his hands. "How do you get your stones to skip like that? I counted fifteen hops on your last throw."

The sunlight shone in his hair and on his shy expression. "It's all in the wrist." He demonstrated for her, and the rock took close to twenty hops before sinking below the surface. Once more she was struck by the ease with which he threw them. "See, there's nothing to it," he said.

"For you maybe." She looked around. They weren't far from a grass meadow alive with blooming flowers in every color. At the far end of the meadow was a small wooden cabin. It, too, looked familiar to her, but not exactly. It was as if it had been thoroughly described to her, not a place she had ever visited. "Is that your cabin?" she asked, pointing.

"Sometimes I stay there," he said, watching her. "You look tired. Would you like a cup of tea?"

His suggestion was a little forward, but somehow, coming from him, it didn't seem rude. There was something disarming about the guy. Not for a second did she feel in danger. Quite the reverse—it was very pleasant to stand beside him in the warm sunlight among the trees.

"I'm just out for a walk." She chuckled. "I couldn't drop in on you. I mean, I don't even know you."

He let his rocks fall to the ground and offered his hand. "My name's Chris."

She shook his hand. "I'm Alison."

"Ali?"

She smiled. "My friends call me that."

"Ali," he repeated to himself, and it seemed as if he liked the sound of her name. He turned in the direction of his cabin. "Well, I'm going to have tea. You can join me if you wish."

She didn't want him to be gone suddenly. "I think I will," she said.

The inside of his cabin was sparsely furnished. He put an old black kettle on a wood stove. He lit a fire with a match scraped along the wall of the stove. "It'll take a few minutes," he said and stepped back outside onto the front porch, where there were a couple of chairs. He sat down and put his legs up on the railing. After a moment's hesitation, Alison sat beside him. He scanned the nearby lake and sighed with pleasure.

"A day like this makes it hard to leave here," he said.

"Do you have to leave? Do you have to get back to work?" She believed she had miscalculated his age. He didn't look much older than she was, but he had an air about him that spoke of greater maturity.

"I'm only back here for a short time, Ali," he said.

"Where are you from?"

The question amused him. He glanced back at the water. "Not so far from here—if you know how to fly."

She laughed. "So you're Peter Pan?"

He laughed softly, nodding. "If you like."

"What kind of work do you do?"

He thought for a moment. "I'm a farmer."

"Really? What do you grow?"

"Seeds."

"No. Seriously?"

"I grow them, and then I harvest them when the time is right."

She couldn't tell if he was kidding or not. She didn't mind if he was. His whole air was so sweet. He was quite enchanting. He brushed a lock of his brown hair aside and stared at her once more. He was waiting for her to speak.

"Where is your farm?" she asked.

"Near here."

"In the woods?"

"In Los Angeles," he said.

She laughed again. "I'd like to see it in the middle of the city. What do you grow? People?"

He continued to watch her. "Yes. You have grown up, Ali."

She stopped, confused. "What do you mean?"

"What I said. You are growing up swiftly. That's why you suffer so much. Sometimes the faster you run, the more you trip and hurt yourself. But the sooner you'll reach your goal."

Now she was totally lost. "How do you know anything about me? I've never met you before. Have I?"

"Yes."

"When?"

"Not long ago. Don't worry. You won't remember me."

Alison leaned back in her seat and felt her breath slowly go out of her body. It was true—she had no memory of this guy. Yet she *knew* him. She didn't understand how both things could be true at the same time.

"What am I suffering from now?" she asked carefully.

"Lack of love. It's always the cause of suffering."

She thought of Tony and their unfulfilled love, and her heart ached. "That's true," she whispered. Then she shook herself. "Who are you?"

He removed his legs from the porch rail and sat up. "I'm a guide. I'm here to guide you."

"To what?"

"You know what."

She bit her lower lip, but she didn't taste blood. She tasted cold water. Her whole body had suddenly gone cold. "You know about the chain letters?" she gasped.

He shrugged. "The letters are not important. It's what they represent."

"And what's that?"

"A chain," he said seriously. "An unbroken chain. It's very ancient—not a happy thing. But it can be broken."

Alison's head was spinning. She had come to this spot by chance. She had only met this guy by chance. Yet he knew of her worst fears. . . .

"How can we break it?" she asked.

"With love," he said simply.

"I don't understand."

The guy's green eyes were penetrating, yet gentle still. It was as if she stood fully exposed before him, her thoughts and everything, but it was OK because he understood her. And appreciated her. That's why she felt so comfortable with him. He radiated unconditional love.

"You do understand, Ali," he said.

"But I love Tony. I want to help him. I want to help the others, but they won't listen to me. Tony won't even talk to me."

The guy raised a finger. "That doesn't matter, either. You have asked for help, and someone will come. Trust this person. But beyond this you must trust what's in your heart. The letters come from a place where there is no heart. There is only pain. None of you must go to that place."

Alison was frightened. "Where is that place?"

The guy hesitated. Alison didn't understand why she didn't think of him as Chris. Then she realized it was probably because it wasn't his real name. It was just something he made up so she could understand. But understand what? Who the hell was this guy?

"It is not far from here, either," he said.

"But this Caretaker has already killed one of us," she said. "How can I stop him from killing more of us?"

"Dying is not so bad as being put in the box."

"What happens when you're put in the box?" Her voice trembled. "Do you go to that place?"

"Eventually. Unless you can get out. But it's difficult to get out once you are inside. Most people never do." The kettle began to whistle inside the cabin. The guy seemed to listen to it for a few moments. Yet he could have been listening to something far off. His gaze focused on a place she couldn't see. He came back to her after a minute, though. "I'm afraid you won't have time to stay for tea," he said, and there was a hint of sorrow in his voice.

"Why not?"

"It is time."

"Time for what?" She stood. "Please, you have to tell me what's happening here. Who are you?"

He stood, too. He didn't say anything but only hugged her, and his arms as they went around her were of great comfort. She felt a warm glow in her chest that spread through her after he let go. But her heart was still in anguish.

"I am your friend," he said. He reached out and touched the hair that hung beside her cheek. "I am your greatest admirer."

"But I don't understand."

"You will. You will act in love. You will do what has to be done."

She began to cry. "I'm afraid. Can't I stay with you a few more minutes?"

He shook his head and turned for the front door. "You have to hurry. Go to where it all began. There are two places, you know. Find them and you will reach the end of the chain." He smiled at her one last time before stepping inside. "Goodbye, Ali."

"But—?"

"Hurry," he said and vanished through the door.

Alison stood for a minute staring at the closed door before opening it and peeking inside. He must have gone out the back way. She saw no sign of him. The whistle of the kettle had stopped. It sat on the wood stove as if it had sat there undisturbed for years. There was no sign of the burning logs. It was as if she had dreamed the entire encounter. She turned and walked back to the lake, toward her car. His words rang true, whoever he was. She had to hurry, even if she didn't know where she was going.

Chapter Nine

Alison was on the main freeway toward her house when she deciphered the mystery the strange fellow had set before her. He had spoken of two places where it had all begun. Obviously the first must be the dusty road in the desert, where they had run over the man. The second had eluded her at first. Neil had started the chain letters. Therefore, the inside of Neil's head must be the second starting point. But Neil was dead. His mind was gone. Yet, she reasoned, he must have sat at home when he composed the chain letters. She would go there, to what was left of the place. She remembered he had burned it down with the man's dead body inside to give the illusion that it was he, Neil, who had been killed by the Caretaker. She didn't want to go to the man's first grave in the desert. She wasn't even sure that she could find it—or what she'd do out in the middle of the desert.

The burned house had months ago been leveled by bulldozers. A grass lot stood in its place. There was plenty of ash left, however. As Alison crept up to the lot in her car, she imagined she was looking at the remains of a bomb blast site—one that had hastily been covered over with sod. She parked and walked across the grass, charred splinters poking at her shoes from between the soft blades. All right, she was here. Now what? Should she sit down cross-legged in the grass and commune with Neil's ghost for answers? She decided she had already met one ghost that day.

Who was that guy? How did he know about the letters?

She wasn't going to answer those questions here. She must have misunderstood the guy's clues. She was returning to her car when she saw a new guy climb out of a car. He had just pulled up. The sun was close to setting, and it was hard to see in the dim light. For a moment she was afraid. What could he want here? It was a vacant lot, after all. She was the only thing there.

"Hello?" he called.

"Yeah, what can I do for you?" she asked nervously.

"What?"

"I said, what do you want?"

He walked closer. "My name's Eric Valence. I'm a police officer."

"You don't look like a police officer. Show me your badge."

He stopped in midstride. "I'm off duty."

"Yeah, right. You look like you're off duty from high school."

Actually, he didn't look bad for a complete stranger. He was slender, but had broad shoulders and a graceful stance. His features were dark, sharp. He looked intelligent, and she wondered if she should be trying to make a fool out of him without first knowing who he was and what he wanted.

"I'm twenty-one years old," he said.

"Isn't that kind of young to be a police officer?"

"What?"

"Can't you hear?"

He tilted the left side of her head his way. "I can hear," he said, insulted.

Yeah, but not too well. God, I'm ridiculing someone's handicap.

She took a step closer to him and spoke louder. "Are you really a police officer? Please tell me the truth."

He hesitated. "I work for the police. My uncle's a sergeant with the LAPD."

"And you just help out every now and then?"

"I'm collecting information for them for a case."

Alison remembered where she was and began to feel nervous. "What kind of case?" she asked.

"I can't go into detail. But I need to find the woman who used to live in this house before it burned down. I've been out to this neighborhood before, but nobody around here seems to know where she's moved to. Do you know who I'm talking about?"

Alison's throat tightened. The police might be on to them already. She had told the group that morning that she wanted to go to the authorities, but it was quite another thing to have the authorities come to them. They'd get no extra credit for turning themselves in.

"I might," she said evasively. "Who are we talking about?"

"Mrs. Katherine Hurly. Do you know her?"

She shrugged. "A little."

He gave her a shrewd look. "Did you know her son, Neil Hurly?"

Alison fought to keep her composure. She was an actress, after all—it should have been easy. But just the sound of Neil's name spoken by someone connected to the police made her face fall and her voice sound unsteady.

"A little," she said.

The guy noted her reaction. He had really turned the tables on her. "Did you go to school with him?"

"Why are you asking me all these questions?"

"I've only asked you a couple of questions. What's your name?"

"Alison."

"Alison what?"

"Alison. Who are you?"

"I've already told you who I am. My name's Eric Valence."

"I want to see some identification."

"I can show you my driver's license."

"No. How do I know you're with the police?"

"You could call them and check me out." He continued to study her. He knew she was worried. He had her over a barrel. "If you'd like to call the police, that is."

"I don't feel like doing anything right now except going home." She turned aside and stepped past him toward her car. He stopped her dead in her tracks with one little sentence.

"I know it wasn't Neil who burned to death in this house," he said.

"I don't know what you're talking about," she told the grass in front of her. He moved up and stood beside her.

"Yes, you do, Alison."

She looked at him out of the corner of her eye. "What do you want?"

"The truth. Who died here? Where's Neil?"

"Neil's dead."

"Where's his body?"

"I don't know."

"What did he die of?"

"Cancer."

Eric was surprised. "He had cancer?"

"Yeah. And if you don't believe me, ask his mother."

"That's just the point I can't find his mother. Can you help me find her?"

"No. You don't want to do that. It would be a waste of time. She doesn't know anything. She thinks her son died in the fire that took place here."

Eric moved in front of her. "But you know differently. Tell me the story."

"No. Why should I? I don't even know you."

"But I know something about you. I know, for instance, that you were involved in a criminal deception."

Alison was indignant. "Are you threatening me? 'Cause if you are, you can go back to the police station and get your uncle and have him come arrest me." She pushed by him. "I don't need to listen to this anymore."

She had reached her car when he caught up with her again. "Look, Alison, I'm sorry. I shouldn't have said what I did. I do want to know what happened here, but I don't want to get you in trouble." He paused and awkwardly reached out toward her. "You look pretty upset. I want to help you. That's all. Please let me help?"

She was going to yell at him again when the words of the stranger at the lake came back to her.

"You have asked for help, and someone will come. Trust this person."

"How can you help me?" she asked quietly.

"I can tell you what I know. You can tell me what you know. We can join forces." He fidgeted awkwardly. "I'm smarter than I look. I'm good at figuring things out."

He sounded so pitifully sincere, she had to smile. "You look plenty smart to me, Eric." She opened the door of her car for him. "Let's go get some coffee. We can talk. But I don't know if you'll believe half of what I have to tell you."

They went to a Denny's Coffee Shop not far from Neil's old house. They got a booth in the corner. Both ordered coffee and pie. Eric confessed what his real relationship was to the police department, which seemed to her to be only that of a hopeful reject. But she was fascinated by how he had used their computers and his ingenuity in piercing through Neil's deception. He told her about the difference in the X-rays and promised to show them to her when she took him back to his car. Even without the stranger's advice, she felt she had to trust Eric. He was within a hairbreadth of exposing everything that had gone on before.

So she told him her tale, starting with the night of the concert and the dead man in the desert. She took Eric all the way through Neil's chain letters, up to the new letters and the death of Fran Darey. Occasionally Eric would interrupt to ask a specific question. Was there another car on the road when they hit the man? Was there a history of mental illness in Neil's family? Did anyone besides Tony see Neil die? How long after Fran's accident was it before the police arrived on the scene? Eric did indeed have a sharp mind. Many of the things he asked, Kipp hadn't even thought of. She answered each of his questions as carefully as she could. She was relieved that he believed her every word. She asked him about his faith in her when she was done.

"I know it must all sound pretty farfetched," she said. "I won't blame you if you think I'm crazy."

He sipped his coffee. He had hardly touched it while she spoke. "I believe you. You couldn't have made up a story like that. It's the most extraordinary thing I've ever heard."

"You asked a lot of questions. Tell me what you think."

He didn't hesitate. "I think you're in serious danger."

In a way it was good to have her beliefs confirmed. Yet his conviction brought her no relief. "You don't think Fran's death was an accident?" she asked.

"Unlikely. She died right on schedule."

Alison nodded weakly. "Fran was always worried about not being on schedule." She sniffed. "So what should we do? Should we go to the police?"

"I wouldn't, but then, I think I know more than most cops. *You* probably should. You need protection."

"Will we get in trouble if we go?"

"Will you go to jail? Probably not. This Tony guy will, though."

"Why him? We were all responsible."

"He was driving when the man was hit. He didn't report it. That's manslaughter." Eric paused. "What exactly is your relationship to Tony?"

"He's my boyfriend."

Eric blinked. "I see."

"I don't want him to go to jail. It's unacceptable." She reached out and touched Eric's hand. "You told me you'd keep everything I said confidential."

The news that she had a boyfriend seemed to have taken him back a step. "Yes, and I will keep my word. But you asked my advice, and I gave it to you. I think you should go to the police."

"You know what I love? I love it that out of everyone in this group, you're the one who's making this suggestion. I just love it, Ali."

"We can't do that. Not yet." She took a breath. "If you know more than most police, what would you do next if you were in my predicament?"

"If you're convinced that the new Caretaker is not someone in your group, then you should concentrate all your efforts on finding out who the man in the desert was. His identity is the missing link. There's a good chance you didn't even kill him. The fact that there was no other car in the area indicates that he might have been dumped there, already dead."

"But then why can't we tell the police that? Tony wouldn't have to go to jail."

Eric shook his head. "I know there was no other car in the area because I believe you. The police won't. You buried a dead man in an unmarked grave and didn't tell anybody about it for over a year. You'll have no credibility with the authorities."

"I see your point."

"Who the man was and how he died is crucial," Eric went on. "If he was murdered, the people who killed him might have had contact with Neil."

"I don't see the logic in that."

"It's obvious. Neil is dead. We must assume he's dead because your boyfriend says he is. But you're getting new chain letters, and they're similar to the ones Neil sent. Therefore, somebody outside the group must have seen Neil's chain letters. This is assuming no one else in your group has turned psychotic, which seems unlikely. It's possible the person who is sending them now is the same one who composed the first ones. Tell me, in the short time you spoke with Neil after you knew he was the Caretaker, did he at any time indicate he had help?"

"I kept wondering and worrying and I tried, but this thing got in my head, and I couldn't get rid of it. I don't know where it came from. It was like a voice, saying this is true and this is a lie. It wouldn't shut up! I had to listen, and I did listen, and then . . . I did all this."

"I don't think so," she whispered.

"You sound doubtful?"

"He did say something that indicated he was being influenced."

"How so?"

Alison repeated the remark Neil had made just before he collapsed into Tony's arms and was carried away. She added, "But it was just something that was in his head. It wasn't like he had a real physical accomplice."

"I'm not so sure about that," Eric disagreed. "If he was mentally ill from a tumor in his brain, then his accomplice could have dominated him in such a fashion that he would be unable, even at the end, to admit that he was working with someone. It's a theory is all. We'll have a better idea which direction to take if we find out who the man was."

"How do we do that?"

"We'll use the computer at the police station. We'll go through all the missing-person files for July of last year. But first tell me everything you remember about the man."

Alison gave him what details she could remember. He had been about thirty years old, Caucasian, handsome, and well dressed in a tan sport coat and light brown slacks. His eyes had been green. She remembered that fact because Neil's had also been green, and Tony had said later that he believed that was one of the reasons for Neil's intense identification with the man. Eric didn't take notes as he spoke. He seemed confident in the power of his memory.

As they were leaving the coffee shop to pick up Eric's car and drive to the police station, Eric asked a single question. "Do you know if Kipp definitely left town?" he asked.

"He promised he would," Alison said.

"Did he give anybody any idea where he was going?"

"Not that I know of. He might have told Tony. They're good friends."

"I hope he didn't," Eric muttered.

"Why not? Tony wouldn't tell anybody."

Eric opened the door to the coffee shop for her. "I hope you're right."

Alison found the ease with which Eric entered the police station and computer room unnerving. Apparently the uncle they had said hello to at the front desk made everything all right.

Alison glanced around anxiously as Eric called up the appropriate files. The computer room was at the back of the station and deserted. Eric commented that none of the people in the station knew how to use the computer like he could.

"With the right programs," he said, "they can uncover almost anything. We're going to use one of them now. Basically it's a filter. It'll eliminate all the people who can't be the man. That's important. You wouldn't believe how many people disappear in L.A. every month."

"Where do they all go?" Alison asked.

"Usually they're wives or husbands trying to get out of unhappy marriages."

"That's sad."

Eric glanced at her and pointed to the computer. "You read as many unsolved murder cases as I have, and you'll see how sad the world can be."

"Why do you do it?"

"What do you mean?" he asked.

"Why do you spend so much time focusing on the worst of humanity?"

The question caught him by surprise. It was as if he had never thought about it before. "I like the challenge of solving a difficult puzzle," he said finally.

"Then you don't do it to help people?"

"Of course I do," he said quickly. "I like people." He added shyly, "I like you, Alison."

She smiled and patted him on the back. "I like you, too, Eric. Now, get to work. The hourglass is running low."

The time has come for your punishment. Listen closely, the hourglass runs low.

A line from Neil's original chain letter. There was something about the cabin where she had met the strange guy that reminded her of Neil. But for the life of her she couldn't remember what it was.

Eric asked the computer to sort through the missing-persons files. It took longer than Alison expected. Eric explained that the files were not all in one place; he had to call up each batch individually. She brought him fresh coffee, which he said he appreciated greatly. He was an interesting guy. As he worked he told her the plot line of every Agatha Christie novel. There were a lot of them.

At close to eleven o'clock Eric finally had a list of six people who met the man's description. They were both relieved the list was short. The previous July must have been a slow month for runaways.

"Now what do we do with this list?" Alison asked.

"We can do a couple of things," Eric said. "We can look up the guys online and try to contact their families. We may even connect with some of the guys. The ones who went home. It would be helpful to eliminate a few of them. There's another program we can use. It takes a name and searches through all the specified editions of the *L.A. Times* for a mention of the name. But it's a slow program. It could take all night to do all six of these people for the whole month of July."

"It's almost eleven," she said. "Do you want to call people now? You might wake them up."

"You're the one who's talking about hourglasses." Eric said.

In fifteen minutes he had pulled up a list of numbers for four out of the six people. He called them. The first person hung up on him before he could get out two words. The second one—a woman—began to cry at the mention of the man on the list. Apparently he had been her husband and had vanished on a hunting trip, only to be found dead a month later outside the cave of a bear. The third one—another woman—laughed when she heard her guy's name. He had left her for another woman, she said, and she was happy to be rid of him. The fourth number rang and rang without a response.

"We still have the two people we couldn't get numbers for," Eric said. He read them out loud off their list—"James Whiting and Frank Smith. Christ, we would get a Smith. The program will be stopping constantly."

"Let's put James Whiting's name in first," Alison suggested.

"Good idea. I hope somebody wrote an article on him when he disappeared."

The program had not been running long—less than an hour—when it flagged that it had found James Whiting in the

July 16 edition of the *Times.* The paper was not on the screen. The checking process was done internally. Eric had to call up the appropriate page. Alison was practically on top of him, she was so anxious.

Then she almost fainted to the floor.

There was a small article on James Whiting with a picture of him. Alison remembered his handsome profile from when he lay flat on his back in the desert. It was ironic—in the photograph he had on his tan sport coat, the jacket they had buried him in. All that the picture was missing was the trail of blood at the corner of his mouth. She pointed at the screen with a shaking finger.

"That's him," she gasped. "That's the man."

"Are you sure?"

Alison swallowed. "I'm sure."

They read the article together.

LOCAL BUSINESSMAN MISSING

Thirty-three-year-old James Whiting, a local record store owner and resident of Santa Monica for the last fifteen years, has been missing from his home for over a week. His wife, Carol Whiting, has no explanation for his disappearance. The Whitings have two children, ages six and three. James Whiting's store, the Sound of Soul, is located on Westwood Boulevard and has been a local favorite for ten years. So far the police have no clues to his whereabouts. If anyone has any information regarding his disappearance, please contact the LAPD.

Alison had to sit down. "He was married," she whispered. "He had two children. And we killed him and never told anybody."

"You don't know that you killed him," Eric said quickly. "I told you there's an excellent chance he was murdered and then dumped in the desert."

Alison shook her head. Her eyes burned. "But we buried him and never told anybody. We could have told the police. Then his wife would have known what happened to him." She began to weep. "She probably sat home night after night wondering where her husband was. We could have at least let her know he wasn't coming home."

"You made a mistake," Eric said. "You were scared. It's done. The best thing you can do for his family right now is try to find out why he was in the middle of the desert in the middle of the night. And whether he was dead or alive when he got there." He handed her a tissue. "We have a lot of work ahead of us."

Alison wiped at her face. "What are we going to do now?"

"Go home and go to bed. James and Carol Whiting are not listed. We'll go to his record store in the morning. I know the place—it's still in business. We'll find his wife and talk to her. Don't worry—you won't have to say what happened in the desert. You can make up another story."

"But the article said she had no idea why her husband had disappeared," Alison said.

"These articles never say anything. She'll have things to tell us, you can be sure of that. If we can get them out of her." Eric turned back to the computer screen. He called up the missing-person file on James Whiting again. He put a hand to his chin and frowned.

"What is it?" she asked.

"What was the date of that concert?" he asked.

"It was the end of July," Alison said. "I could check if you need the exact date."

"I might need it. But note the date of this article. It's the middle of July. James was gone from home about two weeks before you supposedly hit him. Yet you said the blood coming out of his mouth was wet. Therefore he just died then, the night of the concert."

"That's interesting."

"Very. I wonder what James was doing during that missing two weeks—who he was with." Eric pointed at the screen. "This is the most hopeless-looking missing-person file I've ever seen. It has the barest of facts on James. It almost looks as if parts of it have been erased."

"Who would do that?"

Eric turned off the screen. "Maybe the person who killed him."

"But he wouldn't have had access to these records. Right?"

Eric appeared uneasy. "He shouldn't have. But whoever's behind these letters seems to be able to get ahold of whatever he wants. *Whoever* he wants."

Earlier Alison had driven Eric to his car, so they both had their cars with them. But Eric followed Alison back to her house. She protested that it was way out in the valley, but he insisted. When she parked in her driveway, he got out of his car to walk her to the front door. She had called her parents from the police station and told them she was at Brenda's house. They were worried about her, how she was handling the death of Fran. But they still wanted her to go to NYU. They thought the change of scenery would be good for her. She hadn't thought about school for a second since Fran had died.

Eric eyed the dark house. "Are you sure your parents are home?"

"I'd know if they went out of town." She touched his arm. "Really, Eric, I'll be all right. Nothing happens to you until your name comes up on the list. Oh, that's something I forgot to tell you. My name is the only one that isn't on the Caretaker's list."

Eric was startled. "Why didn't you tell me that?"

"I just forgot. Why? I'm sure the new Caretaker knows who I am."

"I'm sure he does. He knows everything else." Eric considered. "This worries me."

She laughed. "I would think it would reassure you. It's no fun being on one of these lists, I can tell you."

He forced a smile. "I understand. I have your number. I'll call you in the morning."

"All right." She started for her front door, then paused. Eric continued to stand in her driveway, thinking. She was happy to have his mind on this problem. He was more resourceful than anybody she knew. A wave of tenderness for him flowed through her. She turned and reached out to give him a quick hug and a kiss on the cheek. "You have sweet dreams," she said.

Her gesture surprised him. He smiled again, but this time with pleasure. "How come it's always the prettiest girls who get in the worst trouble?" he asked.

"I think it's because of the guys they hang out with." She messed up his hair and walked away. "Good night, Eric. Call me early."

"Good night, Ali."

Chapter Ten

Sitting in his car down the street from Alison's house, Tony and Sasha watched Alison hug and kiss the handsome young stranger. And Tony felt a part of him die inside. But this part, as it died, didn't cease to hurt. It just rotted, and in the few seconds that Alison hugged the other guy the filth of it spread through his whole body until he could hardly breathe. Sasha sat silently beside him in the dark. If she knew he was in agony, she gave no sign of it. Tony had to close his eyes. His grief lay on top of him like a boulder, and his anger rocked his soul to its very foundation. That cheating bitch! How long had this been going on? Probably from the time he had first said hello to her. He opened his eyes and watched as the guy walked back to his car. He wondered if the guy had given his girl a feel while his eyes had been shut.

My girl. She's everybody's girl. Whoever wants her can have her.

The guy drove away without noticing them. Tony made a mental note of the guy's car—a red Honda Civic. He had a sinking feeling he'd see that car again. He reached for the key in his ignition.

"I should take you home," he muttered.

Sasha stopped him. "I didn't know we'd see this."

"But you wanted to come here." The streetlight beside them was burned out. He stared at her in the dark. They hadn't sat there long before Alison returned with her date. "Why?"

Her green eyes were on him. "Sometimes a girl gets a feeling about someone just by hearing about her. I had a feeling about Alison."

"What do you feel about her now?"

"That she's a whore."

Tony nodded and started the car. "My sentiment exactly."

The drive back to Sasha's apartment seemed to take an eternity. Had Tony been alone, he might have driven off the road, or into the oncoming traffic. Yeah, better to go out in a ball of fire and take a few others with him. Then, at least, he'd get himself on the front page of the paper. His devastation felt complete. He didn't want to live. He didn't want to breathe.

But he did want to get back at Alison.

Sasha invited him up to her apartment. He begged off, pleading exhaustion, but she insisted. Soon he was sitting on her couch, drinking coffee beside her. He took it scalding black, like her, and felt it burn as it went down. He sat staring at the carpet on her floor. It was gray—the color of his universe. He could think of absolutely nothing to say. Sasha reached over and rubbed his shoulder.

"I think it's time for that massage I promised you," she said.

"It's too late. Another time."

Her fingers worked into his muscles for a moment, then she stood. "You need it now. I'll get my table. I'll set it up out here."

He let her do what she wanted. She had a mind of her own, that was for sure. That goddamn Alison—all this time she'd been pretending to love him, when really he was just another body to jump on. She had made him feel like a piece of meat. She had probably screwed a dozen different guys since they'd started going out. It made him want to vomit to think about it.

Sasha came back with her massage table and began to unfold the legs. "I bought this table especially to work on people," she said. "It cost me four hundred dollars. But it was worth it. You can fall asleep on it if you want, it's so comfortable. Why don't you take off your clothes?"

He looked up. "What?"

"Take off your clothes. I can't give you a massage with them on. I use oil."

He glanced at his watch. It was two-thirty in the morning. "Do I have to take them all off?"

She was enjoying herself. "If you want me to do all of you. Don't be shy. I'll get you a towel to cover yourself."

She left the room and returned with a towel, and then went into the bathroom. He decided if he was going to undress, now was the time. He took off everything except his underwear. Then he lay facedown on the table and covered his lower body with the towel, his bare feet sticking out the bottom. The apartment was warm, and he was as comfortable as a man with a broken heart and a slut for a girlfriend could be. He glanced up as Sasha returned to the living room wearing a white nightgown and no shoes or socks. She carried an unlabeled bottle of lavender-colored oil in her right hand.

"Are you all right?" she asked.

"I'm fine." He lay down again. He heard her pour out a little oil and rub it briskly between her palms. She laid her hands gently on his back, and her touch was soft and greasy. He sighed involuntarily with pleasure. She began to rub the oil into his skin.

"Does that feel good?" she asked.

"Ycs."

"Are you still thinking about Alison?"

"No," he lied.

"You're lying. That's OK. You won't be thinking about her soon." Her hands shifted under the towel, and before he could stop her, she had pulled off his underwear and then re-covered him.

"Hey," he protested.

"You're too uptight," she said, returning to her exquisite

massaging of the muscles along his spine. As her fingers probed deeper, he realized just how tight he was. His back was one huge spastic muscle. It was funny how Alison had never offered to rub his back before. There were a lot of things she had never done for him that Sasha was already doing. Like being a friend when times were tough, rather than a cheating bitch. He just couldn't get that phrase out of his head.

Cheating bitch. Cheating bitch. Goddamn bitch.

Swear words had been invented for times like this.

"I appreciate this," he mumbled.

"You just relax and go on appreciating it. Go to sleep if you want. Alison's nothing. Forget her. She's already forgotten you."

"I want to forget her," Tony whispered. He let her touch travel all over his skin, the scented oil sinking deeper into his pores. Every now and then she'd lightly scratch him, making the nerves at the base of his spine moan with pleasure. But he didn't get sexually aroused. He was too exhausted. It occurred to him, just before he passed out that the oil smelled like the rest of the apartment. It wasn't a particularly pleasant odor. He figured she must have got it at the hospital. He'd have to tell her to use something else—next time.

Tony went to sleep.

The nightmare started where it had left off.

He was back in the vast abyss of despair. The place of red and purple lights, foul smells, and far-off cries. The pit of loud thunder and watchful eyes. He was approaching the huge dark wall, and this time he could see it clearly. It seemed to divide the very universe in two. But what a universe it was. On one side was pain. On the other was only more pain. What choice could he make? All he knew was he didn't want to join the tortured people. He knew they were trapped for eternity.

As he closed in on the wall, he saw that it was riddled with black portals or holes. There was no wind, yet he felt himself being sucked toward one of them, and he was unable to stop himself. His panic grew as the narrow opening swelled into a maw capable of swallowing a battleship. He drifted inside, and the lights and thunder were lost behind him. He was in a vacuum of blackness. Yet the sulfuric fumes had thickened. He felt himself smothering and prayed for it to end, but even as he did so he knew he was in a place where prayers were no longer heard.

But was that true? Or was it just another of *their* lies?

Them. The Caretakers.

Suddenly, in the black void, he could see into a bedroom lit by moonlight flooding into rectangular windows. He saw the place as a slice of reality cut out of his space of nonexistence. But the slice grew as he moved toward it, and soon he was inside the bedroom, although he could still sense the void behind him, waiting for him to return. On the bed lay his friend Kipp, snoring peacefully.

"Kipp," Tony said softly. "Can you hear me? Wake up. Where am I?"

His friend stirred and sat up. "Hello? Who's there?"

"It's me, Kipp. Tony. I'm right here."

Kipp didn't hear him. But he heard something. "Hello? Mary Lou?" Kipp climbed out of the bed in his underwear and walked to the bedroom door, passing right by Tony. Kipp peeked out into the hallway. It was then Tony noticed the noise that had awakened Kipp. He had to assume Kipp hadn't heard him since he didn't seem able to see him.

Am I a ghost? Am I dead?

The noise was coming from downstairs. Kipp started to call out to his aunt again—Tony remembered that Kipp's aunt's name was Mary Lou—when he decided to go investigate the noise himself. Tony didn't like that idea. He ran after Kipp as he made his way down the stairs.

"Don't go outside," Tony said. "One of the Caretakers might be out there. Kipp! Listen to me!"

But Kipp wasn't listening. Still in his underwear, he walked to the front door and opened it and peeked outside. The noise appeared to be coming from the garage. It sounded like someone scratching a rake across the hood of a car.

"Who's there?" Kipp called.

"It's one of them!" Tony pleaded, standing at his friend's side. "Don't go out there."

"Hello?" Kipp called again. He went outside. Tony tried to grab hold of his arms, but he could have been trying to grab his own reflection in a mirror. Kipp strode across the overgrown lawn and entered the garage through a side door.

"Oh, God, stop!" Tony cried.

The raking noise inside the garage had stopped. Kipp fumbled for a light, but when he threw the switch, the garage remained dark. Kipp frowned. His eyes grew wide when he noticed that the paint on one side of his aunt's car had been largely scratched away.

"It doesn't matter," Tony hissed. "Get out of here."

Kipp heard a sound coming from the bowels of the garage. Brave fool that he was, he walked toward it. "Hello?" Kipp said.

A wave of liquid came flying out of the dark directly at Kipp. In a moment he was drenched, and a metal bucket clamored to the concrete floor in front of him. Kipp hardly had a second to register what was happening before a wooden match flared to life, scraped along the side of the ruined car by a figure wrapped in black shadow. Tony's nose was working fine, and the air stunk of gasoline.

"Kipp!" Tony screamed even though Kipp couldn't hear his words.

The shadowy figure tossed the burning match toward Kipp. It bounced harmlessly off his chest without igniting the gasoline, but it landed in the puddle at his feet. Kipp stared down at the tiny orange flame, amazed, but only for a second before he was transformed into a human torch. The flames whipped up his legs all the way to his hair, and the scream that poured out of Kipp's throat rent Tony's heart. Kipp thrashed up and down like a demented scarecrow for several seconds in the worst imaginable pain a human being could experience.

Tony tried to grab him, to hold him, to do something for him. But he couldn't, and it didn't matter anyway. It was too late. Kipp fell to his blackened knees, and his screams began to die as the flesh surrounding his mouth was peeled away in crisp layers. Yet the screams didn't stop for Tony. After he watched his friend slowly die, he was suddenly back in the black portal that ran between the two hells. And the screams of those on the far side of the wall were no longer so distant, no longer so different from human wails. In fact, they sounded very much the same as Kipp did as he passed out of the world of the living. Filled with anguish, devoid of hope, forever forsaken. . . .

Tony opened his eyes and found himself staring up at a strange ceiling. At first he hadn't the slightest idea where he was. Nor did he care. He was just happy the nightmare was over. Never in his worst dreams had he experienced anything so terrible.

Tony moved his head to the side and saw Sasha curled up in a sleeping ball on the couch. The entire evening came back to him in a flash. The relief of waking from the nightmare faded as he remembered Alison's betrayal. How could she have been kissing another man when she said she still loved him? She was worse than the Harlot of Babylon. She was a whore. Sasha had said it right.

Tony sat up and shivered. Except for the towel around

his waist, he was naked. He couldn't imagine how Sasha had managed to turn him over without waking him. But he'd been under a lot of stress lately. He was exhausted. He had to get home and into bed.

The images from his nightmare wouldn't leave him, though. Watching Kipp burn had seemed so real. Tony wondered why he had dreamed Kipp was at his aunt's house, although it would be a logical place for Kipp to run. Kipp had not told anyone where he was going. Hugging the towel around his waist, Tony slipped off the massage table and tiptoed into the kitchen with his phone. He was being silly, he knew, but it couldn't hurt to give Kipp a call and see how he was doing. Tony dialed, and a moment later he had Kipp on the phone. It sounded as if he had woken his friend up. Made sense—it was the middle of the night. Tony didn't mind. It was such a relief to hear Kipp's voice.

"Yeah, what is it, Tony?" Kipp mumbled.

"I wanted to see if you were all right."

Kipp yawned. "I'm fine."

"I'm sorry to wake you. Go back to sleep. Call you in a couple of days."

"Everything cool there?"

"Everything's cool," Tony told him. "Good night. You got your night-light on?" It was a reference to a remark Kipp had made just before Neil had kidnapped him. Kipp laughed quietly.

"Sure do," Kipp said. "Happy dreams, buddy."

Tony set the phone down. He walked back into the living room, still clutching his towel, and found Sasha sitting on the couch. A tunnel of moonlight cut through a nearby window and landed on her legs. But her face remained dark. Her green eyes—he could hardly see them.

"What's the matter?" she asked.

"Nothing."

"Where are you going?"

"Nowhere." He reached for his pants.

"You must be going somewhere." She stood and smoothed her nightgown over her sleek hips. "You're getting dressed."

"I have to go home." He couldn't find his underwear. What had she done with it? She strode across the room and put her hands on his shoulders, interrupting his search.

"Why?" she asked.

"You don't want me staying the night."

In response she reached up and kissed him on the lips. A hard wet kiss. And he kissed her back, and her hand went around the back of his neck, into his hair, and began to pull at his blond strands until they hurt. He yanked away from her and took a breath. She mocked him with a naughty smile.

"Why can't you stay?" she asked again.

Her lips had tasted like pure pleasure. Suddenly he couldn't think of a single reason. "All right," he said. "But I've been told I snore."

She took his hand and led him toward her bedroom. "Who told you that? Alison?"

He hesitated. "Yeah."

"Is that who you were calling?"

"No. I was calling a friend of mine—Kipp Coughlan. He's staying with his aunt in Santa Barbara for a few days."

"Why?"

"There's some trouble that he's trying to stay out of. It's a long story."

They entered her bedroom, and she let go of his hand and pulled back the covers. He couldn't believe what he was doing. He was about to make love to a girl other than Alison. He should have felt no guilt, after what he had seen that night. But he did—plenty of guilt. He felt scared, too, and he didn't know why. Sasha took his hand again and pulled him onto the bed and kissed him some more. These kisses were softer, slower, like the strokes of her massaging fingers when they were not probing deep into his sore body. She scratched her fingernails across his hard belly.

"Tell me your long story," she whispered.

"You don't want to hear it."

"But I do. It's on your mind. I want to put your mind at ease." She nibbled on his ear with her wet teeth. "I want to make you happy."

Tony began to talk. He didn't know why. Maybe because he was exhausted. Maybe because he was in the arms of a beautiful girl. He talked a lot. He told her about Neil and the original chain letters. He even told her about the new Caretaker, and the horrible nightmares he'd been having. Sasha listened silently between caresses and kisses. When he was done, she just nodded and touched him all over, and kissed him so deep he felt as if he were being swallowed whole. But she didn't let him make love to her. She kept her nightgown on the entire night and eventually he fell asleep and dreamed no more.

Chapter Eleven

Eric called Alison early Sunday morning. He had good news and bad news. The new owner of James Whiting's record store was not going to be in till Tuesday, and the help refused to give out his home number. That was the bad news. The good news was that James Whiting's brother was the guy who had bought the store. If anyone knew where James had been during those missing two weeks, it should be him, Eric thought. Eric told Alison to keep her head low and call him if anything happened between then and Tuesday. All day Sunday Alison tried to reach Tony, with no luck. His parents didn't know where he was. That made her worry all the more.

Come Monday there was still no sign of Tony.

He didn't even show up for Fran's funeral.

They buried Fran in the same cemetery where Neil had

been laid to rest. Of course, Neil had been alive at the time of his funeral, and they had unknowingly spent the afternoon mourning the remains of James Whiting. Such could not be said for Fran. As the doctor at the hospital had said, she was as dead as they came. Alison stood dressed in black beside Brenda and couldn't be free of the idea that Fran lay only a couple feet away without her head properly attached. The attending minister spoke about the valley of the shadow of death and lying down in green pastures to rest beside clear waters. It all sounded like a badly written fairy tale to Alison. If there was a God, he was keeping his address secret. Maybe he didn't want to get a chain letter. Alison was beginning to believe the Caretaker was working for the devil. She had had a hellish dream the night before, filled with weird colored lights, sick smells, and tortured souls.

The funeral finally came to an end, and Alison hugged and kissed Fran's parents and told them if there was anything she could do . . . What a futile offer. What could she do for them? Be their daughter? Fran had been their only child. It was all so sad.

Alison said goodbye to Brenda and her own parents and drove home by herself. But as she had on Saturday, she passed by her usual off-ramp and headed for the mountains. An hour and a half later she found herself walking beside the lake where she had met the intriguing stranger. She went to the door of his cabin and knocked repeatedly. There was no answer. She tried the knob, and the door swung in easily. But the inside was not as she had remembered it, not exactly. There was the same wood stove, the same black kettle sitting on top of it. But the place was filled with dust and cobwebs, as if it had been months since anyone had lived there. It made her wonder whether her encounter with the stranger had been a dream—or worse, a hallucination. Yet she knew in her heart that it had been neither. She wondered if she should discuss the matter with Eric. She'd have liked to tell Tony about the mystical encounter. Where could he be? That morning his parents had said he was out doing errands.

Night was falling when Alison finally returned home. She sat in her room and read a book before going to bed. She had trouble concentrating on the story, and when the heroine died unexpectedly at the end, she felt nothing. She was too worried about which of her friends was going to die next. Thank God Kipp had done what he promised and gone away without telling anyone where he was. She had cursed God that morning, and now she was thanking him. She hoped he gave her no more reasons to destroy her faith.

But God did. Or rather, the Caretaker did.

Another call shook her awake in the middle of the night. She turned on the light before picking it up. She knew the news couldn't be good.

"Hello?" she said.

"Ali." It was Brenda, broken and tearful.

"What's happened? Is he dead? He can't be dead, dammit!"

Brenda moaned. "He was at his aunt's. Tony just called me.

The Caretaker got him there. Soaked him with gasoline and set him on fire. Oh, Ali, Kipp's gone."

"Do you want me to come over?" Alison asked.

"No." Brenda's voice suddenly sounded distant. "I'm next on the list. There'll be a letter for me in the morning. Stay away from me."

"But we have to have another meeting of the group. We have to go to the police. Brenda?"

Her girlfriend had hung up. Alison quickly dialed Eric. She woke him up, but he didn't sound mad. She told him what had happened. He cursed softly.

"Tell me the order of the people on the list again?" he asked.

"It's Brenda, Joan, and Tony. Brenda will probably get a letter in the mail tomorrow, the way this Caretaker works."

"You say you guys are going to have a meeting tomorrow?"

"I'm going to try to organize one," she said.

"Make it for the afternoon. I want to come, but I have to do some things in the morning first."

"I don't know if the gang will let you come."

"It doesn't matter. You tell me when and where it is, and I'll show up. They'll have to listen to what I have to say."

"You're going to tell them we have to go to the police, aren't you? We have to put a stop to this."

Eric was evasive. "I hope I'll have a better idea tomorrow about what to recommend."

"Where are you going in the morning?"

"The record store. It's more on my side of town, so you don't need to go. Just stay home and rest. The newspaper office, too. I want to see if I can trace who's been placing these ads."

They had tried a similar tactic with Neil's chain letters. They had been unsuccessful. "Good luck," she said.

"Once you have the meeting set, call and leave the information on my answering machine. And, Ali?"

"Yes."

"We're going to stop this bastard."

"How can you be so sure?" she asked.

"He'll make a mistake. They always do. He may have made one already."

"What?"

He hesitated. "Let me talk to you about it tomorrow."

They said their goodbyes and Alison set down the phone. Tony had called Brenda but hadn't called her. That said a lot about the condition of their relationship. Reluctantly she picked up the phone again and dialed his number. Someone answered quickly on his end, but didn't speak.

"Hello?" she said. "Tony? Are you there, Tony?"

She could hear breathing. It could be his. Then behind him she could make out faint whispering. This did not belong to Tony.

It was a girl.

"Tony?" she cried.

The phone clicked in her ear, and she heard nothing but a dial tone.

Chapter Twelve

The gang met at twelve sharp in the park beside the rocket ship. Once there had been seven. Now there were only four: Brenda, Joan, Alison, and Tony. Alison had had to get Joan to call Tony about the meeting. Tony wasn't returning her calls. Tony sat on the slide across from her and stared at her as if he had never seen her before. But he knew who she was. She had tried to give him a comforting hug and tell him how sorry she was about what had happened to Kipp, but he had brushed her away with a sharp move of his arm. Life was wonderful.

Brenda had received a letter in the morning mail. Kipp's name had gone the way of Fran's—into nothingness. There was an ad in the Personals section of the *Times* for Brenda. Decoded it read:

Cut off your trigger finger and give it to Joan with her letter.

Trigger finger? Brenda didn't even own a gun.

But Joan's dad did. He was a cop.

The gang wanted to start the meeting, but Alison stalled them for a few minutes. She was waiting for Eric to arrive. She had called and left the information he requested on his machine. He didn't disappoint her. Out of nowhere he came walking over a grass hill and strode into the center of the group. Joan and Brenda stared at him, amazed. Strangely enough, Tony didn't seem surprised to see him. Tony shook his head and spit on the ground.

"Hi," Eric said. "I'm a friend of Alison's. I know about the chain letters, but please don't get mad at her. I made her tell me what she knew."

Joan turned to Alison. "Are you out of your mind to bring in a stranger? Don't we have enough problems as it is?"

Brenda had been a decent shade of white before Eric's arrival. Now she could have tried out for the lead role in a play about Casper the Ghost. "Ali," she begged. "What's got into you?"

"Eric discovered that it wasn't Neil who burned to death in the fire in June," Alison said quickly. "He came to me, I didn't go to him. But I'm glad he's here. He's an amateur sleuth, and he's better than most professionals. He's discovered who the man in the desert was."

"Who?" Tony asked tonelessly.

"James Whiting," Eric said. He looked at Tony. "May I sit down?"

Tony eyed him with barely concealed hatred. "Sure."

Eric sat down near Alison. "I'm here to help you guys," he said. "What Alison said is true. She didn't approach me, I approached her. My uncle works for the LAPD. I was going through the police files and stumbled on the fact that Neil had been identified by an emerald ring after burning to death in a raging fire. I knew an emerald would melt in such a fire and figured there had to be something wrong. That started me on my investigation. So far I have kept the confidence of your group. I've told no one about the chain letters."

Tony was amused. "You're connected to the police. Great."

"Only in an unofficial capacity," Eric said smoothly. "But let's not argue about whether I should be here or not. I'm here, and I want to help you out of this predicament."

"What can you do?" Joan asked sarcastically.

Eric turned the left side of his head toward her. "What?"

"Can't you hear?" Joan asked.

"I can hear," Eric said. "Please repeat your question?"

Joan was mean. "You can't help us. You can't even understand what we say."

"I can give you advice," Eric said. "I can point out certain facts that maybe you overlooked. I'll point out one right now. But first I have to ask a question. Who in this group knew where Kipp had gone?"

"None of us," Brenda said. 'That was the point of his leaving."

"Then how did the Caretaker know where to find him?" Eric asked. No one answered. Eric scanned the group. "Someone must have known. How about you, Tony? You were closest to him."

Tony surprised them all. "I knew he was at his aunt's."

"How?" Alison exclaimed.

Tony ignored the question.

"How did you know?" Brenda had to ask.

"I called him and he answered," Tony said simply.

"But how did you know he was there?" Joan asked.

Tony shrugged. "I don't know."

"You're going to have to do better than that," Eric said.

Tony chuckled and spit again. "I don't have to do anything."

"All right," Eric said diplomatically. "Could you tell us if you told anybody else where Kipp went?"

Tony flashed a fake smile. "I don't remember."

"Tony!" Brenda protested. "For God's sake, tell him if you did."

Tony hardened. "Why? This guy's an asshole. He's here to help us? He's here to give us advice? What kind of advice do you have for us, Mr. Amateur Sleuth?"

"I suppose the simplest thing for you to do now would be to go to the police," Eric said philosophically.

"If we do, we'll go to jail," Joan said with no strength in her protest. Indeed, it seemed as if Joan was considering the possibility as they spoke.

"Better to be in jail for a little while than to die," Eric said.

Brenda spoke in a faltering voice. "But this Caretaker could get us even there. Tony wouldn't have told anyone where Kipp was, even if he did know. In jail we could be more helpless."

"That's not true," Alison said. "With the police we'll be safe."

"Safe?" Brenda asked, and her voice cracked altogether. Her opinion of the Caretaker had changed a hundred and eighty degrees since their last meeting, which didn't surprise Alison. "Who can protect us from this monster? I tell you no one can. He pulled Kipp's whereabouts out of thin air. He went there in the middle of the night, lured my boyfriend into the garage, soaked him with gasoline, and then lit him on fire. He did all this without leaving a trace. Tell me what kind of man could do that? Not one that's human, that's who!"

Her words sent a shock through the group, and they fell silent. They had thought such a thing—that their assailant might be of supernatural origin—when Neil's letters had been coming. Of course, they realized how silly they'd been—later. But not much later, because right now, to Alison, there was a ring of truth to what Brenda was suggesting. Eric did not agree.

"Kipp was killed by someone in a human body," Eric said. "There is a rational explanation for everything. It often takes time and hard work to find it, but the truth usually comes out in the end." Eric reached over and patted Alison on the leg. "Now, I went to the paper and the record store this morning. I found out that—"

"I'm getting out of here!" Tony exclaimed, jumping to his

feet and hustling toward the parking lot. Alison got up and ran after him. She went alone. She didn't catch up to him until they were halfway to the cars, at the top of a grassy bluff. He threw off her arm with a cruel swing of his.

"Tony?" she cried. "You have to stop this. You have to talk to me!"

"I don't talk to whores," he muttered, plowing forward.

Alison's breath caught in her throat. "How can you call me that?"

He whirled on her, and his voice and face were savage. He was like a man possessed. "I was there Saturday night when you were kissing your new boyfriend. I saw it all. But that's OK because you see, I wasn't alone. I had a new girl with me." He stabbed a finger in the direction of his car at the bottom of the hill. "I have her with me today."

A young woman with long maroon hair sat in the passenger seat. She nodded and climbed slowly out of Tony's car. She did not approach them, but stood there leaning with one hand braced on the side of the car, dressed entirely in black. She was extraordinarily attractive, but a cruel light seemed to emanate from her straight into Alison's heart. It was almost as if the strange girl were challenging Alison to a duel with invisible steel knives. In fact, Alison felt as if one of the girl's knives had already struck home. The pain in her heart was overwhelming.

"I did not cheat on you," she whispered to Tony.

"Fine," Tony said coldly. "I didn't cheat on you, either,

when I slept with Sasha. All's fair in love." This time he spat on her. "Bitch."

She watched him walk away. The girl—Sasha—didn't climb back into the car until Tony arrived. Then the girl gave Alison one last stab with her weird green eyes and got in beside Tony. Alison watched them kiss. Sasha squashed so hard against Tony's face it looked as if she were trying to eat him alive. Then Alison watched them both laugh and drive off.

Eric walked up to Alison. He offered her a handkerchief, which she took to wipe off Tony's spit from the side of her face. His saliva had a funny smell to it. It reminded her of biology class.

"I'm sorry," he said.

"So am I," she whispered.

"The girls are waiting back at the rocket ship to hear what I've discovered," Eric said. "But I don't know if I want to tell now. This group is extremely unstable. I don't know if we can trust any of them."

"That girl is bad."

"Pardon?"

Alison looked at him. "That girl is bad."

Eric blinked. "I can see why you don't like her."

Alison shook her head and sighed. She felt as if she were already trapped in the Caretaker's box. She couldn't help wondering if everything that had just happened hadn't been planned in advance.

"What did you find out?" she asked.

"Nothing from the paper. They protect the identity of anybody who places an ad, no matter how weird. But the police might be able to go back there later and learn something."

"What about at the record store?" she asked.

"I spoke to James's brother. He was elusive. He knew stuff, but he wasn't talking. He did give me the home address of his sister-in-law."

"James Whiting's wife?"

"Yes. Want to go have a talk with her?"

Alison stared in the direction Tony had disappeared. He had slept with another girl. Her Tony. It was hard to imagine. It was horrible to think about. He must have been put under a spell.

"I want to talk to her right now," Alison replied.

Chapter Thirteen

Mrs. Carol Whiting was not at home when they tried the front door of the tiny redbrick house in Santa Monica. Or maybe she was and her brother-in-law had warned her that he had given out her address. Alison asked Eric what story he had fed the brother-in-law, but Eric was evasive. He just said he had his "ways."

There was nothing to do but hang out near there until the woman came home. Eric took her to a restaurant, but she couldn't even eat her salad. They tried the house again, found no one there, and then Eric took her to a sci-fi film about a future society of humans who wanted to be robots. Alison fell asleep in the movie. She hadn't slept the previous night after hearing about Kipp's death. She did sleep now through two showings of the movie. When Eric woke her it was ten o'clock at night. He asked if she'd been having nightmares. Apparently she had often kicked and clawed at the air while unconscious. But she'd had no dreams that she could recall. All she knew was that her long nap had done little to refresh her.

They went to the woman's house once more.

She was at home and opened the door for them.

"Yes?" she said. "Can I help you?"

She was a short, plump woman with smooth dark features and a nervous twitch in her right eye. She couldn't have been thirty, but she had a streak of gray that split her short hair in two. She looked tired.

"Hi," Eric began. "My name's Tom and this is Amy and we're here to—"

"Talk to you about your missing husband," Alison interrupted.

Eric stared at her in shock. He had told her ahead of time to leave everything to him. But she was tired of deception. The woman had backed up a step.

"I don't understand," she said.

"We know what happened to your husband," Alison said. "We'd like to tell you the whole story. May we come in?"

"You knew Jim?" the woman asked, uncertain.

"No," Alison said. "But I was one of the people who helped bury him."

The woman shuddered. "Who are you?" she asked.

Alison reached out and touched the woman's hand. At first the woman flinched, but as she looked into Alison's eyes, she seemed to relax. Maybe she could see that Alison, too, had been to hell and had yet to come back.

"Please," Alison said. "We mean you no harm."

She studied them for a moment longer before opening the door wider. "Come in," she said.

The woman insisted that they call her Carol. Her brother-in-law had not warned her that they were coming over. Just the same, her children were not at home. They were at a sister's house, which was probably a good thing. Alison figured they wouldn't have got inside with the kids around. Carol was making herself coffee and asked if they would like a cup. They said sure. Carol fussed over them. She was obviously dying to hear what they had to say, but at the same time she was doing everything to postpone it.

There was a picture of the man on the piano. Jim.

When the three of them were seated comfortably in the living room, with Eric positioned with his good ear toward Carol, Alison described what had happened the summer before in the desert after the concert. She kept her story focused on that night alone. She didn't go into the chain letters or Neil's madness. Sitting across from her, Eric began to relax. As she approached the part where they buried the man, she began to cry softly. It was no act. She couldn't get over the fact that she was talking to the man's wife. Carol cried with her as she tried to explain why they hadn't gone to the police.

"We thought of you," Alison said. "I mean, we didn't know

if you even existed. But we knew the man must have family somewhere. We thought we could send an anonymous letter to the police explaining what had happened. But we were afraid it would be traced back to us." Alison wiped at her face. She had shed a lot of tears lately. One of these days they were going to dry up. But today was not that day. Another flood burst out as she thought of covering the man with dirt. "We didn't mean to kill him. It was an accident. We were driving with our lights out and then we hit him and that was that. I'm so sorry, Carol. I can't tell you how sorry I am. All this time you must have wondered what happened to him."

Carol surprised her by reaching out and hugging her, comforting her. This crazy teenager who had destroyed her husband's life. It made no sense to Alison until Carol spoke.

"I have always wondered what happened to Jim's body," Carol said gently. "I would lie awake at night wondering where he lay. But I knew he was dead. I have always known who killed him. Don't be so hard on yourself, Alison. Jim was dead when you and your friends ran over his body."

Alison stared at her in disbelief. "Are you sure?"

Carol sat back in her seat. "Maybe I should tell you my story. It'll put your mind at ease." She put her hand to her forehead. "But those are days I don't care to remember."

"Tell us what you feel comfortable with," Alison said.

Carol shrugged. "I guess I'll have to start at the beginning. Jim and I were married eight years before he met Charlene.

We had a happy life. He had the record store and business was good. We both had the children to play with and love. I was finishing my master's in education at UCLA. I remember the first night Jim mentioned Charlene to me. We were sitting in bed at night reading. He just tossed out her name. He said she was a pretty girl who regularly came into the store and was always asking him to order CDs of bands he'd never heard of. Groups like Dried Blood and Black Sex—real sicko groups. I remember Jim saying that Charlene seemed like such a nice girl to be into crap like that. I just grunted. Jim had lots of odd customers. And that was the last I heard of Charlene for a long time.

"Several months went by and Jim began to change in small ways. He became more impatient with the children and snapped at me frequently. I'm not saying Jim was a saint before this change occurred, but he had always been a nice guy. He really was, and I'm not just saying that because I was his wife. He didn't wish anybody any harm. But his mood had turned sour, and I didn't know how to shake him out of it. He began to suffer from insomnia and took to spending longer hours at the store. It got so that he almost never came home, even when the store was closed. You must think I was pretty stupid, huh? I couldn't see that he was having an affair. But at the time I was worried that he was sick. He'd always been a bit chubby, but now he was definitely on the slim side. I'd put a home-cooked meal in front of him and he'd just pick.

"Then I caught him snorting cocaine in our bathroom one

day. I had come home early from school. I was shocked. The music business is full of drugs, but Jim wasn't that kind of guy. He never put anything harmful in his body. Finally, I thought I understood the changes that were happening in him. He told me that he was barely into the stuff, that it was just a weekend habit. But he was obviously an addict. I checked our bank account. I always let Jim handle the business side of our lives. I was sick when I learned that we were broke. Jim had blown all our savings on drugs. When I confronted him with what I'd found, he promised that he'd get help. I went with him to several clinics, and he seemed to be ready to enter one when I made another shocking discovery.

"I was digging in my garden when I smelled something peculiar. I dug a little deeper and found a green trash bag filled with the remains of desecrated animals. There were dogs and cats and even a skunk. And all of them had been beheaded and their fur shaved with strange symbols. Not for a second did I think they had anything to do with Jim, but when I told him about what I had found, it was all there on his face. He had done those things to those animals! I couldn't believe it. Was this the man I had married? He was behaving like a psycho. I took the children and left for my sister's.

"But Jim called me every night and begged me to come back. He told me be had gotten involved with bad people but that he was getting away from them. He mentioned Charlene's name as one of them. I didn't know who she was until he reminded me. But the way he said her name made me suspicious. I asked him if he was having an affair with her, and when he didn't answer right away, I knew where I stood. That was one thing I wouldn't put up with—unfaithfulness. I swore I'd never see him again and hung up on him. But two minutes later I was missing him worse than I ever had in my life. I drove over to our house and got there just as Charlene was arriving.

"She was pretty. I could see that from where I was sitting in my car up the block. They didn't see me. I watched as she dragged Jim out of the house and into her car. She was laughing all the time like a teenager. They drove away and I followed. They got off the freeway in a section of town where the gangs are very active. I knew I was risking my life just to go there. They parked outside a shabby warehouse, and the girl dragged Jim inside. I keep using the word *dragged.* It was obvious Jim didn't want to go. I'm not saying that to protect him, either. I assumed Charlene was into drugs and that she was taking my husband to meet her connection.

"I sat outside that old warehouse for hours, well into the night. But they never reappeared, and the characters walking by on the street really scared me. Finally I had to go back to my sister's. But I noted exactly where the warehouse was, and the next day I returned there with the police."

"The police let you go inside the warehouse with them?" Eric broke in, surprised.

"Not at first. Two of them checked out the warehouse while

I waited in the patrol car. When they came back outside, their faces were white. One of them had to run into the alley and vomit against the wall. They told me there was nobody inside, and that I didn't want to see what was in there. But, of course, I did want to see. My husband was involved here. I jumped out of the car and ran inside before they could stop me."

"It was a meeting place for a satanic cult?" Eric said.

Carol raised an eyebrow. "How did you know?"

"It fits the pattern," Eric said. "Please go on."

Carol's face showed extreme revulsion. "It stank in there beyond belief. There was dried blood everywhere, and blood that was not so dry. Animal entrails and skins lay everywhere. The walls and floor were covered with bizarre symbols. Many had been painted in blood. There were half-burnt black candles on the floor, as if someone had been celebrating a black mass. I could only stay in there a few seconds before I became hysterical. When I got outside, the officers tried to comfort me. They thought what I had seen had upset me, and it had. But it was more the thought of what Jim had gotten himself into that tore me apart. These weren't bad people he was seeing. They were evil. And I knew they must want something from him, but I didn't know what." Carol looked over at Eric. "Do you know what it was?"

Eric shifted, uncomfortable. "I can guess."

"Go ahead," Carol said. "It's already happened. It's done with."

"The girl Charlene needed your husband to be her victim in a ritual murder," Eric said.

"That can't be true," Alison blurted out. "Things like that don't happen now."

Carol shook her head sadly. "I'm afraid your friend is right. Charlene was an apprentice. She wanted to be a full-fledged witch. To be one she had to murder an innocent. Someone who loved her." Carol lowered her head, and a bitter tear trickled over her cheek. "That girl murdered my husband. She did it so that she could live forever."

"But how do you know that for sure?" Alison protested. "Did you talk to her? Did you see your husband again?"

Carol chewed on her lower lip, and her eyes were focused far away. "I didn't see him again, but I spoke to him once more on the phone. He called me at our house a couple of days later in the middle of the night. I had gone back to living there, by myself. The children stayed at my sister's. I hoped he'd come back. He sounded scared as he told me he was going to try to come home soon, but that he had some business to finish up first. He apologized for getting involved with Charlene. I asked him if he was in love with her, and he was silent for a long time and never did answer the question. Someone came into the room where he was, so he hung up. That was the last I heard from him."

"And did you ever speak to Charlene?" Alison repeated.

"No," Carol said. "But I spoke to her parents."

"Where?" Eric asked. "When?"

"At the morgue, when they came to identify Charlene's body."

"She's dead?" Alison asked.

Carol nodded grimly. "I hate to say it but I'm glad. But let me back up and tell you what happened in the order it happened. The police set up a stakeout on the warehouse. But the cult must have got wind of it because they never went back there. I told the police about Charlene, but that's all I had—a first name and an incomplete description."

"Excuse me," Alison interrupted. "What color was Charlene's hair?"

"Blond," Carol said.

"Oh," Alison said thoughtfully.

"What is it?" Eric asked.

"Nothing," Alison said. "Please continue, Carol."

"The police couldn't find a missing young lady named Charlene. By that I mean there was no missing-person report on such a person. I went ahead and filed a missing-person report on Jim. I had the paper put in a small article about him. That was a waste. Then I had to sit and wait because nothing happened. Two weeks went by. I figured Jim was dead. Then one night I got a call from the police. They wanted me to drive to a hospital out in the San Bernardino Valley. They believed my description of Charlene matched a body that had been brought in."

"That's where I live," Alison said.

Carol nodded. "At the hospital *was* the body of Charlene—I recognized her. Her parents were there, too. Her real name was Jane and she had committed suicide by falling onto a propped-up knife in her own bedroom in the middle of the night, with black candles burning and pentagons painted in her own blood drawn all over her naked body. Her parents found her only a few minutes after she'd died. I can't tell you how distraught they were. And they didn't have good news for me."

"Jane had admitted to killing Jim before she did herself in?" Eric said.

"I should let you tell the story," Carol said.

"I'm sorry I keep interrupting," Eric said.

"I didn't mean that sarcastically," Carol replied. "You obviously have knowledge about these matters. I wish I'd had more—maybe my husband would be alive now. Anyway, you're right. Before her parents went to bed that night, Jane told them that she had killed her lover that night and dumped his body in the desert. She said it so matter-of-factly that they thought she was high on something. They told her to go to bed and sleep it off, whatever it was. Jane's parents had absolutely no idea their darling daughter was involved with Satanism, even though they knew she did drugs."

"What was the date you went to the hospital?" Eric asked.

"July twenty-eighth," Carol said.

Eric looked at Alison. "Was that the night of the concert?"

She thought a moment. "I think it was, yes."

"It must have been," Carol said. Her shoulders sagged with the weight of the memory. "Jane was the girl Jim had been with. I could see that with my own eyes, even as she lay on the cold slab in the morgue, naked, with a big bloody hole in her chest. And if Jane had just killed her lover, it had to mean Jim was dead. It was a relief in a way. I didn't have to worry anymore." Carol began to cry again. "I don't have to worry now."

Alison got up and went over to sit beside Carol and put an arm around her. She almost asked Carol if she had received any strange mail lately. But she figured Carol would have told them if she had. Alison wanted Carol to think it was over. The woman had suffered enough.

"That's my story," Carol said, and she hugged Alison again. "I'm glad you found Jim's body as soon as you did. You didn't do me or my children a great injustice. We knew he was gone. I can understand how a group of kids could get scared and make the wrong decision. At least Jim wasn't left out in the open where animals could have messed with his body. You buried him deep, didn't you?"

"Yes," Alison said. The grave hadn't been that deep. They'd had no tools and the ground had been hard. But she'd say anything to comfort the woman now.

Except for one big thing.

"Do you remember where you buried him?" Carol asked, wiping at her tears.

"I'm afraid not," Eric broke in. "We have no idea. We've tried to find the spot a dozen times and failed."

Carol frowned as she looked at him. "You were there that night, Eric?"

Eric paused. "No, I wasn't there. But I was made aware of what went on. Alison and I are old friends. I'm sorry we won't be able to reclaim your husband's body. But we would greatly appreciate it if you didn't go to the police with Alison's story. It could get the whole group in serious trouble, and there would be no point in it, not after all this time."

Carol nodded. She was a kind-hearted woman. "I understand. I'd like to be able to reclaim my husband's remains, but if it means hurting innocent people, then it's not worth it."

"We weren't innocent," Alison muttered shamefully.

"Mrs. Whiting," Eric began. "Would it be OK if I asked a few blunt questions? Some of them might be painful for you."

Carol sniffed. "No, go ahead."

"Did Jane describe to her parents how she killed your husband?"

Carol's mouth quivered. "Yes. She said she pounded a sharp needle through the top of his skull while he was asleep."

"Did you see evidence of this on Jim's body?" Eric asked Alison.

"Not directly," Alison said. "But there was blood coming out of his mouth."

Eric considered. "A fine needle would hardly have spilt much blood." He returned his attention to Carol. "You mentioned that Jane believed that she would live forever once she made her ritual sacrifice. Why did you say that?"

"It was one of the things Jane told her parents before they

went to bed," Carol said. "To them it was all babble. Jane said she was now ready for immortality."

Eric nodded. "Satan worshipers believe that when they've been fully initiated by their master, they will live a tremendously long life. Jane must have been convinced of the fact."

"But why, then, did she commit suicide?" Alison asked.

"She probably didn't think she'd die when she fell on the knife," Eric said. "Or rather, she probably thought she'd be reborn in her own body, with Satan's help and power. It's in the literature on cults. Murder and suicide are two of the gates into hell's power."

"Maybe there's something to the literature," Carol muttered.

"Why do you say that?" Alison asked.

"Because Jane's body disappeared from the funeral home before they could get it underground. I heard from the police." Carol forced a miserable laugh. "I'm not suggesting that she got up and walked away. The police believe other members of her cult came for the body to use in their ceremonies." The woman trembled. "It makes me sick to talk about things like this. She's dead, God save her soul. If it can be saved."

"Amen," Alison said.

They lapsed into silence. Carol was shrewd. She studied them as they sat digesting her gruesome tale. "Have any members of this cult been bothering you two?" she asked.

"We're not sure," Eric answered quickly. "It's possible. That's why we came here tonight to speak to you. Do you by any chance know how we could get in touch with Jane's parents?"

"I remember their name and the city they lived in," Carol said. "But I never asked them for their address. It wasn't like I wanted to keep in touch with them. They were Mr. and Mrs. Clemens and they lived in Riverside."

Eric glanced at Alison. "We should probably go and leave Mrs. Whiting alone."

Alison nodded and stood. "It's getting late."

Carol got up anxiously. "If any member of that cult is bothering you, I suggest you go to the police immediately. These people have no consciences. They'll stop at nothing to get what they want."

"What do you think they want?" Alison asked.

Carol looked her straight in the eyes. "People's souls." Then the woman grimaced. "I just pray to God they didn't get my husband's."

"Dying is not so bad as being put in the box."

"I'll pray with you," Alison said.

Chapter Fourteen

Eric was anxious to go straight to the Clemenses' house. He had been able to obtain their address online. But Alison insisted they stop and check on Brenda. Her best friend had been in a bad state at the end of the meeting at the park. Alison asked Eric to wait in the car while she ran inside. There was a single light showing in Brenda's window. The rest of the house was dark. The time was a few minutes before midnight. Alison let herself in without knocking. She had done so many times before.

Brenda was lying flat on her back with the music on low when Alison peeked in her room. Brenda glanced over with dreamy bloodshot eyes. There was a half-empty fifth of Seagram's 7 on the night table beside Brenda's head. Brenda seldom got drunk, but when she did, she favored whiskey.

"Ali," Brenda mumbled. "Is that you?"

"It's me." Alison crossed the room and knelt on the floor by her side. "How are you doing?"

Brenda looked at the ceiling and snorted softly. "How am I doing? Just great. They're bringing back what's left of Kipp tomorrow. His mom called and asked if I could help her pick out a casket for him. Can you imagine that? Two weeks ago I went with her to pick out a pair of pants for him." She began to cry, slurring her words. "Now I have to pick out a box to put him in."

Alison hugged her. "I know. It just keeps getting worse and worse. But Eric and I have been busy. We went and spoke to the man's wife. We have a lead on the people who might be behind the chain letters."

But Brenda wasn't interested. "We don't want to mess with that Caretaker. We better do what he says and let him put us in his box, and then maybe he'll go away and leave us alone."

"That's a lousy attitude."

"It's a smart attitude if you're into self-preservation." Brenda winced in pain. A bead of sweat poured off her forehead. "I need another drink." She reached for the bottle with her left hand, although her right hand was closer. Alison snapped the bottle away from her.

"You've had enough to drink," Alison said. "Go to sleep. I'll come see you in the morning."

Brenda persisted in wanting the bottle, although she was too drunk to jump up and take it back. She stuck out her left hand farther. "Just give me the goddamn bottle, Ali," she said.

Alison thought it was weird that Brenda was using her left hand. She was right-handed, like the rest of them. A warning bell went off in the back of Alison's head. She reached down and pulled away the sheet.

Brenda's right hand was covered with a bandage.

A red bandage. The blood was soaking into the top of the bed.

It looked as if she was missing her right index finger.

"Brenda!" Alison cried. "How could you do that to yourself?"

Brenda sat up, her face a mask of fury and fear. "How could I save my life? It wasn't hard. I got drunk enough and got a knife that was sharp enough and cut it off. Then I put the finger in an envelope with the chain letter and—"

Alison pressed her hands over her ears. "Stop it!"

"And I brought it over to Joan. That's what the ad said to do—give it to Joan. I couldn't have mailed it anyway. I put it in a plastic Baggie, but the blood soaked through the envelope anyway."

Alison felt nauseous. "You didn't have to do it."

Brenda grabbed her arm with her left hand. "The hell I didn't! I tell you this Caretaker isn't human. He goes where he wants. He does what he wants. You saw what he did to Kipp. What would he have done to me? Sawed me up into little pieces? It was better to lose just one piece and have it done with."

Alison shook her head miserably. "But you're in his box now."

"Who cares about his goddamn box?"

"But it's difficult to get out once you are inside. Most people never do."

"One day you might care," Alison said sadly. "I hope that day never comes for you. Can I take you to the doctor?"

Brenda glared at her. "I can drive with one hand."

"I think you should wake up your parents."

Brenda snickered. "And show them what I've done? That'll go over great. No, I think I'll wait until morning. When I'm sober. That's when I'll begin to feel the pain." More tears streamed over her face. "I miss Kipp."

Alison couldn't hug her again, and she didn't know why. Maybe it had something to do with her bloody finger. Maybe it was because she thought Brenda—

Was already damned?

When Neil had sent out his chain letters, the tasks he had assigned had each been personally distasteful to the recipient. These new tasks seemed to follow a similar pattern, except each task was personally damning. Fran had loved her puppy more than anything. Kipp had loved his sister more than anybody. And Brenda loved herself, her body—she was incredibly vain. But her vanity had now taken a serious blow. For the rest of her life she would be disfigured.

"I have to go" was all Alison could say. She set the bottle of whiskey down and left Brenda crying.

Eric was waiting impatiently in the car. He wanted to go to the Clemenses'. But when Alison told him what had happened, he thought they should go to Joan's house first. He was concerned that the Caretaker had broken his own pattern. He now wanted the letters brought to the next person.

"It's a small change," Alison said.

"Yes. But he may be trying to accelerate the cycle," Eric said.

"Why?"

"I don't know." He stared straight ahead out the car window. The nighttime sky was ablaze with white light. "It's a full moon tonight. Maybe it has an occult significance for the Caretaker."

"Do you believe the Caretaker is connected to this Satanic cult Carol described?"

"I honestly do," Eric said. "The tasks listed in the paper have all had a ritualistic torture quality to them." He grimaced. "Brenda really cut off her finger?"

"It looked like it. But let's not talk about it." She tapped on the dashboard. "Let's drive. Let's go see Joan."

But Joan wasn't home, and they only succeeded in waking Joan's father, who was in a grumpy mood. Mr. Zuchlensky was a big, tough man who wasn't to be messed with. He stood in the doorway in his shorts, with his hairy stomach sticking out.

"Which one are you?" he demanded.

"I'm Alison Parker," Alison said. Eric was still in the car. "I'm the one your daughter can't stand."

He grunted. "You're the one who stole her boyfriend away, right?"

"He was never her boyfriend. She just thought he was. But

I'm not here to argue about it. Do you have any idea at all where Joan went?"

"Nah. She was here until that other girl came over. What's her name?"

"Brenda?"

"Yeah, that's the one. She came over here with her hands wrapped in a towel. What a kook. Joan left right after her."

"Did she take anything with her when she left?"

"Not that I know of. I didn't actually see her. I was watching the news. That was tough what happened to those two friends of yours. I was sorry to hear about them."

Alison began to turn away. "Thanks, Mr. Zuchlensky. I'm sorry I woke you."

"It's all right. You try to stay out of trouble, you hear?"

"Yeah. Sure."

Alison noticed that the little metal door on Zuchlensky's mailbox at the end of the driveway was lying open.

Eric and Alison were at odds about where they should go next. He still wanted to talk to the Clemenses. She wanted to check on Tony. She was worried that Joan had gone to Tony's house—bearing strange gifts. She thought she was being logical. Tony didn't live that far from Joan. The Clemenses lived all the way out in Riverside, closer to her house. But Eric was insistent.

"He's probably not at home," Eric said as he restarted the car.

"Are you saying that he's with that girl?" she asked, hurt.

"I'm saying we need more information before we confront Tony. The Clemenses can give us that information."

"But he could be in danger."

Eric ignored her. He was heading for the freeway.

"Dammit Eric, you saw that he spit on me today. That's not the Tony I know. That witch has done something to his mind." She tried to grab the steering wheel. "I love him! I'm not going to let him die!"

Eric pushed her aside and quickly pulled over to the side of the road. He sat breathing deeply for a minute. He must be furious with her. She had almost yanked them into the oncoming traffic.

"I'm sorry," she said.

He sighed. "Alison, has it ever occurred to you why you might not be at the bottom of the list?"

She frowned. "We've talked about it."

"Not really." He reached out and put his hand on her knee. "It could be that the Caretaker knows you won't be around when he gets that far."

She was incredulous. "Are you saying that Joan's going to kill me?"

Eric shook his head and put the car back in gear. "I'm saying that it could be worse than you think."

It took them almost an hour to drive to the Clemenses'. They went to the door together. Alison didn't understand how people could continue to live in the same house where their daughter had impaled herself on a knife. She felt creepy walking up to the front porch.

Eric had to knock on the door for a long time to get an answer. Finally an elderly man appeared and peered at them through the torn screen. The Clemenses lived in a poor section of town and were obviously of modest means. Alison decided it had to be the same house Jane had died in. The man's bathrobe seemed to be in as poor shape as the screen.

"Can I help you?" he asked.

"Yes," Eric said. "We're here to talk to you about the group your daughter Jane was involved with. They've been causing us trouble, and it's important that we find out everything we can about them."

"Who are you?" the man asked.

"We're a couple of scared kids," Alison interrupted. "Please, Mr. Clemens, we know it's weird stopping by like this in the middle of the night. But we need your help."

"Did you know Jane?" the man asked.

"No," Alison admitted. "But we know of her. We know how she died. We know the man she killed before she died."

The man trembled at her remarks. "She wouldn't have hurt anyone before she got involved with those monsters." He opened the door for them. "Come on in. You both look decent. If I can help you, I will."

"Have we woken Mrs. Clemens?" Alison asked as she and

Eric stepped inside. There was a muskiness to the house that Alison found distasteful. She glanced down the short narrow hallway as Mr. Clemens padded into the living room and took a seat. Jane's room must be down there, she thought. A chamber of horrors. How many times had the Clemenses sat in their quiet living room while Jane got loaded in her room and played music from Black Sex and painted pentagrams on her floor with cats' blood?

"There is no Mrs. Clemens," Mr. Clemens said. Sitting in the light of the living room, he looked close to sixty. They must have had Jane late in life, or perhaps she was adopted. "My wife died shortly after Jane."

Eric sat near Mr. Clemens, with his left ear toward the man. Alison had noticed that Eric relied on sight almost as much as his "better" ear to understand what people were saying.

"May we ask how she died?" Eric asked.

"She was in Jane's room one night dusting. I never went in there myself. I couldn't bear the memories. She let out a single scream and was lying dead on the floor when I got to her." Mr. Clemens shrugged. "The doctor said it was a heart attack."

"It must be hard for you living here all alone," Alison said.

Mr. Clemens coughed painfully. He sounded ready to have a heart attack himself. "It's hard," he agreed quietly. "Who told you Jane killed a man?"

"Mrs. Carol Whiting," Eric said.

Mr. Clemens twitched. "The poor woman." He paused. "What can I tell you?"

"The name of any of Jane's friends who might have been involved in the cult with her?" Eric asked.

"Jane didn't have any friends," Mr. Clemens said simply. "She was a loner. She was pretty as pie, but boys didn't ask her out. Girls didn't call her up. I never understood why. I don't understand now. I think if she had had a few decent friends, her life might have taken a different course." He paused again. "But that wasn't to be."

"She must have had somebody she talked to?" Alison said.

"Sure, she did," Mr. Clemens said, and there was bitterness in his voice. "The people in that cult. But I don't know any of their names. I don't want to know any of them."

Eric and Alison looked at each other. Had they hit a dead end already? Jane Clemens was their only lead. But then Alison glanced past Eric and Mr. Clemens to a cluster of family pictures standing on a dusty shelf at the top of an old bookcase. She couldn't make out much detail from where she sat, but a flash of green in the photograph of a young woman's eyes caught her attention.

Alison stood and slowly crossed the room. Suddenly she felt as if she were walking through a space where the normal laws of reality no longer applied. The red and purple lights of her nightmares flashed in her mind. The horrible smells and the crushing despair. They surrounded her as she walked across the simple living room of a poor man living in Riverside, California.

She reached the cluster of family photos.

She picked up the one of the beautiful girl with the green eyes. The eyes that shone like polished emeralds, like a cat's eyes. Alison didn't have to ask. She knew intuitively that the photograph had been taken after Jane Clemens was already involved in the cult. Jane's eyes were bright, but the light they put out was as cold as the black water at the bottom of a well. Jane was blond, Mrs. Whiting had been right about that. But who was to say Jane couldn't dye her hair later in life?

Like, say, after she was dead?

Dye her lovely blond hair a deep, dark maroon.

Maroon—the color of the girl's hair in Tony's car.

The faces were the same. Identical. Jesus help them.

Dear dead Jane Clemens was sleeping with Alison's boyfriend.

"Oh, God," Alison moaned. She dropped the photograph, and the glass caught the edge of the bookcase and shattered in many pieces. Eric was at her side in an instant. It was a good thing. Alison felt the room spin and go dark, but Eric caught her before she could fall.

"What is it?" he demanded, holding her upright in his arms.

"It's her," Alison whispered.

"Who's her?" Eric asked.

Alison had to take a deep breath. She opened her eyes, and Eric helped her into a chair. Jane Clemens's picture had fallen facedown on the floor. Alison nodded for Eric to pick it up.

"It's her," she repeated.

"You've met Jane before?" Mr. Clemens asked from his seat on the other side of the room.

Eric picked up the photographs and shook the glass off. "Who is this?" he asked.

"You didn't get a good look at her this afternoon," Alison said. "I did."

"What are you talking about?" Eric asked.

"Jane is the same girl who was in Tony's car," Alison said.

"Hold on just a second," Mr. Clemens said, and he was angry. "My daughter has been dead for over a year."

"I saw her today," Alison said firmly. "She's back."

Mr. Clemens stood and waved his hand in disgust. "I want you people to leave. Now."

"Alison," Eric began. "I don't think this is the time to be mixing people up. Mr. Clemens was nice enough to invite us into his—"

"I tell you I saw her!" Alison shouted. "She's dyed her hair, but it was her. I would recognize those eyes anywhere. Listen to me, both of you, Jane killed James Whiting as part of an elaborate ritual to gain physical immortality. Her body vanished from the mortuary. Mrs. Whiting said it in jest, but I think it was true, I think Jane got up and walked out of that mortuary."

Eric took Alison by the hand. "I'm sorry about this, Mr. Clemens. She's had an upsetting last few days. I'll take her home. Thanks for your time." He practically pulled her toward the door. "Goodbye."

"She's alive!" Alison called back toward the old man. "I think she's the one who gave your wife a heart attack!"

If Mr. Clemens answered, Alison wasn't given a chance to hear it. Eric had yanked her out the door, down the steps of the porch, and onto the sidewalk. He was angry, but so was she. She shook him off when he stopped beside her car. She had been letting him drive it all day.

"You have no right to drag me around like I was your dog!" she shouted at him.

"And you have no right to scream at a broken-hearted old man that you have just seen his daughter who's been dead for over a year!" Eric shouted back.

"She isn't dead! She's alive!"

"Jane Clemens was seen lying naked in a morgue with a huge hole in her chest!"

"Then she's come back from the dead! All I know is I saw her this afternoon! She's the Caretaker! She's the one who's sending us these chain letters!"

Eric quieted. "You don't know what you're talking about."

Alison also calmed down. She glanced up and down the block. The houses were all old and shabby. In the bright moonlight they looked like cardboard shacks. They were alone on the street. Their solitude sank deep into Alison's soul. Was there no one who could help them out of this nightmare?

Satanic sacrifices and now the walking dead. And the chain kept going, from one link to the next.

"A chain. An unbroken chain. It's very ancient—not a happy thing. But it can be broken."

How? *With love* was all he would say.

The guy she loved was in the enemy's camp. But she had felt love in the stranger's presence in the mountains. It had been a beautiful thing. Sweet and innocent, free of all blemishes. It had been unworldly.

And yet it had been familiar. As familiar as the guy himself.

Where had she seen him before?

Why had she driven to that particular place?

Alison strained to remember back to the day after Neil died. The day she and Tony had gone for a walk near her house. The first day they had been sure it was all over. Tony had said something to her that was important. But what? Try as she might she couldn't. . . .

Then Alison had it.

"We went to the mountains. It was a pretty place, next to a lake. Neil liked it. I used my parents' credit card and rented a cabin. . . . We stayed there the whole week. . . . The Caretaker, the man, all that garbage was gone. We didn't even talk about it. . . . Mainly we just sat by the lake and skimmed rocks and that was good. I fixed him up this old cushiony chair next to the water, and he was comfortable enough. . . . He was sitting in it yesterday morning when he died."

She had driven to the spot where Neil had died! Tony had talked about the place later, in more detail. She had known how to get there subconsciously. And she had gone right there when things had looked the darkest. Why? Because she knew she'd get help? Who had helped her?

"I am your friend I am your greatest admirer."

Tony had described Neil as her greatest admirer.

After Neil's first funeral.

Neil had been buried a couple of times.

But had two times been enough?

Alison knew now who the guy at the cabin reminded her of.

Neil. It *had* been Neil, and yet someone else, too.

Another form of Neil Hurly.

Like Tony's girlfriend was another form of Jane Clemens.

Oh, God, it just keeps getting worse.

"Did you hear me, Alison?" Eric said.

Alison came back to the sidewalk as if from a million miles. She grabbed ahold of Eric. "We have to go out to the desert where we buried the man," she said.

"Why?"

"Because Neil told me I had to go there. He said I had to go back to where it all began. That's where it really all started. We have to dig up the man's grave and see if Neil's body is buried there."

"When did Neil tell you that?"

"You don't want me to answer that."

"But you said Tony buried Neil in the man's grave in the desert. What makes you think Tony was lying?"

"I don't think Tony was lying. I just think Neil's body might have disappeared."

"Why?"

Alison looked up at the full moon. She was confident she would be able to find the place. And they would have plenty of light to work by. "For the same reason Jane Clemens's body disappeared," she said.

Chapter Fifteen

Tony dreamed of the inside of the box. But it was only a metaphor—his unconscious wrestling with the impossibility of it. Because the box was unimaginable to mortals. No one who went in it returned to tell of the tale. Or so they said.

They. The Caretakers.

Tony was inside a metal box that was approximately the size of his own room. This made sense because his physical body was actually lying asleep in his bedroom. But his soul was sweating. He was locked in a seamless metal jail that was suspended in a caldron of flames.

There seemed no way out.

But that was a lie. Everything that happened in the box was a lie.

He was so hot. He paced from featureless wall to featureless wall, and as the temperature steadily increased, he began to scream for help. It was then that Brenda suddenly appeared in one corner of the metal room. He had no idea where she'd come from. She carried a long silver knife.

"Brenda!" he cried. "What are you doing here? Do you know how to get out of here?"

She handed him the knife and stared at him with whiteless eyes—twin black marbles in a flat face. "Oh, Tony," she said. "We just have to open our hearts. That's what they all say, you know."

"Then we can leave here?" he asked.

She flashed a fake grin. He wished her eyes would return to normal. He didn't know what the hell was wrong with them. "Sure. Then we can leave together," she said.

"Who are they?" he asked, although he believed he knew the answer to that question.

"It doesn't matter," she said, wiping away a bead of sweat that actually looked more like a drop of blood. He noticed for the first time that her hands were bleeding and that she was missing several of her fingers.

"What happened to your hands?" he asked.

"I don't know," she said. "Let's just get out of here. We can talk about it later. It's hot!"

He turned the knife over in his hand. "What am I supposed to do with this?"

"Open our hearts, Tony baby." She ripped open her blouse. He could see her bra. It was a mess. She had splattered blood on it from her severed fingers. She pointed to the center of her chest "Just stick it right here, and I can forget this place," she said.

"You mean, you want me to kill you?" he asked, horrified.

"It's not that way, Tony. You just have to open my heart. It's a simple operation. Go ahead, I don't mind." She reached for his hand with the knife in it. "Please hurry."

"No," Tony said, aghast. He pulled his hand away. "There must be another way."

Brenda's face suddenly became ugly. The change was dramatic. Her flesh actually took on lines and wrinkles that made it look like a witch's mask. Her voice came out high and cruel.

"You cut out my heart, or I'll cut out yours, little boy," she snapped. Magically another knife appeared in her hand, one longer than his. She stabbed at him, and Tony dodged to the side. Instinctively he slashed back with the knife she had given him. His aim proved true. He caught her in the center of her rib cage. The blade sunk in all the way to the hilt, and he felt warm fluid gush over his hand. Brenda's face relaxed, turning to normal. But a mess of blood bubbled out of her mouth as she sank to her knees in front of him.

"That hurts," she gasped in surprise as she died.

Tony looked down at the bloody knife in his hand.

He couldn't believe he had just killed someone. A friend at that.

He couldn't understand why it felt so good.

Then he was outside the metal box. He was floating in the abyss of red and purple lights, loud throbbing, and choking fumes. As before, he was closing on the vast dark wall. A huge black portal grew larger before him, and he felt himself being sucked inside. The lights vanished and all was silent. Once more he saw a slice of a bedroom, held up against a starless void. He moved steadily into the scene, and soon the room was all that existed. Yet the memory of where he had just come from stayed with him, and it was enough to terrify him.

He was in Neil's bedroom, and Neil was trying to screw up the courage to call Alison and ask her out. Tony watched as Neil dialed the number twice and then immediately hung up. Finally, on the third try, Neil was able to stay on the line long enough to have Alison pick up.

"Hello," Neil said. "Alison? This is Neil Hurly. How are you doing? That's great. I'm doing fine, thanks. The reason I called—I was wondering if you would like to go to a movie with me this Friday? Oh, you're busy. That's OK. How about Saturday? You're busy then, too? That's OK. How about next weekend? Oh, I see. Yeah, I know how that is. Well, I just thought I'd give you a call. Goodbye, Alison."

"Wait a second!" Tony yelled as Neil started to put down the phone. He strode across the room and snapped the receiver out of Neil's hand. "Let me talk to her." Tony raised the phone to his ear and mouth. "Hello, Alison? This is Tony. Would you like to go out to the movies this Friday? You would? That's great. When should I pick you up?" Alison gave him a time, and he hung up. He turned back to Neil. "See, that's the way to do it, buddy. You just be me, and everything goes perfectly."

But Neil wasn't listening. He'd already stood and begun to walk out the door. But he turned at the last moment and sadly shook his head at Tony. Tony wasn't sure what he had done wrong, other than steal his best friend's girl.

Then Tony was back in the metal room—in the box.

Alison was standing before him. She had a silver knife in her hand.

It was murderously hot inside the box.

"Tony," Alison said sweetly. "You've really opened my heart to what love is all about." Then she raised the knife and tried to stab him in the chest. But he was ready for her tricks. Brenda's witch had taught him well. He dodged to the side and managed to trip Alison. She fell forward and landed on her own knife. She rolled over on her back, and he saw that the blade stuck straight up out of the center of her chest. There was blood everywhere, especially in her hair. It gave her black curls a special maroon color. She smiled up at him, and blood gurgled out the sides of her mouth.

"Fooled you, didn't I?" she said, and her voice was different from Alison's. He realized it was Sasha who was lying on the floor in front of him. He watched in amazement as she yanked the knife out of her chest and tossed it aside. She reached up, and he helped her to her feet. She brushed her hands off on her black pants, but the blood didn't go away.

"I thought you were Alison," he said, confused.

"They always think that," Sasha said. She took his hand again. "Come. It's time. We have to go."

He took her hand reluctantly. This last murder had not felt so good as the first. He could have sworn it had been Alison in the room with him.

"Where are we going?" he asked.

She smiled. "They always ask that."

"Who are they?" he asked.

She laughed. "You are they. We are they. It makes no difference where we're going." She leaned over and whispered in his ear. "Soon you'll be in the box."

"But I thought this was the box," he said. It felt hot enough to be the box.

She giggled. She couldn't stop giggling. The sound of it began to make him feel sick. "Oh, no," she said finally. "This place is only to warm you up. You have no idea what the box is like."

Then she took his hand and led him away—to the other side of the wall. And soon the screams he heard were his own, and they never stopped.

Tony awoke and stared at his own ceiling. He turned over in bed and saw Sasha curled up in a ball beside him. She slept like a cat, he thought. He swung his legs off the side of the bed and sat up. His mouth was dry, and he had a headache. He must be getting sick. His entire body was soaked with sweat.

He stood and walked to the window and looked out at the deserted nighttime street. It looked like an alien planet. He didn't even feel he belonged in his own body. He hurt all over. He had gone to bed early only to awake at midnight and find Sasha standing over him. Before he could speak she had pressed her finger to his lips and whispered in his ear that she wanted his love. She had slipped into the bed beside him, and they had done the nasty deed, and it *had* been nasty. He had never experienced such passion with Alison, but it had taken its toll. He had passed out almost immediately afterward. Once more Sasha had refused to undress completely. She had kept her black blouse on. Indeed, she still had it on. It was the only thing.

Studying her sound asleep on his bed, Tony felt a sudden digestive spasm. The contents of his stomach welled up in his throat. He barely made it to his bathroom. He vomited up everything he had eaten for dinner and then some. He was catching his breath when Sasha came and knelt by his side. She leaned over and kissed him hard on the lips, vomit breath and all. She patted him on the back.

"Is my darling not feeling well?" she asked.

"I had a nightmare," he mumbled. It was just coming back to him. "I think it made me sick."

"What was it about?"

"I don't want to talk about it."

She grinned. Even in the unlit bathroom her green eyes glittered. He was reminded of the dead man in the desert. Of course, his green eyes had been flat as the ground he had been lying on.

"But I want you to talk about it," she said. "You will talk about it."

He smiled with her, although he felt far from smiling. "I have no choice in the matter?" he asked.

She continued to stare at him. Another wave of nausea swept through his body. "No," she said.

It was one little word. *No.* He had heard it a million times in his lifetime. But he had never heard it spoken the way she had just said it. There was a power in her voice that pushed a button deep inside him, one he didn't know he'd had. Maybe he hadn't had it until she'd come over that night. Their lovemaking had been passionate, but he couldn't say he'd enjoyed it. One of the reasons he felt sore was that she had scratched his back so badly in the throes of love.

Like a cat.

Her green eyes, green even in the dark, continued to hold him.

He told her about his nightmare. He remembered it all.

When he was done, she seemed happy. She patted him on the back again. Then she said something that shocked him to the core.

"Did I tell you I met Neil?" she said.

"What? No. When?"

"I met him in the desert where you buried the man. He had brought flowers to put on the man's grave. It was two months after you killed the man with your car, Tony."

"It wasn't my car," Tony said.

Sasha smiled. "But you were driving. You were responsible. Neil told me the whole story. I made him. He sounded so sad. I wanted to do something for him." She leaned closer. "Do you know what I did for him?"

Tony could not imagine. Everything she said blew his mind, which was already pretty well blown. "No," he said.

She moistened her lips with her tongue. Once more he smelled her smell. It wasn't really a hospital odor at all. He had just thought that because she had told him it was. But he was beginning to understand she didn't always tell him the truth. For some reason he was reminded of biology class in high school.

"I kissed him," she said.

His stomach rumbled. "Why?"

"I kissed him to make him feel better. I kissed his head. I kissed his knee. Do you remember he had a sore knee?"

"Yeah. He had a bone tumor in his leg. He ended up with a brain tumor. That's what killed him." Of course, Neil had not had these tumors two months after the incident in the desert. He had only developed them later.

"He was in a lot of pain," Sasha said sympathetically. "I made him feel better. He needed a friend. He felt awful about what you had done to the man. I talked to him regularly about it." She chuckled. "I talked to him even when he didn't know I was talking to him."

"But this thing got in my head, and I couldn't get rid of it. I don't know where it came from. It was like a voice. . . ."

"Did you know about the chain letters?" Tony asked, shocked.

"I know many secrets." Sasha sat back on her heels. "I kissed Neil, and now I've kissed you. But I've done more for you than give you a kiss, and now you'll do more for me than even Neil did." She cocked her head to the side. "I believe we have a visitor."

He could hear nothing. "What are you talking about? What did Neil do?"

"Shh," she said. "Listen. There it is. Someone's here."

She was right. Someone was knocking softly on the front door. He stood and grabbed his robe and hurried downstairs. Sasha didn't follow him. He opened the door, half expecting to find Alison. But it was Joan. She carried a brown paper sack in her right hand.

"Hi," she said flatly. "I have something for you." She thrust out the bag. "Take it. Do what you want with it. I'm sorry I'm late with it. I had to—go somewhere first before I could bring it over."

He took the bag reluctantly. "What's going on here?"

Joan spoke like a robot. "Brenda brought me her chain letter. She did what she was told to do. I'm doing what I was told to do."

"Who told you?" Tony asked.

"There was a note in my mailbox. One for me, one for you. Yours is in the bag, with the gun."

"What gun? What do I need a gun for?"

"It's my father's. Read the Caretaker's note. You're going to need everything I gave you."

Sasha suddenly appeared at Tony's side. Joan's eyes widened when she saw her, and she took a step back. Sasha grinned a mouth full of teeth.

"Is it loaded, Joany?" Sasha asked.

Joan swallowed. "I know you," she said.

"You're going to know me better," Sasha said. "You've done what you were supposed to do."

Joan trembled. She stammered. "I didn't hurt anybody."

Sasha laughed. "You just keep telling yourself that. Get out of here, worm. I'll come for you later." Sasha shut the door in her face. She turned to Tony. "Open the bag."

Tony searched inside the bag. If he hadn't just thrown up, he would have done so then. Joan had brought her dad's gun, all right. It could even have been loaded—he hadn't checked. Joan had brought it over with the trigger pulled back.

With a bloody severed finger.

"Brenda," Tony breathed. The gun fell from his hand onto the floor. It was fortunate it didn't go off. The finger bounced loose. Sasha reached down and retrieved them both. She pocketed the finger and flipped open the revolver chamber. It was fully loaded.

"It's hers," Sasha cackled. "Oh, Tony, we are going to have fun tonight. Hurry, read your small service. I'm going to help you perform it."

Tony reached into the bag again and withdrew a crumpled purple paper. He read in the shaft of white moonlight that shone through the window beside the front door. He didn't have to decode it.

Blow Alison's brains out.

He dropped the note in horror. "I can't do that."

Sasha was amused. "Why not? Do you know what your dear Alison is doing right now? She's on her way with her new boyfriend to dig up Neil's body. She's going to turn it over to the police. She's going to put you in jail, Tony."

Tony put his hands to his ears. "Stop it! She wouldn't do that to me!"

"She's doing it as we speak." Sasha pulled his hands down and placed the revolver back in his palm. "You're going to have to kill her. If you don't kill her, she'll destroy you."

"But Ali—"

"Is a whore," Sasha said, sweeping in closer so that she was practically whispering in his ear. But the funny thing—he wasn't sure if she was speaking at all. It seemed as if her thoughts were simply inside his head. That they were the same as his thoughts. Yes, that was the way of it.

"She's a whore, and she's spent the night screwing her new boyfriend and laughing about what an asshole you are. Now she's digging up Neil's body so that she can put you in jail so that she

can screw anybody she wants while you rot away."

"Is this true?" Tony whispered, standing frozen in shock. This new voice was a revelation to him. It knew so many secret things. It had been there for months, he suddenly realized. Ever since Neil had died. It was funny how long it had taken for him to hear it clearly.

Sasha kissed his ear, briefly sticking her tongue inside, and said, "It's all true, my love."

"I would have to see it for myself," he heard himself say.

"You will see it. I promise you. We will go there now."

"You will see your whore digging in the mud, and you will take the gun and put a hole in her brain and bury her in the mud, and then you will be my love. We will make love on her grave, and it will be like heaven."

He turned his head toward her and felt her tongue slide over the side of his face. Her eyes stared at him only inches away—twin mirrors hung in a featureless box. Her smell was overpowering—the stink of the morgue.

"Who are you?" he asked.

"The Caretaker. The one who takes care of you."

Sasha smiled. Her mouth did. But her eyes didn't change. They never did. They just watched. She was the Observer, the Recorder. She was also the Punisher. He had to listen closely. The time had come for his punishment. She brushed her hand through his hair. "I'm your greatest admirer," she said.

Chapter Sixteen

Alison found the spot without having to search. Even with the passage of time and the dark, there were still visible signs: tire tracks on the road that the winter's worst had failed to obliterate, scraped rubber on the asphalt that would probably be there at the turn of the century. But had there been no evidence, she would still have recognized the place where Tony had lost control of the car. For her, as well as for Tony, it was haunted, and her ghost, as well as the man's, often walked there at night. Alison and Eric parked their car, grabbed their shovels, and climbed outside.

"How far off the road did you bury him?" Eric asked. They wouldn't need flashlights. The moon shone in the sky like a cold sun.

"Fifty paces, straight out," Alison said. "Come on."

"What are we expecting to find?" Eric asked, following beside her as they strode through the sticky tumbleweeds. Alison remembered the night it all began—the howling wind, the dust in their eyes. That night the area was bathed in serenity—but it was as false a peace as that achieved by suicide. They had given themselves a death sentence that night a year ago when they had tried to pretend to the world they hadn't killed anybody. The irony of it all was that they hadn't. The man had already been dead. If only they had known!

"An empty grave," Alison said.

"But if we don't find anything, how can we be sure we weren't digging in the wrong spot?" Eric asked.

"I'll know."

"But what will the empty grave prove?" he persisted.

Alison stopped. "I tell you I met Neil up in the mountains."

"But you said he had terminal cancer. Even if Tony lied about him dying, he would have died shortly after."

"He's alive," she said. "He died and he came back."

"Alison, people don't come back to life. It's just fantasy."

She raised her eyes to the big round moon. She thought of the enchanting love of the stranger. She remembered the knives that had stabbed outward from the girl's eyes.

"Maybe they come back as something other than people," she said.

A minute later they entered a small clearing in the field of tumbleweeds and cacti. The latter stood around them like frozen sentinels. They had counted fifty paces, and here the soil was grossly uneven. It should have been. Tony had buried Neil only two months earlier.

"This is the spot," she said. "Neil's body should be right beneath us."

"I have to tell you I'm not looking forward to this," Eric said.

"It doesn't matter. You're already in this too deep." She pulled off her coat. The evening was cool, but she knew that soon she'd be sweating. "Let's get to work."

They had bought their shovels at an all-night grocery store and were lucky that the place had any shovels at all. But the quality of the shovels matched the quality of drugstore jewelry. A couple of feet into the ground and the wooden handles were coming loose from the metal spades. Eric muttered something about coming back later with better equipment, but Alison tossed a shovelful on his pants. Keep digging, brother.

The soil was a mixture of dirt and sand. It was not tightly packed—another sign that they had found the right spot. Working together they were down to five and a half feet in a hurry. Eric raised his shovel for another deep plunge. Despite his complaints, he was a hard worker, stronger than he looked. His spade stabbed into the earth, and it made a squishing sound.

As if it had plunged into something that had once been alive.

"Oh, Christ," he muttered. He was afraid to pull the shovel back out. He looked over at Alison, who had suddenly frozen in the moonlight at the sick sound. The two of them were standing head deep in the grave.

Neil's body is still here. He didn't rise from the dead.

Was she wrong about Jane Clemens as well?

An arm swung out of the night above them.

It struck Eric hard across the head, and he crumpled at Alison's feet.

She screamed, then all at once her scream choked in her throat.

Tony Hunt, her dearest love, accompanied by Jane Clemens, witch from hell, appeared above her at the edge of the grave. Tony was carrying a baseball bat, and a black revolver stuck out of his belt. He peered down at her with eyes cold as Arctic frost. The girl beside him giggled.

"We won't have to do any digging," she said. "We'll just cover her over. Both of them." She turned to Tony. "Do you believe me now?"

"It's true," he said softly, his voice void of any inflection.

The girl raised her arms above her head, stretching. "Kill her now, Tony. It'll give us that much longer to roll in the mud above her corpse."

Tony dropped the bat and pulled the revolver out of his belt.

"Wait!" Alison cried. "Tony, listen to me. This girl has lied to you. She's not who she says she is."

Tony aimed the gun at Alison. "I know that. But you aren't who you say you are. You lied to me. You're a whore."

"No!" Alison pleaded. "I never cheated on you. I just gave

Eric a quick hug and kiss good night. I would have done it right in front of you, and you'd never have minded. Tony! Don't kill me!"

"You did do it right in front of me," Tony said grimly. He cocked the revolver. "Say goodbye to life, Ali."

"Say goodbye to life, Ali."

The thought floated into Alison's mind like an echo from a shout in a canyon. But it wasn't her own thought. It came from the outside. She recognized that fact immediately because there was a harshness to it that pained her. She glanced up at Jane Clemens, who was posed above the grave as if she were being photographed for a men's magazine. Jane had Tony under some kind of mental control. Alison said the first thing that came to her mind, that belonged to her alone.

"Tony," Alison said. "She made Neil do things the same way she is making you do things. She's the Caretaker."

Tony's aim wavered. The mention of Neil threw him for a second. He blinked and looked around, seeming to discover for the first time where he was.

"Neil was the Caretaker," Tony said, confused.

"No," Alison said. "Neil was a pawn of the Caretaker. We've all been pawns. The girl standing beside you is the Caretaker. Look at her. Does she look human?"

Tony glanced at the girl. She ignored him at first. She stopped posing and moved around to the far side of the grave. She appeared unconcerned about Tony hesitating. Arrogance dripped from her every pore.

"You can climb out of the hole if you want, Ali," the girl said. "I won't kick dirt in your face."

Alison boosted herself out of the hole with difficulty. She brushed the dirt off her pants and stood upright. She was at the head of the grave, with the girl on her left and Tony on her right. Tony looked as if his plug had been pulled. For the moment the girl was not feeding him any evil thoughts. But Alison knew that moment wouldn't last.

Her shovel handle stood just below Alison's right foot. She must have set her shovel upright when Tony clobbered Eric.

"What's your plan, Jane?" Alison asked the girl.

The girl chuckled at the question. "I am not Jane. Jane is in the box. Jane will be staying in the box."

"Is that what you've planned for all of us?" Alison asked.

The girl gestured to Eric—almost invisible at the bottom of the hole—and at her. "You two are just props," she said. "You'll go no farther than this grave."

"But Tony?" Alison asked.

The girl sighed with exaggerated pleasure. "Ah, Tony. He's mine, all of him." She kicked a clod of dirt into the hole. "I'll take his body to places he's never imagined."

Alison shuddered. "Will he still be inside it?"

The girl nodded her approval. "Very good, Alison. You see the greater goal. Another Caretaker will come, and then another. An endless chain of them, you might say. There are so many of us who want to come out and play."

"And the chain letters?" Alison asked.

"An initiation process," the girl said. "It prepares people to welcome us into their hearts."

"By damning their souls," Alison said bitterly.

"Gee. That sounds impressive," the girl said, mocking.

"And if they don't get ready, they die?" Alison said.

The girl giggled. "There are worse things."

"The box," Alison said.

"You think you know about that," the girl said, and now the tone of her voice became serious, almost sad. "But you don't. None of you know." She was silent for a second, introspective, then she shook herself and laughed lightly. She gestured to Tony. "Kill her now, my love. Kill her slowly."

"Kill her so that she suffers. Blow off bits of her at a time. I want to see her squirm like a wounded animal."

Tony raised his gun as if he were a stringed puppet. The barrel of the revolver shone in the silver light of the moon. "Kill my love," Tony mumbled. Once more he cocked the hammer.

Then the girl let out a shout of surprise.

Alison twisted toward her to watch her topple into the hole.

Eric had grabbed the witch by the leg!

Tony's aim wavered. The dull, confused expression returned to his face as he watched his master fall into the grave. "Sasha?" he said.

Alison took advantage of the confusion. Bending down, she grabbed the top of the shovel handle and snapped it into her hands. Tony was just beginning to turn back to her when she let fly with a wide sweeping arc. The spade caught the tip of his revolver and sent it flying into the tumbleweed. Stunned, Tony turned to retrieve it. He must have been totally out of it. He didn't even see the blow coming that Alison delivered to the back of his skull. It sent him to the ground.

In the grave the girl was wrestling with Eric. She was winning. Eric let out a howl of pain as the girl stood up to climb out of the hole. Alison brought the shovel down on the top of her head, too. The girl grunted and fell backward.

Now what?

Alison realized she had done as well as she was going to do with one shovel. Both she and Eric had already lost the element of surprise. Tony was stunned, but recovering swiftly. She could whack him again, but she was afraid of doing him serious damage. The witch was already getting back up. Alison considered searching for the gun, but it would take her at least a minute to find it in the weeds. She glanced down at Eric. Whatever the girl had done to him, he wasn't going to be of any help in the next ten seconds. She had no choice, and she hated it. She had to take care of herself. She had to make a run for it.

Alison dropped the shovel and leapt across the grave. She took off for the car. The jagged tumbleweed tore at her legs, but she didn't let them slow her down. She ran as if she had the devil on her heels, and maybe she did. She had parked with the driver's side facing the gravesite. She was running so fast she did the majority of her braking by slamming into the car. Frantic, she threw the door open and jumped inside. But she didn't have her keys. Where were her keys? She couldn't remember. They were in her pocket. Yes! She stuck her hand in the pocket and pulled them out. But then she made the horrible mistake of sticking the wrong key in the ignition. She yanked it out and dropped the whole key chain to the floor.

Alison had just leaned over to find the keys when a fist came through the passenger window above her.

Shattered glass spewed over her. A hand like a claw grabbed her by the hair.

"Ouch!" Alison cried as she was yanked upright.

"Going somewhere?" the girl asked, standing just outside the window. Her grip on Alison's hair was enough to make Alison feel as if she were about to have the top of her skull ripped off. But the girl was not in the best of situations, either. She did, after all, have her arm stuck through a mean broken window. In fact her arm was already lacerated in a half dozen places.

But she wasn't bleeding. Instead, the cuts dripped a foul-smelling fluid. Alison had smelled the odor earlier in the day when Tony had spit on her. Then she had just caught a whiff of it. Now the stink of it flooded her nostrils.

Embalming fluid.

Jane Clemens had been embalmed before the Caretaker had taken possession of her body.

"Go to hell," Alison said. She jammed the right key in the

ignition and turned it over. The girl tried tightening her hold on Alison's hair, but Alison was already slamming the car into gear. It jerked forward, and Alison felt a thousand hair roots yanked out of the top of her head. But flooring the accelerator had worked. The girl let go.

Oh, but the pain of losing so much hair at once. It sent such shock waves into Alison's central nervous system that she simply couldn't drive straight. The car raced straight forward but then immediately veered back off the road and got stuck. She had plowed into a mess of tumbleweed—sort of like Tony had done when he had gone off the road the summer before. Her head struck the steering wheel, and a black wave crossed her vision. But she didn't let herself faint. She threw the car in reverse and backed out of the wall of weeds. But as she flew backward she hit something hard—maybe a body. For a moment she had the horrible thought that she had run over Tony. She fretted between racing off and checking. The indecision cost her precious seconds. Finally she turned and glanced over her shoulder.

It was at that instant that the car door was ripped off its hinges.

The girl stood in the moonlight three feet to Alison's left, dripping embalming fluid from her crushed guts and grinning from ear to ear. There was a tire mark across her tattered black blouse. Alison saw how the girl could have survived the wreck with Fran. She must have been in the car with Fran, after all.

"You're a feisty devil," the girl said. "I like that."

She reached inside the car and grabbed Alison by the throat.

"Please," Alison croaked, but she was asking the wrong monster for mercy. The girl yanked her out of the car as if she were made of paper. She threw Alison in front of her, in the direction of the grave.

"Don't make me carry you," the girl warned.

Eric and Tony were waiting for them at the grave. Eric had recovered his wits, and Tony had found his gun. At the moment he had it pointed at Eric's head. The girl suddenly shoved Alison from behind, and Alison fell at Tony's feet. Dirt pushed into her mouth. Blood seeped over the side of her head from her clump of missing hair. She spit and looked up. Tony had the barrel of the gun pointed at her head.

"All right," she whispered. "I give up."

"Good," the girl cackled. "We are about to start carving you up anyway. It's a good time to give up."

Alison got up slowly. She didn't know how to reach Tony. She stared deep into his eyes and saw another person at work. She had felt this way once before, when talking to Neil in the throes of his madness. How had they gotten to Neil? With Fran. With the one girl in the whole world who loved him.

"How can we break it?"

"With love?"

"I don't understand."

Now she understood. Now she knew what to do.

She remembered her nightmares.

Tony could not be put in the box.

She loved Tony. She really did. It would be all right.

"Can I ask something before I die?" Alison asked.

"Of course," the girl said. "You can ask things *while* you're dying, if you can stop screaming. The night's young. We'll play a while before you go in the ground."

"You've got serious psychological problems," Eric told her.

"Yeah," the girl said. She poked Eric in the gut, and he doubled up in pain. "We'll play with you as well."

"Stop that!" Alison cried.

"I don't think so," the girl said.

"All this, from the very beginning, was to prepare us?" Alison asked.

"Yes," the girl said. "But I had to step in. I had to get you to Column Three. Neil couldn't take you that far."

"Because Neil wouldn't," Alison said. "He had a good heart. He got away from you in the end."

The girl stared down into the grave. She spat out a mouthful of embalming fluid. "It doesn't look to me like he got very far."

"Tony," Alison said, turning to her boyfriend, and now she was crying. It was hard, what she had to do—so hard. She needed him to help her. "I can help you. Let me help you."

Tony blinked and a tremor went through the length of his body. "You lied to me," he said, but it was without force.

"But beyond this you must trust what's in your heart."

"This thing here lied to you," Alison wept. "It lies to you

in your own mind. You have to listen to me with your heart. You know me in your heart, Tony. You put me in there and kept me safe and warm. You told me that once when we were alone together."

Tony fidgeted. He looked at the girl, then back at Alison. "You came here to get the body to bring to the police," he mumbled. "You turned against me."

"Yes," the girl said.

"No," Alison said. "I was always on your side. I'm on your side now." She took a step closer to him. The tip of the black barrel was practically touching her, pointed directly at her heart. "I love you. I'll always love you."

But even as she spoke the words, she knew it was no use. The girl stood at Tony's right, smirking. She was confident. No doubt she had fought similar battles over the course of centuries and always won. The stranger had said the chain was very ancient.

"Alison," Tony said, and there was pain in his voice but no strength. Alison knew it would take strength to break the chain. The strength that love gave.

Alison whipped her hand up and folded her fingers around Tony's right hand. His index finger was pressed to the trigger. She pressed it tight. Yes, it was *she* who pulled the trigger. Not her boyfriend.

Alison heard a loud roar. She felt a painful slap.

Then she was lying flat on her back, staring up at the sky.

Tony and Eric and the girl were peering down at her.

The girl looked more shocked than the guys.

"What did you do?" she asked in disgust.

Tony's face crumpled. "Alison?" he cried.

Alison smiled through her pain. "Tony."

"You witch!" Tony swore, turning on the girl. Before the girl could react he pressed the gun to the side of her head and pulled the trigger. There was a flash of orange light. The girl toppled out of sight. Tony dropped the gun and knelt beside Alison. He reached out for her.

"What have I done?" Tony moaned.

"Don't move her," Eric cautioned Tony, trying to stop him.

"Let him take me," Alison whispered, and now the pain was coming in red tidal waves. She felt as if her chest had exploded, which it had. She could feel a mess of blood under her blouse, dripping down her belly. "I want to die in his arms."

Tony began to weep. "You're not going to die." He bit his lip and hugged her face to his shoulder. "Oh, God, what have I done?"

Alison was having trouble breathing. But she managed to smile. It felt good to be held by him again. "You didn't do anything. I did it. No one can put you in the box. You're free. You're—" It was difficult to get out the words. "You're mine."

Tony continued to hold her, but he shook them both as sobs racked him. He implored Eric, "Can't you do anything for her?"

Eric was sad. "There's nothing we can do."

Alison felt herself growing faint. The pain was receding into the distance. She closed her eyes, and Tony eased her back onto the ground. It was good to lie down and be still. It had been a long time since she had had a chance to rest. Now she could. She was at peace. She had done what had to be done. That was the best that anybody could do.

Far away, a million miles perhaps, she heard footsteps. Someone was approaching. But she couldn't get her eyes to open to see who it was. Yet she knew it was someone good, and she felt happy.

Epilogue

Tony and Eric watched the stranger walk out of the dark with a mixture of awe and fear. He was nothing to look at—a slightly built guy with sandy brown hair and an innocent expression. Yet he walked with power. The white light of the moon shimmered around him. They rose as he stepped into their small circle.

"Who are you?" Tony asked.

The stranger didn't say anything for a minute. He just stared down at Alison as she lay dying on the ground. But his eyes—they were warm and green, somehow familiar to Tony—were not unhappy. Finally he looked at them.

"I am a friend," the stranger said.

"Can you help my girlfriend?" Tony asked. A stupid question. Nothing could help Alison now. Any fool could see she was dying.

"Your madness has passed," the stranger said. "You're all right now."

Tony nodded. His heart was broken, his girl was dying, but suddenly he felt lighter. The stranger spoke the truth—a great burden had been lifted from his shoulders. He looked down at the girl in disgust, a bundle of stinking fluid and blood lying beside the grave. He couldn't imagine how he had ever gone to her.

"I'm all right," Tony agreed. He gestured helplessly to Alison on the ground and began to cry miserably. "But Ali isn't."

The stranger seemed unconcerned. He stepped over to the fallen girl with the bloody head. Incredibly her ruined body had begun to stir. This didn't disturb the stranger, either. He stood over the grotesque heap until something began to worm its way out of the dead girl's mouth. It was black and slimy. It looked like a slug, but it was as big as a snake. The thing stuck its head into the nighttime air, then focused on Alison's dying figure. Suddenly it darted out of the girl's mouth, and its full length was revealed, more than five feet long. It dashed straight for Alison. But the stranger was too quick for it. He slammed his heel down on the head of the snake, crushing it. The thing rolled over in the mud and fell into the hole and was gone.

"Did you see that?" Tony gasped to Eric.

"No," Eric said.

"That thing that just came out of the witch's mouth," Tony said.

"I didn't see anything," Eric said, confused.

The stranger regarded both of them with calm. "This Caretaker is gone. It will not return. And Alison has passed a great test. She is ready for great things. There's no need to grieve over her. She'll be in good company soon." The stranger turned to walk back into the desert. "Goodbye, Eric. Goodbye, Tony."

Something in the way the stranger said his name touched Tony in a deep way. He *knew* that voice. It was the voice of a friend, the voice of *his* friend. But that was impossible, Tony told himself. They were standing beside the grave of that friend. He had buried the guy.

The stranger sounded like Neil.

Tony jumped at him, catching the guy by the hand just before he was out of their circle. "Neil!" Tony cried and threw himself to the ground at his feet. "Don't leave me. Don't let her leave me."

The stranger slowly turned and lay his hand on Tony's head. His touch was soothing beyond belief. Tony felt his sorrows melt beneath those magical fingers. But there were so many sorrows—and the stranger was in a hurry.

"Your friend has to go," the stranger said. "He only came back to offer what help was allowed. But it was enough. The chain is broken. Life will go on. Your life will continue." He patted Tony's head. "Be strong."

Tony could not be strong. He couldn't bear a future without Alison. "No. I want to go with you. I want to be with Alison, wherever she is. There's nothing for me here without you two." Tony kissed the stranger's hand. "Please? Let me go?"

The stranger slowly shook his head. "You're alive. You have to live. It is the way of things."

Tony stared into the stranger's face, and he could not remember when he had ever seen such love.

Alison had told him to listen to his heart, not his head. Well, deep inside he felt there was nothing that the stranger's love could not do.

"Heal her," Tony said. "Before she dies."

The stranger was silent for a moment. Then he raised his head to the stars. For a long time he stood like that and if he breathed, he didn't show it. Finally he patted Tony on the head again. He smiled a playful smile.

"You want a miracle?" he asked.

"Yes!" Eric cried, coming over and joining them. "I would love a miracle. I've never seen one before."

The stranger laughed easily. Tony pressed the guy's hand to his forehead. "Please?" Tony begged.

The stranger took his hand back and knelt in front of Tony. He put both his hands on Tony's shoulders and bid Eric to come closer. "I'll tell you a secret," he said to both of them. "Joan took a long time to bring the gun to your house, Tony, because she first had to find blanks to fill it with. She never did the bidding of the Caretaker. She fooled the Caretaker."

Eric and Tony glanced back at Alison, and at the fallen girl. "But Alison is dying," Tony protested. "That witch is dead. The revolver must have been loaded."

Eric interrupted. "But Tony, you pressed the revolver to the girl's temple when you pulled the trigger. Even if it was loaded with blanks, it could still have killed her. Most people don't know this, but blanks shoot out quite a formidable wad of paper. At high speed it can be lethal. The temple is the weakest part of the skull."

"But what about Alison?" Tony asked. "She's bleeding. She's dying."

"The same thing," Eric said. "She pressed the tip of the barrel flush with her chest. Even a blank would have torn up her skin pretty bad. But the wound shouldn't be fatal." Eric glanced at the stranger, who seemed to intimidate him. "Is that true?"

The stranger nodded. "It is the truth. See it how you wish it." He closed his eyes briefly before reopening them. "Alison can stay with you. That much is granted. It is all right." He stood. "Go to her. Take care of her. I am leaving now."

Tony reached out and shook the stranger's hand. He looked him straight in the eye, and this time the impact wasn't so overwhelming. Tony felt as if he were merely saying goodbye to an old friend.

"Will I see you again?" Tony asked.

"Someday," the stranger promised. Then he turned and walked into the night and was gone. Tony and Eric hurried over to Alison. She was still breathing. In fact, she appeared to be gaining strength. Tony helped her to a sitting position, and she opened her eyes.

"Am I dead yet?" she asked.

"No," Tony said. "You're going to be fine." He felt under her blouse in the area of her wound. Eric was right. Her flesh was badly torn, but the bleeding was slowing down. He applied pressure to the wound. He could not find a bullet hole. Yet he could have sworn when she was first shot— There had been that powerful recoil. . . .

"Is she going to live?" Eric asked hopefully.

"I think so," Tony said. "I honestly do."

Alison jerked in his arms, then relaxed. "I think so, too," she said. She smiled sheepishly at Tony. "Who was here?"

"I don't know," Tony said, raising his eyes to the brilliant moon. "A friend. Someone wonderful." He nodded to Eric. "Let's get her to a hospital."

Eric helped Tony lift Alison into his arms. As they walked back toward the car, Eric suddenly stopped. "I'd like to check the revolver and see if it really does have blanks in it," Eric said.

"You think maybe it didn't?" Tony asked.

"I just want to know for sure," Eric said, turning. Tony stopped him.

"Don't check," Tony said. "Let's see it how we wish it." He leaned over and kissed Alison on the forehead. She sighed and snuggled warmly into his arms. "To me it's a miracle," he said.

TURN THE PAGE FOR
A PEEK AT
CHRISTOPHER PIKE'S
NEWEST NOVEL:

CHAPTER ONE

ONCE I BELIEVED THAT I WANTED NOTHING MORE THAN love. Someone who would care for me more than he cared for himself. A guy who would never betray me, never lie to me, and most of all never leave me. Yeah, that was what I desired most, what people usually call true love.

I don't know if that has really changed.

Yet I have to wonder now if I want something else just as badly.

What is it? You must wonder . . .

Magic. I want my life filled with the mystery of magic.

Silly, huh? Most people would say there's no such thing.

Then again, most people are not witches.

Not like me.

I discovered what I was when I was eighteen years old, two days after I graduated high school. Before then I was your typical teenager. I got up in the morning, went to school, stared at my ex-boyfriend across the campus courtyard and imagined what it would be like to have him back in my life, went to the local library and sorted books for four hours, went home, watched TV, read a little, lay in bed and thought some more about Jimmy Kelter, then fell asleep and dreamed.

But I feel, somewhere in my dreams, I sensed I was different from other girls my age. Often it seemed, as I wandered the twilight realms of my unconscious, that I existed in another world, a world like our own and yet different, too. A place where I had powers my normal, everyday self could hardly imagine.

I believe it was these dreams that made me crave that elusive thing that is as great as true love. It's hard to be sure, I only know that I seldom awakened without feeling a terrible sense of loss. As though my very soul had been chopped into pieces and tossed back into the world. The sensation of being on the "outside" is difficult to describe. All I can say is that, deep inside, a part of me always hurt.

I used to tell myself it was because of Jimmy. He had dumped me, all of a sudden, for no reason. He had broken my heart, dug it out of my chest, and squashed it when he said I really like you, Jessie, we can still be friends, but I've got to go now. I blamed him for the pain. Yet it had been there before I had fallen in love with him, so there had to be another reason why it existed.

Now I know Jimmy was only a part of the equation.

But I get ahead of myself. Let me begin, somewhere near the beginning.

Like I said, I first became aware I was a witch the same weekend I graduated high school. At the time I lived in Apple Valley, which is off Interstate 15 between Los Angeles and Las Vegas. How that hick town got that name was beyond me. Apple Valley was smack in the middle of the desert. I wouldn't be exaggerating if I said it's easier to believe in witches than in apple trees growing in that godforsaken place.

Still, it was home, the only home I had known since I was six. That was when my father the doctor had decided that Nurse Betty—that was what my mom called her—was more sympathetic to his needs than my mother. From birth to six I lived in a mansion overlooking the Pacific, in a Malibu enclave loaded with movie stars and the studio executives who had made them famous. My mom, she must have had a lousy divorce lawyer, because even though she had worked her butt off to put my father through medical school and a six-year residency that trained him to be one of the finest heart surgeons on the West Coast, she was kicked out of the marriage with barely enough money to buy a two-bedroom home in Apple Valley. And with summer temperatures averaging above a hundred, real estate was never a hot item in our town.

I was lucky I had skin that gladly suffered the sun. It was soft, and I tanned deeply without peeling. My coloring probably helped. My family tree is mostly European, but there was an

American Indian in the mix back before the Civil War.

Chief Proud Feather. You might wonder how I know his name, and that's good—wonder away, you'll find out, it's part of my story. He was 100 percent Hopi, but since he was sort of a distant relative, he gave me only a small portion of my features. My hair is brown with a hint of red. At dawn and sunset it is more maroon than anything else. I have freckles and green eyes, but not the green of a true redhead. My freckles are few, often lost in my tan, and my eyes are so dark the green seems to come and go, depending on my mood.

There wasn't much green where I grew up. The starved branches on the trees on our campus looked as if they were always reaching for the sky, praying for rain.

I was pretty; for that matter, I still am pretty. Understand, I turned eighteen a long time ago. Yet I still look much the same. I'm not immortal, I'm just very hard to kill. Of course, I could die tonight, who's to say.

It was odd, as a bright and attractive senior in high school, I wasn't especially popular. Apple Valley High was small—our graduating class barely topped three hundred. I knew all the seniors. I had memorized the first and last name of every cute boy in my class, but I was seldom asked out. I used to puzzle over that fact. I especially wondered why James Kelter had dumped me after only ten weeks of what, to me, had felt like the greatest relationship in the world. I was to find out when our class took that ill-fated trip to Las Vegas.

Our weekend in Sin City was supposed to be the equivalent of our Senior All-Night Party. I know, on the surface that sounds silly. A party usually lasts one night, and our parents believed we were spending the night at the local Hilton. However, the plan was for all three hundred of us to privately call our parents in the morning and say we had just been invited by friends to go camping in the mountains that separated our desert from the LA Basin.

The scheme was pitifully weak. Before the weekend was over, most of our parents would know we'd been nowhere near the mountains. That didn't matter. In fact, that was the whole point of the trip. We had decided, as a class, to throw all caution to the wind and break all the rules.

The reason such a large group was able to come to such a wild decision was easy to understand if you considered our unusual location. Apple Valley was nothing more than a road stop stuck between the second largest city in the nation—LA—and its most fun city—Las Vegas. For most of our lives, especially on Friday and Saturday evenings, we watched as thousands of cars flew northeast along Interstate 15 toward good times, while we remained trapped in a fruit town that didn't even have fruit trees.

So when the question arose of where we wanted to celebrate our graduation, all our years of frustration exploded. No one cared that you had to be twenty-one to gamble in the casinos. Not all of us were into gambling and those who were simply paid Ted Pollack to make them fake IDs.

Ted made my ID for free. He was an old friend. He lived a block over from my house. He had a terrible crush on me, one I wasn't supposed to know about. Poor Ted, he confided everything in his heart to his sister, Pam, who kept secrets about as well as the fifty-year-old gray parrot that lived in their kitchen. It was dangerous to talk in front of that bird, just as it was the height of foolishness to confide in Pam.

I wasn't sure why Ted cared so deeply about me. Of course, I didn't understand why I cared so much about Jimmy. At eighteen I understood very little about love, and it's a shame I wasn't given a chance to know more about it before I was changed. That's something I'll always regret.

That particular Friday ended up being a wasteland of regrets. After a two-hour graduation ceremony that set a dismal record for scorching heat and crippling boredom, I learned from my best friend, Alex Simms, that both Ted and Jimmy would be driving with us to Las Vegas. Alex told me precisely ten seconds after I collected my blue-and-gold cap off the football field—after our class collectively threw them in the air—and exactly one minute after our school principal had pronounced us full-fledged graduates.

"You're joking, right?" I said.

Alex brushed her short blond hair from her bright blues. She wasn't as pretty as me but that didn't stop her from acting like she was. The weird thing is, it worked for her. Even though she didn't have a steady boyfriend, she dated plenty, and there wasn't a guy in school who would have said no to her if she'd so much as said hi. A natural flirt, she could touch a guy's hand and make him feel like his fingers were caressing her breasts.

Alex was a rare specimen, a compulsive talker who knew when to shut up and listen. She had a quick wit—some would say it was biting—and her self-confidence was legendary. She had applied to UCLA with a B-plus average and a slightly above-average SAT score and they had accepted her—supposedly—on the strength of her interview. While Debbie Pernal, a close friend of ours, had been turned down by the same school despite a straight-A average and a very high SAT score.

It was Debbie's belief that Alex had seduced one of the interviewing deans. In Debbie's mind, there was no other explanation for how Alex had gotten accepted. Debbie said as much to anyone who would listen, which just happened to be the entire student body. Her remarks started a tidal wave of a rumor: "ALEX IS A TOTAL SLUT!" Of course, the fact that Alex never bothered to deny the slur didn't help matters. If anything, she took great delight in it.

And these two were friends.

Debbie was also driving with us to Las Vegas.

"There was a mix-up," Alex said without much conviction, trying to explain why Jimmy was going to ride in the car with us. "We didn't plan for both of them to come."

"Why would anyone in their right mind put Jimmy and me together in the same car?" I demanded.

Alex dropped all pretense. "Could it be that I'm sick and tired of you whining about how he dumped you when everything was going so perfect between you two?"

I glared at her. "We're best friends! You're required to listen to my whining. It doesn't give you the right to invite the one person in the whole world who ripped my heart out to go on a road trip with us."

"What road trip? We're just giving him a three-hour ride. You don't have to talk to him if you don't want to."

"Right. The five of us are going to be crammed into your car half the afternoon and it will be perfectly normal if I don't say a word to the first and last guy I ever had sex with."

Alex was suddenly interested. "I didn't know Jimmy was your first. You always acted like you slept with Clyde Barker."

Clyde Barker was our football quarterback and so good-looking that none of the girls who went to the games—myself included—cared that he couldn't throw a pass to save his ass. He had the IQ of a cracked helmet. "It was just an act," I said with a sigh.

"Look, it might work out better than you think. My sources tell me Jimmy has hardly been seeing Kari at all. They may even be broken up."

Kari Rider had been Jimmy's girlfriend before me, and after me, which gave me plenty of reason to hate the bitch.

"Why don't we be absolutely sure and invite Kari as well," I said. "She can sit on my lap."

Alex laughed. "Admit it, you're a tiny bit happy I did all this behind your back."

"I'm a tiny bit considering not going at all."

"Don't you dare. Ted would be devastated."

"Ted's going to be devastated when he sees Jimmy get in your car!"

Alex frowned. "You have a point. Debbie invited him, not me."

On top of everything else, Debbie had a crush on Ted, the same Ted who had a crush on me. It was going to be a long three hours to Las Vegas.

"Did Debbie think it was a good idea for Jimmy to ride with us?" I asked.

"Sure."

I was aghast. "I can't believe it. That bitch."

"Well, actually, she didn't think there was a chance in hell he'd come."

That hurt. "Love the vote of confidence. What you mean is Debbie didn't think there was a chance in hell Jimmy was still interested in me."

"I didn't say that."

"No. But you both thought it."

"Come on, Jessie. It's obvious Jimmy's coming with us so he can spend time with you." Alex patted me on the back. "Be happy."

"Why did you wait until now to tell me this?"

"Because now it's too late to change my devious plan."

I dusted off my blue-and-gold cap and put it back on. "I suppose this is your graduation present to me?" I asked.

"Sure. Where's mine?"

"You'll get it when we get to Las Vegas."

"Really?"

"Yeah. You'll see." I already had a feeling I was going to pay her back, I just didn't know how.

CHAPTER TWO

I WAS AN IDIOT TO GET IN ALEX'S CAR. BUT I WAS NOT fool enough to sit in the backseat between Ted and Jimmy. Debbie ended up sandwiched between the boys, where she looked quite content.

It was two in the afternoon by the time we hit the road. Our parents had insisted on taking us three girls to lunch, but it was only fun as long as our appetites lasted. We were anxious to get to Vegas. Also, there was tension between Alex's and Debbie's parents.

It was rooted in the UCLA fiasco and the ugly talk surrounding it. The truth was Debbie had only been accepted by the University of Santa Barbara—an incredibly beautiful campus, in my humble opinion—and she had graduated second in our class, while Alex had finished thirty-eighth. Alex made no effort to soften the tension, wearing a UCLA T-shirt to lunch.

Out of the five parents present, my mom was the only one who did much talking.

No one was jealous of me. I had finished tenth in our class and my SAT scores equaled Debbie's, but I hadn't bothered to apply to college. It was a money thing, I didn't have any. And I couldn't apply for financial aid because my father was rich.

Silly me, I kept hoping my father would suddenly remember he had a daughter who had just graduated high school and who needed six figures just to get an undergraduate degree. But so far he had not called, or written, or e-mailed me.

My mom didn't appreciate his silent rejection. She bitched about it whenever she had a chance. But I took the rejection in stride. I only cried about it when I was alone in my bed at night.

I hardly knew my dad but it was weird—I missed him.

"I enjoyed your speech," Jimmy said to Debbie as he and Ted climbed aboard in a deserted parking lot far away from any stray parental eyes.

"Thank you," Debbie said. "I was afraid it was too long. The last thing I wanted to do was bore people."

Christ, I thought. Her thirty-minute speech had been twenty minutes too long. I knew because neither Alex nor I could remember the last twenty minutes.

Debbie had spoken on the environment, of all things. What did she know about that? She had grown up in a goddamn desert.

We didn't have an environment, not really, just a bunch of sand and dirt.

"Your point on the impact of methane versus carbon-dioxide gases on global warming was important," Ted said. "It's a pity the tundra's melting so fast. I wouldn't be surprised if the world's temperature increases by ten degrees in our lifetimes."

"Won't happen," Alex said, swinging onto the interstate and jacking our speed up to an even ninety. She always sped and often got stopped by the cops. But so far she had yet to get a ticket. Go figure.

"Why do you say that?" Ted asked.

"We'll never live that long. We'll die of something else," Alex said.

"Like what?" Jimmy asked.

Alex shrugged. "That's my point. Here we're worrying about carbon dioxide raising the temperature and now it turns out methane is the real culprit. That's the way of the world, and the future. You can't predict nothing."

"Anything," Debbie muttered.

"Whatever," Alex said.

"What are you majoring in at UCLA?" Jimmy asked Alex.

"Psychology. I figure there's going to be a lot of depressed people pretty soon."

"You plan to cash in on their sorrows?" Debbie asked.

"Why not?" Alex replied.

"You're so altruistic," Debbie said sarcastically.

Alex laughed. That was one of her great qualities—she was almost impossible to insult. "I'm a realist, that's all." She added, "Jessie thinks the same way I do."

"Not true," I said. "No one thinks the same way you do."

Alex glanced over. "You have the same attitude. Don't deny it."

"My attitude changes from day to day." Ever so slightly I shifted my head to the left, to where I could see Jimmy. I added, "Today I feel totally optimistic."

Jimmy was dressed simply, in jeans and a red short-sleeved shirt. His brown hair was a little long, a little messy, but to me it had been a source of endless thrills. It might have been because it was thick and fine at the same time, but when I used to run my fingers through it, I always got a rush. Especially when he would groan with pleasure. One night, I swear, I did nothing but play with his hair.

His eyes matched his hair color, yet there was a softness to them, a kindness. People might think "kind" an odd word to apply to a guy but with Jimmy it fit. He was careful to make the people around him feel comfortable, and he didn't have to say much to put others at ease.

When we had dated, the one thing I had loved most about him was how he could sit across from me and stare into my eyes as I rambled on about my day. It didn't matter what I said, he always made me feel like the most important person in the world.

It had been early October when he asked me out. He came into the city library where I worked and we struck up a conversation in the back aisles. I knew he was dating Kari so I kept up a wall of sorts. I did it automatically, perhaps because I had liked him since our freshman year.

He must have sensed it but he didn't say anything about being broken up with Kari. It was possible they were not formally divorced at that exact moment. He kept the banter light. He wanted to know what I was going to do after graduation. He was in the same boat as me. Good grades, no money.

He left the library without hitting on me for my number. But a week later he magically called and asked if I'd like to go to a movie. I said sure, even before he explained that he was free and single. He picked me up early on a Friday and asked if I felt like going to Hollywood. Great, I said, anything to get out of Apple Valley. We ended up having dinner and watching three movies at the Universal CityWalk. We didn't get home until near dawn and when he kissed me good night, I was a total goner.

First love—I still feel it's the one that matters the most.

We spent the next ten weeks together and it was perfect. I was in a constant state of joy. It didn't matter if I ate or drank or slept. I just had to see him, think of him, and I'd feel happy.

We made love after a month, or I should say after thirty dates. He swung by on a Saturday after work. He was a mechanic at the local Sears. My mother was at work at the nearby Denny's, where she was the manager, and I was in the shower. I didn't know he was coming. Later, he said he'd tried knocking but got no answer. That was his excuse for peeking inside my bedroom. But my excuse, for inviting him into my shower, I can't remember what it was. I don't think I had one.

It didn't matter—once again, it was perfect.

I felt something profound lying in his arms that I had never imagined a human being could feel. I was absolutely, totally complete, as if I had spent my entire life fragmented. Just a collection of cracked pieces that his touch, his love, was able to thrust together and make whole. I knew I was with the one person in the world who could allow me to experience peace.

Later, when I tried to explain my feelings to Alex, she looked at me like I was crazy, but I sensed she was jealous. Despite her many lovers, I knew that she had never felt anything close to what I had with Jimmy.

Six weeks after our shower, he was gone.

No, that would have been easier, had he just vanished. Had he died, I think it would have been simpler to bear. But no, I had to see him every day at school, Monday through Friday, with Kari—until she graduated early, at the end of January. He told me he had to go back to her. He didn't say why. But watching them holding hands across the courtyard, I couldn't help but feel the smiles and laughter he shared with her were all fake.

But Alex said they looked real to her.

And she was my best friend. I had to believe her.

"Jessie," Jimmy said, startling me. It was possible my discreet peek out of the corner of my eye had accidentally lengthened into a long, lost stare. Had he caught me looking at him? He was too polite to say. He quickly added, "Do you guys know where you're staying?"

"At the MGM. Aren't you? That's where our class got the group rate." I paused. "Don't tell me you don't have a reservation."

He hesitated. "I wasn't sure I could get off work this weekend. By the time my boss finally said okay, I tried calling every hotel on the Strip but they were booked. I thought when we got there I'd see if there were any cancellations."

"That will be tricky on the weekend," Debbie warned.

"No biggie—you can always stay with us," Alex said.

A tense silence ensued. Ted must have immediately shorted out at the thought of Jimmy sleeping in the same suite as me. The idea drove me nuts as well, but for radically different reasons. Debbie was annoyed that a guy might be staying with us period. Despite her lust for Ted, she was a prude. She glared at Alex and spoke in a deadly tone.

"Nice of you to volunteer our accommodations."

Alex ignored the sarcasm. "Hey, the more the merrier." I knew what was coming next. Alex was never going to let me get away without putting me on the spot. She glanced my way and smiled wickedly. "Let's vote on it. Jessie, you okay with Jimmy sleeping in our suite?"

I had to act cool, I thought, it was my only escape.

"As long as we get to use his body in whatever way we see fit."

Alex offered me five. "Amen to that, sister!"

I gave her five while the three in the backseat squirmed. Ted turned to Jimmy. "If you get stuck, stay with me and Neil. We can always call down for a cot."

"You're rooming with Neil Sedak?" Alex asked, stunned. "That guy's never stepped out of Apple Valley in his life. Plus he was our class valedictorian, which means he's got to be a nerd."

"You have something against nerds?" I asked.

"I love nerds!" Alex said. "You know me, I'm never ashamed to admit my best friend works at the library. But I'm talking about Ted's rep here. Ted, if you spend a night with Neil, everyone will assume you're unfuckable."

"Hardly," I said. "I know two girls who've slept with Neil."

"Who?" Alex demanded, getting out the first half of the word before suddenly grinding to a halt. I smiled at her knowingly.

"Is someone forgetting a certain confession?" I asked.

Alex acted cool. "Confession is private."

"Oh, my God, Alex. You didn't," Debbie squealed with pleasure. Screwing Neil the Nerd went above and beyond the UCLA admission-man rumor. This one would be all over Las Vegas before the weekend was done. Alex cast me a dirty look.

"Tell her it ain't so," she ordered.

"It's possible it ain't so," I said. There was more truth to

Alex's remark than I let on. I *was* a bit of a nerd. The reason I worked at the library was because I loved to read. I was addicted. I read everything: fiction, nonfiction, mysteries, sci-fi, horror, thrillers, biographies, romance novels, all the genres, even magazines and newspapers. It was probably why my brain was stuffed with so much arcane information.

"Explain that I was only joking about Neil," Alex insisted.

The sex secrets of Alex and Neil could have gone on another hour if Jimmy hadn't interrupted. He was not a big one for gossip.

"I don't give a damn about Neil's sex life," Jimmy said. "But I do appreciate your offer, Ted. If I get stuck for a place to stay, I'll give you a call."

"No problem," Ted said, a note of relief in his voice. He reached in his pocket and pulled out a card. "Here's a fake ID if you plan to gamble."

"Great." Jimmy studied it. "This license looks real."

"It's not," Ted warned. "Don't use it at the MGM's front desk to check in. It'll fail if it's scanned. But don't worry about gambling at the other hotels. I haven't seen them scan IDs on the casino floors."

"How do you know?" Jimmy asked.

"He's been to Vegas tons," Alex said. "He's a master card counter."

"Wow." Jimmy was impressed. "Is it hard to learn?"

Ted shrugged, although it was obvious he enjoyed the

attention. "It takes a good memory and hard work. But you don't have to be a genius to do it."

"You should teach us all this weekend," Debbie said, a bold comment coming from her. Ted shrugged.

"I can teach you the basics. But it takes hours of practice to make money at it. And the casinos keep changing the rules, making it harder to get an edge."

"The bastards," Alex muttered.

We reached Las Vegas before sunset so we weren't treated to the famous colorful glow suddenly rising out of the desert night. It was a curious phenomenon, I thought, but during the day Las Vegas looked far from imposing. Just a bunch of gaudy buildings sticking out of the sand. But I knew when night fell, the magic would emerge, and the town would transform itself into one gigantic adult ride.

Alex drove straight to the MGM, where we checked in to our room, a decent-sized suite with a view of the Strip and three separate bedrooms—plus a central living area that came equipped not only with a sofa but a love seat. The price wasn't bad, one hundred and fifty bucks: fifty bucks when split three ways. Still, the weekend was ruining my savings. The library was not exactly a high-paying place to work.

With the sofa and love seat, we had room for another two people. But Jimmy, damn him, was too much of a gentleman to impose. He also seemed reluctant to take Ted up on his offer. He tried his best to find his own room, using our hotel-room phone to call several hotlines that supposedly could find you a suite on New Year's Eve. But it was all hype; it was Friday evening at the start of summer and Las Vegas was bursting at the seams. Jimmy struck out.

"This couch is softer than my bed," Alex said, sitting not far from where Jimmy had just finished dialing. I was glad we had temporarily left Ted—who had gone off to find his own room. Alex, it seemed, was determined that Jimmy stay with us.

"We settled the sleeping arrangements in the car," Debbie said, studying the minibar. Because it was filled with tiny bottles of liquor, and we had checked in to the room using our real IDs, the bar should have been off-limits. But Ted had managed to bypass the locking mechanism before departing for his quarters. I was glad, I loved minibars. The snacks tasted ten times better to me, probably because they cost ten times as much as they were supposed to.

"When we talked about it in the car, we didn't know this suite would be so large," Alex said.

"We only have one bathroom," Debbie growled.

"Do you plan on spending the weekend throwing up?" Alex asked.

Jimmy interrupted. "Hey, it's okay—remember, I've got Ted's room as a backup. Don't worry about me."

Alex went to reply, but then her eyes slipped from Jimmy to me. Her unspoken message couldn't have been clearer. She wasn't worried about Jimmy, she was worried about me. Or else she was trying to force the two of us back together, which, in her bizarre mind, was the same thing.

It didn't matter. The elephant standing in the room had just quietly roared. It could no longer be ignored. Jimmy and I had to talk—soon, and alone. But I felt too nervous to say it aloud. I stood and caught his eye, and headed toward my room. Jimmy understood, he followed me and shut the door behind him.

Before I could figure out where to sit, or what I should say, he hugged me. The gesture caught me by surprise. I didn't hug him back, not at first, but when he didn't let go, I found my arms creep up and around his broad shoulders. It felt so perfect to stand there and listen to his heartbeat. Yes, that word again, I could not be free of it when I was around Jimmy.

The hug was warm but chaste; he didn't try to kiss me. He didn't even move his arms once he had ahold of me. Although we were standing up, we could have been lying down together, asleep in each other's arms. I don't know how long the hug lasted but it felt like forever . . . compressed into a moment.

Finally, we sat on the bed together. He was holding my hands, or trying to, but I had to keep taking them back to wipe away the silly tears that kept running over my cheeks. He didn't rush me to speak. But he never took his eyes off me, and I felt he was searching my face for the answer to a question he had carried with him a long time.

Of course, I had my own question.

"Why?" I said. The word startled me more than him. It felt so blunt after our tender moment. The question didn't offend him, but he let go of me and sat back on the bed, propping himself up with a pillow.

"Do you remember the day we drove to Newport Beach?" he asked.

"Yes." It had been during Christmas break, a few days before the holiday. I wasn't likely to forget because it was to turn out to be the worst Christmas of my life. He dumped me December 22. Then I hadn't known what to do with the presents I had bought, or the ones I had made for him. In the end, I hadn't done anything. I still had them in my bedroom closet. They were still wrapped.

"When we got back to Apple Valley, Kari was waiting at my house." Jimmy paused. "She said she was ten weeks pregnant."

I froze. "We were together ten weeks."

Jimmy held up a hand. "I never slept with her once I was with you. I never even kissed her."

"I believe you." And I did—he didn't have to swear. Jimmy was incredibly rare; he didn't lie. I added, "Did you believe her?"

"She had an ultrasound with her."

"That doesn't mean it was yours."

"Jessie . . ."

"Saying, 'I'm pregnant, Jimmy, you have to come back to me.' That's like the oldest trick in the book."

"I know that. I know Kari's not always a hundred percent

straight. But I just had to look in her eyes. She was telling the truth."

I crossed my arms over my chest. "I don't know."

"And she was showing a little bit."

"At ten weeks?" I asked.

"It might have been twelve."

"And it might have been a folded-up pillowcase."

He hesitated. "No. She lifted her shirt. It was for real."

"And she wanted to keep it."

"Yes. That wasn't an issue."

"She wanted you back. That was *the* issue."

He lowered his head. "I don't know. Maybe."

It was a lot to digest. It was a minute before I could speak.

"You should have told me," I said.

"I'm sorry. I wanted to, but I felt it would hurt you more to know she was having my baby."

I shook my head. "You've been good so far, real good, but that, what you just said, is nuts. Nothing could hurt worse than that call I got. Do you remember it? 'Hello, Jessie, how are you doing? Good? That's good. Hey, I've got some bad news. I don't know exactly how to tell you this. But Kari and I are getting back together. I know this is sort of sudden, and the last thing I want to do is hurt you, but Kari and I . . . we're not done yet. We have stuff we have to work out. Are you there, Jessie?'"

He stared at me. "God."

"What?"

"You remember it word for word."

"I'll remember it till the day I die."

"I'm sorry."

"Don't say that word again. Tell me why."

"I just told you why. She was pregnant. I felt I had to do the right thing and go back to her."

"Why didn't you tell me the truth?"

"I was ashamed, it's true, but I honestly thought the truth would hurt you more."

"That's so lame. Didn't you stop to imagine how I felt? You left me hanging. Hanging above nothing 'cause I knew nothing. One moment I'm the love of your life and the next a cheerleader has taken my place."

He nodded. "It was dumb, I made a mistake. I should have explained everything to you. Please forgive me."

"No."

"Jessie?"

"I don't forgive you. I can't. I suffered too much. You say you felt you had to do the right thing so you went back to her. Let me ask you this—were you still in love with her?"

"I was never in love with Kari."

"Were you in love with me?"

"Yes."

"Then what you did was wrong. So she was pregnant. So she wept and begged you to come back for the sake of your child. That doesn't matter. I was more important to you, I should have been more important. You should have said no to her."

"I couldn't."

"Why not?" I demanded.

"Because when she rolled up her shirt and I saw that growing bump, and realized that it was true, that it was mine, my flesh and blood, I knew I had to take care of that baby."

"Bullshit."

"You're wrong, Jessie. At that moment, nothing mattered more to me than that child. And yes, forgive me, but it mattered even more than us."

I stood. "Get out."

He stood. "We should talk more."

"No, leave. This was all a . . . mistake. Go stay with Ted."

Jimmy stepped toward the door, put his hand on the knob. He was going to leave, he wasn't going to fight me. That's what I liked about him, how reasonable he could be. And that's what I hated about him, that he hadn't fought for me. I was the one who had to stop him.

"Where's the baby now?" I asked. Kari had graduated at the end of January and left campus early. I assumed she'd had the child.

But Jimmy lowered his head. He staggered.

"We lost him," he said.

"She had a miscarriage?"

"No." The word came out so small. I put my hand to my mouth.

"Don't tell me she had the baby and it died?" I gasped.

He turned and looked at me, pale as plaster. So frail, so hollow. I felt if I said the wrong word, he'd shatter.

"His name was Huck. He lived for three days."

"Why did he die?" I asked.

The wrong words. Jimmy turned, opened the door, spoke over his shoulder. "You're right, I should go. We can talk later."

He left; it was amazing how much it hurt. It was like he was breaking up with me all over again. It was then I wished I hadn't said the "why" word. We should have left it at the hug.

ABOUT THE AUTHOR

CHRISTOPHER PIKE is a bestselling author of young adult novels. The Thirst series, *The Secret of Ka*, and the Remember Me and Alosha trilogies are some of his favorite titles. He is also the author of several adult novels, including *Sati* and *The Season of Passage*. Thirst and Alosha are slated to be released as feature films. Pike currently lives in Santa Barbara, where it is rumored he never leaves his house. But he can be found online at christopherpikebooks.com.

THE FALLEN
THE FALLEN AND LEVIATHAN
1
THOMAS E. SNIEGOSKI

THE FALLEN
AERIE AND RECKONING
2
THOMAS E. SNIEGOSKI

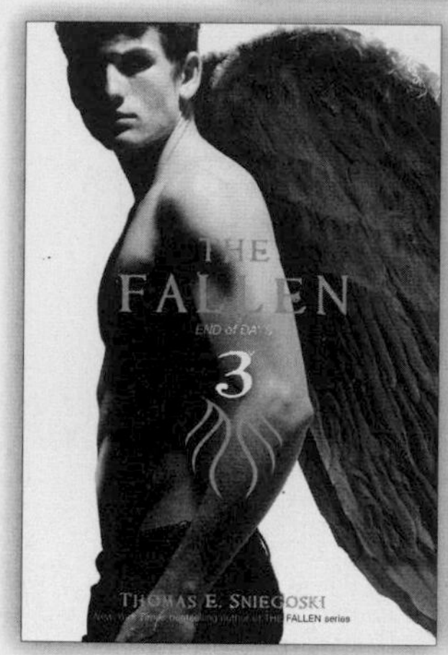
THE FALLEN
3
THOMAS E. SNIEGOSKI

THE FALLEN
4
THOMAS E. SNIEGOSKI

THE FALLEN
ARMAGEDDON
5
THOMAS E. SNIEGOSKI